Home Cries the Soul

©Whisperwood Holdings, LLC

This is a work of fiction. Names, characters, business, events, and incidents are the product of the author's imagination. Any resemblance to actual persons, living or dead, or actual events is purely coincidental.

To my husband, Tim, you are forever my Boaz.

Acknowledgments

No book is ever done in a silo, and I must thank each and every person who has helped me realize my dream. First and foremost, my husband Tim. I will never forget when I told him I wanted to write a novel. He was in the shower, and I was anxiously hollering over the shower noise. His response was typical Tim and one reason I love this man so dearly. He said, "Let her rip potato chip." And so, with his support and endearing quotes, I have done just that.

To my guru and friend, Melissa who has shown me how to follow my dreams, tap into my creativity, and lean into that which scares me. As I sit here writing this, nothing is truer… I am scared to death. But I am leaning in and getting to the other side; there is where I will find that which I am seeking, freedom.

To the first readers of my novel and their feedback, Kathleen, and my lovely niece Alicia. Both gave advice, which I have used to better hone my readers' enjoyment.

To Kimberly, who willingly stepped in to edit my writing. I am forever indebted to your ability to understand "grammatically correct" and provide constructive criticism.

To Judy and Jennifer, my BFF's who did not laugh or make fun of my new passion for writing and creating. You have no idea how your acceptance encouraged me.

To my children, Erin and Ethan, you are never too old to follow your dreams. Thank you for your love and support.

And finally, to Dave Ramsey, whose newsletter presented using KDP as a platform for authors as a good side hustle. I hope he is right!

Prologue

It's the summer; the night is sultry and hot. The cicadas are humming, and sweat is pouring off the two people dragging a body across the cotton field. The boy runs to the shed procuring a wheelbarrow. He grabs the torso, the girl his feet. With a great deal of effort, they lift the dead body into the wheelbarrow. Both take a handle and start to push. Digging into the ground with the toes of their tennis shoes, they push with all their young strength.

"What are we doing? What are we gonna do?" whispered the girl. Tears are streaming down her face.

"It's gonna be ok. Let's just dump the body next to the slave cabin. It won't be found for a while. Should give us enough time to figure something out. If we have to run, we do. I got some money stashed away. But we go back to our lives until or unless we have to run."

"I don't know. What if we get caught?"

"Not gonna happen. Come on! We are almost there." It takes both of them to lift the handles and steer the cart across the dirt path. The man is heavy.

They stow the body next to the slave cabin. They then take his watch, ring, wallet, shoes, belt, anything that might identify him. They even have the presence of mind to cover him with some shrubbery and corn stalks. They walk to the river.

The tide is up. She puts all the dead man's belongings in a bag she steals from the Beauregard's boat. She puts a rock in the bag to weigh it down and tosses it in the water. The bag floats for a moment before sinking. The teenagers watch as the bag sinks to the bottom, praying the tide and the pluff mud will cover up the crime.

"That is as good as we can do. We have to go," says the boy.

They look at each other and look around the plantation. He takes her hand and squeezes it before running across the field and back to their respective lives. Fear and panic, and a certain amount of relief are nipping at their heels.

Chapter 1

Present Day

"Laura Lynne, can I get you anything before I head home for the evening?" asks Marguerite, the housekeeper God himself sent to help keep Laura Lynne and Grays' hacienda running smoothly each day.

"No, Marguerite, thank you." Laura Lynne smiles over her shoulder and waves her hand in Marguerite's direction. "I am good. Go see your family. Give Jose and little Pepe a hug from me."

Laura Lynne relaxes against her new outdoor furniture, leaning back. She stares at the stars, sipping her tea. The phone buzzes; it is her husband, Gray.

"Hey, handsome! How was the sales conference?"

"I rocked it baby! Sold over 100,000 in the first two hours! No clue what we ended up selling. But I am beat! How was the trip home? Everything good at the ranch?"

"It was good. Glad to be home. Not gonna lie though, love doing the whole 'book tour' thing. Still can't believe I am a published author. I was just sitting here thinking I needed to pinch myself to make sure I wasn't dreaming."

Three years ago, Laura Lynne ditched her 12-hour shifts at the hospital and followed her dream. She set up a home office and quickly authored three books chronicling her experiences as a menopausal, southern woman drenched in wine and scandalized by divorce. Laura Lynne struck a chord with Generation X readers.

"Baby, we live a sweet little life. You hear from the kids?" Gray asks. Between them, Gray and Laura Lynne have three adult children.

"Only Savannah, our little mother. Since she became pregnant, I am the smartest person in America right now! She had her follow-up ultrasound and little man is doing fine. She is still feeling pukey, but she sounded happy. I know she is super excited to be a mom. Didn't hear from anybody else. You?"

"No, but with boys, no news is good news."

"Ok, Gray. I love you. Get home safe. I am not planning to go anywhere for a while. Time for me to get serious about my next installment of the Bluebird Chronicles. You go out there and knock'em dead."

Laura Lynne and Gray purchased their ranch in New Mexico the previous year, looking for a new spot away from the hectic pace of the big city and humidity of Atlanta. With the children grown and the ability to work from anywhere, Whisper Creek offered everything they were looking for at this stage of their lives. They were in those years before full retirement and after the children are grown. Whisper Creek is 125 acres of creeks, hills, wildlife, hiking trails, and a pool.

Laura Lynne and Gray were blessed to keep on their staff Marguerite and her son, Jose, when they purchased Whisper Creek. Marguerite cares for the house, and Jose the grounds. They live in the small town of Verde, about five miles down the road. Laura Lynne and Gray also employ Ashley and Lenny to round out their small family. Ashley is Laura Lynne's personal assistant and master of all thing's social media, and Lenny helps Jose when he is not handling the security of Whisper Creek. Both reside in the newly built guest houses far enough from the main dwelling to ensure privacy, but close enough if there is a need. And, in this case, there always seems to be a need.

Laura Lynne smiles into her nearly empty mug of tea. She is living a life she could not have imagined for herself 15 years ago. She thought the dream she had when she was a child growing up cocooned in wealth and privilege on a plantation in Mississippi was long dead. But, gazing up at the stars, she could remember doing the same thing as a little girl when life was simple, when she was innocent of just how cruel life and human nature could be.

Shaking her head at the thought, as if to divert her mind of the tract it had taken, Laura Lynne pushes herself to stand heading inside. She is suddenly exhausted and feels dirty, just like she always gets when she thinks too much about Mississippi. It's time for a hot shower and a good night's sleep.

* * *

Laura Lynne wakes with the birds and dons her favorite walking outfit, a wide brimmed hat and linen pants. It's her best version of the Boho Chic Grandmother that she wants to cultivate before the arrival of her grandson. "No need to look like an old fogey just because I am one," Laura Lynne thinks as she grabs her yoga mat and heads up the hill to her favorite meditation spot. Laura Lynne found yoga during her divorce experience as a panacea to craziness. Meditation during sunrise, and asana to greet the day have become Laura Lynne's way to show gratitude and humble herself before the universe. "And if momma heard me say what I just thought, she would lock me up in the loony bin," Laura Lynne mumbles as she finishes her last down dog.

Laura Lynne rolls up her mat and repacks it in her mat sack, a gift from Savannah. Savannah is the oldest of Laura Lynne's children, and a bit of a mother hen, coordinating family activities and remembering birthdays. Unlike Beau. Beau is a 'do today, do tomorrow' kind of guy, not really much on planning. It is amazing how great the kids have turned out after the tumultuousness of the divorce. Water under the bridge at this point, Laura Lynne shakes her head, refusing to dwell on those most difficult years.

The hike down is quick and invigorating. Laura Lynne heads to the kitchen, ready for a bit of breakfast. Marguerite is already there, preparing for the day. "Good morning, Miss Laura Lynne. How was your walk?"

"Lovely, thanks for asking." Laura Lynne walks toward the counter and nearly trips over Pepe, Marguerite's grandson. "Oh, well, hello my love! I didn't see you there."

"Story." Pepe holds up his arms toward Laura Lynne. He loves it when Laura Lynne regals him with stories of her childhood, growing up on the river in Mississippi. Pepe stays most days in the house with his grandmother, as Jose is a single dad. Laura Lynne loves helping the family, and Pepe is a doll baby.

Smiling, Laura Lynne scoops him up, "Absolutely. Mind if I grab some tea first? Then, you can tell me which story you want to hear."

***

After several hours in her office working on her next book installment, Laura Lynne pushes back from the computer and does a few stretches at her desk. The book is going well, but writing about her separation and divorce takes an emotional toll. There is a light tap at the door. "Come in!" she calls.

"Hey honey, I am home!" Gray is standing in the doorway.

"I wasn't expecting you for another few hours," Laura Lynne exclaims as she makes her way to the door for a hug and snuggle. Gray wraps his arms around his wife, nuzzling her ear and kissing the top of her head.

They entangle in a big hug and a deep kiss, his hands cupping Laura Lynne's butt cheeks. She is in the place she wants to be. Their relationship is a solid one, built on mutual trust and respect. Gray is a Capital P, Provider and Protector. His nature is to simply provide and protect those people God has entrusted into his care. Laura Lynne had no idea how much she craved and wanted this type of love and security. Not that there had not been issues, Gray too was divorced, and both brought baggage to the relationship.

"Pineview called. They called me after they couldn't get in touch with you." Disengaging, Gray goes to Laura Lynne's desk and picks up her phone, turning it back on. The phone lights up like a Christmas tree. "Here, call them back. They didn't tell me what the problem is."

"They called me? Why on earth did they not call Scarlet?" Laura Lynne and her mother have been on merely tolerable terms since Laura Lynne was a teenager. Laura Lynne's older sister, Scarlet Huger handles all things mom-related.

"One way to find out."

"Hello? This is Laura Lynne Atkins. My mother is Melanie Beauregard and I have a message that I needed to call?"

"Oh, yes, thank you Mrs. Atkins," says the voice on the phone. "Your mother has been a handful today. We were unable to reach Mrs. Huger and you are our second contact."

"What seems to be the issue?"

"Well, it is all about the dead body that was found at Tea Olive Plantation. Nobody seems to know anything more about it, and Miss Melanie is all out of sorts. We hoped maybe you could calm her down. Let me put her on."

"Wait…" but the nurse was already putting Laura Lynne on hold. Laura Lynne looks at Gray. "A dead body?"

"I heard." Laura Lynne has the phone on speaker. Her momma picks up.

"Laura Lynne, is that you?" Laura Lynne doesn't get a chance to respond. At 75 years old, Melanie Louise Cooper Beauregard has been raised to understand she descends from royalty. Her demeanor and attitude reflect this belief. "These awful women are calling me a murderer! Did you know about the dead body? Well of course you don't. I have no idea why they called you. Scarlet is the only one who knows anything and Gabriel won't pick up the phone either." Laura Lynne starts to speak, and the line goes dead as her mom hangs up.

"Well, that is interesting." Laura Lynne looks at Gray. "Your thoughts?"

"If it had been anything you need to deal with Uncle Gabe would have called, or at the very least Scarlet, or even Avery. Don't you imagine?" He walks out the office door but stops before getting too far. "But the nurse did mention a dead body."

"There are dead bodies at Tea Olive. We do have a cemetery on the property. It is pretty old. And then there is the old slave cemetery. But it is more likely the bones are from an animal, but I probably need to find out. I am guessing it is gossip in small-town Mississippi."

The Beauregard and Cooper, two of the most prominent Venice, Mississippi families, merged when Laura Lynne's mother and father married. Their wedding was the social event of the year and was attended by the Governor of Mississippi. After the marriage, Melanie and her new husband, Sawyer moved into the Residence at Tea Olive Plantation with her parents. Laura Lynne's mother lived in the house until the Parkinson's she developed had made it impossible for her to reside in the mansion with its narrow doorways and stairways. Her doctor recommended after her fall two years ago she be moved to Pineville. The siblings agreed it was the best option.

"Maybe a leftover from your Poppy Cooper's days," says Gray as he escorts Laura Lynne toward the back porch.

Poppy Cooper, better known as "Coop", is notorious along the coast and intercoastal waterways, a modern-day pirate and land-grabber who died years ago. He was 90. The reading of his will was perhaps the most dramatic moment of Melanie's life so far, except maybe, well, Laura Lynne's entire life. Poppy deeded the land to Sawyer instead of his son, Gabriel Lynne Cooper, Laura Lynne's namesake. This caused shock waves throughout the family, as Gabe is the oldest son and subsequent heir. However, Sawyer rectified this upon his own death, deeding the land back to Uncle Gabe. The transition of The Residence from Sawyer to Uncle Gabe has been anything but smooth. Melanie is still fuming, even though her children are the only heirs and will one day inherit the house and plantation. It's not like Uncle Gabe kicked her out. He kept things as they had always been, other than taking over one of the many bedrooms for his own quarters.

Uncle Gabe is quite the Southern Gentleman, an ancient bachelor who warded off many Southern Belles over the years, only to find himself the sole proprietor of The Residence and apparently considered a very eligible bachelor once again. Laura Lynne wouldn't be surprised if he were trying to ward off well-meaning widows by spreading rumors about a dead body simply to find peace.

"No need to dwell on it, Laura Lynne. Come on, Marguerite left us a charcuterie board and some fruit. Why don't we pour ourselves a drink and take this to the back veranda?"

Laura Lynne smiles. "That sounds lovely."

"Now, sit down and tell me how the writing is going, I will grab the food and beverage." Kissing Laura Lynne passionately on the lips, Gray heads to the kitchen.

Laura Lynne thinks about her writing. How is it going? Good question. At 53 years old, Laura Lynne did not begin writing until her kids were grown and she had a moment to think deep thoughts. Writing stories about her experiences seemed a good place to start. She just always felt she struggled with things that others did not. She wanted to incorporate her experience as a southern woman, married too young, now divorced, a Jesus Follower, yoga instructor, spirit guide believer, vegetarian, and sober sister. She felt like she had a unique perspective and, much to her surprise, her stories resonated with a lot of people. Laura Lynne's first book focused on her relationship with alcohol and was published as an indie book. It gained momentum and a fan base that picked up speed. Over the past two years, Laura Lynne has been a guest speaker at multiple conferences, and recently done her first book tour.

"Well, I would say it is going well, though it is difficult. I decided to focus on separation and divorce, sort of a handbook of handling the emotional roller coaster," Laura Lynne takes a bite of a cheese and cracker while Gray sits in a chair next to her.

"I think you know best. I prefer not to dwell on that time of my life." Gray wiggles about in his chair. "These seem comfortable enough. You like them?"

Laura Lynne smiles and snags an olive, popping it in her mouth. Nothing dries up conversation with her amazing husband as quickly as talking about his divorce. "I love them."

Laura Lynne's phone is buzzing. It is a phone number with an area code in Mississippi. She picks up. It's her Uncle Gabe, mother's younger brother by two years. "Hello?" Laura Lynne listens for a moment. "Uncle Gabe? Where are you calling from? Is everything okay?"

"Laura Lynne, you know I wouldn't have called if there had been anyone else available."

"What is it Uncle Gabe? I talked to Momma earlier, and she was making no sense. Some rambling about a dead body at Tea Olive?"

"Well, you see, that is why I am calling. I have been brought into the police station for questioning about the skeletal remains we excavated yesterday. I tried to tell them about the slave cemetery, but nobody seems to be listening." He sounded unruffled and calm. Laura Lynne, on the other hand, went into panic mode.

"Ok, Uncle Gabe I am on my way. Stay there and stay quiet. I will call Lally." Laura Lynne looks at Gray as he rubs her back.

"Oh, there is no need. He has already been here. I have a hearing first thing in the morning."

"They arrested you?" Laura Lynne barely whispers. Even at 73 years old, Uncle Gabe has stayed fit, in body and mind, but the years farming have taken a toll. "Okay, Uncle Gabe, I will be there as quickly as I can."

"Now darlin', there is no need to panic. This nice young man is taking good care of me. Pretty soon I am going to convince him to play some chess with me. I'm fine, sweetheart, but I do need your help."

"I will be there tomorrow. I love you Uncle Gabe."

"Hmmph, I love you too baby girl."

Laura Lynne hangs up and reaches for Gray's hand. Laura Lynne's head is spinning. Gray looks at her with concern and a bit of fear. He knows his wife's past; there are no secrets between them.

"Looks like I am going to Tea Olive. We knew it would happen one day. Looks like today is the day. Well, tomorrow anyway."

"Okay honey, I will book the flights. I just need to maneuver some stuff around so I can join you."

"Gray, I love you with my whole heart, but I need to do this on my own. Some dragons you must slay by yourself." Gray is not happy about this. He is all but crushing Laura Lynne's much thinner hand in his grip.

"That is not true. You don't have to do this alone. You have me now."

"I know I do. And that is what makes me strong. Gray, it is hard to explain. I guess I just need to prove to myself I can do it by myself."

"You have nothing to prove. To anyone."

Laura Lynne pats his hand and smiles into his eyes. "Gray, I do. Please let me do this my way."

He relaxes his hold and puts his forehead on Laura Lynne's, "Understood, but you call me the *minute* you want me to join you, and I will be there."

"I know it, and I will. I am going to need every superpower I possess to walk into that police station tomorrow," Laura Lynne says as she stares into Gray's beautiful blue eyes. "It has been 40 years Gray. Forty years since Daddy drove me to the airport, and I swore I would never return."

Laura Lynne gets up from the table and walks out into the night, gazing at the stars, Gray at her side. Laura Lynne knows, as she had known many times throughout her life, that this decision was a crossroads. She hopes she is picking the correct direction.

Chapter 2

Sitting on the plane to Mississippi, Laura Lynne begins to feel the fear and panic she has managed to keep at bay. Gray insisted on driving her to the airport, then encouraged her to text the children. Gray was adamant she keeps the children abreast of the current family situation. Laura Lynne simply did not want to involve them until she had to. And she didn't want to explain herself. But she caved and texted a brief missive about Uncle Gabe. She had no more than hit send when Savannah called to confirm she was going to Mississippi. She did her best to answer her questions, reiterating she knew very little. In the end, she hung up the call with her head aching and her nerves on edge.

***

Summer 1985

Laura Lynne is 15 this summer. Summertime in the Deep South is hot, and humid, and the air is heavy, even when the sun sets. But Laura Lynne loves it. She loves the way the sun beats down on the earth, heating the ground and causing the pluff mud to release its pungent odor of decaying plant life. To her, there is no better smell on earth, and no better place to live than Venice, Mississippi.

At 5'8" Laura Lynne is tall and thin, gawky for a teenager. No boobs and no butt. Laura Lynne's momma assures her she looked the same at 15 and not to worry, Laura Lynne will fill out soon enough. Laura Lynne's mother is beautiful, regal, and cultured. She is tall, and lean, and wears her lush chestnut brown hair in a French twist which nicely complements her long face and deep blue eyes. As any child who grows up in a world of privilege and wealth, Laura Lynne chooses to trust her mother, waiting patiently for the day she looks more like a woman than a bean pole.

Laura Lynne's oldest sister and the oldest of the four Beauregard children, Scarlet, is the family anomaly. She doesn't look like anyone but herself. She has blond hair, luscious curves, and big boobs. Very big boobs. Much to their momma's frustration, she has resorted to strapping them into a corset so the school uniform buttons will not gape. This has been met with modest success.

Laura Lynne is roused from her musings by the ringing of The Residence bell. Queenie, the house maid, is signaling the Beauregard children in from their various locations on the farm. The bell is attached to a decorative iron pole and was originally used on the plantation schoolhouse. When the plantation had a schoolhouse. Now, it was used to summon children, call for help, bring the workers in from the field for meals, and fire. Each need has a specific number of dongs. Laura Lynne waits to hear all three bell dongs before leaving her perch on the Angel Oak tree overlooking the river. It is her favorite spot to daydream. Tonight, the Beauregards are expected at the Country Club for the annual fund-raising gala for her school, Moseley Hall. It is the same school her parents attended and their parents before them. Everybody will be there, including Laura Lynne's best friend Grace.

Grace Cunningham, and her little brother Grady live at Cotton Mill plantation. Their property line is shared with Tea Olive. Grace's father owns the Piggly Wiggly grocery store, but that is just his side hustle. The Cunningham family has raised and ginned cotton for generations. There are several plantations along the river, but Tea Olive Plantation is the largest, oldest, and most prosperous. The current property is over 2000 acres and has been in the Cooper family since 1798.

The original Cooper, Dean Nathaniel Cooper, headed to the Mississippi territory as soon as the Pinckney treaty was signed. He was a part of the first migration of settlers and fought in the Creek War of 1814. He purchased land and immediately began planting cotton, marrying, and having 12 children, all but two of them surviving adulthood. Over the years, the property expanded as did the family wealth. The main crop has always been cotton, though currently Laura Lynne's daddy was interested in diversifying to include farming the Beauregard sweet potato. In truth, Uncle Gabe has been the one pushing the sweet potatoes. He manages all the farming, while Laura Lynne's daddy handles the business.

"Girl child, you better hurry on inside, get ready for the gala. Your momma laid out your dress. Let Pearl know when you are ready for your hair to be done," Queenie says as Laura Lynne enters the back courtyard.

"Yes, ma'am," Laura Lynne replies, "Is there any sweet tea left?"

"Lord child, is there any sweet tea left? You catch a fever out there on your thinking tree? Of course, made some fresh. You go on and head upstairs and get a shower. I'll have Pearl bring it up to you."

Queenie and her daughter Pearl take care of The Residence. Queenie's family has been in Mississippi almost as long as the Coopers, Queenie's ancestors having been captured and sold into slavery, a fact not discussed in the Beauregard household but common knowledge, nonetheless. Queenie and her husband, Lincoln live in a cabin about a mile north of The Residence. They have five children. Pearl is the oldest and is Laura Lynne's second-best girlfriend.

Laura Lynne sighs as she enters her sage green and rose bedroom. Her mother has put out the ugliest dress in Laura Lynne's closet. It is navy blue with a huge lace collar and a million buttons down the front, making her look like a pilgrim. "I am not wearing that nasty thing. Momma can just have a fit; I am not on the freaking Mayflower," Laura Lynne mumbles under her breath as she rustles through her closet and finds a simple white, sleeveless sundress. She pulls it out of the closet.

"Girl, Miss Melanie will have a fit if you don't wear that peasant outfit," says Pearl as she walks through the door carrying a pitcher of tea and two glasses, one for herself and one for Laura Lynne. "Though it is mighty ugly, and long sleeves in this heat? You gonna pass out on the dance floor after one dance with the handsome Buck," she continues in a sing songy voice that suggests Pearl knows of Laura Lynne's attraction to the boy.

"I don't care. That thing makes me look like a little girl. I am not wearing it, and you are right. I will die of the heat, Buck or no Buck."

"Well, I will let you fight that battle with your momma. Better go get ready. It is getting late, and I still need to do your hair."

Laura Lynne rolls her eyes. "I can do my own hair, too."

"Well go on with your own self then! I will go see if Momma needs help with Miss Scarlet."

Laura Lynne sticks out her tongue at Pearl as she heads to her bathroom. Pearl laughs and sashays out of the bedroom. Laura Lynn's bathroom is her favorite place in the house with a white antique tub as the center piece, a hand-painted China sink and a gilded mirror. The bathroom is the reverse of the bedroom, with pink and rose as the dominant colors and sage green as the accent. She looks at herself in the mirror and begins to get ready. She can hardly wait to see Grace….and Buck.

Laura Lynne sits smugly between her brothers on the front seat of Tripp's truck. She leans over and puts her head on Tripp's shoulder while he is driving. Tripp is Laura Lynne's older brother by one year. Laura Lynne and her mother had nearly come to blows when Laura Lynne refused to wear her mother's choice of clothing, but then Tripp stepped in and sided with Laura Lynne. She was forever grateful.

"Thanks, Tripp. If you hadn't come to the rescue, I would have been miserable tonight."

"No problem baby girl, but you owe me one, and I plan to collect tonight."

"Absolutely. What is happening tonight?"

"A group of us are going to the ridge during this shindig and I may need cover. Doubt anybody will miss us, but just in case." He glances at Laura Lynne and their little brother Avery who is listening intently. "You too squirt, you able to keep a secret?"

"Hell yes!"

"Avery Rhett Beauregard! Momma would skin your hide for cussing!" Laura Lynne slaps his leg while Tripp laughs. Avery is four years younger than Laura Lynne and idolizes his older brother, the star quarterback and town golden boy.

Tripp fist bumps Avery and squeezes Laura Lynne's knee. "Loosen up Laura Lynne! You are getting worse than Scarlet." Tripp is shaking his head. "We Beauregard's have to stick together. Nothing this town would like more than to see one of us fall off the very high Tea Olive pedestal."

"Truer words," Laura Lynne replies, "Okay, I got your back, but it is not an even trade. I expect you to back me up on the next ugly dress momma tries to make me wear!"

The three laugh as they pull up under the overhang of the Venice Country Club. All three pile out, handing the keys over to the valet. Tripp leans over and whispers into Lamar's ear, slipping the valet a 20.00 bill.

"The party has arrived!" Avery says as he attempts to match his brother's swagger through the doors of the country club.

"Wait! Escort me in you idiot! Momma is right behind us!"

Tripp turns and bows slightly, extending his arm to his little sister and giving her a wink, "Next year Buck will have the honor!"

Laura Lynne blushes and slaps at her brother, it is impossible to keep a secret in this family.

The three siblings immediately disperse to find their friend groups, Laura Lynne spotting Grace and heading in her direction. Laura Lynne has always envied Grace's petite figure and blue eyes.

"I thought you would never get here! Buck has been asking for you!"

"He has not!"

Grace is nodding her head, "He has! And look, here he comes now, with my man!" Laura Lynne turns around and sees Buck and Charlie walking toward the pair. Charlie and Grace have been together since elementary school, though they cannot officially date until Grace turns 16. "Just play it cool. Charlie tells me he really likes you. Wants to 'go with you.'"

"Really?"

"Hey beautiful, want to dance?" Charlie sidles up along Grace, rubbing her back and gently steering her to the dance floor. Grace looks over her shoulder at Laura Lynne and shrugs her shoulders, mouthing, "Sorry," as she flows easily into a waltz.

"I asked Charlie to do that," Buck is leaning over slightly, speaking directly into Laura Lynne's ear. He is one of the few boys tall enough to accomplish this feat. Laura Lynne loves it. It makes her feel petite and feminine.

"Why would you do that?"

"Wanted some time with you by yourself. Thought maybe you and I could 'go together.' You know, kinda like Grace and Charlie."

"You did, did you?" Laura Lynne brazenly turns her head, causing Buck's mouth to gently brush against her temple.

"Well, seems like we like each other enough to give it a try?" Buck drops his hand to the small of her back. "Come on, let's dance. Make Miss Witherspoon proud."

Janice Witherspoon is the town spinster and Cotillion teacher. All students at Moseley Hall are subjected to her classes on social etiquette, decorum, and learning the waltz.

"Sure." Laura Lynne walks onto the dance floor for her very first dance with a boy other than her father or brother, except in Miss Witherspoon's class.

Buck expertly maneuvers Laura Lynne around the dance floor, "Hey, you're pretty good. You didn't learn this in Miss Witherspoon's!"

Buck laughs. "My mom loves to dance, been dancing with her since I could walk." Buck pauses briefly and says, "Sir. Ma'am."

Laura Lynne looks over as her parents dance up alongside them. Laura Lynne tries to hide.

"Enjoying yourself young man?" Sawyer Avery Beauregard II looks directly into Buck's eyes, and, to Buck's credit, he does not flinch. Laura Lynne's father is a strapping man, the epitome of tall, dark, and handsome. To Sawyer's delight and their children's dismay, he is often compared to Gabeie Kennedy's father, Black Gabe Bouvier.

"Yes, sir. Very much."

"Jeremiah do not forget you are dancing with my baby girl. She is to be treated as such." Laura Lynne rolls her eyes. Could this get any more embarrassing?

"Understood Mr. Beauregard. I will treat her with care."

"Good enough. You two enjoy yourselves." Sawyer looks into Melanie's eyes as he leads her across the dance floor. "Can I interest you in a drink before the auction begins?"

Laura Lynne puts her forehead on Bucks chest. "I am absolutely mortified."

Buck is laughing. "Don't be, I expected it. I am surprised Tripp and Avery haven't done the same thing." He leans close to Laura Lynne's ear, as he dances with her into the next song. "And if it makes you feel better, my mother has been eyeing us this entire time. I expect she has a thing or two to say as well."

Laura Lynne sighs and matches him step for step. Her stomach clenches, her heart beats a mile a minute, and she feels giddy. So, Laura Lynne thinks, "This is what it feels like to be in love."

Charlie and Grace flow past. Charlie calls out in passing to Buck, "Leaving in ten."

Buck nods, "Got it," and explains to Laura Lynne, "Some of the guys from the football team are cutting out and heading to the ridge. I would invite you to come but Tripp would skin me alive."

"He told me earlier. Asked me to cover for him. I owe him one. I can't come. Momma and Daddy watch me like a hawk anyway. Sometimes, I think it would be easier to have been born a boy."

Buck looks down at her, smiling that wicked smile, and runs his hand gently up her back. "Well, I for one am certainly glad you are not a boy." He escorts her to the edge of the dance floor and bows slightly over her hand. "Thank you for the dance, Miss Beauregard."

Laura Lynne laughs and does an exaggerated curtsy, "My pleasure, Mr. Huger. Wow, wouldn't Miss Witherspoon be so proud?"

Buck steps a bit closer and gives Laura Lynne a brief hug. "Listen, after the auction, before everyone packs up, meet me near the first tee, at the Magnolia tree. Bring Grace and I will bring Charlie." Buck then shyly mumbles, "If you want, that is."

"I can do that," Laura Lynne readily agrees, knowing full well what happens under the Magnolia tree. It is where the teenagers go to make out.

"Come on, Buck, we gotta go. The boys are already out in the car," Charlie says as he grabs Buck's arm and steers him toward the exit. Laura Lynne smiles and does a little wave as they leave the ballroom.

Laura Lynne hunts down Grace to tell her what all happened with Buck. The girls are in the bathroom gossiping and putting on more lip gloss.

"I told you he liked you! And the great thing about Buck is your parents can't object. He comes from good people," Grace is puckering her lips in the mirror as she talks.

"Tell me about it. My mother was all but drooling when she and Daddy danced over. I could see the wheels working in her head, 'my little Laura Lynne has a Huger interested in her. Well, she could do worse.' She was all but planning my wedding."

"Well, I expect to be the maid-of-honor, and I am telling you now, I am not wearing a lavender dress.

I don't understand people who love lavender. It is an old lady color."

"What? Would you hush up? Now you are making me nervous. Come on, we need to get out there before the fun is over," Laura Lynne steers Grace by the elbow out of the bathroom. "So you will come with me to meet Buck?"

"As long as Charlie is there, but if he does not show up, I am not going to hang around and watch you two make out," says Grace as she heads to the sophomore class section of tables.

"Deal," says Laura Lynne as she sits amongst her friends, her heart racing as she thinks about her first kiss ever and with Buck Huger. And, as much as she hated to admit it, Grace was right. Her momma will absolutely approve of the match. Buck is the only son of Robert and Suzanne Huger. Mr. Huger is a prominent businessman, and Mrs. Huger was a former Miss Mississippi pageant winner, both from long lines of Mississippi blue blood. Buck and his family live at Twin Oaks Plantation.

Laura Lynne nudges Grace, who is busy getting the gossip from the cheerleaders at the table. "Pay attention. Your daddy is getting ready to start."

"Did you know that there is a new guy coming to school this year? Name is Clay Newhouse, coming from Natchez. Some big wig football player. Apparently, his daddy does computer farm equipment. You know anything about that?"

"I didn't know his name, but Daddy mentioned Mr. Newhouse bringing the farming industry into the computer age. Told Tripp he needed to make his son feel welcome. I think his mother is a teacher or something."

"Well, apparently he is top-notch, grade A, hunk material," Grace replies and sighs, "I do hate my father being the auctioneer every year. He practices at home for a month leading up to the gala. Drives Momma and me batty."

"I love it. He is a scream," says Laura Lynne as she turns around to watch the festivities.

Every year, Mr. Cunningham gets the crowd excited and plays to the audience as jeers and cheers are hurled at him. As the largest fund-raiser for the private school each year, the parents open up their check books and ante up. The auction items range from hunting and fishing trips to handbags and jewelry. The students join in on the commentary, egging their parents on. The auction lasts close to two hours, and as the last item is being brought out, Laura Lynne sees her mother signaling her.

"I have to go, Momma is waving me over." Laura Lynne looks at Grace. "What do I do?"

"Make an excuse and meet me outside. Tell her I started my period and made a mess, and I need your help," says Grace. "Or, I don't know, something. You are not ditching Buck."

The auction concludes and everyone starts to get up. Laura Lynne makes her way to her parents. Her mother is obviously ready to leave. "Come on, Laura Lynne, say goodbye to your friends. It is time to go home."

"Everybody is staying for a while longer and I don't want to leave yet. Besides, Tripp can bring me home. He doesn't mind."

"Where is that boy? I haven't seen him all night."

"He and the other football players are playing pool in the game room. I saw them go in about halfway through the auction," Laura Lynne smoothly covers for her brother. "Come on Mom, please? Grace is here. It will be fine."

"Oh, all right, but you listen here young lady, you behave yourself. Never forget you are representing the Beauregard *and* Cooper name. I will not tolerate any shenanigans from you," this is delivered with a smile on her face, but a stern look in her eye, giving the impression of a pleasant conversation. This was Melanie Beauregard's talent, the ability to project the façade of a southern lady no matter the circumstances.

"Yes, ma'am." Laura Lynne is already backing away from her mother, turning quickly to catch up with Grace before her mother can change her mind.

"There you are! Come on!"

Grace and Laura Lynne start jogging toward the Magnolia tree. There are already a few couples lip-locked together. Grace and Laura Lynne are looking around, trying to see Buck and Charlie. It is dark; there are no lamps or lights, only the moon.

"Ahh!" Grace and Laura Lynne scream as both are grabbed at the waist, Grace by Charlie and Laura Lynne by Buck. The boys are laughing, pulling them up against their chests.

"Calm down! It is just us!" Out of breath and obviously a few beers in, the boys are flirtatious and fun, "Did y'all have fun at the auction?"

"You scared me to death Charles Davis Hawkins!" Grace is laughing and swatting at Charlies arms, flirting back with aplomb, "How do you plan to make it up to me?"

Charlie leans over whispering in Grace's ear. She giggles and the two head over to the darkness of the Magnolia tree.

"Well, I guess they have made up," says Laura Lynne.

"What about you? Did I scare you to death?" Buck pulls Laura Lynne snugly against his chest. With a start, Laura Lynne realizes Buck has an erection, and instead of pulling away, she is enthralled, wiggling a little closer. Buck groans, turning her around, "Come here, Laura Lynne, I need a kiss."

He cups her neck with his hands, tilting her chin up, rubbing his thumbs along her jaw line to her ears. He leans forward and gently places his lips on hers. They are soft and gentle. Laura Lynne closes her eyes and sinks into the kiss. Sensing her acquiescence, Buck deepens the kiss, gently probing with his tongue. Laura Lynne allows access, and a sensual dance of tongues, teeth, and lips ensues. Laura Lynne is breathless when Buck releases her.

"God, you taste so good. Come on, let's go where it is a bit darker," Laura Lynne is all in. She loves how her body is feeling, sensual and alive. Buck pulls her to the shadows and dips his head for another taste of her. Laura Lynne stands on tiptoe deepening the kiss, beginning to caress Bucks chest, allowing her hands to travel to his sides as Buck cups her hips and pulls her tightly against his groin. Laura Lynne feels his erection, hard and thrilling, against the juncture of her thighs.

"What in the hell, Buck! That is my little sister!" Buck is pulled off of Laura Lynne, and she is left bereft and confused. "She is only 15. Hands off!"

Tripp curls his fist and starts to swing. Laura Lynne grabs his arm. "Tripp! Stop it! Stop it!" He all but lifts her off the ground as he attempts to strike Buck on the jaw. "This is ridiculous! Stop it!"

By this point Charlie and several of the guys from the football team have joined in the fray. Laura Lynne is once again mortified by the men in her life. Buck is not backing down. He reaches for Laura Lynne, shielding her with his body. "Tripp, I know she is your little sister, but we were just kissing, nothing more."

"There sure as hell had better not be anymore! And stop shielding her from me! I am not going to hurt my own sister. Laura Lynne, you better get over here with me right now! We are leaving." He jerks Laura Lynne back by the arm and starts marching her toward the parking lot. "This is not over Huger!" Tripp gives Laura Lynne a little shake, "I came to find you as *apparently* I am bringing you home. Momma caught me on her way out, but I couldn't find you anywhere." He stops and releases her arm, pacing back and forth. "What are you doing making out with that guy?"

"I don't have to explain myself to you Sawyer Avery Beauregard the third, Mr. High and Mighty!"

"Well, you better start explaining, or I am telling Dad."

"You wouldn't dare!"

"You try me, Laura Lynne! Buck Huger is a player. He is just interested in you because you are a Beauregard! You are setting yourself up to be nothing more than locker room gossip!" He gets right in her face, "You have got to be smarter than this! I am telling you he is no good." He takes a deep breath, leans his head back, regroups and in a gentle voice says, "You promise me you are going to stay away from him. He is not at all what he appears to be." He leans a little closer. "Promise me Laura Lynne, I have never lied to you. I am not now."

"God, Tripp! It was just a kiss! And I think he is cute, and he is nice to me! Besides, Momma is thrilled because he is a Huger."

"Jesus Christ!" Tripp retorts as he grabs her hand and walks toward his truck. "Now promise me. I mean it."

Laura Lynne gets into the front seat of the truck. "What do you know about him that I don't?"

"Plenty." As he starts up the car, he turns slightly in his seat. "Listen, there are some great guys at Moseley; Buck Huger is just not one of them. He plays dirty, on and off the field. I don't want you near him."

Trusting her brother, but still irritated enough to provoke him, Laura Lynne replies, "I promise, Tripp. I do! I trust you. But he is a really good kisser."

"Do I need to go back and break his jaw?"

Laura Lynne smiles, secretly pleased by her brother's reaction but surprised by the revelation. She would have to ask Grace. Maybe Charlie knew something.

***

Present Day

"It is fine, Gray. I finally got a rental car and am just headed to one of the hotels outside of Biloxi. It has been a really bad travel day."

"I know baby. I'm sorry. Let me at least book you a hotel. I can do it while we talk; got the app up already."

Laura Lynne's flight was delayed several hours due to a mechanical issue, causing her and the other passengers to be loaded and unloaded from the plane. Once reloaded, the plane sat on the runway for another hour. Once in Biloxi, the rental car agency had released her car, thinking she would not arrive until the next morning. It had been a series of issues all day long. She was finally in her car, loaded and heading out of the airport.

"Okay, love, I got you one about 20 minutes down the road. Sending you the location now," Gray is talking as Laura Lynne hears him type. Laura Lynne's phone pings.

"I got it. Listen, I want to plug this in and just head down the road. I will call you when I get there. I love you."

"I love you more than that! Be careful and text me as soon as you get there."

"I will, love."

Laura Lynne plugs in the address to the GPS and heads down the road. She has no idea how Uncle Gabe is doing or how the bond hearing has gone. Scarlet is not answering her phone or receiving texts. It is as if her phone is turned off. Avery and his family are on a Caribbean cruise, and Laura Lynne does not want to interrupt their fun. With one special needs child and two teenage daughters, they deserve a holiday. Besides, there is nothing for them to do. Tripp is off fighting some war and impossible to reach. She doesn't even have up-to-date contact information.

So, it is up to Laura Lynne to sort this all out, and right now, she is just exhausted. Before the flight, Ace Lally, the family attorney, reached out and reassured her he was looking after Gabe. However, there is not much he can do until the bond is set. Laura Lynne pulls into the hotel and unloads her bag. Maybe she could think more clearly after a decent night's sleep.

"You must be Laura Lynne Atkins." The receptionist at the front desk looks extremely bright-eyed for the late hour. "It is a pleasure to have you. Would you like some waters for your room?"

"That would be lovely. It has been a really long day."

The receptionist, Sally, according to her name tag, handed Laura Lynne two bottles of water and a room key. "I hope you don't mind my asking, but did you write Bluebird Chronicles?" Sally is looking at Laura Lynne shyly.

"Yes, that's me." Laura Lynne is always surprised when someone recognizes her name or photo. It is still surreal.

"I read your book for a class I am taking in nursing school. I didn't even know grey-area drinking was a thing." Sally smiles. "Can I have your autograph?"

"Uhh, sure." Laura Lynne hastily scribbles her name on the hotel stationary Sally produces. "Maybe you can get some extra credit."

"That is my plan. Could use it. Between work and school, my grades are not the greatest."

Smiling, Laura Lynne nods. "Been there and done that. Just do one day at a time; you will get there."

Laura Lynne heads down the hallway shaking her head. Her book is mandatory reading in nursing school? Crazy.

Chapter 3

Laura Lynne is on the road by 6AM. Sleep is basically non-existent. Instead of fighting it, she gets up, takes a shower, and grabs a banana and Diet Coke from the breakfast bar at the hotel. She still has three hours on the road before she arrives in Venice.

Once loaded and back on the road, Laura Lynne's mind wanders to her sweet Uncle Gabe, her mother's only brother. A confirmed bachelor, Uncle Gabe has spent his entire life in Venice, Mississippi besides his time in Clemson University and serving one tour of duty in the Korean War. Momma claims the war changed him, made him gentler, and more compassionate. He spends endless hours in the fields, nurturing the plants and spending less and less time with people. Laura Lynne had overheard her grandmother, Birdie, and her momma worrying over him, but over time being out in nature amongst his plants seemed to heal his soul. His agricultural degree from Clemson made him the perfect fit for managing the farming side of the Cooper Estate. Uncle Gabe and Sawyer have grown Tea Olive Plantation into a thriving farm, rivalling the wealth of the era when Cotton was King.

"Okay, gotta pee. Kind of proud of myself, made it all the way to Wisteria," Laura Lynne says to herself, parking the car and undoing the buckle. She continues to converse with herself, "And I would *love* another Diet Coke."

As Laura Lynne is washing her hands in the surprisingly clean gas station bathroom, she gazes at herself in the mirror. Between yesterday's travel adventure, really more like the seven stages of hell, and the lack of sleep last night, Laura Lynne critically examines her features. Not too bad considering. Laura Lynne has a fleeting thought that after 40 years, most people in Venice would probably not recognize her. Shaking her head, she silently chuckles. Who was she kidding? Venice is a small town, memories are long, and Laura Lynne looks exactly like her momma did at her age. The Cooper gene pool runs strong and deep.

Taking a deep breath and squaring her shoulders, Laura Lynne opens the bathroom door and heads straight to the soda machine. There is nothing better than a super large Diet Coke with light ice in the sultry summer heat of Mississippi. As her drink is fills up, Laura Lynne catches a glimpse of the newspaper stand. There, on the front page above the fold of the local paper is a picture of Uncle Gabe standing in front of his gardens at Tea Olive, with the iconic Cooper Estate wrought iron gates in silhouette.

"Crap!" Laura Lynne's drink has overflowed and is making a mess. Hastily grabbing napkins and a lid, she walks toward the end of the counter, hoping to get a better view of the paper. Wiping down her hands and the sides of her fountain cup, she reads the headline in bold type, "High Society Bachelor Arrested for Murder."

"You gonna buy that drink, hunny, or wear it?"

This from the middle-aged woman smoking her cigarette and drinking coffee while she waits on customers behind the counter. Since Laura Lynne is the only customer in the store and her car is the only one in the parking lot, it seems a good time to pump "Dorothy" for some information.

"Looks like both!" Laura Lynne puts the drink and a copy of the Wisteria Chronicle on the counter. "Looks like there's quite a bit of intrigue going on in Venice today."

"Intrigue? Oh, you mean the dead body. Yeah, my husband works construction with some of them boys that found it. Said it weren't nothing but bones. That'll be 3.46."

"So, do you think the old guy did it?" Laura Lynne hands her a five.

"Wouldn't put it past any of them rich people. No tellin' what happens on those big ol' plantations. Probably plenty of dead bodies out there." She hands Laura Lynne her change.

"Keep the change. Probably owe you that much for all the napkins I used." Laura Lynne smiles as she picks up her drink and newspaper. "Thank you so much!"

Laura Lynne hops in her rental car, turns on the air conditioner, and begins to read the article. It is mostly speculation. She learns one new, and seemingly pertinent fact. There is a new sheriff in town, a guy by the name of Gerald Thomas, from Boston. For as long as Laura Lynne can remember,

Bubba Westerman was sheriff of Venice County. He was a tobacco chewing, bald man with a beer belly hanging over his pants, and Laura Lynne was pretty sure her daddy had him on the payroll. He always turned a blind eye to the Beauregard boy's antics, bringing them straight home if there was a run-in with the law. Nothing ever serious, but trouble seemed to surround Avery, and Laura Lynne knew at least one time when Tripp was hauled in for public intoxication. Bubba and his wife, Frances, were regulars at the various dinner parties and social events hosted at The Residence. Laura Lynne attended school with their oldest daughter, Candy.

Laura Lynne texts Gray and then starts the car. She is on the road when he calls her back, "What's up buttercup?"

"It has already been picked up by the local papers, Gray. I just stopped at the Wisteria Whistle-Stop Gas Station, and Uncle Gabe's picture is staring back at me from the Wisteria Herald!"

"That doesn't seem so surprising Laura Lynne. From what you told me your family is pretty prominent down there." Gray is calm and soothing.

"Ahhh! I am just super frustrated. And emotional. This whole thing has been a lot harder than I have let on, Gray. I am not sure I can do this." Laura Lynne's voice starts to quiver, "If I did not love my Uncle Gabe so much, I wouldn't be here. I don't think I am ready."

Gray lowers his voice, "Sweetheart, you are the strongest person I know. I think it is just the opposite. I think it's well past time you face your past. Too many coincidences for God not to be involved, or your Aunt Eileen. Wouldn't put it past her to be pulling some strings in heaven to get your butt back to Venice."

Laura Lynne starts to chuckle, "Truer words." Taking a deep breath, she says, "God, I hate being strong."

"You want me to catch a plane and head down, sweetheart? I can be there sometime in the next day or so."

Taking another deep breath, Laura Lynne shakes her head, "No. *No*! I can do this. The newspaper article just made it a little too real. Wasn't expecting media coverage in the first 24 hours, but your right, probably the biggest thing to hit these parts in a while."

***

Within an hour of hanging up with Gray, Laura Lynne drives down Main Street in Venice, Mississippi. It has been nearly 40 years since she was last on this street, and the town has grown during her absence. The main street has undergone a revitalization and now hosts a brewery, art gallery, wine bar, bookstore, and bakery. Just like many small towns in America, the love affair with Main Street is being reignited. People are tired of the anonymity and standardization of the big box stores. They crave unique, quaint, and creative. The Venice County Sheriff's Department sits at the end of the main street. It, too, has undergone some updates.

Laura Lynne parks her rental car in an empty parking space at the side of the building and collects her thoughts. She can barely believe she is back in Venice. It is real now; no turning back. She does a quick inventory of herself. Her stomach is surprisingly calm, but her heart races, and she notices sweat dripping under her arms.

Putting the car in park and turning off the engine, she exits the vehicle and is immediately swamped by the overwhelming heat of the Delta. The air is strangely familiar and comforting. Gathering her purse and cell phone, Laura Lynne walks to the front door of the building. Unlike her brothers, Laura Lynne has never been inside the sheriff's department.

The door is heavy, and the force of the air conditioner makes it even more difficult to open. Laura Lynne puts some weight into it, forcing the door to swing open. She heads to the front desk, barely looking around her. Now that she is here, she just wants to get to her Uncle Gabe.

"Excuse me, I am Laura Lynne Atkins, Gabriel Cooper's niece. I am here to pick him up."

The woman turns around. Her hair is bleach blonde and teased to within an inch of its life. She has bright blue eye shadow, pink lips, and a pink outfit. She looks like cotton candy or a middle-aged Barbie doll.

"Sugar, have a seat. I will let the Sheriff Thomas know you are here."

Laura Lynne finds it hard to quit staring at the bundle of pink fluff. She can't tell if she is 40 or closer to 60. And her outfit is a mini dress with a pink feathered neckline and matching pink boots. Even the boots have feathers. Laura Lynne can't help but smile. She smiles back, she seems kind. She picks up the phone and presses some buttons, informing the sheriff of Laura Lynne's arrival. She nods and puts the phone back in the cradle.

"Miss Laura Lynne, the sheriff is ready. Come on back. And your Uncle Gabe is fine, just tired." Laura Lynne walks around the counter and through the swinging door. Cotton Candy escorts her toward the back room where she assumes there is a holding cell or cells?

"I am sorry. I didn't catch your name?"

"That's because I didn't throw it! Beth Anne Bodeen."

Bodeen. Now, that is a name Laura Lynne is familiar with. They live on what her momma would refer to as the "wrong side of the tracks." But then anyone who did not own 100 acres of land and carried a DAR card was considered "wrong side of the tracks" to Laura Lynne's momma.

Beth Ann uses her very long, very fake fingernails to peck at the door. Surprisingly, they are not painted pink, but instead seem to be decorated with tiny red hearts. She must have received some sort of acknowledgement because she enters a code into the keypad by the doorframe and opens the door.

Beth Anne stands to the side and ushers Laura Lynne through.

"Thank you, Beth Ann. It was nice to meet you."

Laura Lynne finds herself not in a holding cell but in the sheriff's office. The man standing behind the desk is young, tall, and thin, with sharp features from his nose to his elbows. Hard angles and no muscle, just skin and bones. Laura Lynne suspects he was horribly bullied as a child, probably why he chose law enforcement. The name plate on his desk says Gerald "Jerry" Thomas. He extends his hand to Laura Lynne for a handshake, and it is immediately obvious he is new to the South. He has not learned the etiquette rules.

"Hello Miss Beauregard, it's nice to meet you." Laura Lynne struggles to understand the quick dialect and the thick Boston accent. "I am sorry its bad news that has brought you back."

Laura Lynne nods. She does not return the handshake. Southern women do not shake hands; they nod. "Yes, well, thank you. I have not been Miss Beauregard for quite a while. It's Mrs. Atkins now. I really just want to get my Uncle Gabe and take him back to The Residence. I will be staying there with him until this is all cleared up."

"Well, there is the small matter of a bond. Apparently there has been a reluctance from your family attorney to provide the funds per your Uncle Gabe's request."

"Well, we need to sort this out. Is Ace Lally here? What is the bond amount?"

"One million dollars."

"What? For a 73-year-old man? He is not going to flee. Surely, he is eligible to be released on his own recognizance. He has no prior criminal record. My Uncle Gabe is an upstanding citizen and has never travelled further than Clemson University! And he is a veteran for God's sake!"

"Mrs. Atkins, I agree with you, but the judge thought differently."

"The judge? And who exactly is the judge these days? Surely it can't still be Sal Monroe? He must be retired by now."

"Well, you are half right. It is a Monroe, but its Sal's son, Chandler who is the presiding judge, has been for going on 15 years, took over for his father. Ol' Salvadore Monroe is still alive and well."

Laura Lynne rolls her eyes. No doubt father and son are in cahoots. The Monroe family has been in a Hatfield's and McCoy's type war with the Coopers since Moses was a child. No need to fight it. Just need to get Uncle Gabe. No wonder Uncle Gabe wouldn't let our family attorney, Lally, post the bond. There is too much pride and water under that bridge. "Could you please point me in the direction of the nearest bail bondsman?" Laura Lynne turns to leave. "And can someone please tell my Uncle Gabe I am here and working through this for him? I don't want him to worry."

***

It takes another couple of hours, multiple phone calls with Gray, and attempts to reach Scarlet, but finally the bond is secured. Laura Lynne hated to do it, but she put The Residence up as collateral. Apparently, the Cooper Estate is rich in land, but not in liquid cash. It was the best she could do for now.

"And just where in the hell is Scarlet? Leaving me here to handle this, and Tripp! He is out somewhere playing war games when he should be here acting as executor of the trust. It is high time he took over from Uncle Gabe or if he doesn't want to do it, pass it on to Avery! It is like the entire family disappeared overnight!" Laura Lynne is ranting in her car to no one in particular as she has spent the last four hours dealing with the bureaucracy. And she is hungry. That banana from breakfast is long gone.

Laura Lynne returns to the police station. Beth Ann is still at the counter, as pink and bubbly as ever.

"Hi again Laura Lynne. You ready to collect your Uncle Gabe? I just received word that the bail has been posted and he is free to go."

Laura Lynne nods. She is just too worn out to do more. Beth Ann takes her back to collect Gabe. He is playing chess with one of the deputies. And winning, of course. Laura Lynne looks at him from behind. He is ramrod straight, legs crossed, foot dangling, hands crossed on his top leg. He could have been in the front parlor at The Residence. He is wearing the traditional Southern Gentleman garb, complete with a bow tie. He turns around when he hears Laura Lynne enter the room.

"Laura Lynne, come here darling. Meet this nice deputy who has kept me busy playing chess."

Laura Lynne walks over to the table, places her hand on Uncle Gabe's shoulder, leans down, and kisses his head. She is so glad to see him. The last 24 hours had been turbulent, but underneath it all was the nagging worry about Uncle Gabe. He is no spring chicken. Laura Lynne glances up and meets the deputy's eyes. He looks familiar, but she can't quite place him.

"How much has he taken you for?"

"We are up to $50. Glad you got here before I owed him another 50. It's Grady Cunningham."

Laura Lynne takes a good look. Grace's baby brother? He definitely had the look of a Cunningham. "Your daddy owned the Piggly Wiggly? You are Grace's little brother? Good grief, how are you?" Laura Lynne laughs, reaching over and holding on to his outstretched hands. It is so good to see a familiar face.

Patting her hands and standing from his chair, Grady smiles, "That's me. Daddy still owns the Pig. Goes to the store every day and Grace still lives on the farm with Charlie and their son, Trey." Uncle Gabe is smiling at us, but I can see in his eyes and his bearing that he is exhausted.

"Grady, good to see you again. I would like to take Uncle Gabe home now. Bail has been posted," Laura Lynne steps to the side so her Uncle Gabe can stand, "Maybe we can catch up another time?"

"Of course, and Laura Lynne, it is good to have you back in Venice, no matter what the circumstances. Things were never the same after you left."

Laura Lynne drops her head, gathering her emotions as a fresh wave of sentiment washes over her. She really had some good friends and good times growing up here. She didn't realize how much she had missed them until just now. She doesn't make eye contact or acknowledge his comment. "Grady, thank you for looking after Uncle Gabe. And could you please let Grace know I am in town? I left a number where I can be reached with Beth Ann. Come on, Uncle Gabe, let's get you home."

Ever the gentleman, Uncle Gabe acknowledges all the staff, paying particular attention to Beth Ann. Their flirting is obviously nothing new and Laura Lynne finds out Beth Ann's son helps out at Tea Olive, after school and during the summers. In fact, he was the one who found the remains and started this entire chain of events.

"Beth Ann, you tell that boy of yours this is not his fault! Have him at Tea Olive tomorrow, same as usual."

Beth Ann tears up. "Oh Mr. Gabe, he has been so torn up about it! He hasn't slept and has texted me 100 times today. I keep telling him you are fine, but he feels awful guilty."

"Have him at the house. He is a fine lad. I will make sure he knows." And with that, Uncle Gabe walks through the front door and out onto the sidewalk. Once the door closes, he stands still, closes his eyes and takes a deep breath. He bows his head and Laura Lynne hears him whisper, "Thank you Jesus," before he straightens up, opens his eyes and heads to the parking lot.

Uncle Gabe sits heavily in the front seat of the car. He looks at Laura Lynne with concern in his eyes. "I didn't know who else to call. This is bad, Laura Lynne. I know you don't want to go to Tea Olive. I am sorry I had to ask."

"It's okay Uncle Gabe. It's time. Forty years is long enough."

.

Chapter 4

Summer 1985

"My momma sure does *piss me off*! I mean why do I have to miss the county fair and Sweet Potato Festival to go babysit for Dr. Butler? I told her he was a lech, and she just laughed me off! Like, I should be *pleased* he gropes me and flirts with me. The man is like *old,* like 40 years old. It is disgusting. But NO! I have to do what I am told, and there is nothing more to say. So, there goes my Friday night fun," Laura Lynne rants on her way to the front gate to meet Grace, kicking rocks and generally in a foul mood. Her mother had just told her she would be babysitting for Dr. Butler's niece and nephew *this Friday,* even though she knew she had plans with Grace.

And hadn't Laura Lynne told Dr. Butler this when he had asked her last week when she was working her summer internship at the hospital? The job she had worked hard to get and was so excited about had turned into a nightmare thanks to the lecherous Dr. Butler. Laura Lynne's mother couldn't understand why she would want to work at the hospital with sick people. But Laura Lynne loved volunteering as a candy striper last year at Venice Regional Hospital and thought maybe she wanted to pursue nursing as a career. Not that Momma understood why any woman wanted a career, in her eyes there was nothing more important than being a proper wife and mother. College was simply a way to achieve your MRS degree.

Laura Lynne finds another rock to kick, swinging her foot with all her might and using her favorite cuss word, "Shit! Shit! Shit! It just is not fair!" There was just something off about the handsome Dr. Butler. He made her uncomfortable. And he was overly flirtatious with not only her, but all the females he encountered at the hospital. Some of the girls thought it was cute and fun, but not Laura Lynne. He turned her stomach. She did her best to avoid him, but it seemed every time she turned around, he was somewhere close by, with some body part touching her. Laura Lynne even tried explaining this to her momma, but she was having none of it.

"It is nothing for you to help this young man out Laura Lynne. He needs a babysitter, and you are certainly qualified to do it! I was appalled when he came up to me after the hospital board meeting and told me you had refused to help him! I raised you better than that!" As Laura Lynne started to protest, Melanie plowed on. "And don't tell me about your plans for the fair. I don't care." Then she uses her favorite phrase, "Don't ever embarrass me like that again Laura Lynne Cooper Beauregard, not ever again!"

Laura Lynne shakes herself from her foul mood. Grace is pedaling up Tea Olive Lane, waving and smiling. She is wearing shorts and a T-shirt with cute sandals. Laura Lynne can see the tie from her bathing suit around her neck, "Hey girl! Good news! Charlie and Buck are taking the boat out today. Might be they stop by your dock on their way out."

"Great," Laura Lynne says forlornly.

"What? I thought you still liked Buck, even after Tripp's big brother stunt at the club." Grace witnessed the entire debacle and agreed with Laura Lynne that her brother was being overprotective. Even Charlie was surprised at Tripp's reaction, as the three of them hung out regularly.

"No, it's not that. Momma just told me I have to babysit on Friday night, so I can't go with you to the fair." Laura Lynne begins walking beside Grace as she slowly pedals toward the house.

"What? Why? That sucks. Buck and Charlie have plans to be there," Grace replies.

"I know, right!" Laura Lynne proceeds to tell Grace about her conversation with her mother over breakfast. Grace already knows about Dr. Butler, so she is in full agreement.

"Can't you get out of it some way?"

"I don't know how. Think maybe we can change the plans to Saturday night?"

"I can ask, but darn! That just sucks!" Then, smiling, Grace points to her basket, "But let's not think about it right now. We will worry about it later. Let's get to the dock before we miss the guys."

The boys stop by the dock, tying off and getting out. Well, Charlie got out and flirted with Grace, snagging her boiled peanuts, and drinking from her Diet Coke. Buck stayed on the boat, much to Laura Lynne's dismay. Apparently, Tripp's warning had its desired effect. "Hey Laura Lynne, probably best if we just stay friends. Tripp's one of my best friends. I shouldn't be poaching on his little sister."

So that was the end of Laura Lynne's summer romance, over before it even started. And, to make matter's worse, Grace couldn't change her plans to Saturday. She had company coming into town. So, Laura Lynne was left to babysit two kids she had never met at the house of a man she thought was a creep. Her mother had even lectured her on the way over to the house.

"Laura Lynne, I am surprised at you! Dr. Butler has been very good to you this summer. Making sure you have that internship, working at the hospital. You need to be more appreciative. Babysitting for one evening is simple enough."

And Laura Lynne was shamed into silence, bit her tongue, and kept quiet just the way she was raised to do.

Melanie drops Laura Lynne off as she heads to check the DAR booth at the fair.

"Be sweet Laura Lynne!" Laura Lynne rolls her eyes as she gets out of the car.

The niece and nephew, 5-year old twins, Denise and Dennis, meet Laura Lynne at the door. Dr. Butler is very aloof and formal, introducing Laura Lynne to his fiancé, Margaret, his sister, and his brother-in-law. They have dinner reservations at The Calhoun House, so Laura Lynne receives last-minute instructions and they leave.

Since the kids have eaten and bathed, it was just a matter of settling them down in front of the television to watch *The Smurfs* on the VCR. It takes Laura Lynne a minute to figure out the VCR, as Melanie does not approve of any type of technology at The Residence. Mostly because it is ugly and disrupts the cultured aesthetic of her home. But Dennis just pushes her aside, inserts the tape and hits play. By the end of the movie, the kids are sleepy and easily go off to bed. Laura Lynne had listened endlessly about the kids' adventures in Uncle Ken's pool and they are worn out. Laura Lynne pulls out her required summer reading book, *Alas, Babylon*, and reads on the back porch until the adults return. Dr. Butler's sister, Andrea, volunteers to take her back to Tea Olive.

"Laura Lynne, I hope you don't mind. I have always wanted to see The Residence, especially the gardens. I have driven by the gates and never been in!"

The drive back to Tea Olive is quick, and Andrea is nice and talkative. She raves over the house and gardens, which Laura Lynne finds a bit disconcerting. Laura Lynne understands other people, especially those from off, find it charming and gracious, but to her, it's just home. By the time Laura Lynne gets to her room, she has convinced herself that Dr. Butler's behavior is off-putting, but harmless.

***

Two weeks later Laura Lynne comes in from spending the day at Grace's and heads straight to the kitchen. Grace's June is no match for Queenie in the kitchen. Laura Lynne has her nose in the refrigerator when she hears her momma's clackety-clack heels coming down the hallway. She spots the egg salad and places it on the counter when Melanie comes through the swinging door.

"Thought I heard you, Laura Lynne! What are you doing?" Laura Lynne is scooping egg salad into her mouth directly from the bowl. "Can you not get a plate? You are getting worse than your brothers!" Melanie stares, but Laura Lynne just keeps shoveling it in. "Listen Dr. Butler called today to ask if you could babysit for his niece and nephew again this Friday night. I told him it was fine." She is waiting for Laura Lynne to object.

"It is," Laura Lynne says with her mouth full. "Easiest $50 I ever made." Laura Lynne has almost saved up enough money this summer for a car of her own, just a clunker, but her dad had helped her find one they both agreed on. Neither had told Melanie yet. Scarlet and Tripp share the Volvo, but Laura Lynne wants her own car. This babysitting gig will bring her closer to the finish line.

"Good! He said he would pick you up at around 5:30. Home by 10PM. Same as last time."

He arrives as scheduled and Laura Lynne goes out to the car, Momma waving from the door. He smiles as she makes her way into the car. He circles the driveway and heads down Tea Olive Lane, toward the gates. He is quiet, the radio is playing Journey's *"Any Way You Want It,"* and Laura Lynne sings along in her head, comfortable in the air-conditioned Mercedes. By the time the song ends, they arrive at Dr. Butler's classic brick ranch house. He lives in town, close to the hospital, but in a nice neighborhood. Melanie calls it a "gentrified' neighborhood.

Dr. Butler pulls in and Laura Lynne gets out of the car, heading to the door. He opens it and then closes it behind him, Laura Lynne looks around. It is eerily quiet, and Dr. Butler has yet to say a word.

"Where are Denise and Dennis?"

Dr. Butler clears his throat, "They are on the way. They are going to be a bit later than expected but I didn't think you would mind waiting with me. Go out to the back porch and I will bring some snacks. Do you want a Diet Coke?" Laura Lynne is a fanatic for Diet Coke.

"Sure. No ice, please"

It's a beautiful night. The air is thick but there is a decent breeze. Dr. Butler brings out the Diet Coke in a glass with no ice, a whiskey for himself, some cheese, crackers and a cut-up apple. They talk about work and discuss Laura Lynne's summer reading. It's pleasant.

"Dr. Butler, excuse me. I need to run to the ladies' room." Laura Lynne is starting to feel funny and heads to the bathroom. She started her period yesterday, but these stomach pains were not the cramps she had grown to expect each month. Laura Lynne feels the soda start to come up the back of her throat, and barely makes it to the bathroom before vomiting. She heaves and vomits until there is nothing left. Her eyes are watering and snot is dripping from her nose. Laura Lynne can't remember the last time she was so sick! After rinsing out her mouth and throwing some water on her face, Laura Lynne opens the door to see Dr. Butler standing there.

"You don't sound so good. Stomach hurt?" Laura Lynne nods, scared to open her mouth in case she hurls again. "Lie down on the couch. I will call your mom to let her know what is happening."

"I am so sorry, but I don't think I can babysit the kids tonight. I just want to go home."

"Don't worry about that. I will call and cancel. They were running late anyway. Probably be relieved." He escorts Laura Lynne to the couch to lie down, putting a throw over her. She immediately falls asleep.

"Wake up Laura Lynne. Come on sweetie, I know you don't feel good, but we need to get you home." Melanie says as she gently shakes Laura Lynne. Laura Lynne is confused and feels woozy.

"Momma I threw up."

"Yes, dear, Ken told me. Let's get you home."

"What happened to my clothes?"

"I have them in a sack sweetie. You got vomit on them. Just keep the blanket on. We will have it washed and returned to Ken tomorrow." Laura Lynne wobbles as she stands up, but the nausea has subsided. Her entire body aches. She hobbles out the front door.

"Ken, thank you for calling! I am sure it's just a bug. I am so sorry your evening got ruined."

Laura Lynne does not hear Dr. Butler's reply. She doesn't care. She just wants to get home. She has never felt so sore and achy. Getting in the car, mumbling apologies, Laura Lynne feels awful. She lays across the front seat, placing her head in her mother's lap.

Melanie rolls down the window and calls out to Dr. Butler, "Thank you for looking out for her!"

"No problem. Hope she feels better soon. Laura Lynne, see you at work on Monday!" Laura Lynne is mute, staring at the dashboard clock while her mother gently rubs her hair off her forehead. The clock says 9:00. How is that possible? But before Laura Lynne can finish the thought, she feels the nausea begin to bubble up.

"Momma, pull over!"

Laura Lynne's tone was warning enough. Melanie pulls off the side of the road. Laura Lynne pushes the car door open, hangs her head over the seat, and dry heaves. There is nothing left in her body to vomit.

Chapter 5

Present Day

Laura Lynne and Gabe pull up to the gates of The Residence. The gates are an imposing structure made elegant by the beauty of the iron work, truly a masterpiece. The gate was commissioned by Gabe's father, the notorious Coop, whose love and respect for fine things is evident throughout the estate. However, the entrance gates to Tea Olive were designed by Charles Reichert. Charles Reichert commissioned a local blacksmith, Christopher Werner, to create his design. The gates are ornate, with gorgeous finials, and vines that look like the branches of a Tea Olive Tree in the shape of a "C." On top of the stone structures that secure the gates hinges, two beautiful pineapples stand tall and proud. The pineapple is a symbol of "welcome" and a typical and often seen ornament to grand, old, southern homes. These gates have been featured in many newspaper and magazine articles over the years, most recently gracing the cover of Southern Living's Christmas edition. When the gates open, the sight does not disappoint. The gardens are as gorgeous as the gates, graced by Magnolia trees, Camellia bushes, and too many azalea bushes to count.

"Uncle Gabe, the place looks amazing! The gardens are stunning."

He looks over at Laura Lynne with pride, though the pride quickly turns to chagrin. "Yes, well, thank you. I am afraid it was my gardening projects that got us into our current ordeal."

"Really? Why is that?" Laura Lynne and Gabe arrive at the front door. There, standing on the front step waiting is Laura Lynne's second best friend growing up, Pearl. She was now the head of the household and looks every inch like her mother.

"We will talk later. I want to rest," Gabe says, looking every bit his age.

"Of course, let's get you inside." The car door opens, and Laura Lynne is embraced in the familiar arms of Pearl. Laura Lynne closes her eyes, smelling the scent of magnolia blossoms and lemon. She takes a deep, shaky breath as the events of the last 48 hours wash over her.

Pearl pats her gently on the back, whispering softly in her ear, "Now, now, everything is going to be okay. You are home now."

Pearl steps back and Laura Lynne sees the tears in her eyes. Both in their 50's and no longer the young, vibrant children they were when they last saw each other. Laura Lynne's eyes well up, they are the same, but different. Older, wiser, and with a few more wrinkles and gray hair. Laura Lynne whispers, "I have missed you, Pearl. I am so glad you are here. Been wondering how I was going to make it up those stairs and into The Residence."

"We will do it together, Laura Lynne." Pearl walks around the front of the car. "But first Mr. Gabe." She hustles over to help Gabe from the car. "Now

Mr. Gabe, you have quite a story to tell! And I just bet you are hungry. What did they feed you? Bread and water?" She holds onto his arm, guiding him toward the steps. "Not to worry, Victoria's been in the kitchen all morning cooking your favorites. Got a hungry-man's brunch planned for you!"

Gabe smiles, the first since leaving the sheriff's department, "Glad to be home Pearl."

While Pearl assists Gabe up the stairs and into the house, Laura Lynne takes her first look at the home of her ancestors. The home her mother was born and she grew up in. Laura Lynne allows the tears to fall as she gazes at the plantation house, elegant and grand. The stately columns, front porch, and balcony. The gas lanterns on either side of the 12-foot mahogany front doors flicker at Laura Lynne, quietly beckoning her up the stairs of her childhood home. Laura Lynne wipes her eyes, clears her throat and whispers to herself, "I can do this."

Laura Lynne stands at the base of the stairs for so long that Pearl is back after depositing Gabe in his study. "Laura Lynne, go see your uncle. He needs you." She hesitates on her way to unload Laura Lynne's luggage. "You want to hold hands? Walk up those stairs together?"

Laura Lynne shakes her head, silently taking her first step up the stairs, thinking about her promise to herself the last time she walked down the stairs to a future no longer so carefully defined by her parents. She was a scared and confused little girl.

***

Summer 1985

"Laura Lynne, I need to get your mother in here. I am concerned with the test results," says Dr. Goldbug, Laura Lynne's pediatrician since the day she was born and also a classmate of her mother's.

Laura Lynne nods. "All right."

Laura Lynne shivers in her little cotton gown, sitting on the exam table, wondering if she is dying of cancer. She had been feeling bad for over a month: sore throat and nausea. Laura Lynne was lethargic and grumpy, choosing to stay in bed most of the summer. Her mother had had enough and hauled her to the doctor against Laura Lynne's vehement protests. She just wanted to be left alone.

Melanie walks into the room. She comes over to Laura Lynne and without a word, opens her palm and slaps Laura Lynne firmly across the face, the sound ricocheting around the room. She is furious. "You little whore," she hisses as Dr. Goldbug pushes Melanie to the side, standing directly in front of Laura Lynne.

"Melanie! Stop it!"

Laura Lynne is stunned, not even crying. Her mother never hit or slapped her. Discipline was meted out as a pop on the leg or grounding. Laura Lynne is clutching Dr. Goldbug's arms from behind. "What is it? What is wrong with me?"

"Melanie Beauregard, are you going to behave, or do I need to send you outside? You will not hit one of my patients. I don't care if you are her mother," says Dr. Goldbug firmly as he issues his warning.

Melanie says nothing, sitting stiffly in the chair by the wall. Her eyes are steely, her mouth a straight line. Her body is rigid. She is clutching her purse tightly enough to make her knuckles white.

Satisfied, Dr. Goldbug turns to his patient, "Laura Lynne, I know what is making you feel so bad, and the good news is we can give you medicine and clear it all up. I need to call the nurse in so we can do a vaginal exam."

At this Melanie jumps from her chair, startling Dr. Goldbug into turning around and facing the wrath of Laura Lynne's mother, "Absolutely not! Sydney, I won't have it!" Tears start to flow down Melanie's cheeks. "There will be *no gossip*, there will be *no nurse*, you will do this with me in here or I will take her somewhere else where *nobody* knows us. She will *not* be the downfall of our family."

"Melanie…" Sydney Goldbug takes Melanie by the shoulders and propels her back to her seat. "You are making this ten times worse than it is. Get yourself together."

Turning back to his patient, Dr. Goldbug takes a deep breath. "Laura Lynne, look at me, not your mother." Laura Lynne can't seem to stop staring at her mother, she has never seen her this mad before, and Laura Lynne still has no idea what is wrong with her. Dr. Goldbug gently turns Laura Lynne's chin toward his calm, gentle eyes. "Sweetheart, you feel bad because you have two venereal diseases, gonorrhea, and chlamydia. But to make sure you are not pregnant and to ensure there are no other symptoms telling me something different, I need to do a full work up."

"What? I can't have VD! I have never even had sex!" Laura Lynne turns her head toward her mother, "Momma! They got this all wrong! Something is not right. It is not possible." Dr. Goldbug says nothing; his eyes fill with compassion, and it is obvious he does not believe a word Laura Lynne is saying. "Dr. Goldbug, I have never had sex!"

"Well then, that is what this exam will tell me."

***

The drive home is horrible. Melanie is silent. She does not speak, look, or acknowledge Laura Lynne's existence. She has a fierce grip on the steering wheel. Her eyes are steely, looking straight ahead.

Laura Lynne tries, "Momma, I haven't…" It's as far as she gets. Melanie is having none of it. She gives her a withering look, hushing Laura Lynne so hard she spits.

Laura Lynne turns her head to look out the window. It looks like any other August day in Mississippi, but in Laura Lynne's heart she knows her life will never be the same. The exam reinforced Dr. Goldbug's suspicions, Laura Lynne's hymen was no longer intact. She is not a virgin. But Laura Lynne doesn't see how that is possible. She knew about sex. She and Grace have talked about it a lot. But she has never *experienced* it. She tried to tell Dr. Goldbug and her momma, but neither were listening. Dr. Goldbug just nodded knowingly, as if he had heard it all a million times before.

As soon as Melanie parks the car, Laura Lynne is out and running up the stairs, flying through the house up the stairs to her beautiful sage green and rose room. She flings herself on the bed and cries, deep wrenching sobs. The exam had been awful. Laura Lynne is still traumatized from the stirrups and the speculum.

"I am going to be as gentle as possible Laura Lynne, but I imagine you are hurting pretty good from the looks of things. Before you leave, I will give you some ointment to put on this raw skin. It should soothe the irritation." Laura Lynne flings the white bag with the instructions and tube of ointment across the room. It hits the door.

There is a soft knock at the bedroom door. Laura Lynne ignores it. The door opens slightly, and Tripp peers his head in. "Laura Lynne, are you okay? What is going on?" Laura Lynne is unable to answer.

Tripp walks to the bed and sits down next to Laura Lynne, gently petting her hair and rubbing her back. Laura Lynne squeezes her eyes tight, but she is ashamed to tell her big brother what just happened at Dr. Goldbugs office.

The door slams open and Tripp and Laura Lynne jump. Momma is there with Pearl. Pearl has her trunk and a suitcase. Laura Lynne sits up, "What's going on Momma?"

"You are going to your Aunt Eileen's. I have called her. She is willing to take you in." Eileen is Melanie's younger sister and lives on a horse farm in South Georgia.

 "What? I don't want to go! Momma, I haven't done anything wrong!"

While protesting Melanie is combing through Laura Lynne's closet, tearing things off the hangers, and throwing them at Pearl. She is a fury, a hurricane, causing destruction and terror in her wake. Tripp jumps off the bed and confronts Melanie.

"Momma! Stop! What are you doing?" She turns around, arms swinging, hangar in hand. Tripp ducks and the hangar barely misses his head. He wraps his arms around her body, as if to tackle her, and they sink to the floor, Melanie sobbing. Tripp looks at Pearl and yells, "Go and get Daddy, now!" Pearl is not used to Tripp giving her instructions, and she looks at Miss Melanie for confirmation. Tripp gets firmer. "Pearl, go and find my Daddy now. I need his help. I have Momma. Laura Lynne, it's going to be okay. Go to the kitchen and stay with Queenie. Maybe make some tea."

Running down the stairs to the kitchen, Queenie stands at the doorway, arms open for Laura Lynne. For Laura Lynne, this was the first human contact today that is not clinical, scary, or accusatory. Queenie sways from side to side, her warmth and smell like fresh baked Snickerdoodles and rich vanilla enveloping Laura Lynne. Eventually, Laura Lynne stops weeping. Queenie, matter-of-fact as always, ushers Laura Lynne into a seat at the kitchen island, placing a plate of cookies and some sweet tea in front of her. Nothing sweet tea and Jesus can't fix in Queenies eyes. Laura Lynne pushes the plate to the side and lays her head on the counter, closing her eyes and wishing the day was not happening.

The screen door opens and closes, the sound of Sawyer's boots on the hardwood floors echoing through the house. The fact Queenie does not comment on Sawyer traipsing through the house in dirty work boots is a testament to the severity of the situation. Tripp comes down the stairs and to the kitchen, sitting next to Laura Lynne, stroking her hair, and reassuring her. "Don't worry Laura Lynne, Daddy will make it right." While they wait, Tripp eats all the cookies and drinks the tea, it seems that no matter how bad the situation, Tripp is always up for a snack.

Eventually, the sound of their parents' quiet footsteps coming down the stairs meets their ears. "Come to the study, Tripp, Laura Lynne," says Sawyer, his baritone voice carrying to the kitchen.

"Come on. Let's get this over with," Tripp stands up, and Queenie reaches over the counter, squeezing Laura Lynne's arm gently.

"Everything will be fine, just fine, Miss Laura Lynne," Queenie reassures her.

Laura Lynne looks desperately at Tripp as they head to the study. "Promise me you will not leave me? No matter what happens?"

"I promise." Sawyer gives Laura Lynne a hug. She snuggles in close and Tripp whispers, "You know you can tell me anything, right?" Laura Lynne nods but remains silent. "Okay, well, let's get this over with."

Melanie and Sawyer Beauregard are seated on the two leather chairs opposite the dark brown leather sofa. Sawyer signals his two children to sit down. He looks tired and sad. His eyes are red, and his mouth is set. He is not pleased with the current situation. Melanie, on the other hand is stoic, her eyes staring straight ahead gazing over the top of Laura Lynne's head, her hands placed in her lap, her spine straight. They have made up their minds about something.

Daddy confirms Laura Lynne's suspicions. "Based on the current circumstances, and as yet unknown test results, your mother and I agree it is best to send you to Aunt Eileen's for a few weeks." Laura Lynne slowly lifts her head; she had been staring mindlessly at her feet. She starts to speak, but Sawyer holds up his hand. "There will be no discussion. This disgrace cannot be exposed. It will ruin the entire family's standing, not to mention the damage to Scarlet and Tripp. We need to salvage what we can of your reputation, though I doubt this will help." Sawyer leans forward and places his elbows on his knees, templing his fingers. "Do you have anything to say in your defense Laura Lynne?

Can you explain how, after all we have done for you, you allowed this to happen?"

Tripp reaches out, squeezing Laura Lynne's hand, a show of solidarity. Laura Lynne sniffles, "But that is just it, Daddy, *nothing* happened! I swear to you on Grandma Birdie's bible I have never *slept* with anyone!" Tears run down Laura Lynne's face.

Sawyer shakes his head, "Laura Lynne, I am not going to tolerate you sitting in this house flat out lying to your mother and me," he says in a resigned voice as he stands to exit the room, holding out his hand to Melanie. "Now go pack your things. We need to get to the airport."

Laura Lynne looks to her mother for help, but Melanie just ignores the pleading look and tears Laura Lynne cast in her direction. As her parents leave, Laura Lynne sinks to the floor on her knees, begging and pleading for another chance for them to believe her. And, though her parents stop on their way out, neither say anything or even make a move to comfort her. It is as if she has been cast out of the family.

"I hate you! I will never forgive you! If you send me away, I will never come back!" Laura Lynne continues to sob, fighting for the life she has always known. "Momma! Daddy! Don't do this to me! I swear I am a good girl!" Laura Lynne runs after them, grabbing at her father, pulling at his sleeve, begging.

"Laura Lynne! Enough!" Sawyer bellows loudly and thrusts Laura Lynne away, causing her to fall.

Tripp instantly runs to her, holding her close, rocking back and forth on the floor while Laura Lynne cries, heaving and wailing.

"Shh, shhhh! It's going to be okay, Laura Lynne. You love Aunt Eileen! Besides, you will be back before you know it. All this will blow over. Just wait and see," Tripp says, rocking and murmuring until eventually, Laura Lynne is completely worn out and her body goes limp. "Come on baby girl, let me help." Sawyer picks up Laura Lynne and carries her to her room, placing her on her bed where she curls up into a ball.

Pearl is instantly at her side, rubbing her head and covering her with a blanket, "Is she okay, Tripp? What in the world is going on?" Laura Lynne starts shaking uncontrollably.

"I don't know Pearl! You saw what I did! What the *fuck*!"

"Stop it, Tripp. You aren't helping anything." Pearl looks up as Queenie enters the room. "Thank God Momma, Laura Lynne is in bad shape."

"I know it, Pearl. You and Tripp need to head on out now. I need to talk to Laura Lynne." Tripp hesitates, loathing to leave Laura Lynne in this state. Queenie reassures him, "I promise I will take good care of her. Go on now!" Pearl pushes him out of the room, closing the door behind them.

"Laura Lynne, I am not leaving! I am in my room right next door if you need me!"

"That boy, he sure is a good one." Queenie comes to the bed, sinks into the mattress, and pulls Laura Lynne over onto her lap like she is five instead of fifteen. "Can you tell me what happened baby girl?" She rubs Laura Lynne's hair out of her face. "I think I can guess, but I'd like to hear it from you. But you hear me good. I love you no matter what you tell me."

Laura Lynne finally looks at Queenie, the woman whom she has trusted with all her secrets growing up, and she knows she can tell Queenie anything. She tells her everything about the doctor's visit, the drive home, her mother's slap, the whole sordid tale. Queenie listens quietly.

When Laura Lynne runs out of words, Queenie just continues to rub her head, "You believe me don't you Queenie?"

She nods. "If you tell me that is the truth, then that is the truth. You have never lied to me before, no reason to start now." She pauses in her stroking and gazes into Laura Lynne's red and swollen hazel eyes. "You sure you and Mr. Buck didn't do more than kiss?"

Laura Lynne sits bolt upright, "Yes!" She looks at Queenie accusatorily. "You said you believed me!"

"I do! I do! It's just something doesn't add up, that's all," Queenie tries to back track, but it is too late. Laura Lynne realizes even her most trusted confidante thinks she is lying.

"I want you to leave now, Queenie. I need to pack."

"Now Miss Laura Lynne, don't be that way. I was just making sure is all."

"Go, Queenie, now. I mean it. I don't want you here! Leave!" Laura Lynne starts pushing Queenie's considerable bulk off the bed, pushing her to the door, closing and locking it behind her. "I hate you!"

Chapter 6

Present Day

Laura Lynne walks up the front steps, realizing she is on a pilgrimage of sorts. She is revisiting a part of her life, long dead. Sensing her hesitation, Pearl comes along beside Laura Lynne, luggage in hand. "Come on, Laura Lynne. Aren't you ready to stop hiding from the past?"

"Whether I am or whether I am not doesn't seem to matter. Looks like the past has found me."

"It sure has a tricky way of doing just that. Come on. I was here when you left; glad I get to be here to welcome you back home. Sorry your Momma and Daddy aren't here to do it for you."

"Truthfully, Pearl, if they were I probably wouldn't be here. Not sure I am ready to see Momma again. Talking to her on the phone is one thing. Seeing her face to face, well, that's another."

"You're not a scared 15-year-old anymore Laura Lynne. Time to own your own power." She reaches out to hold Laura Lynnes hand, smiling. Laura Lynne smiles back, locking palms and swinging their hands back and forth like they did as children. Climbing the remaining stairs together, Laura Lynne gives Pearl a squeeze and releases her hand.

"I need to do this on my own, you understand?" says Laura Lynne.

Pearl nods and goes through the open door, leaving Laura Lynne on the front porch, calling over her shoulder. "Just so you do it!"

Laura Lynne smiles, shakes her head, takes one more look over her shoulder, turns toward the door, straightens her spine and walks over the threshold and back into her childhood. Laura Lynne looks around the foyer, tilting her head to gaze at the ornate crystal chandelier installed by Grandma Birdie, a purchase made in France on her and Coop's 'wedding tour' in 1932. It hangs in the center of the 30-foot ceiling, spraying sparkles of light on the walls of the two staircases that lead up to the second floor. The staircases have always reminded Laura Lynne of arms, reaching down on either side of the room. Her heart catches as she remembers the myriad of times, she and her brothers had ridden down the banisters much to her mother's dismay.

"There! You did it. Now, go see to your Uncle Gabe. He's in the study. I will bring some tea and lemonade unless you still prefer a Diet Coke?"

"A Diet Coke would be great. Thank you, Pearl." Laura Lynne starts to follow Pearl into the kitchen.

"Where do you think you are going? You have no business being in the kitchen with me and Victoria! Go see your uncle in the study. He wants to talk to you."

"Great," thinks Laura Lynne, "the study, my all-time least favorite room in the entire house. Just where I want to spend my time!' She sighs, muttering, "Oh well, may as well slay this dragon too."

Laura Lynne changes course and heads toward her dad's, well Uncle Gabe's study now, Laura Lynne supposes. As she approaches the open pocket doors, Laura Lynne can see her uncle propped up on the couch, a blanket over his lap. He is sipping a mug of coffee.

"Laura Lynne, please come sit down with me." Gabe pats the seat next to him, urging Laura Lynne to join him. She walks over to the couch thinking of the last time she sat in this very same spot, on this very same couch. "I need to tell you about the corpse."

Laura Lynne sits next to him. "You sure you are up to this? It can wait."

"No, I want you to hear it from me. Plenty of speculation and gossip around already. I want you to have the facts. Besides, it will give us a chance to catch up." He sips his brew and casts a sidelong glance at Laura Lynne. "What do you think of the house?"

Sighing, Laura Lynne sits down next to Gabe. "It looks the same. I have missed it."

"Yes, well your heart will always yearn for home, and with Cooper blood, that means Tea Olive," Gabe says this without inflection, as if it is a simple fact. Uncle Gabe leans his head against the back of the couch, settling in for his story.

"It is really all my fault. I have no one to blame but myself. I was in the middle of a project, and I got careless. I should have been more careful."

"What project?"

"I had run across the original renderings for the front garden, drawn by no one other than Dean Beauregard, the original in 1860. The plans were never completed, more than likely because of the Civil War. It doesn't really matter, but I thought it would be fun to finish the job." Raising his head, Gabe points to the desk. "The drawings are on the desk if you want to look."

Laura Lynne goes to the desk, the scroll unrolled and open on top of the desk, a replica of the Resolute found in the Oval Office. "Is that a fountain in the middle?"

"Well, a fountain probably, but a water feature, and here in lies the rub. To have a water feature you must have water and to get water to the front of the house, you have to dig. I hired excavators to do the heavy work. They began digging ten days ago, without incident. Then, Tuesday," says Uncle Gabe as he taps his head, "Wait, was it Tuesday? What day is it today? No, no, Thursday they came across a bone."

"What kind of bone?"

"Well, at first, we were not sure. It could have been an animal bone. I was not thinking human until I saw where they found the bone." Gabe points over his head toward the south side of the property.

"Well, you saw the crime tape when we drove in. It's over by the old slave quarters. At first, I thought maybe a slave, but the corpse had on a belt buckle. You know, like one of those ones you get at a rodeo."

Laura Lynne nods her head. Like most of the plantations along the Mississippi River, Tea Olive Plantation owned slaves. Unlike many of the plantations, Tea Olive has several of the original cabins, or quarters, still standing and preserved. The one-room buildings were made of logs, a living history of the brutal conditions endured by the enslaved persons who worked the fields and enriched the landowners. Queenie and Lincoln's people were once slaves in and around Tea Olive. A blight on Mississippians for certain, but a fact of Southern history.

"When I realized it was a person, I told them to cover it back up. I did not want to disturb the bones any further. I should have called it in to the sheriff's department immediately, but I didn't. I don't really know why, worried this would happen I guess."

He sheepishly looks at Laura Lynne.

She replies, "Yes, you really should have, Uncle Gabe." Laura Lynne comes back to sit next to him, taking his hand. "Unless you are trying to hide something."

In a quiet voice, Gabe whispers, "I wasn't thinking of myself, Laura Lynne. I was more worried about your father or maybe one of your brothers or sister."

Laura Lynne nods. "I thought the same thing myself, or maybe Poppy Cooper. You think your daddy would have done such a thing?"

"Oh, yes, no doubt about it. Could be him, right enough." He sighs. "I know for certain it was not me and that was the only thing I knew."

"Well, it wasn't me either," Laura Lynne replies, "That narrows it down a bit."

Smiling, Gabe pinches her cheek. "That is good to know." He resumes his story. "So, we put the dirt back over the hole and I sent everyone home for the day. The next thing I know, Sheriff Thomas is at my door with a search warrant and an arrest warrant." He finishes the story. "And here we are."

"What did Lally have to say?"

"Garfield read the warrant. I called him immediately. He said everything was in order and to let them do the search. His son Ace came with me to the sheriff's department while he stayed here, overseeing the search warrant." He takes a sip of coffee. "All he could tell me is the remains were human, appeared to be a man, and the belt buckle was from modern times." Gabe shakes his head. "I am worried about this, not for myself, but why is there a corpse on the property?"

"Have you asked Momma?"

"Good Lord no! Melanie? I am going to leave that to you, but she may know something. Not that she would ever tell us, but she lived here for 75 years. Not much would have gotten past her."

"Okay, I will ask, or maybe if I ever get in touch with Scarlet, she can ask. She was always Momma's favorite." Laura Lynne walks over to the bar, pouring herself the Diet Coke Pearl left while they were talking. "Where is Scarlet anyway? I have not been able to reach her. Is that usual?"

"Not that unusual," Gabe replies vaguely.

"What does that mean? She disappears regularly? I need you to expound on that a bit."

Pearl sticks her head in again. "Y'all ready for something to eat? Victoria set you up on the back porch, but if you would rather, I can bring the meal inside."

"No, no, the back porch is perfect, Pearl. I have been cooped up inside for too long." Gabe unwinds the blanket from his long legs, pushing himself to standing. "Come on Laura Lynne, nobody makes chicken and waffles like Victoria."

Following Gabe to the back porch, Laura Lynne sits across from her uncle at the table, waiting for him to say Grace. They bow their heads, and Gabe expresses gratitude for the abundance and for his current freedom. "Dig in, Laura Lynne."

Laura Lynne looks at her plate of waffles and strawberries, no chicken in sight. "What about the coroner's office? Any word from them?"

"Said it could take weeks. They need to bring someone in from Jackson to do the official autopsy. You know we don't have the equipment to do things proper here."

Laura Lynne cuts her waffle, loading her fork with the fresh berries and cream. "Then, we wait. I will call Lally in the morning and find out what the next steps might be." Laura Lynne takes a bite and closes her eyes in bliss. "Lord, these are good." Chewing and swallowing, Laura Lynne continues, "I will go see Momma this afternoon, maybe bring her by for cocktails."

The two discuss the updates to Tea Olive, The Residence, and the businesses Gabe invested in during the town's renovations. As executor of the estate trust, Gabe manages all the business affairs including purchases, sales, stocks, and land. It is a large task, especially for a man in Gabe's advanced years. As tradition dictates, Tripp will be the next executor of the estate, upon Gabe's resignation or death, whichever comes first.

Finishing their meal, the two lean back in their chairs, contemplating. Long silences with Gabe are not unusual or uncomfortable. Laura Lynne waits to speak, watching as her Uncle Gabe leans his head back and takes a deep breath.

"Are you good here? I think instead of waiting until tomorrow, I will go to town and try to talk to Lally and catch up with Grady Cunningham. I also need to try and connect with Scarlet and Avery. It is time to call in the calvary Uncle Gabe, and see what everyone knows, or in my case, doesn't know."

"Yes, I think that is a fine idea. I need to go out to the gardens for a while. That cell was rough on my soul. I need my flowers."

"Don't you want to rest?"

His laser beam gaze falls on his niece, and she knows she stepped in it. "Laura Lynne, I have been cooped up in a jail cell the size of a matchbox for the last 36 hours. I want to be outside." Getting up and heading to the mud room, he admonishes her. "Now stop your fussing."

"Yes, sir." He has a valid point.

Laura Lynne watches Gabe get his boots on, fretting anyway. John comes to the door. "Figured you would want to spend some time with your flowers, Mr. Cooper."

"Just so, John, just so."

John nods his head in Laura Lynne's direction, "M'am."

"John, this is my niece Laura Lynne. Laura Lynne, this is John."

"It's really nice to meet you, John." Laura Lynne smiles at Uncle Gabe. "I know you told me not to fuss, but take it easy out there today. Plenty of time for you to play in the dirt tomorrow."

"You are as bad as your Momma, always fussing." He gets up and heads to the door. "I don't need a caretaker, Laura Lynne, just my flowers." And with that, he takes off out the back door, spry as a young man.

Laura Lynne watches the two men stroll off toward the barn, deciding there is no sense worrying about him. He is going to do what he wants to do.

Besides, John is with him. He seems like a responsible person.

Laura Lynne walks through the house, popping her head into the kitchen. Pearl and Victoria are both there, working on a shopping list. "Ladies, thank you for a wonderful brunch! And how did you know I was a vegetarian? I don't remember telling you!"

Pearl smirks. "We have our ways, don't we, Victoria?" Pearl elbows her daughter, smiling.

"Well, it is appreciated. Listen, I am going to get Momma today. Bring her by this evening for cocktails and dinner. Can you handle it? I know it's last minute, and Momma will expect something nice."

"Of course, be nice to have Miss Melanie home for a few hours. We were just working on a menu for the week with you back home. Any special requests?"

"Maybe some of your Momma's shrimp and grits? Oh, speaking of Queenie, maybe I can see her tomorrow. I want to tell her how sorry I am about Lincoln and Pearl, you too. I am sorry I was not here for the funeral."

"Thank you, Laura Lynne. He died the way he wanted to, at home with his children. Cancer ate him up on the inside, but his brain was still good. He was ready to be called home."

Laura Lynne nods, changing the subject. "John seems like a nice enough man. He's got Uncle Gabe out in the garden. If I am needed, call or text me on my cell phone. Here." Extending her hand, she takes the pen from Victoria, smiling. "Let me give you the number." She proceeds to write it down on the grocery list. "Thanks, ladies, y'all are the best."

Heading into town, Laura Lynne takes the road to the family cemetery next to the Cooper family chapel. The chapel is small, seating fewer than 100 people, and was built in the 1800s. It has all the customary aspects of a chapel, steeple, bell, and pulpit, but its claim to fame is the Lalique stained glass window purchased in France by Julian Cooper. The cemetery is in the side yard and is the place of rest for all Cooper family members. It is also on the National Historic Registry.

Laura Lynne parks the car, gets out, and walks toward her father's grave marker. As she walks by the church, she reminisces about the special occasions the family celebrated in the chapel: christenings, weddings, funerals, and the high holy days. Laura Lynne should have been married here. She and Grace used to dream of white weddings and babies in this very spot. She and Jimmy eloped. Laura Lynne didn't even consider returning to the chapel. Besides, her father was not a fan of Jimmy's. Laura Lynne grimaces, thinking how right he was to be concerned.

Laura Lynne turns the corner of the chapel, walking toward the center of the small family cemetery. She has always loved it here—peaceful and beautiful in a serene and majestic way. There are azalea bushes and live oak trees with moss hanging from the branches like women's hair, blowing in the breezes coming off the river. Laura Lynne notes the wildflowers and honeysuckle that drape the stones and climb the statuary as she makes her way to stand beside her father's marker, Sawyer Avery Beauregard II, 1944-2018.

Chapter 7

Summer 1985

Laura Lynne is sitting in the Cadillac on her way to the airport. Silent tears slide down her face. She does not attempt conversation. There seems nothing left to say. She and her father drive in stony silence, parking the car, retrieving the luggage from the trunk, and walking toward the ticket stands. Laura Lynne watches as her father pays for a one-way ticket to Atlanta. The attendant glances with concern at Laura Lynne and her tear-streaked face, but she, too, says nothing. Laura Lynne is miserable, all this because of one kiss, a sweet stolen moment behind the Country club.

On their way to the gate, Sawyer sits Laura Lynne down in a quiet corner of the airport. "Laura Lynne, I am going to give you one more chance to come clean with me. I need to know who did this to you." He takes a deep breath. "Was it Jeremiah?"

Laura Lynne looks at her father, emotionally exhausted. "Why? Is that what Tripp told you?"

"No, Tripp never said anything to me. But I am not stupid, Laura Lynne. Stop acting like I am. I know what happens under the Magnolia trees at the club. Your mother and I saw you head out there with Grace."

This was news to Laura Lynne, and here she thought she and Grace were being so clever!

"Buck and I, we kissed, but only for a moment. Tripp came out there and saw us, nearly tore Buck's head off and marched me back to his truck! Daddy, I swear to you I have never *done it* with anyone! I don't know why no one will believe me! I am not a liar!" Laura Lynne begins to cry harder, fat tears rolling down her cheeks.

"Laura Lynne, I *know* better. Dr. Goldburg told your mother you were no longer…," stumbling over the word, her father harshly whispers, "*intact*." He takes hold of her hands, "So if it was not Jeremiah, then who was it? Laura Lynne, I need to know."

"Nobody!" Laura Lynne releases all the pent-up emotion and anger in her, screaming it in her father's face, and for the second time in 24 hours, Laura Lynne receives a slap across her cheek.

Stunned and quivering, Laura Lynne holds her cheek with her hand, balled up in the chair, her legs up to her chest. She looks like a child. "I expected this from Momma, but not from you, Daddy, never from you."

Regret in his eyes, her father stands up, "Well, I gave it one last try. I did my best. You continue to lie and fabricate stories we all know are false. You have to face the consequences." He reaches down and, grabbing her arm, he hauls her to her feet. "Come on, let me drop you off at the gate. It should be boarding in a few minutes."

Laura Lynne shakes her father's hand off her arm, wiping her nose with her forearm and rubbing her eyes with her hands. "I need to find the bathroom first."

Looking at her for the first time with compassion, her father walks toward the ladies' room. "I will be right here, and if you are not out in five minutes, I am coming in to get you."

Laura Lynne escapes into the bathroom, running to a stall and flinging it open. She feels awful. Her girl parts are all itchy, and when she pees, it burns, hurting so bad she groans and whimpers as she opens her purse, searching for the cream Dr. Goldbug prescribed. Cleaning up, she gazes at her reflection in the mirror, unable to recognize the face staring back at her.

***

Laura Lynne gazes at the ceiling of her room at Aunt Eileen's, wishing she could somehow crawl into a hole and die. She doesn't want to be here. Laura Lynne loves Aunt Eileen; she is super hip and new agey, but Laura Lynne wants to be at home in her own room at Tea Olive. As much as Laura Lynne wants to roll over and snuggle back under the covers, nature is calling. She moves like an old lady, aching from head to toe. Exhausted, as if she has not slept a wink, Laura Lynne glances at the clock radio on the bedside table calculating, twelve hours of sleep has not occurred.

Laura Lynne stumbles across the floor, finally arriving at the bathroom door. Flicking on the light, she opens and closes her eyes as if she is a mole coming out of its hole. She relieves herself and then, spotting the extravagant shower, turns on the shower head. Standing under the hot spray, Laura Lynne revisits the events of the previous 24 hours, barely understanding how she is standing here and why everyone thought she was now, as her mother so bluntly put it, *defiled.* The shame and pain, the culmination of the events and travel, well up inside of Laura Lynne. She curls up on the shower floor, sitting under the hot spray, and closes her eyes.

"Laura Lynne! Laura Lynne! Honey, are you okay?"

Laura Lynne opens her eyes. She has been lying so long on the tile that the shower water has run cold. She begins to shiver but still doesn't move or call out. The bathroom door opens slowly. "Laura Lynne?" Spotting her niece on the floor shivering, Eileen runs to the shower, turning it off. "Oh baby girl, poor thing, hold on. Let me get you a warm towel." She grabs a towel out of the basket, opens it up, and pulls open the glass shower door. She sinks to her knees, cradling Laura Lynne in her lap.

"Shhh, shhh, sweetie, everything is okay. Auntie is here, shhhhh, shhhh," cradling Laura Lynne, whispering quietly, kissing her head, offering comfort.

The two of them remain on the floor until Laura Lynne finally asks, "Why doesn't anyone believe me?"

"That is not true, Laura Lynne. I believe you."

Laura Lynne's eyes pop open, "You do? No, you don't. You don't even know what happened."

"I have a good idea, and the truth is, none of it matters." Aunt Eileen strokes Laura Lynne's hair. "The only thing that matters is you. Come on, baby girl, what do you say we get off the bathroom floor and get some dry clothes on? I have breakfast waiting for you on the porch." Glancing at her watch, she chuckles, "Well, more like lunch now."

Laura Lynne nods as they both awkwardly get to their feet. Eileen puts her hand under Laura Lynne's chin, looking directly into her eyes. "I know everything seems really bleak right now, and you are scared, but I am not going anywhere. You can stay at River Oaks as long as you want, understand?"

Laura Lynne nods.

Aunt Eileen continues, "Can you get dressed by yourself? Or do you want me to help?"

"I'm good," Laura Lynne says quietly. Then, looking fully at her aunt, the first hint of a smile creeps across her lips. "I think maybe you need to change too."

Her aunt looks down at herself, dripping wet in her flowing outfit of poncho pants and matching blouse. "Guess I do." Smiling, she shrugs, practical as always. "Meet you on the back porch?" She turns to walk out. "Now, don't make me come and get you, Laura Lynne. If you are not downstairs in 20 minutes, I am sending up Martha."

Twenty minutes later, Laura Lynne is walking gingerly downstairs wearing loose warm-up pants and a sweatshirt, praying the discomfort will go away. Instead of the medicine making things better, her redness and swelling are worse. Now, there is an odor. Not only is Laura Lynne mortified, but she is also scared. What if she has cancer or something? And Dr. Goldbug got it all wrong; maybe she is dying. She has a moment where she relishes the thought of her parents suffering her imminent death. It would absolutely serve them right.

Aunt Eileen is waiting, tea in hand. Aunt Eileen doesn't like coffee. She drinks tea and Diet Coke, another reason Laura Lynne loves her so much. She has a Diet Coke sitting on the table for Laura Lynne. As she gently sits across the table, Aunt Eileen assesses the situation quickly. Handing her a cushion, she says, "Here, sweetheart, sit on this. It will help." Gratefully taking the pillow, Laura Lynne sits down and immediately takes a swallow of Diet Coke. She is parched. Silently watching her, Eileen waits until Laura Lynne puts the glass down, "You okay, baby girl? You look mighty uncomfortable."

Laura Lynne leans over the table and whispers, "I don't think it is getting any better. The medicine is making things worse, and now it," she lowers her eyes and barely whispers, "smells bad down there."

Aunt Eileen waits until Laura Lynne lifts her head, her eyes wet with unshed tears. "You look at me right now, Laura Lynne." Passionately grabbing Laura Lynne's hands, Aunt Eileen continues, "You don't ever be ashamed to tell your Auntie *anything*! You hear me? I am no prude, and I am *not* your momma! You have nothing to be embarrassed about!" She leans closer. "*Nothing* you tell me, Laura Lynne, *nothing* will shock me or be shared with *anyone* without you telling me I can. I have heard it all. I have experienced most of it." She leans back and clears her throat, waving at the food on the table. "Well, go ahead and eat something."

Laura Lynne looks at the food, "I am not very hungry. I feel nauseous."

Aunt Eileen hits a button on the porch intercom system, "Martha, can you possibly make some broth for Laura Lynne? She is not feeling very well this morning." Eileen waits for acknowledgment before disconnecting.

"You want to tell me about your day yesterday? Or would you prefer to hear about mine?"

"Yours."

Sensing a fun story, Laura Lynne settles in for a recounting of her aunt's day. And she does not disappoint, regaling Laura Lynne with stories about the horses, the cowhands, and ranch life while Laura Lynne sips the mug of broth brought in by Martha during the tale. She finishes her story, "And then my lovely big sister, your mother, calls me to ask if you can stay with me awhile, and I readily accepted. I love having you here, Laura Lynne." She refills her teacup. "Are you ready to talk about it now?"

Nodding and with hesitation, Laura Lynne slowly tells her story of the last 24 hours, finishing with, "And then Daddy tells me unless I was truthful, I could not come back home. But I *am* telling the truth! I swear!" Throughout the entire telling, Laura Lynne is gazing into her mug, refusing to look directly at Aunt Eileen. And when she did look, Laura Lynne was not sure what to make of it.

Aunt Eileen is furious, absolutely furious. She is up out of the chair, pacing around the porch. "I have a mind to call up that horrible sister of mine and give her a piece of my mind! Calling you a whore? And Sawyer! Slapping you?" She looks at Laura Lynne. "Shipping you off to me as if you were now no longer *worthy* of being at Tea Olive, of all the nerve!"

Of all the reactions, having Aunt Eileen mad on her behalf is not one Laura Lynne was expecting. And it felt really good to have someone in her corner. Laura Lynne leans back in her chair, picking up a muffin and biting in, the tang of lemon exploding over her tastebuds. She eats the entire muffin, watching her aunt pace and rant, until finally, Aunt Eileen loses steam. "You done now?" Laura Lynne says.

"Not by a longshot, but I am for now." Smiling, Eileen comes by Laura Lynne's chair, ruffling her hair. "Glad my diatribe activated your appetite."

"Martha makes the best muffins. These are even better than Queenie's."

"Hummph, high praise that. Martha will be tickled." With a plop, like all the air has been let out of a balloon, Eileen sits down. "Okay, let's deal with first things first. I want you to see my doctor. Not to say anything bad about Dr. Goldbug, but he is a small-town doctor. Might be worth getting a second opinion." Sensing Laura Lynne's hesitation, she continues, "Her name is Lydia. You can trust her. She is also a personal friend. And, until you start feeling better, it is hard to think about anything else." She waits for Laura Lynne to nod her head in agreement. "Okay, let me make some phone calls. Maybe she can see you today. Why don't you just lie down on the chaise lounge until I get this figured out?"

Laura Lynne pours herself another Diet Coke and walks slowly to the chaise lounge. She pulls the blanket over her, curling up and falling asleep instantly.

"Come on, baby girl. I am sorry. Need to wake up. Dr. Lydia can see you today. We have about 30 minutes."

Laura Lynne gazes at her aunt's beautiful face. "What time is it?"

"3:30, sweetheart. You slept two hours. Come on, sleepy head, wash up and let's get on the road."

The two arrive at the doctor's office. Laura Lynne is intimidated by the skyscrapers and the traffic of a big city. She is ushered to the back immediately. Aunt Eileen stays out in the waiting room, a privacy Melanie would never afford one of her daughters.

But she just smiles, waving Laura Lynne away, saying, "Laura Lynne, you are a young woman now. You don't need your old Aunt Eileen hovering over you. Dr. Lydia will take good care of you. Besides, the two of you can talk privately, woman to woman. I love you. You got this, but call me if you need me." She pulls out her newest addition of *Southern Living* and begins flipping through the page.

Laura Lynne likes Dr. Lydia immediately, appreciating her gentle, straightforward approach. A large, athletic woman with gray sprinkled throughout her black hair, she sports huge, round, black-rimmed eyeglasses over her gentle brown eyes. She makes Laura Lynne feel very comfortable before calling back her nurse to complete her exam. She talks the entire time, telling her about the horse she has recently purchased from River Oaks named Jezebel. She pushes back from the exam table, taking off her gloves. "Okay, Laura Lynne, need just a few minutes to get these results. I am going to have Rose get Eileen from the waiting room." Rose nods and heads out while Dr. Lydia helps Laura Lynne sit up.

Shortly, Eileen is ushered through the door, and Dr. Lydia sits her next to Laura Lynne. Eileen wraps her arms around Laura Lynne's shoulders, and the two look expectantly at the doctor as Rose hands her the lab test results. "So, here is the news. Laura Lynne, you have three infections, not two, which is why the treatment Dr. Goldbug gave you is not working effectively. During my exam, I noted some growths around your cervix and confirmed you have what is commonly referred to as genital warts, in addition to chlamydia and gonorrhea."

Silent tears run down Laura Lynne's cheeks. Eileen snuggles her closer to her side. "Okay, Lydia, what do we need to do?"

"With your permission, we can go ahead and perform cryosurgery, basically freezing the warts. This will kill the virus, and the warts will slough off, but it removes the problem within about a week."

Nodding, Eileen asks the question foremost on her mind, "Is it possible Laura Lynne is pregnant?"

Shaking her head, Dr. Lydia continues, "No, she is not pregnant. Her test came back negative." Eileen is visibly relieved, "Laura Lynne, can you look at me for just a minute, sweetheart?"

Laura Lynne raises her tear-drenched eyes. "We are going to figure this out, but first, we need to make you well. Unchecked, these types of infections can have negative long-term effects, including infertility."

Laura Lynne nods, laying her head on Eileen's shoulder. "Will you stay with me? Please."

"Of course," Eileen says as she looks and gains Dr. Lydia's consent, "I will be right here holding your hand the entire time."

"While we are getting prepped, Rose is going to give you a shot of Rocephin to treat the gonorrhea and an oral dose of Doxycycline. Would you like something to help you relax? I can get you something mild."

Laura Lynne is staring listlessly, not able to engage. Eileen answers for her, "I think that would be helpful. She is about tapped out, Lydia."

"Okay, we will get this done as quickly and easily as possible."

The next hour is a blur to Laura Lynne. After she administered a muscle relaxant, Laura Lynne drifted in and out of consciousness, enjoying the feeling of weightlessness and the release of tension from her muscles. Once completed, Dr. Lydia motions Eileen out to the corridor while Rose finishes cleaning up and keeping an eye on her patient.

"Eileen, something happened with your niece. For all intents and purposes, her symptoms present as a typical sexual encounter with one or more partners. I even swabbed her throat, and it came back positive for gonorrhea." She leans against the wall. "Emotionally, she is a wreck, but that could be because she knows something and doesn't want to talk. Or she experienced a trauma and has repressed the memories."

"I know, and I have no idea what to do. I will take any recommendations."

"I have a friend who is a psychiatrist, works with children and young adults. I think Laura Lynne might benefit from some counseling."

"I thought about that, but I don't want her labeled or drugged up." Eileen shakes her head, "She's a really good kid who just caught a really bad break. There is no need to ruin her future."

"Well, if you change your mind, give me a call. She is pretty conservative. And honestly, if Laura Lynne were my child, I would be sending her to Dr. Thurgood. And Eileen, I say this as a friend. If that child does not get some help, I don't suppose she will have much of a future."

"Okay, give me her number, I will make an appointment."

Chapter 8

Present Day

Laura Lynne makes her way back to the rental car, pulling out her phone and calling Scarlet one more time. As if waiting for her call, Scarlet picks up on the first ring. Laura Lynne and Scarlet's relationship has been very rocky since Scarlet's marriage to Laura Lynne's former teenage crush, Jeremiah "Buck" Huger. Laura Lynne was not invited to the wedding, not that she would have attended anyway. They married as soon as Scarlet graduated from Ole Miss, four years after Laura Lynne was sent to live with Eileen.

"Laura Lynne, what is going on?"

"Scarlet, where have you been? We have been trying to reach you for three days!"

"Don't you fuss at me, little miss big britches! I am left here to deal with Momma and Uncle Gabe 365 days a year while the rest of you live your lives as if they don't exist! If I make myself unavailable for a few days, then you or Avery, or even Tripp, can pick up the slack!"

"Well, you picked a fine three days to relax and rejuvenate! Next time, a heads up would be helpful."

"Oh, really? You ready to take on some of the responsibility around here?"

It's a valid question.

Laura Lynne takes a deep breath, "Truthfully? I am really not sure yet. Check with me after I see Mom today."

"Wait! Are you in Mississippi? What is going on?"

"Yes! Where have you been? Lord, Scarlet, you live up the road, and you didn't know Uncle Gabe was arrested?" Scarlet lives north of Venice on land the Hugers gave her and Buck as a wedding gift, about halfway between Venice and Wisteria. "I bailed Uncle Gabe out of jail yesterday, had to put The Residence up as collateral." Laura Lynne fills her in about the corpse, the sheriff's department, Uncle Gabe's declaration of innocence, and Momma's dramatic phone call. Then, the tough question. "Scarlet, do you have any idea who this could possibly be? You have been here the longest. Any dead bodies that Daddy or Poppy would have been hiding?"

There is silence on the phone. Laura Lynne figures Scarlet is digesting the current circumstances.

"No, I cannot think of anyone, though it would not be out of the range of possibilities for Poppy Cooper. Daddy, no, I doubt it. His worst crime was cheating on Momma, and I sure didn't do it." Scarlet's voice turns soft. "How are you doing Laura Lynne? How is Tea Olive?"

Laura Lynne is surprised by the questions. She and Scarlet have not been on personal terms since the summer of '85. The two have corresponded, had discussions about their parents, and most recently, about putting Momma in assisted living, but that was two years ago. Since then, the two had exchanged birthday and Christmas cards, nothing more.

"It's good. I am okay. I am surprised by how little has changed."

"Isn't that the truth? Okay, what do you need me to do?"

"I am not sure yet. I was really hoping you might have an idea about the corpse. The autopsy will be sometime over the next week or so. They ended up taking the body into Jackson. So, we wait. The only thing we are certain of is his gender. The corpse is a man. I am headed into town to see if I can catch up with Grady Cunningham. I think he might have more information than he was telling me at the station. And, Scarlet, we have to consider a lawyer for Uncle Gabe—somebody in criminal defense. I don't have a clue who that might be. But the Monroe men are all over this, and we need to expect trouble. Ace Lally cannot handle it."

"Buck might know. Let me ask."

"That would be great. Scarlet, actually, I do have a favor to ask." She is silent. "Can you go to the assisted living place and talk to Momma? She needs to know what is going on, but it needs to be done in private. Maybe you can bring her to The Residence for cocktails around 5 PM? That way, it will look like we are having a normal evening. I don't know…something nice, so her friends think everything is good?"

"Oh God, I didn't think of Momma's friends. Okay, you're right. It's better if I do it. I can call and tell her we are having a celebratory dinner to welcome you home or something like that. I will pick her up in the Cadillac. She loves riding in her old Cadillac. May as well brighten her day and mood before we hit her with this one."

"Well, I am wondering if she might know something. Melanie Beauregard is neither naïve nor stupid. She knows better than any of us how this family works. And let's face it, the Beauregard family tree is not exactly free from illegal activities either."

"True, very true. Listen, Laura Lynne, I have to go. Are you going to call Tripp and Avery, or do you want me to do it? I am not even sure where Tripp is these days. I haven't spoken to him in months."

"Let's just talk about it tonight over cocktails and with Momma and Uncle Gabe. It can wait another few hours. See you this evening." As Laura Lynne goes to hang up, she hears Scarlet on the other end.

"Laura Lynne?"

"Yes?"

"I am glad you are home. I can really use the help. And I was always sorry the way things worked out for you…and for me." She disconnects.

That is the weirdest thing to say. What does she mean how things worked out for her? She got everything she and Momma ever wanted. The name, the house, the social standing, the two kids, everything. Laura Lynne shakes her head, putting the comments aside. She has no time to dwell on them now.

As Laura Lynne drives into town, she sees a bustling hub of activity—a vast improvement from her teenage years when Main Street was dying. Magnolia Mall was the place to hang out, eat Chick-fil-A, and "cruise" the parking lot on Saturday night. Laura Lynne spots the brewery, a few high-end clothing stores, and a wine bar. Even the old movie theater has a fresh, retro look. Laura Lynne continues driving until she spots the Venice Gazette newspaper office. On a whim, Laura Lynne pulls into a vacant parking spot in front of the building and parks the rental. The best place to find information about the happenings in the town is a small-town newspaper. Might be worth scouring the backlog to see if any information emerges about Tea Olive's new resident, "Dead Doe."

Laura Lynne exits her rental. She closes the car door and locks it before walking slowly down the street, absorbing her old hometown as she makes her way to the coffee shop called Magnolia Café. The café is busy. The outdoor tables are filled with customers, obviously the town hub. Laura Lynne senses the change almost immediately as if a hush goes over the crowd as she makes her way to the front of the shop. She glances around to see what is causing everyone to stop what they were doing. Seeing no one behind her, she realizes she is the cause. Small-town gossip is alive and well in Venice, MS.

Grateful at times like these for her mother's strict rules on propriety and Laura Lynne's own sense of pride, she slowly walks toward the entrance. With her gaze steady and calm, Laura Lynne acts as if she is not aware she is the center of attention. Laura Lynne overhears one woman loudly "whisper" across the table to her friend, "That's the youngest daughter, isn't it? Lord, things must be pretty bad for her to come back here. Rumor has it she was a teenage mom, shipped to Atlanta, never came back. Bless her heart."

Zoning in on the woman sharing her tidbits of information, Laura Lynne spots what her momma would refer to as a "wannabe." She has obvious wealth, new money, and is from somewhere north of the Mason-Dixon line. She is trying to be something she can't be, but wants to be: a Southern Lady. This woman is dressed to impress in a gorgeous Lily Pulitzer sundress, matching hat, and heels. Pearls are dripping from her ears and lying around her neck. Her hair is pulled back in a bun. And, Laura Lynne admits, she is beautiful. However, she looks like she is going to the Kentucky Derby instead of grabbing a coffee. She is too overdone.

Laura Lynne turns toward the woman, who has leaned back in her chair, gazing at Laura Lynne as if waiting for her reaction. She was obviously the current town bully. Laura Lynne sighs. She really wishes she could have her tea before giving this woman a lesson in manners. "So, you are the current town 'mean girl?' I wondered who was playing the role these days. Used to be Candy

Westerman, but I understand she stopped her bullying ways, and she is as sweet as her name." The woman starts to object. Laura Lynne simply puts her hand up. "Listen, I don't have time for this and have no clue who you even are, and I don't care. It is obvious you are new to town and the South as no self-respecting Southern woman would be so gauche or so overly dressed on a Wednesday morning at Magnolia Cafe."

Miss Wannabe gazes at her beautifully lacquered nails and too sweetly replies, "I have no idea what you mean, Laura Lynne. Nobody here was talking about *you!* You must have misheard me, though it is not at all surprising considering how exhausted you must be. You know, with what all is going on with your poor Uncle Gabe."

Laura Lynne acknowledges this woman has skills, but then so does Laura Lynne. "Wow, that is impressive. Somehow, in one sentence you presented yourself as someone who is familiar enough with me and my family to be on a first-name basis. We are not. We never will be."

Reinforcements in the form of Laura Lynne's childhood best friend walks up to Laura Lynne and exclaims, "Laura Lynne Cooper Beauregard is that you? Grady told me to keep an eye out as my best friend in the entire world was in town!" Grace envelopes Laura Lynne in a big hug, talking nonstop, "It is so good to see you! I have missed you!"

Pulling away, she looks at Laura Lynne, smiling, "What are you doing standing out here? The cool crowd is inside, come on let's get you something to drink and you can join us."

Grace casts a dour look over her shoulder and escorts Laura Lynne into the coffee shop. "That Natalie Johnson is a horrible person. I didn't notice you had been caught in her clutches, or I would have gotten to you sooner."

"Well, I appreciate it. I was getting ready to give her an appropriate dressing down. But honestly, I just don't have the energy to deal with her ilk today." Looking at the menu, Laura Lynne continues, "But she definitely seems like a nasty bit of goods."

"Truer words. But if she went after you already, she has you in her crosshairs. I would watch my back if I were you."

"What is her deal?"

"Breezed in from Boston about 20 years ago. Her husband, Brad is the VP of Banks Construction. Nice enough guy. Plays golf on occasion with Charlie. Natalie on the other hand, fancies herself a Southern belle. Even attempts a Southern drawl." At this Grace rolls her eyes. "And has remade herself into her version of a Steel Magnolia." Grace smirks. "Wouldn't be so bad, but she is mean with it. I have yet to find a kind bone in that woman's body."

At the counter, there is a young girl with braids and a nose ring. Somehow the combination makes her look artsy. "Hey, Mrs. Eubanks, what can I get y'all?"

"Hi, Amanda. Are you about ready for school to end? Ready for the summer?"

"Busy with the school play. I am working on the sets."

"With your artistic eye? I bet you'll do a great job. Okay, what do you recommend? Never mind, just give me my usual. Laura Lynne?"

"Large hot tea, Earl Grey, no milk."

The artsy Amanda rings the women up and then heads to the coffee maker. She is wearing overalls cut off as shorts with striped leggings underneath, and black clog shoes. She has her own confident wardrobe style.

The two women stand to the side, waiting for their orders. Laura Lynne gazes around the café while Grace discusses the exuberant Amanda, who is currently in her literature class. She is a thespian and is the only daughter of the Wheelbarrow bookstore owner, Diane. While Grace chatters on, Laura Lynne notices the new additions to their old haunt. There are now soft pastel-colored tin panels for the ceiling, and the walls have been painted cream to accent the refinished mahogany wood floors.

"Here you go ladies," Amanda says as she hands them their beverages.

Grace escorts Laura Lynne to a cozy nook. The nook has two cushy chairs, surrounded by bookshelves overflowing with books. The bookshelves feature a sign from *Wheelbarrow Books* proclaiming, "Reading gives us someplace to go when we have to stay where we are."

"This is a super cute place. Are the pastries any good?"

Grace closes her eyes and sighs. "Only divine! Just looking at them causes my waistline to expand!"

Laura Lynne smiles, looking at Grace's slim and petite figure as envious as she was as a teenager. "You are as beautiful as ever, inside and out." Laura Lynne sips her tea. "Do you have time for all this? Aren't you in here with a group of people? I don't want to take up all your time."

Laughing Grace smiles. "No, no, I just made that up to make Nasty Natalie jealous. I stopped by to pick up coffees for the real estate office. With spring break in full swing, I am attempting to get some listings together. I swear, next year I am going to retire from teaching! Too much for this old girl."

"You love it. I can tell. Bet you are great at it. How is Charlie? And your parents?"

For the next ten minutes, Grace catches Laura Lynne up on her husband and their son, Trey. He graduates from Ole Miss this year and will follow in the Eubanks family's footsteps, farming and running the Piggly Wiggly. "He is a great kid, and my parents are good, still living in the house at

Cotton Mill. They would love to see you. Of all my friends, Momma always favored you."

Nodding, Laura Lynne says, "I have missed them and you. I am so glad we ran into each other. It has been too long."

Grace's eyes tear up. "Laura Lynne, what happened to my best friend all those years ago? And now? What can I do to help?"

Looking at her thoughtfully, Laura Lynne puts down her tea. Grace puts down her coffee and the two hold hands, leaning over close to each other. Laura Lynne softly speaks, "I am so sorry I hurt you. I was not allowed to say good-bye. It broke my heart." Laura Lynne inhales, taking a deep breath. "I went to my Aunt Eileen's and never came home." Squeezing Grace's hand, she continues, "One day, maybe I will be brave enough to tell you what happened. I am just not strong enough yet." Laura Lynne looks back at her, tears overflowing. "You understand?" Grace nods.

Squeezing her hands one last time, Laura Lynne leans back in her chair. Both ladies grab napkins, dabbing their eyes and blowing their noses. The sweet Amanda discreetly comes to their corner with fresh drinks and a box of Kleenex, making the two women giggle. The heavy moment is over.

"Oh God Laura Lynne! I am so glad you are back!" Sipping her coffee, Grace asks, "What can you tell me about the goings on at Tea Olive?"

"Not much really. You probably know as much as I do. The coroner won't have results for a while, so there is very little to go on." Thoughtfully, Laura Lynne gazes into her tea. "Uncle Gabe claims he doesn't know anything, and I believe him. Scarlet, the same. I certainly didn't kill anyone." Smirking as she raises her cup to her mouth, Laura Lynne continues, "Doesn't narrow the field by much."

"Have you asked Miss Melanie? I imagine she may know something."

"Scarlet is bringing her to The Residence tonight under the guise of celebrating my homecoming. We hope to pry out what information we can from her over whisky sours and macaroons."

"What about Tripp and Avery? You hear from them yet?" Grace picks up her coffee, takes a long drag, closes her eyes, and smiles softly. Grace dated Tripp in high school during her "make Charlie jealous" stage. It worked.

"I haven't heard from Tripp in years, five to be exact. When Daddy died. His military career keeps him busy, but mostly I think he stays away on purpose- like he has to prove something. I don't know Grace, none of us stayed close. I have a number for his lieutenant in case of emergencies. Probably getting to that point. And Avery stays in touch with me. He won't come back here unless he has too. And it will just be him. He will not subject his wife and children to Momma again. He made that clear."

Grace leans over and pats Laura Lynne's knee. "I am sorry your sister and brothers are distant. Growing up I didn't think anything could bust up the Beauregard clan. You were all so close. I am so sorry I was wrong."

Smiling sadly, Laura Lynne pats Grace's hand. "Me too, Grace. Me too."

The two chat about Laura Lynne's new husband and her children, becoming a grandmother. And Laura Lynne's book, which Grace has read and wants to be sure she gets her copy signed.

"I thought it was very brave of you to write, but then you have always been very brave. I am glad you are home." Grace gathers her coffee mug and stands. "I have to run. My co-workers are going to wonder where their afternoon coffee and pastries are." She looks seriously at Laura Lynne, "I know you know this, but plenty of people in this town wouldn't mind seeing your family taken down a notch or two." She glances toward the front door, "Watch your back."

"Noted." Laura Lynne reaches her hand out to Grace, "Grace, thank you."

"Nothing to it. Just don't leave again without saying goodbye."

Laura Lynne pulls out her phone, checking messages and emails, noting the time. She only has about thirty minutes before she needs to head back to Tea Olive. The time spent with Grace causes her to rearrange her scheduled plan for the day. Not that she minds. Laura Lynne retrieves her teacup, placing it in the wash basin on her way out the door. No sign of Miss Mean Girl.

Unable to pass up a bookstore, Laura Lynne decides to spend her thirty minutes in *Wheelbarrow Books*. Walking through the front door, Laura Lynne sees a woman who can only be Amanda's mother. Diane is working on a book display at the front window. And, to Laura Lynne's delight and dismay, she realizes it is her book, "*The Bluebird Diaries*."

"It still makes me jolt when I see my book in a bookstore, much less the window display." Laura Lynne walks toward Diane, the gorgeous, mystical, woman sporting a nose ring, and who has her hair all bundled on top of her head in a loose knot. She is gorgeous. Holding out her hand, businesswoman to businesswoman, Laura Lynne says, "I am Laura Lynne Atkins, and you must be Diane."

Diane shakes Laura Lynne's hand with a firm grip and looks her in the eye. "I am. You look like your mother, though your aura is completely different, a lovely indigo for you. Highly intuitive and wise. Seems accurate for an author."

Laura Lynne smiles wide. Diane reminds her so much of her Aunt Eileen. "And what color is my mother's?"

"These days, she is more a soft grey, but when I first met her, she was a bright orange. Age affects us in many ways. It is nice to meet you, Laura Lynne." She glances around the shop. "Please make yourself at home unless I can help you in some way?"

"No, no, I just had some time to kill. It is hard to pass up a bookstore. Always been one of my favorite ways to pass the time."

Laura Lynne wanders around the shop, enjoying the books stacked to the ceiling. Mozart is playing softly in the background and Laura Lynne wishes she had time to sit in one of the comfy chairs reading a cheap romance novel instead of preparing for battle. She will see her mother for the first time in nearly forty years tonight. She wished she was excited by the prospect. Instead, she is dreading the meeting.

Chapter 9

Fall 1985

Laura Lynne has been at Aunt Eileen's for several weeks. Her parents insist she stays away from Tea Olive until things "settle down." Sawyer confronted Buck's parents, even after Laura Lynne's vigorous defense of him. Buck, of course, adamantly denied any type of encounter other than the kiss, even after Robert, Buck's daddy, took his belt to him. Sawyer demanded he be tested, threatening to destroy the Huger family if proper measures were not taken. Robert took Buck to Dr. Goldbug, and sure enough, the results were negative. Buck's "I told you so" left Robert furious with himself over being bullied by a Beauregard. He began a vicious campaign against the Beauregard family, and apparently it is working. Melanie has been kicked out of the Junior League and removed from her duties as President of the local chapter of the DAR. There are no social invitations. Tensions are high, gossip is rife, and nobody thinks it is a good idea for Laura Lynne to come back. Unless, of course, she is willing to disclose her lover.

Laura Lynne hears Aunt Eileen on the telephone. "Sawyer, she swears she has not had sex with anyone! And, honestly, I believe her. I don't think she remembers that she has. The psychiatrist that Dr. Lydia recommended is not available for another two weeks, so at this point I agree that she stays here with me. She can go to school here. There are several good ones. And I don't mind. I enjoy having her with me. She is no trouble at all." Plans are made without Laura Lynne's consent or even opinion.

Laura Lynne is physically better. The medicine and surgery resolve the physical symptoms. Mentally it's another story. Laura Lynne prefers staying in her bed, refusing to bathe. She eats only enough to keep a bird alive. Today she attempts to be productive by reading '*The Grapes of Wrath*'. Here, in the world of John Steinbeck, Laura Lynne is transported to another world. A world where people help each other, and families stand up for one another, and no one is left behind. Laura Lynne loves the book, the escape. She spends the next two weeks reading one book after the other, holing up in her room.

One morning, there is a knock at the door and before Laura Lynne can acknowledge it (not that she would have), Aunt Eileen is standing next to her, hands on hips. "Laura Lynne, this has gone on long enough. You are a ghost in this house, hidden up here in your room, expecting Martha to bring your meals and clean up after you. It ends today."

Laura Lynne's eyes begin to tear. Noticing, Eileen sits on the bed. "Sweetheart, I know. I do, and honestly no one is more disappointed in your parents than I am. But you have to live your life, and if you let yourself, I think it can be a good one here with me." Hugging her niece, Eileen sits back, her nose wrinkled. "But first, a shower."

Eileen hovers over Laura Lynne like a mother hen, helping her walk to the shower, worrying over how thin she has become, how limp her hair is, and how sad her eyes have become. "I thought we might go to Whistledown today and look at the litter of puppies from their Beatrice. Would you like a puppy Laura Lynne?"

Hearing nothing, Eileen soldiers on. "It would be yours to keep, take care of, name, all the things. What do you think?"

Whispering, Laura Lynne asks, "Can she be an indoor dog? Stay with me in my room?"

"Well, of course! If that is what you want."

"I do. I truly do. Momma never let us keep animals in the house."

"Well, your mother is not here to make the rules anymore. I am. And the rule of my house is dogs are a welcome addition to the household."

Leaning in for a hug, Laura Lynne wraps her emaciated arms around her aunt. Eileen holds tight, her eyes wet from unshed tears. Patting her on the back and putting on her matter-of-fact voice, Eileen clears her throat. "Go on then, get your shower. I will wait in the bedroom."

"I love you, Aunt Eileen."

"I love you too, baby girl."

That afternoon, Laura Lynne came home with not one puppy, but two. Eileen just couldn't separate the only two girls in the litter of Golden Retrievers.

In the spirit of celebrating Southern literary great Harper Lee, they named their new family members Maudie and Scout. Laura Lynne dotes on both girls, but in the end, Scout is her dog. Her constant companion. Scout becomes the first step in her healing journey. There is just something so comforting about the wiggly warm body and constantly licking tongue that soothes Laura Lynne's battered soul.

Laura Lynne also begins her sessions with Dr. Mabel Thurgood, the psychiatrist Dr. Lydia recommended.

"Laura Lynne, it's nice to meet you. My name is Dr. Thurgood. Why don't you have a seat? Would you like your aunt to stay?"

"No, just us is fine."

Aunt Eileen nods and comes over, kisses Laura Lynne's head, and whispers, "I am staying right outside in the waiting area. I will be there when you are done. Love you, baby girl."

As the door shuts, Laura Lynne looks over at Dr. Thurgood. "This time is yours Laura Lynne. You can talk to me about anything you want. I want you to understand I will not share anything you tell me with *anyone* unless I fear you will harm yourself or someone else."

"Yeah, right," Laura Lynne thinks to herself. Since the beginning of this entire debacle, anything Laura Lynne has said has been shared with her parents. Not that anyone actually believes her. But Laura

Lynne does have one question. "Do you think I might be crazy? Like Momma's Aunt Augustine, who hears voices and talks to the air like there is somebody there?"

Dr. Thurgood looks at Laura Lynne thoughtfully, kind dark brown eyes steady. "No, Laura Lynne, I don't think you are crazy. Our minds are really wonderful things. When something traumatic happens that is just too difficult to process, sometimes our mind blocks that memory until we are ready to deal with it. I think maybe that happened to you. And it's my job to help you process those feelings, those emotions, so your brain will let you remember. So, no, I don't think you are crazy. I think you are traumatized."

"So, something bad could have happened to me, and I just don't remember it? Like rape? Somebody could have raped me, and I didn't know?" Laura Lynne's voice rises and cracks, her breathing heavy.

"Laura Lynne, look at me." Laura Lynne looks at her, panic setting in. "Laura Lynne, look at me. We are going to figure this out together. You are a strong, smart girl. You are not crazy. I believe you. Do you understand me? *I believe you.*" Slowly, the panic begins to subside. "Deep breaths, Laura Lynne. Slow deep breaths, very good." Dr. Thurgood is so reassuring; and so pleasant. She is not embarrassed, or mad, or anything. She is just peaceful. And Laura Lynne begins to have hope.

Once the panic has abated, Dr. Mabel asks, "Do you have these panic attacks often?"

"Not often, no, but sometimes. Sometimes when I think about what might have happened to me, I get scared, and my chest hurts; my throat closes off. Am I weird?"

"No, not at all. Perfectly normal." Dr. Thurgood leans back in her chair, laying her pencil across her pad of paper. "Laura Lynne, tell me what brings you to my office today."

And with those words, the events of the last month unfurl. Laura Lynne leaves nothing out, including her feelings about her parents kicking her out of Tea Olive. It is as if a heavy burden is being lifted off her chest with every word. Laura Lynne even threw in some cuss words to see if Dr. Thurgood would get riled. She didn't. She just kept listening. Laura Lynne experiences all the emotions from fear to anger to defiance to shame and then resignation. When she has nothing more to say, she sits quietly, feeling empty, like a sponge that has been wrung out.

"Well, now, do you think I am as crazy as Aunt Augustine?"

Dr. Thurgood allows herself the first smile of the entire session, laughing gently. "No, I don't. I think you are a brave, smart, strong girl who is overcoming a lot in the best way she knows how. But I do think I might be able to help you if you let me."

Laura Lynne begins seeing Dr. Thurgood three times a week until school starts. Once she starts classes, the therapy visits will move to weekly.

Until then, Laura Lynne begins journalling some of her thoughts and feelings as one of the recommendations from Dr. Thurgood. She thinks it might help to process some of her feelings if she could write them out. Recently she has mostly been writing about her fear of starting a new school.

"How do you feel about school starting?" Dr. Thurgood asks during one session.

Laura Lynne shrugs her shoulder. "Ok, I guess. I don't know why I can't go back home and go to Mosley Hall. I want to be with my friends."

"I completely understand. But let's talk about your first day of school tomorrow. It will be hard to be the new kid in town. Especially at a small private school with lots of cliques and it may be difficult to find your footing. You have made a great deal of headway in the last couple of weeks. I want you to keep that momentum."

Walking down the halls of Robert E. Lee on the first day of school is completely intimidating. Laura Lynne thinks she should have paid closer attention to Dr. Thurgood's concerns. Luckily, she is not the only new girl, so she has someone to walk with between classes and a lunch partner for the first couple of days. Not that she was all that concerned with making friends. Laura Lynne was certain her parents would be by to get her any moment and whisk her back to Tea Olive.

But two weeks into the school year Laura Lynne's hopes are dashed. After a phone call with her parents, Laura Lynne is so devastated that Dr.

Thurgood makes a house call. Her parents are unrelenting in their pursuit of the "truth." Unwilling to bend to their daughters' continued pleas, her tears, or her begging, she is not allowed back into the fold until she discloses who has "ruined" her.

Aunt Eileen, Laura Lynne, and Dr. Thurgood sit in the cozy kitchen nook while Martha pours tea and serves cookies. Eileen is livid and Laura Lynne is shattered. Having a good understanding of the situation, Dr. Thurgood asks, "Laura Lynne what do you want to have happen here? Besides going back to Tea Olive?"

Laura Lynne just shrugs her shoulders, her eyes wet with tears, her nose running. Eileen pulls closer to Laura Lynne and holds her hands. "I have done everything I know to sway your parents, Laura Lynne. Even Mabel called and spoke to them." Eileen glances at Dr. Thurgood.

"And to be completely honest, Laura Lynne, I am not sure it is a good idea to send you to your parents given their current state and behaviors. I think the environment could prove very difficult for you, especially considering their ultimatum."

Eileen takes the baton. "And we both think it best if you stay here with me indefinitely. I love having you here. You are already enrolled in school. You have Maudie and Scout, and you have me and Mabel." Eileen takes a deep breath. "Well, what do you think?"

Laura Lynne whispers softly, "I think I don't have a choice. May I be excused please?"

"Laura Lynne...," Dr. Thurgood starts to intervene as Laura Lynne stands from the table.

"It's ok, really, I am fine. I appreciate all y'all have done for me. I just need some time alone. I will be upstairs in my bedroom."

As Laura Lynne shuffles out of the kitchen and heads up the stairs, she hears Eileen say, "My bitch of a sister and her sorry-assed husband are more worried about their, their, their...friends, and what they think than their own child! It is appalling! I have never been more ashamed of them!"

Laura Lynne turns around. "Don't be too hard on them. I let them down. I knew the rules. Even if I don't know *how* what happened to me happened. But I put myself in a situation that allowed it to happen. Somehow, someway." Laura Lynne shrugs her slim shoulders. "But, even though I love my parents, after this, I don't think I can ever see them again. Would that be all right? To never see my parents again?"

Eileen jumps up from the table and runs over to Laura Lynne, hugging her with all her might. "If that is what you want, then you have my permission to wait until you are ready. But when you are ready, we will face them together. You and me baby girl, we got this."

As Laura Lynne heads up to her room, Scout at her heels. She feels a sense of relief to realizes she does not have to face her parents again. She doesn't have to listen to their accusations, or, worse, sit in their stony silence. She curls up in her bed, Scout laying over her lap. She gets her journal and begins to write, pouring out her heart. But this time is different. This time she is resolved. Resolved to prove her parents' wrong.

Chapter 10

Present Day

Laura Lynne and Gabe are standing at the top of the stairs when Scarlet pulls up with Melanie for Laura Lynne's welcome home dinner. Gabe is dressed in khakis, a button-down shirt, and a bowtie. Laura Lynne is wearing a maxi sundress with tropical flowers. Gabe hustles down the stairs to open Melanie's car door, and Laura Lynne stays put. She has not seen her mother in person but once, since 1985. Melanie has not met her grandchildren, though she has spoken to them on birthdays and holidays over the years.

As Melanie emerges from the car, Scarlet goes to the trunk to retrieve Melanie's walker. A broken hip with the last fall at The Residence kept her hospitalized for weeks before her transition to assisted living- no need for a repeat performance.

"Scarlet, I am not using that thing. I have my cane."

Laura Lynne sees Scarlet take a deep breath. "Okay Momma, let me help you with the stairs."

They slowly take the steps. Laura Lynne takes the opportunity to get a good look at her mother. She is still regal and intimidating, even though her shoulders are stooped and her back hunched. Her hair is professionally colored and coiffed: the same mahogoney brown Laura Lynne remembers growing up. And tonight, for Laura's welcome home dinner she is wearing a pretty, light pink sheath with a matching cardigan thrown over her shoulders. Pinned at her chest is a pearl brooch alongside her DAR pin and matching pearl earrings. She has on panty hose with white tennis shoes.

At the top of the stairs, Melanie stands directly in front of Laura Lynne. Laura Lynne does not blink, holding her mother's gaze for the first time since she was a teenager. Melanie's eyes are no longer the steely, deep blue of her youth, but are still piercing and unforgiving.

"Hello, Momma."

"Laura Lynne."

Sensing the discomfort, Gabe reaches around Scarlet for Melanie's hand. "Scarlet, I can take Melanie from here." He switches places with Scarlet. "You two girls catch up. Melanie and I are going to have a Tom Collins to celebrate." Looking over his shoulder, he winks at Scarlet and Laura Lynne as he escorts Melanie inside. Pearl meets them at the door, dressed in all white and looking every bit like her mother. Laura Lynne rolls her eyes, and Pearl bites her lip.

Leaning toward Scarlet, Laura Lynne whispers, "I thought for a minute Pearl was Queenie."

"In that getup? I am not surprised. Mother insists Pearl wears that hideous thing as if it is still the 1950s. I told Pearl she didn't need to, but she said she didn't mind. Her mother was proud to wear her uniform every day, so she gets a kick out of it when she puts it on."

Laura Lynne turns to fully face Scarlet. "Hi, Scarlet, it's good to see you." Scarlet is as beautiful as ever, but there are dark circles under her eyes. She is terribly thin, but coiffed and properly turned out for this evening's festivities. Not a hair out of place, her blonde hair in a fashionable bob and she is wearing a smart jumpsuit in blue. She also has on pearls, of course, and cute strappy sandals. Her makeup looks professionally done. She does not look 56. "You look gorgeous as always. Thanks for getting Momma."

"It is not a problem, though the vultures at the assisted living facility were circling." Rolling her eyes, she continues, "Though not a big worry as Momma can easily hold her own." Scarlet takes a moment to collect herself and holds out the walker to Pearl. "Thank you, Pearl. Do you mind stashing it in the mudroom for me? She says she doesn't need it, but the nurse at Pineview told me she needs to use it. Her balance is shaky due to the Parkinson's. It was hard enough getting her to wear tennis shoes, so I wasn't going to argue about the walker. I figure that between all of us we can keep her upright."

Squaring her shoulders, she looks over at Laura Lynne, gently rubbing her cool hand along Laura Lynne's forearm. "Come on Laura Lynne, let's get this over with."

The two Beauregard girls walk through the main entrance of The Residence together for the first time since the two girls were in high school. The significance did not escape either of them, but neither did they dwell on it. Walking toward the sitting room, Scarlet whispers, "I have missed my sister."

To Scarlet's surprise, Laura Lynne begins fanning her eyes, which are moist with tears. "Damn it Scarlet! I was doing so good and then you go and mess up my make-up!"

"Young lady, the rules of this house have not changed. No cussing. I don't care how old you are." Gabe lifts his drink, "But I am letting it go just for tonight. John, mix these ladies a drink."

Smiling, Laura Lynne looks at John. "Just some unsweetened tea for me, please, no ice."

Everybody turns and stares at Laura Lynne. She has just committed not one, but two sins in the span of one heartbeat. Every home in Mississippi has gallons of cold, sweet, iced tea at the ready for guests and family. It is, after all, the house wine of the South. Clearing his throat, John replies, "I will need to get with Victoria as we don't seem to have that. Would a water work?

Nodding, Laura Lynne shakes her head to herself. She knows better. She makes her way over to the small spread of appetizers, and she grins, grabbing a cold piece of shrimp and dipping it in cocktail sauce. Putting it in her mouth she catches her mother's eye. Melanie is giving Laura Lynne the same look she gave her when they were together in Dr. Goldbug's office, the one that shows her disdain. Laura Lynne looks straight at her and pops another shrimp in her mouth, acting bold even though what she really wants to do is hide or worse, beg for forgiveness.

As Laura Lynne takes a seat across from her mother, Pearl comes to the sitting room with Laura Lynne's glass of unsweetened, room-temperature tea. "Oh Pearl, you didn't have to go to the trouble. Water is fine!"

"No trouble, Miss Laura Lynne." Pearl takes a step back, and dropping her head, turns to Melanie and says, "Ma'am" before making her way out of the room. Laura Lynne's stomach turns. When the two were growing up, this type of behavior was normal and expected from Pearl and, well, all the servants. Today, it just makes Laura Lynne realize how much she has grown up and changed since she was here last. In a good way.

Seeing her mother disdainfully eyeing her glass, Laura Lynne remarks. "I don't drink alcohol, I prefer my drinks room temperature, and I don't like sugar in my tea. A lot has changed since I was here last."

"Humph," Melanie replies.

At this, Gabe launches into farm news and his business dealings in town. He has dealt with his sister for many years. He knows better than anyone how to smoothly engage Melanie by asking her opinion on matters related to Tea Olive. The two have a lively discussion regarding the price of cotton and upgrades to the farm equipment. Laura Lynne is surprised by her mother's obvious business acumen. She had no idea her mother knew about anything other than hem lines and social functions.

At exactly 6:30, Pearl comes to the door, signaling it is time to withdraw to the dining room. Melanie, as the matriarch, proceeds the guests where she sits at the head of the beautifully laid out dining room table.

"I see you used the Royal Albert," Melanie comments as she is helped into her seat by Gabe and John, "a lovely choice."

"Thank you, ma'am." Pearl waits patiently to the side as Scarlet and Laura Lynne stand behind their chairs. "I know it is one of your favorites."

Once everyone is seated, Pearl pours a bit of wine into Gabe's glass, waiting for his approval before pouring it for the rest of the family. Laura Lynne declines by discreetly placing her hand over her wine glass. This, of course, is not missed by the sharp-eyed Melanie. Victoria arrives with the first course, a light cucumber soup, cold. She has Melanie taste it before receiving the nod of approval to serve the rest of the family.

As soon as the family is alone, Melanie launches her first missile. "Laura Lynne, you finally decided to grace Tea Olive with your presence. Is it as you had hoped it would be?"

Laura Lynne knew it was coming and, in fact, prepared herself. Well, at least she thought she had prepared herself. Girding her loins and biting her tongue, Laura Lynne says simply, "It's just as lovely as ever."

"And if you have returned to Tea Olive, then you must be ready to tell me the truth. I believe that was your father and my stipulation to your return."

"I never lied to you Momma, never once told you anything but the truth. You and Daddy just didn't believe me. Besides, Uncle Gabe owns Tea Olive now and he asked me to visit. I agreed it was time for me to return."

Scarlet looks over at Laura Lynne with compassion and a bit of steel. Laura Lynne did not expect to see either reaction from her. "Momma, enough! You will not ruin tonight's meal and Laura Lynne's return. Laura Lynne is a full-grown woman and has a right to her own privacy."

"Scarlet is right Melanie. Leave the child alone."

Melanie is impervious, though she stops her barbs when Pearl returns to remove the first course, and Victoria serves the main course of red beans and rice with a side of collards and fresh cornbread. She goes through the same routine with Melanie and, once satisfied, serves the rest of the family.

As she sets down the plate in front of Laura Lynne, Victoria whispers, "Miss Laura Lynne, I made yours to your specifications." Laura Lynne gives her a quizzical look, and she mouths, "No meat."

"Thank you."

"You have special dietary restrictions now, other than no alcohol, no ice, and no sugar?" Melanie intones.

Laura Lynne responds back with a bit of cheekiness, "Yep, no meat. It's not really a restriction. I just choose not to eat meat; haven't for 25 years."

Before Melanie can respond, Gabe chimes in. "A smart and healthy idea, Laura Lynne! Thank you, Victoria."

Melanie waits for Victoria to leave, and the family is alone, though Pearl probably has her ear pressed up against the door listening. Melanie begins, "Scarlet, you, and Laura Lynne will always be my daughters, regardless of your age. Lying and hiding things from me will never be tolerated."

Nodding, Gabe says, "Very good then sister. I agree; lying and hiding things should not be tolerated in families. Keeping this in mind, perhaps you can help shed some light on a puzzling problem we have here at Tea Olive. You see, last week, the excavators uncovered a corpse near the old slave cabins. For some reason beyond my own ability to understand, they think I had something to do with it. Any idea why that might be? Or better yet, who that might be?"

Scarlet and Laura Lynne glance across the table at each other, their mouths slightly open. Scarlet carefully puts her fork on the plate, placing her hands in her lap. Laura Lynne quickly closes her mouth and ducks her head. Nobody but nobody talks to Melanie Louise Cooper Beauregard in that tone. Not ever.

Except, obviously, Melanie's younger brother and the current trustee of the estate, Gabriel Lynne Cooper because he was not finished. "Perhaps you offed somebody with that scathing tongue of yours?"

Scarlet kicks Laura Lynne under the table. Laura Lynne kicks back. This is more fun than going to the movies, though Laura Lynne wishes she had some popcorn and a Diet Coke to enjoy the show. Before Melanie could answer, Pearl comes in to remove the plates, followed closely by Victoria with dessert: Mississippi Mud Pie. John is in the doorway with the coffee pot ready to pour, or for reinforcements. Laura Lynne is not certain at this point.

The table is cleared, and coffee is served for everyone except Laura Lynne, who instead is given hot tea. Melanie is unable to let this slide. She must comment. "No alcohol, no sugar, no meat, no *ice* and no coffee, divorced. I see Eileen's influence put crazy ideas in your head about what is acceptable for a Southern lady. I should have never sent you there."

Laura Lynne froze, wadding up her napkin in her lap. "You are absolutely right, Mother. You should have never sent a frightened, 15-year-old to her aunt's house. I couldn't agree more. But don't ever say another ugly word about Aunt Eileen in my presence. For most of my life, she was more of a mother to me than an aunt. But I am not that scared, little girl anymore. Your nasty tongue won't work on me. I need neither your love nor validation, so instead of trying to get the focus off of you with your barb at Aunt Eileen, how about you answer Uncle Gabe? Did you kill somebody? Because honestly, I have not one doubt in my mind you are mean enough to do it."

Melanie is not easily rattled, but by this point her glasses are quivering on her face with pent-up rage. "Ashamed, Laura Lynne. I was ashamed of you at 15 and even more ashamed now."

Laura Lynne's eyes begin to tear, and her lip begins to quiver. She knew it in her heart, but now hearing it directly from her mother's lips cuts straight through her heart. "The feeling is mutual."

"Stop it! Stop it! Both of you, don't say things you cannot take back." Scarlet waves her arms and is as pale as a ghost. "I won't have it!"

The suddenness of her outburst shocks the entire table. Uncle Gabe wades in, "I started this. I apologize."

"Don't you dare apologize, Uncle Gabe. You did nothing wrong. Just said what we have all been thinking these many years." By this point, Scarlet has command of the table. Her color is returning. "Laura Lynne, let me apologize for our mother's very poor behavior and even worse manners on your first night home in over three decades. She is completely out of line, though I am certain her intent was not to make you feel unwelcome or unwanted."

"I am very certain it is exactly what she intended. But not to worry, Scarlet, she failed. She only succeeded in validating what I have always known." Looking at Scarlet with sympathy, she says, "I was the lucky one. I got away. And now, I have lost my appetite. Please excuse me. I need a breath of fresh air."

And with that, Laura Lynne walks out of the dining room, through the back door, and down the porch steps. Once clear, she takes off and runs to the river dock, tears flowing. When would she ever learn? When would she figure out that no matter what she did, no matter how many degrees, how many books, or how amazing her children were, her mother would always find fault? She would never apologize, never admit she was wrong, never. The one thing Laura Lynne craved the most, what her young heart yearned for and never received, was her mother's unquestionable, unconditional love.

Sometime later, Laura Lynne feels a warm hand on her shoulder. She is sitting on the edge of the dock, swinging her legs, looking out over the river.

"Mind if I join you?" a voice says from behind.

Glancing up, Laura Lynne sees Pearl dressed in jeans and a t-shirt. "Of course," Laura Lynne responds. Pearl sits next to Laura Lynne, swinging her legs to match Laura Lynne's rhythm, just like when they were girls. Laura Lynne asks, "At what point do we stop craving our mother's love? Even when we know we won't get it?"

"Now you don't think your Momma doesn't love you, do you? She does, plain and simple. She doesn't understand you. She is hurt because she thinks you are lying to her, but she loves you," Pearl says.

"She sure has a funny way of showing it."

"She does, that is for certain. Miss Melanie, well, she is a bit of a cold fish, for certain. Not to make excuses for her behavior, but things were not good for her once you left. She and your daddy, well, they never got over it."

Laura Lynne looks at Pearl. "You listened at the door?"

"Well, of course! Just like always!"

Snickering, Laura Lynne starts to laugh. "Pearl, God! I nearly swallowed my tongue when Uncle Gabe asked her if she killed anybody! Scarlet was kicking me under the table. I was shoving red beans and rice in my mouth and nearly choked! Scarlet was all but slack-jawed. And there Uncle Gabe sat, cool as a cucumber, calling Momma out on her bad behavior."

The two women start howling with laughter, hugging up on each other, each talking over the other as they recount another part of the horrible dinner hour. Pearl picks up the tale, "And, God! John and Victoria! Mortified by the conversation and yet strangely drawn to hear the outcome! Did you see John at the door with the coffee pot? I wasn't sure if he was going to pour the coffee or wallop your Momma over the head with it?"

This sent them into another gale of laughter. Mopping at her eyes, Laura Lynne looks at one of her oldest friends, "I have missed you, Pearl! And, please, don't ever wear that horrible uniform again. It made me ashamed of my mother all over again. Promise me."

"That is a promise!"

As the two quiet down, holding hands and looking back over the river, Laura Lynne asks, "Think she and Scarlet have left yet?"

"Oh, didn't I tell you? Scarlet stood up when you did and told me to get her mother's walker. She was taking her back to Pineview. When Miss Melanie started to protest, Scarlet gave her a look that would have silenced the devil himself. She told me to have you call her when you were up to it."

"What about Uncle Gabe? The whole point of the evening was to find out what momma knew about the corpse."

Pearl shrugged. "I don't think he cares at this point. He and your momma are like oil and water. Hard to believe they are siblings. I think he was just happy to see her go."

Laura Lynne nods then glances over at Pearl. She asks, "What is going on with Scarlet? She seems different. Not that I have much to compare it with.

I have seen her so little over the years. But she does not seem like herself."

"I don't really know Laura Lynne. Best to ask her, don't you think?"

"You are probably right. Pearl, I am exhausted. I want to go to my room and pass out. Do you ever feel like you accomplished nothing and yet so much happened?"

"Every day of my life, girlfriend, every day of my life."

***

Laura Lynne gets out of her shower. Her bedroom and bathroom are the same as they were when she was here as a teenager. As she dries herself off, she glances at herself in the mirror, saddened by all the unnecessary years of absence. She mourns the youth she should have had, the one her parents had so perfectly sculpted. Shaking off the melancholy, she notices her phone lighting up. Glancing at the screen she sees a text from Gray. He is anxious to hear about her first day. Scrubbing off, she puts on some lotion that smells like the soap she just used in the shower; a mandarin orange and magnolia blossom combination which smells divine. She walks to the bedroom and slips on her pajama set. She texts Gray, "I have one more call to make, then will call you. I am fine.' Gray sends a thumb-up emoji sign.

Laura Lynne thumbs through her contacts and calls her baby brother, Avery. Avery currently lives in

North Carolina with his wife, Justine, and their three children. Their oldest son, Junior, has Down syndrome. And he is also the reason for the falling out between Melanie and Avery. Melanie did not want Avery to "waste" the family name on a child who was not "normal." Better to wait. Needless to say, Avery was justifiably mortified by her sentiment. But Melanie, being Melanie, refused to back down or apologize. Things between them have been frosty ever since.

Placing the call, Avery picks up on the second ring. "Hey, big sis, how's the famous author?"

"Well, that's the thing. You are not going to believe where I am currently sitting."

"On the sunny beaches of Hawaii, dreaming up your next best-seller while sipping a mocktail and talking to your favorite brother?"

Laughing, Laura Lynne responds, "Don't I wish! No, I am currently sitting in the window seat of my old room at The Residence, looking out at the moon rising."

"You're at Tea Olive?! No way. You told me you would never return! What, did somebody die and not tell me about it?"

Laura Lynne was silent.

"Wait, somebody died? Was it Momma?" Avery's voice rises about three octaves and cracks at the end. Regardless of their falling out, when Avery was a boy Melanie doted on him. He was the favorite, as the baby she coddled him. He was also four years younger than Laura Lynne, with a few miscarriages in between the two.

"No! No! Avery, slow down. Momma is fine. She was here tonight for my celebratory welcome-home cocktail and dinner party. She is as ornery as ever!"

Avery cuts in, "Then who died?"

"Well, that's why I called, and I am sorry to interrupt your vacation."

"Vacation ended two days ago, Laura Lynne. What's going on?"

Laura Lynne catches him up on the corpse and Gabe's subsequent arrest. "Any ideas who this might be?"

He is silent for a few minutes, thinking back over the years. "I do remember vagrants being an issue on the river when I was eleven or twelve. They would hitch a ride on a log, steal a boat, ride in on whatever floated. Not sure if they were homeless, druggies, or just river runners, but Daddy took Tripp and me aside and told us to keep our eye out. He hired one of Lincoln's sons, not sure which one to patrol the dock and river. Never heard anything afterward. Tripp might know more. You able to get in touch with him?"

"Honestly, I haven't tried yet. Hoped I could handle this without involving everyone but looks like it is a bit more complicated than I first anticipated."

"Considering Daddy's history with women, have you thought about some woman's husband or boyfriend, maybe even a pimp? Seems like a longshot, but it is a thought."

Laura Lynne sighs. Her father's mistresses were not a secret, but he was discreet. "I would have no idea where to even begin."

Avery's voice takes on a distant tone. "I met one of them once. A long time ago, would have been after you were sent to Aunt Eileen's. Daddy took me to Mobile with him, to do some business there. She was at a diner we stopped at for a meal. Their interaction was almost intimate, more than cordial. Neither of them acknowledged it, just said hello. But I could tell."

"You don't happen to remember her name, do you?"

"Virginia, but he called her Ginny. Don't remember a last name." Avery changed the subject, "Listen, do you need me to come to Tea Olive? I can maneuver some stuff around. I am sure Justine could handle Junior and the twins for a few days."

"Thanks Avery, but at this point there is really no need. We are just waiting for the coroner's report. If that changes though, I will reach out. Might just go ahead and have a plan in case things go south in a hurry."

"So, Sissy, how are you handling your first trip back home?" His voice is gentle, radiating concern.

"Much better than I had imagined all these years. Nothing has changed, but then everything has changed. But, being home, in Venice on the plantation, has been bittersweet."

"Good. Listen, I have to run. It's time for Junior's nighttime routine and tonight is my night. Keep me posted, would ya? And don't let Momma get to you."

"You're a fine one to talk! Talk at ya later. Oh, and if you think of anything else, give me a call."

"Right oh! Love ya, baby girl."

"Love you too, baby boy."

As Laura Lynne hangs up with Avery, she settles into her bed, pulls up the covers and dials her husband. Gray answered on the first ring. His strong voice and love nearly brought Laura Lynne to tears. She is not aware of how close to the emotional edge she is hanging on until then.

Chapter 11

Laura Lynne slept surprisingly well for her first night back in her old room, old bed, old life. It was probably pure exhaustion, but she wasn't one to look a gift horse in the mouth. Looking at her clock, it is still just 5:00AM, but she knows the house will wake up soon. Farmers do not sleep in, and Gabe is definitely a farmer. Slipping downstairs to heat up some hot water for a morning cup of tea, she runs into Gabe running the coffee maker.

"You're up early, baby girl. Have a hard time sleeping?"

Coming up behind Gabe, Laura Lynne gives him a hug and kiss on the shoulder. He pats her hand absently. She lays her head on his back and says, "I slept surprisingly well. I love you, Uncle Gabe."

"I love you too. Glad you are home."

Knowing Gabe is not one for emotional displays, Laura Lynne walks toward the tea kettle, turning on the burner. She fills the pot with water. "What are your plans for today, Uncle Gabe?"

"Mostly plan to work in the front garden, but this morning, I am meeting with Malcolm to discuss planting season. I think he is interested in organic farming, though he won't come right out and say it. He has been taking some courses."

Malcolm is Lincoln and Pearl's oldest son. He has been the foreman of Tea Olive since his father stepped down. Laura Lynne says, "Hmmm, really? Any other plantations that have gone organic?"

"None around here."

"What do you think?"

"Don't know yet. It would be a risk. Don't want to risk an entire crop. We will see what he has to say." Taking a sip of coffee, Gabe asks, "What about you? What are your plans for today?"

"I think I will head into town, talk with Lally, and see what he thinks of this McElhanney fellow. Maybe talk with Grady. Not sure, really." Picking up the kettle from the stove, Laura Lynne begins to ease into asking her Uncle Gabe about Virginia, Ginny. "Talked to Avery last night. He doesn't know anything about the dead body, but he did remember having a problem with vagrants when he was eleven or twelve. He also mentioned something else, something that may mean nothing, but well anyway…"

"Spit it out, Laura Lynne. I got crops that need tending."

"So, he thought maybe one of Daddy's mistresses might have something to do with it. Like maybe a husband, a boyfriend, or a pimp." Laura Lynne casts her gaze sideways. "Avery said he met one of them, a woman named Virginia, though Daddy called her Ginny."

Gabe is quiet for a moment. "Yes, I know about Virginia, though I doubt she has anything to do with the current situation."

"What do you know?"

"Nothing I want to discuss this early in the morning. We can talk at breakfast." And with that, Gabe heads out the door.

Laura Lynne stirs her tea thoughtfully. Uncle Gabe is probably right. But now Laura Lynne's curiosity is peeked. Why would Uncle Gabe know about one of her father's mistresses? Shrugging her shoulders, Laura Lynne picks up her tea and heads upstairs to get ready for the day.

Pulling up her computer and sitting at her old desk, Laura Lynne opens the top drawer and is shocked to see all her papers, notes, letters, and cards dating back to her sophomore year at school. She begins opening other drawers and realizes nothing has been touched. It is as if her desk has been waiting patiently for her return. She opens several of the folded notes, mostly from Grace, passed to each other in the hallways of the school. Reading through them, she realizes how innocent she was of the real world, how naïve and overprotected.

She plugs in her computer and gets to work on her emails, mostly from Ashley and her publisher. There is discussion about another book in her Bluebird series, another type of memoir. The publisher feels her divorce might be a valuable addition. Laura Lynne has hesitated to take this step. Her divorce was tumultuous and uncomfortable, worse for the children. She does not want to reopen raw wounds. And, yet a raw look at the first year of separation would be interesting. Laura Lynne is intrigued.

Closing her laptop, Laura Lynne picks up her now cold tea and heads to the closet. Her wardrobe is limited at best. Without Laura Lynne's knowledge, Pearl unpacked her luggage and ironed all her clothes. Smiling, Laura silently thanks her old friend while she pulls out an outfit of yellow capri pants, a sleeveless white button-down, and sandals. Pulling her hair back in a high bun and fastening her pearl earrings, she gives herself one last look in the mirror. Not bad for 53.

Laura Lynne stops at the kitchen to refresh her tea and smells what can only be defined as bliss. As she opens the door, she spots the culinary marvel, Victoria. Laura Lynne has yet to officially meet her, so she clears her throat as she enters, not wanting to disturb the magic happening on the stovetop. Victoria glances over her shoulder and smiles widely, "Hi Mrs. Atkins. Momma has told me all about you. She couldn't be more thrilled to have you home. What can I help you with?"

"You can start by calling me Laura Lynne. You are the spitting image of your grandmother standing at the kitchen stove. Gave me a bit of a start when I opened the door. And I don't need a thing, just want to heat up my tea bag, Victoria. May I call you Victoria?"

"Of course, ma'am."

"Don't let me interrupt whatever amazing creation you are making. It smells divine."

"Leftover chicken and waffles for the men. They appreciate a good meal."

"Men?"

"You will see. I don't want to ruin your uncle's surprise. I guess he wants you to meet everyone, so he is bringing them to breakfast." Turning back to the stove, Laura Lynne realizes that is all the information she is going to get. Topping off her tea, she heads to the back porch where the table is set for five. Laura Lynne settles down on the rocking chair, sipping her tea, watching the plantation wake up. She cannot resist taking a picture and sending it to Gray and the kids.

Laura Lynne stands as she sees Gabe on his side by side, a teenage boy and John riding shotgun. Galloping up on his horse, Pearl's brother Macolm follows along. Laura Lynne waves and waits patiently while the foursome disappears into the barn. It gives her time to assess John. She knows little about him, though her uncle has had nothing but glowing comments about his work ethic and his good nature. He is handsome, tall, and strong with chiseled features and a slightly crooked nose, broken one too many times. He keeps his gait to Gabe's slower stride, walking with his hands in his pockets. Laura Lynne notes the cowboy boots with approval. He reminds her of the many cowboys her aunt employed on River Oaks. She imagines he sits a horse as well as Malcolm.

"Ma'am." John takes off his baseball cap, revealing curly brown hair.

"Laura Lynne, please." Laura Lynne says as she walks straight up to Malcolm and gives him a big hug. His grin splits from ear to ear, "Hey there, Malcolm, long time no see."

He ruffles her hair as he steps back. "You too, glad you are back home. Miss seeing you running around the fields and playing at the dock with Miss Grace."

Malcolm is a few years older than Pearl and spent most of his childhood in the field with his father. The two did not spend time together, but Malcolm was much like his father. He was built like a spark plug, solid and sturdy with a gentle nature, his eyes gleaming and always quick with a grin. "I am real sorry about your daddy, Malcolm. Lincoln was a mighty fine man."

Seeing the obvious discomfort come across his face, Laura Lynne turns to the young man standing quietly between John and Gabe. "And you must be young Liam? I met your mom yesterday in town."

"Ma'am."

Liam has blond hair and blue eyes like his mom, but the resemblance stops there. He's a strapping young man, lean and muscular, maybe 14 years old, with buck teeth and ears that dominate his shaved head. Liam is wearing overalls, a long-sleeved T-shirt, and work boots. By the look of his shoe size, Laura Lynne suspects he had a lot more growing to do. He's the exact opposite of the Cotton Candy convection Laura Lynne met at the sheriff's office.

"I was just telling Liam this mess with the corpse has nothing to do with him finding the bones. I should have reported them to the sheriff straight away. Doesn't matter now. What's done is done. Let's both just forget about yesterday and have some breakfast."

"Yes, sir!"

The men devour the meal of waffles and chicken. The conversation centers around the crops. Malcolm and Gabe tell tales of drought, boll weevils, farming with horses, and the new-fangled tractors. The others listen and eat while the two reminisce. Laura Lynne enjoys the camaraderie that is so obvious between them. Her heart warms to know how close the two men have become.

After demolishing the rest of the meal, Gabe stays behind as the three men, well two men and one boy, head back to the fields. Laura Lynne waits patiently while her uncle sips his coffee, working out in his mind how to begin a delicate conversation.

"I didn't get to tell you yesterday, but I am so glad you are home. Way things were left with your momma and daddy; well, I just can't tell you how much I appreciate you coming to help when I called."

"I am glad you called, Uncle Gabe. It is time, well past time, for me to come home. This just forced my hand. I was wondering though, why didn't you call Scarlet? I mean, she is closer, and she helps out with Momma all the time. I am glad you called. I was just surprised, is all."

"I tried calling her. She didn't answer. I left a couple of messages." Uncle Gabe is vague in his answer. "Laura Lynne, Scarlet's been carrying the burden alone for long enough. She's got plenty of troubles of her own. No need to add my own."

"What kind of troubles does Scarlet have?"

"Not for me to share. Scarlet will tell you if she wants you to know. Just be sure you extend some grace there. She's been dealing with Melanie her whole life. That alone should be explanation enough. You get in touch with Tripp?"

"No haven't tried yet. I only talked to Avery. And as I mentioned earlier, he did not kill anyone, and his only two ideas were vagrants and a spurned husband or maybe a pimp. He mentioned this Virginia or Ginny. Said he met her in Mobile at a diner once when he and Daddy were there on business. He didn't know much else. But it is obvious you know more, a lot more."

Nodding thoughtfully, Uncle Gabe says, "Your father confided in me about Ginny years ago. Your daddy's exploits were not a secret, even from Melanie. But Ginny, she was different. After you left, things changed between your parents. Sawyer wanted you home, but Melanie was adamant. Then, by the time she agreed, it was too late. You were off living a life of your own. Your daddy never forgave Melanie. He found solace where he could."

Laura Lynne slowly shakes her head, thinking how much damage had occurred that long ago summer. "Is there anything else you can tell me about her?"

Gabe clears his throat. "I have her address. When your father passed and left me in charge of the trust, he requested Ginny be, well, 'looked after.'"

"What does that mean? She got money?"

Nodding, Gabe is looking at his hands. "He calls it a monthly stipend in his will, but I have been wondering if it is perhaps blackmail money."

"Blackmail? About what?"

Gabe looks Laura Lynne in the eye, "Young lady you know as well as I do this family has secrets- many of them. We are not some lily white, died in the wool, holier than though monks and nuns for God's sake! We are human! And your father was human. He made mistakes. He may have confided in her. I really don't know." At this point, Gabe is up from his seat, pacing the porch. His distress is obvious. "I have no idea what this woman knows or doesn't know. In the meantime, I pay the monthly stipend."

Laura Lynne is taken back by her uncle's vehemence, "Uncle Gabe, ok, all right. You have a right to be upset. Hell, I am upset! But I agree, you are doing the right thing!"

"Don't you dare cuss in this house Laura Lynne! I don't care how old you are, I will take you across my knee!"

At this, Laura Lynne smiles and giggles, "Yes, sir. I apologize."

Gabe sits down heavily. "This has been on my mind for the past five years. You are the only one who knows. Well, you and Melanie. I had to tell her. She needed to know." Taking Laura Lynne's hands, he squeezes them. "We have to protect the family, Laura Lynne. I need your help."

"That is why I am here. Looks like I am taking a trip to Mobile." Sighing, Laura Lynne squeezes Gabe's hands, "I am assuming she still lives in Mobile?"

"Yes. I even checked online, and the address is connected to a home in what looks like a fairly nice neighborhood."

"You send a check? Why don't you wire it or send it online?"

"The money is not accounted for in the books and is from a separate account your father set up. I am assuming he is trying to protect the trust. It is why I think it may be blackmail money."

"So, Scarlet and Tripp don't know?"

"They know of her, certainly, but I don't know if they know who she is or ever met her. I never asked, and they have never told me."

"Uncle Gabe, I have to tell my sister and brothers. It is their legacy as well as mine. I don't want to make decisions without all of us being on board. No telling what can of worms a visit to this Ginny could open up."

"I have given you the secret to do with as you see fit, Laura Lynne."

"Any more secrets you want to share before I head into town? Might as well unburden yourself, Uncle Gabe," Laura Lynne teases her uncle.

"Oh, plenty of secrets, baby girl. Plenty. But I think this is enough for today." He gets up and walks toward the edge of the porch. "Be careful who you trust, Laura Lynne. A lot has changed in Venice since you were here, but a lot has stayed the same." He looks into the distance. Then he grabs his hat on the porch banister, places it on his head, and ambles off toward the barn.

Laura Lynne looks at her phone and plugs in Tripp's name, dialing the number. He is not available to take her call, but Lt. Colonel Beauregard would get word there is a family situation. Captain Young did inform Laura Lynne it could take several days. She thanks him and hangs up, wondering what daring mission her brother is on this time.

Laura Lynne sticks her head into the kitchen on her way to collect her computer before leaving. "Victoria, thank you for the amazing breakfast. May I ask where you learned to cook like that?"

Victoria smiles. "Thank you. Learned mostly from Grandmama, but I went to culinary school. Hope to one day open my own place. Need to wait, though. Momma needs my help for a while longer."

"Well, if this morning's breakfast is any indication of your capabilities, I have no doubt it will be a huge success." Waving her phone, Laura Lynne tells Victoria, "I am headed into town this morning. Uncle Gabe is out in a field somewhere. If I am needed, don't hesitate to call."

"Don't worry Miss Laura Lynne. I know you don't know John very well, but he is a good man. He looks after Mr. Gabe and doesn't let him do too much." She carefully folds the creamy mixture into a square of dough she has rolled out on the counter, "I'm glad to finally meet you. My momma has talked about you for years. She was right, too. You have a light about you that brightens up a room when you walk in. Nice change of pace for this old building. Sometimes feels like the weight of our combined ancestors are all jammed up in these walls. Like the place needs airing out." She looks at Laura Lynne, "Maybe you are the one to do it."

Laura Lynne takes her time on the way into town. There are few things she likes better than driving and thinking. As her head is spinning with the information about Ginny, she decides to tuck it away into a corner so she can concentrate on the current situation in Venice- the corpse. Laura Lynne makes the decision to refer to the corpse as "Dead Doe." That is enough to think about, no need to borrow trouble.

As she plans her day, Laura Lynne begins to believe the best approach to gathering any information she can is to research Venice news starting the year she left, 1985. Dead Doe's clothing articles are from then, so it seems as good a time as any. Plus, since she was not here after 1985, she can follow the town's news and events. It is a place to start.

Approaching town, Laura Lynne sees the offices for the town newspaper, *The Venice Gazette*. Without hesitating, Laura Lynne pulls into one of the many empty parking spaces in front of the building. Laura Lynne fondly remembers perusing the pages of the Gazette when growing up, reading all the gossip, high school sports news, politics, and society pages.

Upon entering the building, Laura Lynne sees an attractive white-haired woman manning the front counter. She has lively green eyes and looks to be around 65, rail thin, wearing a lavender wrap-around dress with a matching cardigan sweater. She is leaning over the counter with her glasses perched on her nose, reading a book. As Laura Lynne draws closer, she looks eerily familiar.

"Good morning, Miss Wright? Is that you?" She peers over her glasses at Laura Lynne and that is all it takes. She has no doubt. Miss Wright was her English teacher from Moseley Hall. She taught Laura Lynne on several occasions, but the one year that stands out the most was her freshman literature class. "It is you! It's me, Laura Lynne, Freshman English!"

"Of course, I know who you are! Been keeping tabs on you for a while now, well, all the Beauregard children. How is your Uncle Gabe faring? Heard about all the drama at Tea Olive. Sorry it happened, but I just bet you Gabe and Melanie are pleased as punch you are back home!" Miss Wright is as bubbly as ever.

"Yes, it is good to be back. You still teaching at Moseley? Surprised to see you behind the counter here."

"I retired last year, but still help with the drama department. I run the counter here just to get out of the house. Decided retirement is not for me, at least yet."

"This might be a long shot, but I thought it was worth an ask. I was wondering if the microfiche from the years 1980-1990 might be available. Not sure if they are archived here or in the library?"

"They are here. Why do you need them? This have anything to do with the current dealings at Tea Olive?"

With her Uncle Gabe's warning ringing in her ears, Laura Lynne nods. "No clue what I am looking for. Do you remember anything from those years?"

"Nothing more than most folks," she averts her gaze. "Truth be told Laura Lynne, the gossip and scandal from those years was about the Beauregard's, specifically you. Lots of speculation there. Kept the gossips of this town busy for a long time."

"I have no doubt. Momma made that more than clear to me."

Miss Wright lifts her eyes, "Didn't mean to bring up bad memories, sweetheart. But you did ask."

"I did. So, let me ask a different question. What do I need to do to view those archived newspapers? I would also like to subscribe to the newspaper. I am guessing you are online as well as delivered?"

"Oh, yes, went digital when the 'conglomerate' took over from Matt Waring. You can just go online and subscribe. It's quite simple. As far as the microfiche, can you come back tomorrow? It will take me some time to gather the boxes, but I can set up an office here for you to look at them. Nobody but me here these days."

"Really Miss Wright? That would be super helpful. What is the earliest I can be here tomorrow?"

"My day starts at 8:30. The front office opens at 9. Why don't you come around 8:45? Does that work? And, Laura Lynne, why don't you call me by my first name, Mary? Little less formal and more comfortable for me. Makes me feel less like a school marm!"

"All right, I will! No promises I won't forget on occasion. Thank you for all the help. Not sure if this will even turn anything up, but it's a place to start."

"My pleasure." Laura Lynne turns to walk out the way she came in, and Mary says to her back. "I enjoyed your book, Laura Lynne. Very inspiring. You are much stronger than you think."

Tears fill Laura Lynne's eyes as she pushes open the door, glancing over her shoulder. "Thank you….Mary. That is high praise coming from you." She smiles and nods, puts her glasses back on her nose, and picks up her book. She looks the same when Laura Lynne leaves as she did when she arrived, bent over the counter reading.

Laura Lynne's phone rings. It is Savannah. Her heart lifts as she answers, sliding behind the wheel of her car. "Hang on a second Savannah. I have to crank the car and turn on the air conditioner. The humidity is brutal." As she gets situated, she transfers the phone to the car's Bluetooth. Laura Lynne is proud of herself for figuring this out, and it only took one FaceTime phone call with Gray. Laura Lynne says, "Hey, sweet baby girl. How are you feeling?"

"Super nauseous, but good. Thanks for asking but I am calling you for *deets!* Your text messages didn't tell me very much. What's happening?" Savannah replies.

Starting from the beginning, Laura Lynne tells her everything that has happened in the last 36 hours, excluding her father's mistress. Savannah is listening raptly. Laura Lynne can tell she is taking notes. She is, after all, her child. "What about you, Mom? How are you handling being in Venice? Is it wonderful or awful?"

"Honestly, I am not sure I have had time to process my feelings yet. It's been so busy with Uncle Gabe and Momma, Scarlet, and the sheriff's station,…but overall, I feel good. No panic, no anxiety, no fear. I think there is some anger and regret over years lost, but truly I just don't know yet."

"You want me to come, Mom? I don't mind and really do want to see Tea Olive."

"I do want you to come, just not yet. I do want you to see Tea Olive. It's as wonderful as the stories I told you growing up. I want you to see my thinking tree. But not right now. I am not sure how long all this is going to last, and if there is a trial or something even more difficult, I need you here then. Can you start looking at your calendar and maybe clearing some time in about 4-6 weeks?"

"I am tentatively scheduling it as we speak. It would put us there early to mid-May. Is there anything I can do for you?"

"Yes, there is. Can you please call Ashley and update her on what is happening here? Tell her I will be in touch over the next day or so. I need to do some stuff with her on the blog and navigate the PR stuff when this hits the press. She needs to be forearmed."

"Yep, got it. Anything else?"

"Can you reach out to Beau and relay everything I just told you?"

"Sure. Anything else?"

"I can't think of anything else right now. Savannah, I love you, but I need to go. I have been sitting in a parking lot for 20 minutes. People are going to talk."

"Okay, love you, bye." She hangs up. You can always count on Savannah not to have a long, drawn-out goodbye.

Laura Lynne decides she needs caffeine and a good book as she gets out of the car to walk down Main Street toward Magnolia Café. Along the route, Laura Lynne notes the changes to the town she remembers with such fondness, and sadness. Most of the buildings have been upgraded in some distinct way: a new day spa where the drug store used to be, a yoga studio in the old clothing store, and Mr. B's pharmacy with its 1950's soda fountain even got a face lift. But the feel of the town, the people walking by nodding and smiling as they amble past is the same. Laura Lynne arrives at the café. Amanda is at the counter, "Earl Grey for you Miss Laura Lynne?"

"Not today, Mandy. Do you mind if I call you Mandy?"

"I prefer it!"

"Great, Mandy, can I have just an unsweetened black tea, light ice, with a lid and a straw? Gonna go over to your Momma's and look through the books."

After procuring her tea, Laura Lynne walks to Wheelbarrow Books. The tinkle of the bell above the shop door greets her entrance. Diane waves as Laura Lynne heads to the shelves, meandering through the shop. Nothing catches her eye until she arrives at the Local History section. Laura Lynne's eye rests on a picture of the gates at Tea Olive as she scans the bookshelf. Picking up the book, Ghost Stories of Venice, Laura Lynne scans the back cover and notes the author, Ron Adams. Picking up the book, *Ghost Stories of Venice*, Laura Lynne scans the back cover and notes the author, Ron Adams. "That is odd," thinks Laura Lynne, "There are no ghosts at Tea Olive that I know about."

She heads to the counter and Diane. "Find something? Oh, Ron Adams' book. It's a fun read; gives history, legend, and spirits. Basically, sums up the South. You know Ron Adams? He was a reporter at the Gazette for years before he turned book author."

"Really? Not sure I knew that." Laura Lynne pulls out her credit card and completes the transaction. Diane starts to put her book in a bag. "No need for a bag. If you don't mind, I will just stick it in my purse."

"Don't mind a bit. Here you go."

"Thanks. And, Diane, thanks for displaying my book so prominently in your window. I am flattered."

"Afraid it won't be there for long. It's all but sold out. I ordered some more, but with all that's going on over at Tea Olive, well, the Beauregard family is a hot topic. And besides, I like the book. One of the perks of being the owner is I get to display my picks and personal favorites."

"All the same. Thank you. Have a great rest of your day." Diane waves Laura Lynne away and gets back to her computer.

Laura Lynne decides to stop by Lally's office, but he is not in. Gone for the day. Checking her phone, Laura Lynne realizes that time has gotten away from her. It is late afternoon and time to head back to Tea Olive and Uncle Gabe. Feeling like she accomplished nothing, she calls Gray. No help there. He is busy at a show and can't talk for long. Putting away her phone and walking to the car, Laura Lynne is at a loss as to what to do next to "protect the family." She needs answers but doesn't know where to get them.

Chapter 12

Spring 1986

"No, I am not going. They can't expect me to root my life up and go back to Tea Olive after I haven't been allowed home for a year! I have plans this summer, Aunt Eileen! I finally have some friends. I don't want to go back. It will mess everything up! Besides, they don't believe me and think I am lying or keeping secrets. I hate them, and I am not going back!" Laura Lynne had just gotten off the phone with Melanie. She would like Laura Lynne to come home for two weeks over the summer.

Laura Lynne is not interested. She has a good routine at River Oaks, and she feels and looks much better. She has even cultivated some friendships at Robert E. Lee, going to football games and movies together. And to be honest, Laura Lynne is not over being mad. Her parents, particularly her mother, has been hell-bent to keep her away from Mississippi. Laura Lynne does not trust her change of heart. Besides, when Laura Lynne pressed her, asking if she could see Grace and her other friends, her mother admitted she would be expected to stay at The Residence and be with family.

"Laura Lynne, you are almost 17. It's completely your decision. Your parents can't force you to do anything anymore. If you don't want to go, then you won't go. I will do whatever you want to do. I do think, at some point, you need to see your parents, though. Maybe we can meet in the middle. Have them come here for a visit. They can see how well you are doing."

Laura Lynne has no desire to see her parents, but Aunt Eileen is right. Eventually, she needs to face them again. A compromise, and maybe they will bring Avery.

"Okay, but I want to see Avery. They have to bring him along. I miss my baby brother."

Laura Lynne talks to Avery several times a week. At 13, he will start high school next year, attending Moseley Hall for the first time sans sibling. He has had a difficult year living in Tripp's shadow. Tripp's senior year has been filled with accomplishments and awards, the town's favorite son. Star quarterback, star forward, and Salutatorian; he is brilliant on and off the field. Avery does not compare.

Two months later, all the details have been worked out, and Laura Lynne's parents, with Avery in tow, will be arriving for a weekend in June. School is over. Laura Lynne has remained adamant she will not return to Mississippi. Melanie is shocked by her daughter's refusal to do as- directed, a first for both of them. But Laura Lynne is no longer the naïve little girl who left Tea Olive broken, alone, and afraid. She has developed a backbone, and it is made of steel. In this regard, she is more like her mother than she cares to admit.

In preparation for their arrival, Martha has spent weeks airing out the rooms, worrying over menus, and basically driving Eileen and Laura Lynne to the barns. Melanie and Sawyer have never been to River Oaks and probably never would have visited if not for the current circumstances. Running plantations and being a farmer does not allow for vacations. Besides the occasional trip to Mobile, Beauregards stay close to home. Life is Tea Olive Plantation.

The one stipulation Laura Lynne requested is keeping Dr. Mabel Thurgood close by during the visit. Laura Lynne trusted Mabel's counsel and besides, this gave Mabel a chance to spend some more time with Ben. Ben is one of Aunt Eileen's farmhands, but also a dear friend. She gave him a job and sobered him up over 20 years ago. He has been devoted to her ever since. To Eileen's delight, Ben and Mabel were a couple. Mabel spent most weekends in Ben's house near the upper field, close to the orphaned animals. One of Eileen's passions is rescuing orphaned animals and Ben takes care of them. Laura Lynne often wonders if Eileen has so easily taken her in because she views her as one of her orphans.

Today, putting all thoughts aside of the upcoming visit from her parents, Laura Lynne is going to town to buy her first car with her own money. Laura Lynne meticulously researched until she found something she and her aunt could agree on: a 1979 BMW 320i, rust-colored, 200,000 miles, new tires.

"I will pay for the license and car insurance, but for anything else, you will have to foot the bill," says Eileen. Laura Lynne nods excitedly and Eileen continues, "You need something to get you back and forth to the vet clinic, plus you deserve it. You have worked hard all year, even though I know it's been tough."

"I want to do this myself, Aunt Eileen."

"You will, sweetie, but if you want to be taken seriously, I probably need to at least show my face. I promise I will let you do all the negotiating."

"Promise? I know you love to haggle." Aunt Eileen is fierce when it comes to the farm auctions and a competitive bidder.

"Promise. Now let's go buy you a car!"

Two hours later, Laura Lynne is a proud car owner. Aunt Eileen is true to her word, staying silent through the whole process. Laura Lynne pays cash, all but emptying her bank account. Sliding behind the wheel, Laura Lynne is certain it is all worth it. She decides to name the rust-colored car Ginger.

"Let's go celebrate with some ice cream. Meet you at the Frozen Cow Juice Stand? A hot fudge sundae sounds good right now."

"Meet you there!" Laura Lynne shuts the car door, buckles her seat belt, turns on the radio, and smiles at Aunt Eileen. "I can't believe it! My own wheels!!"

Aunt Eileen laughs and waves, shouting, "Meet you there! And *be careful*!"

Driving down the road with the wind in her hair, Laura Lynne is excited about the summer for the first time in a long time. She has secured a job at the vet clinic, working with Dr. Lucille Vanderbilt. Dr. Lucy is a regular visitor at River Oaks, caring for the horses and the orphans. Laura Lynne loves following her around and watching her work. She needed some summer help and asked Laura Lynne if she was interested. The job paid minimum wage, and the work was hard, dealing with all forms of excrement, the occasional bite, and more than a few scratches. But Laura Lynne jumped at the chance, working weekends toward the end of school. She will be full-time after her parents visit this weekend.

The day finally arrives, and everyone is nervous. Even Scout and Maudie sense the tension, though they remain stoically at Laura Lynne's side. A lot has occurred over the past nine months. Laura Lynne had a birthday, celebrated holidays, and completed an entire year of high school with little to no parental involvement. And Laura Lynne has changed too, and not just physically.

The rental car pulls up in the driveway, and Avery jumps out of the car, giving Laura Lynne a big hug. "Sissy! You are so tall! But still skinny!" Laura Lynne laughs as she hugs him. He has grown a foot and is beginning to fill out, showing signs of manhood. His voice is changing, cracking when he teases.

"You big giant, what is Queenie feeding you? You have grown a foot and gained 50 pounds. I think you are going to be even bigger than Tripp!" Laura Lynne pulls him closer and hangs on.

Avery whispers in her ear, "It's going to be fine. We will see Momma together." He releases his grip and grabs Laura Lynne's hand as the two walk toward their parents. "Momma, Laura Lynne still has the Cooper good looks."

Laura Lynne leans forward and kisses Melanie on the cheek. "Hi, Mother, it's good to see you."

"You too, Laura Lynne." She is as nervous as Laura Lynne. "Avery, help your father with the bags."

"I'll help you, Avery. I will show you to your rooms." Laura Lynne heads to the back of the car, where Sawyer has the trunk open and is pulling out the luggage.

"Your Aunt Eileen tells me you got a new car, Laura Lynne. How about after we get settled and have supper, you show me what you ended up with," Sawyer says.

"Yes, sir." Laura Lynne picks up one of the suitcases and grabs the hanging clothes. Avery has two more suitcases. "You got everything, Avery?" It's a ton of luggage for two days.

"I think so. Momma packed like we were going to the Queens' coronation in England, four bags for two days? Three of the bags are Momma's." He looks over at Momma and gives her a big wink. "Aunt Eileen! Hey!"

Aunt Eileen is at the top of the stairs, cocktail in hand. "Is that little Avery? What are you feeding that boy? You sure do make pretty babies, Sawyer!"

Sawyer bee-lines it straight to his sister-in-law and gives her a hug, taking a sip of her drink.

"I absolutely do, Eileen. I absolutely do. Now, where are the refreshments? The flight and drive were good, but Hartfield Airport gets busier every year."

Melanie walks to the top of the stairs and gives Eileen an air kiss. "Martha has everything set up on the back porch. There is a nice breeze, and we can see the horses. Laura Lynne, you help Avery with the bags and then show him all our strays! Y'all can catch up while us old people get reacquainted."

"Come on Avery!" Laura Lynne and Avery head upstairs to the second floor. Martha has set up three bedrooms and two bathrooms. Sawyer and Avery will share the Gabe and Jill bath and Melanie will have the en suite. Aunt Eileen didn't say, but Laura Lynne knows it's because her parents are not getting along. As the two enter the second bedroom, Martha comes up the stairs.

Martha waves her hands and says, "Y'all shew now! I will unpack everything. You have about an hour and half before you need to be back and ready for supper. Now scat!"

The two do not have to be told twice. They take off down the stairs and out the front door, running across the grounds to the farm. Ben and Mabel are there, sitting outside at the picnic table. Laura Lynne is surprised to see tea and lemonade, cucumber sandwiches, watermelon, and cheese cubes. It's the kid's version of cocktails before dinner. They wave Avery and Laura Lynne over.

"Avery, this is Dr. Mabel and Mr. Ben. Dr. Mabel, Mr. Ben, this is my little brother Avery."

Avery nods at Mabel. "Ma'am." Then he sticks out his hand to Ben.

Ben grips it. "How was the trip in?" Everyone sits at the picnic table, and Mabel pours tea and tells stories about Ham, the orphaned pig. Ben adds his narrative, and pretty soon, everyone is laughing and devouring the snacks. Avery meets the notorious Ham and all his orphan friends.

"I like them. They seem really nice," Avery says as he and Laura Lynne walk across the field, taking their time back to the main house.

"Mabel has been great. Not sure what I would have done without her. Now, Mabel and Ben are dating. Guess I was sort of their matchmaker."

Avery gives Laura Lynne a side hug and pets her hair. "Missed you, Sissy."

"Missed you too, Av."

Avery and Laura Lynne join the adults on the back porch. Melanie is subdued, but Sawyer and Eileen are entertaining each other with horse stories. Martha comes to the door, saying, "Miss Eileen, supper is ready."

"Thank you, Martha! Okay, gang, let's take this party to the dining room. Avery, did you enjoy the animals? Get to meet Ham?"

Avery talks animatedly with Eileen as the group walks to the table. Sawyer puts his hand at the base of Laura Lynne's spine, guiding her to the table. Laura Lynne is a bit surprised he is treating her like a lady and no longer like the little girl who would grab his hand on the way to dine. Supper is much like cocktail hour. It's as if everyone agreed to take an evening off and not have any heavy conversation. Melanie joins in appropriately, but she does not commandeer the conversation as she normally does at Tea Olive. Aunt Eileen is the lady of the house, and Melanie understands her place.

As the meal ends with a key lime pie for dessert, Sawyer pushes himself away from the table. "Laura Lynne, why don't you show me this car of yours?"

"Yes, sir." Laura Lynne places her napkin on the table and pushes her chair back. Avery starts to get up as well.

"Avery, please stay and entertain the ladies. Laura Lynne and I are going to have some father-daughter time." Avery glances at Laura Lynne in concern, not wanting to leave her on her own with their father. Laura Lynne gives a little shrug. "Laura Lynne can take you for a spin tomorrow."

Sawyer and Laura Lynne walk out the mud room door toward the barn. As Eileen's gift to Laura Lynne, she had one of the stalls in the barn cleaned out for Laura Lynne to park Ginger.

"So, this is her? Looks like you chose well! How does she drive?" Laura Lynne starts to hand him the keys. "No, no! It's your car; you drive." Smiling and climbing behind the wheel, Laura Lynne gets in. Sawyer bends his long frame into the passenger's seat and says, "Let's keep it to the farm for tonight, Laura Lynne."

Laura Lynne backs out of the garage and drives around the house to the back acreage. There are dirt roads and horse paths throughout the property. Laura Lynne decides to head to the high pasture, downshifting as she heads up a steep grade. The sun is beginning to set. Laura Lynne rolls down the windows and turns up the music, allowing the pleasure of driving to encapsulate her. Laughing out loud, Laura Lynne shakes her hair as the cool breeze blows through it and the dust flies up behind her wheels. She feels her father's stare and shouting over the loud music. Sawyer points to the curve in the road. "Pull over, Laura Lynne. Let's walk around a bit."

Nodding, Laura Lynne slows down and puts the car in park. She turns down the music, and not waiting for Laura Lynne to turn off the engine, Sawyer jumps out of the car. He flings open the driver's side car door and hauls Laura Lynne out of the car and into his arms. He rocks back and forth, murmuring into Laura Lynne's hair, "I am so sorry, so sorry, so sorry."

Shocked, Laura Lynne is frozen refusing to reciprocate. She pushes Sawyer away from her as panic wells up, "Daddy, stop it! What are you doing?"

Sawyer goes still. Pulling his head back, he looks at Laura Lynne. His eyes are full of tears. Laura Lynne's eyes are full of panic as she frantically tries to take a step away. Sawyer immediately releases her, turns, and takes several steps back, away from Laura Lynne and the car. With his back turned, he searches his pocket for his handkerchief, wiping his eyes and blowing his nose.

"I am sorry. Are you okay? I didn't mean to scare you."

"I'm okay. I just…you frightened me."

"I know. I just, I don't know, seeing you here, all grown up. I don't think your Momma and I did right by you. We just didn't know what to do. Now, it's like I am company instead of your father. Ben and Eileen are teaching you all the stuff your momma and I should be teaching you! It messed me up a bit. I just wanted to hug it all away and start over again. We aren't going to be able to do that, are we?"

"No, Daddy. It can't be undone. All I can do is move forward. What you and Momma did? Not believing me? Kicking me out of the house? Those things hurt. How could I possibly trust you again?"

Sawyer finally turns around, facing Laura Lynne. "I thought you lied to us. You still haven't told us what happened. But I don't care anymore. I just want you home where you belong."

"I did *not lie*! I don't know what happened! All I know for sure is you hurt me in the worst possible way, and even if Momma let me come back, I wouldn't! I will never go back. Not as long as I live! You threw me away, Daddy! You *blamed* me! If it had been Tripp or Avery, you would have supported them 150%! Because, as you say, "Boys will be boys." But because it was me and I was no longer a *good* girl in your eyes, you treated me like trash!" Laura Lynne is screaming at him, stomping her foot, tears pouring, spitting out the words with conviction…and it felt *good*!

He stares at his youngest daughter, stunned into silence. How could he have messed up so badly? "You're wrong, Laura Lynne. Your Momma wants you home, too, and I never threw you away. I sent you away. I was trying to protect you."

Laura Lynne sighs, angrily wiping her nose and mouth with the tail of her shirt. "No, Daddy, you and Momma were protecting yourselves and the Beauregard name."

"Isn't that what I just said? You are a Beauregard, too."

"Not anymore. I was going to tell you and mom together, but I may as well tell you now. I am staying here this summer and working at the vet. Aunt Eileen said I could stay as long as I want. I don't want to transfer again before my senior year; I just want to finish at Robert E. Lee. That is my plan. I have no intention of coming back to Mississippi. I told you that when you put me on the plane last summer, threatening me when I was sick and scared to death. I meant it." Laura Lynne opens her car door and gets in. "I am going to the house."

"You go ahead. I will walk back."

Starting the car and making a U-turn, Laura Lynne glances in the rearview mirror. Sawyer is standing with his hands on his hips, watching her as she drives down the hill. Instead of going to the main house, Laura Lynne drives to Ben's cottage. Mabel is on the front porch swing, standing as soon as she sees the car as if waiting for Laura Lynne's arrival.

Laura Lynne turns the corner too quickly and veers off the driveway into the field, slamming on the brakes as she comes to an immediate stop. Ben has been watching from the doorway and bounds across the porch straight to Laura Lynne. He reaches through the open window and grabs the keys, turning the car off. Ben opens the door, and Laura Lynne crumples into his arms, feeling safe and secure once again. He picks her up as if she is a bag of feed and brings her to sit on the porch swing. Mabel gently wraps her in a blanket and pulls up a chair. "Baby girl, I am going to make you some tea. It's going to be all right," says Ben.

"Ben, let Eileen know Laura Lynne is with us, will you, please?" asks Mabel.

Mabel says nothing as she waits for the tears and the emotions to calm. When Ben comes out with the hot tea, Laura Lynne sits up straight. The storm seems to have passed.

"Thanks, Ben. Sorry about that," Laura Lynne says as she waves her hand toward Ginger.

"We will talk about your driving later. Ready to tell us what happened?"

Taking a deep breath and a sip of tea, Laura Lynne sits back on the swing and recounts the events of the night. She unburdens on two of the people she trusts most in the world. They listen without interrupting.

When she is done, Mabel asks gently, "How do you feel about all this? Be sure you are not acting out of spite, Laura Lynne, but out of a sense of what is best for you emotionally and spiritually. Although I don't agree with your parent's actions, I do believe in their minds what they were doing was out of love and a sense of duty and protection."

"Mabel, I was repelled by my father. When he grabbed me to give me a hug, something he has done hundreds of times, I went into a panic. I was scared. I didn't feel protected; I felt in danger! It was the weirdest reaction."

"Not really; you have been protecting yourself for a long time. He invaded your personal space without permission. It's a normal reaction."

"I don't think it's spite. I just don't want to deal with people who still think I have done something wrong, or worse, think I am hiding something and lying about it. I can't imagine it would be comfortable there anymore. I have a routine here and some friends. I have a job now. It doesn't make sense to start over again."

"I think that is reasonable."

The three sit in companionable silence until Laura Lynne finally says, "Well, I would rather eat Ham than go back to the house, but I need to get back. I am done hiding."

Ben gets up and goes inside, coming back out with his hat and keys, "I am following you home; don't argue."

"I won't. Too exhausted." Looking at Mabel, Laura Lynne gives a slight smile. "Thank you for validating me and telling me I am not crazy."

"That's easy. You are not crazy. You sure you are okay to drive?"

"I am fine." Laura Lynne hugs Mabel's neck, "Thank you."

"You are more than welcome."

Eileen is waiting in the kitchen when Laura Lynne gets to the house. "Mabel called. Told me what happened. You okay, Laura Lynne?"

"Surprisingly, I am. At least, I think I am. Where's Momma? Did Daddy make it home?"

"Not yet. Ben went to find him. Your Momma turned in about an hour ago. She took Avery with her. We are alone for now. You want to talk about it?"

"No, not really. I unloaded on Mabel and poor Ben. But, Aunt Eileen, I am never going to see eye to eye with Momma and Daddy on this, ever. I am not going back to Mississippi with them. I could never trust them again, and they don't trust me. It's that simple and that difficult."

She doesn't say anything, just walks over and pets Laura Lynne's hair, rubbing her back and kissing the top of her head. The lights from Ben's truck shine through the kitchen windows, and the sound of a car door slamming and footsteps up the stairs to the back porch are all Sawyer's.

"I am going to bed. I don't want to see him again tonight," Laura Lynne says. Aunt Eileen nods, giving her one last lingering kiss on the head before stepping away and heading to the back porch. Laura Lynne hears the screen door open and quietly close. She doesn't wait around to hear their discussion.

As Laura Lynne approaches the second-floor landing, the guest room door opens, and Avery sticks his head out. His hair is thick and dark like Sawyer's, but his facial features are all Cooper: narrow nose, hazel eyes with a gentle slant, and a narrow-pointed chin. He is curious, "Sissy, what happened? Y'all been gone forever. You okay?"

"I am now. Exhausted. Talk tomorrow? How about I come get you to help out with the orphans in the morning? Rosebud needs milking, and they all need to be fed. It'll be fun."

Avery's eyes light up. He nods. "I want to feed Ham."

"Absolutely. Night, little bro." Laura Lynne blows him a kiss and heads upstairs, feeling blessed

Melanie didn't choose to stick her head out to check on things. One parent was plenty tonight.

Chapter 13

Present Day

Laura Lynne arrives promptly at the Gazette at 8:45. Mary is eagerly waiting for her arrival. The two women greet each other, and Mary escorts Laura Lynne to the corner office. Mary says, "This used to be Matt Waring's office. But now that we are all online, very few people actually come to the office. So it's all yours for as long as you need." Mary is wearing baby blue today, an identical outfit as yesterday, just a different color. She is lively and excited. "I spent some time last night going through the Moseley Hall yearbooks. I remembered a few things from around that time. Nothing that really stood out, just students who were troublemakers, or dropped out, got pregnant. Some teachers who came and went. I marked them with sticky notes and jotted a bit of information about them for you."

"Thanks, Mary. I have no idea what I am even looking for, but at least I am doing something."

"Let me show you how to work the microfiche, and then I will get out of your way." Mary walks closer to the desk as Laura Lynne sits in the chair, putting her bag on the floor. "It's really quite simple, hasn't changed since you were in high school." She grabs the first box and pulls out a spool of film. "Each box is labeled, starting with 1980. There are quite a few boxes." She points to the filing cabinets, stacked on top are around 20 boxes. "All in all, I located a total of 43 boxes covering the ten-year period." Mary expertly feeds the microfiche into the projector, demonstrating how to advance and reverse the film. "Once you get through these, I will bring in the next batch. If you figure out what you are looking for and need me to help, I would love to. I don't do much all day at that front desk, though I do enjoy the time to read."

Staring at the stacks of boxes, Laura Lynne realizes an assistant to go through all this would be helpful. Especially someone with Mary's skill set. "Really? That would be great! Thank you. I think I am going to need all the help I can get."

"Okay, I will leave you to it."

Laura Lynne spends the next four hours looking at the microfiche film from 1980. It is tough going simply because she does not know what she is hoping to find. Laura Lynne stops on an article about a local girl who has been missing for 48 hours. She later turns up wandering along the railroad tracks, bruised, suffering a head injury, and wearing torn and dirty clothes. There are no pictures, and the information is sparse. Laura Lynne makes notes on her pad, citing the reporter as Ron Adams. Mary gently knocks and pops her head in the door.

"I am closing for lunch. Want to join me? Or I can bring you back something."

"Really? That would be great. I finally found something. I have no idea if it means anything. Do you remember a girl who was found at the railroad tracks in 1980? She had been missing for two days."

Mary walks in and comes to the desk. Laura Lynne pulls up the article for Mary to read.

"It wasn't a Moseley Hall girl. I would have known about that. Must have gone to the public school. It's not ringing a bell, but let me think about it while I grab us something to eat. I usually just go down to the square and choose from one of the food trucks. I have a fetish for this gouda and pear grilled cheese sandwich with fresh arugula."

"Venice has food trucks?"

Mary laughs. "Well, yes! We aren't that small town anymore! There are two or three that have made a name for themselves locally, but "Cheese Louise!" has currently won my affections. What can I get you?"

"Let me guess. Louise is the creator of these cheesy delights?" She nods as Laura Lynne laughs. "God, I love the South! I will have what you are having and the largest unsweetened tea with no ice you can find." Laura Lynne picks up her phone and opens the case. She always keeps a $20 bill tucked behind the credit cards. Laura Lynne hands the money over to Mary.

"Comin' right up!" Mary leaves the office and Laura Lynne hears the lock close on the front door. Taking advantage of the empty office, Laura Lynne gets up from her desk and performs some basic yoga poses. She hops up on an empty desk, assumes the lotus position, closes her eyes, and levels out her breathing. Allowing her brain to relax, Laura Lynne spends the next ten minutes meditating. The discovery of the missing girl is causing Laura Lynne's anxiety to spike. Some hidden fear is clawing its way up her throat. The nagging feeling doesn't let up, even after performing a few sun salutations. Giving in, Laura Lynne sits back at her desk and begins scrolling again.

There are several articles about the expansion of the hospital and the new services that would be provided, including an entire new wing devoted to maternal and child health and wellness. Laura Lynne is startled to be staring at the grainy, black-and-white picture of the monster in her nightmares. The newest member of the physician resident team, Dr. Kenneth Butler. Laura Lynne stares hard at his picture, remembering him as young, charismatic, and good-looking, a ladies' man. She has kept tabs on him since Savannah's birth and even seen a picture or two, but the years have not been kind. He is old now, bald, fat with a flabby jaw line. Laura Lynne shakes off the ick creeping into her mind, determined to make a note in her legal pad, then move on.

She is saved from her reverie when Mary appears with her lunch. "Here you go, dear. Been thinking about that little girl, and nothing has come to mind yet. I need to man the front desk. The line at Louise's is getting longer; word is out!"

Laura Lynne smiles as she hands her the change and places the food on the table, accompanied by the beautiful sight of a 44 oz Styrofoam cup filled to the rim with unsweetened tea. Laura Lynne grabs the cup and takes a large swallow.

"Thank you so much, smells wonderful." She nods and hurries off. Laura Lynne opens the bag and pulls out the carefully wrapped sandwich. She bites into the heavenly-smelling concoction and rolls her eyes. "God, that is good," she mumbles aloud. She finishes off half the sandwich, deciding to save the other half for tomorrow. Wiping her mouth and taking one more swig of tea, Laura Lynne repositions herself in front of the screen, determined to get through 1980 before the office closes at 5.

Laura Lynne notes a bar fight, a car accident, and the purchase of the old Bostwick place. Not certain what this has to do with Dead Doe, Laura Lynne makes notes and references the names in the articles. Picking up the phone on her desk, she hears a ringtone and presses the key that says, "front desk." Mary picks up, "What did you find?"

"Hey! It works! Wasn't sure when I didn't hear a ring."

"No ring tone, it is just a flashing light. Can I help you with something?"

"The old Bostwick place? I saw it was sold in 1980 to some investors with plans to renovate, but as I recall, it was abandoned up until the day I left. The Halloween before, Grace and I had scared ourselves silly running up and touching the front door of the house, nearly killing ourselves in the process."

"Not sure about any sales, but I can tell you the place has never been renovated. The house completely fell to the ground a few years back. Nothing much left but the original chimney."

"Okay, thanks. And Mary? Are you sure I am not bothering you?"

"I am sure. In fact, I am making a few notes about your questions."

"Oh, that would be great. Okay, well, if you are sure. Thanks."

Laura Lynne continues through the last reel and finds a follow-up article to the missing little girl found near the railroad tracks. As reported by Ron Adams it reads, "The young girl with almond eyes recalls heading to the grocery store on South Street to buy some eggs and milk for her mother. She remembers nothing else until she is found two days later wandering the railroad tracks."

This time, Laura Lynne gets up and walks out to the front desk. Mary is sitting at the counter, book in hand. Today's novel is a steamy romance. At least the cover appears to be very steamy. "Mary, sorry to bother, but I found a follow-up article on the railroad girl from 1980. See if it helps." Laura Lynne reads the information she copied down. Mary purses her lips and takes off her glasses.

"No, still not helping. But back then, "almond eyes" was code for Asian descent. That could be helpful. Not too many Asian people here in 1980. Certainly, none in Moseley Hall. And you said she was headed to the South Side grocery? I would guess she lived near that area, so I am sure she was probably quite poor. I doubt even above the poverty line. Probably why there is so little said about her in the paper, would not have been considered that odd in that part of town. Sad, but true. Especially then. I could reach out to the librarian at Venice High School and see if she has a copy of a yearbook from then. We might be able to find a name."

"Really, Mary? That would be great. Also, I was wondering if there was a way to copy off the articles from the microfiche, like a digital download or even a paper copy?"

"Not sure about that, but have you tried just taking a picture of it with your phone? Might be you can upload the image to your computer and then convert it into something usable."

"God, Mary, you are brilliant! I have no idea why I didn't think of that. Ashley is a guru with IT. I bet she can figure something out for me." Laura Lynne sits heavily on the stool next to her. "I don't even know what I am doing. I feel like I am trying to find a needle in a haystack but have no idea what I would do with the needle if I found it."

"No word from the coroner's office, I take it?"

"Nothing and our attorney keeps telling me until we do have some information, it's pointless to do anything. He feels confident Uncle Gabe is just a scapegoat at this point. Uncle Gabe swears he knows nothing, and I believe him. He is such a gentle spirit."

"Yes, I nearly laughed out loud when I heard about his arrest. It was just so ridiculous! More likely, his daddy was involved. That was one mean man, and your Uncle Gabe bore the brunt of his mean."

"Why do you say that, Mary?" Laura Lynne looks at her with curiosity. She knows her Poppy Cooper is notorious in these parts, not above breaking the law when he felt the need, but she had never thought of him as mean. He must have been in his 70s when Laura Lynne last saw him, still commanding, certainly, but never mean.

Mary looks startled, like she was talking out of school. "Nothing, Laura Lynne, just talking." She pats Laura Lynne's hand and avoids eye contact. She squeezes her hand and waits, forcing her to look at her.

"It's okay. I am not mad. I want to know."

"It's just something my mother shared with me. I am not even sure how the topic of Gabe came up, but she mentioned that she and Gabe attended school together at Moseley—shared the same classroom in elementary school. He came to school a few times with bruises and even a black eye. The worst was a broken arm. She intimated that Gabe was 'clumsy,' but everyone knew his daddy was using him as a punching bag. Gabe wasn't like the Cooper men. He was gentle, more like Birdie, his mother's people. She thought maybe he was trying to toughen him up, make him a 'man.'"

Child abuse, what a family legacy. Add one more victim of Laura Lynne's grandfather. Laura Lynne sighs deeply. "I am glad you told me."

"It's just my mother's perception, or more her Momma and Daddy's perception. Rumors. I don't want you to think my momma or I are gossipers. Toward the end of her life, she liked to talk about her growing-up years. A lot of times, it was the only thing she remembered."

"I know Mary. I am not worried about you fanning the flames of the local gossip mill." Laura Lynne gets up and walks back to her office space. "I am going to work about 30 more minutes. Want to get done with 1980. Tomorrow, I have an errand in Mobile, but is it okay if I come back on Friday?"

"Sure, I will try to have those yearbooks from Venice High here for you."

Laura Lynne smiles and heads back to her microfiche. She finishes the year, finding one more article on the Winter Country Club Gala with photographs. Laura Lynne sees her parents in their formal wear. She takes pictures of the photos and the article, uploads them to her email, and sends everything to Ashley with a request to make it all user-friendly. She knows Laura Lynne is a luddite, or a technophobe, whatever, but if it's not in a Word document she doesn't know what to do with it. Packing up, Laura Lynne glances at the wall clock. She has spent the last seven hours bent over a desk, viewing reels of film. At this rate, she has another 63 hours left of film to review.

"Thanks, Mary. Have a great rest of the day! I appreciate the help."

"My pleasure, you are the most fun I have had at this job!" She waves and goes back to her romance novel.

On the drive home, Laura Lynne calls Scarlet. Laura Lynne needs to ask her what she knows about this Ginny person. Hopefully, she can convince her to join her on the trip to Mobile. Scarlet picks up right before it goes to voicemail, her speech garbled. Laura Lynne can barely understand her.

"Scarlet, is that you? You sound awful."

"I know. Had a tooth crack and partially fall out yesterday. The dentist did some work on my mouth today. Half my head is numb, starting with my lips. Sorry I sound awful, but I wanted to see if you knew anything new?"

Laura Lynne tells her about her research at the Gazette. She agrees it would probably not bear much fruit, but it was something to do. She, too had no recollection of a possible Asian girl who turned up at the railroad tracks in 1980. Laura Lynne finally asks, "Scarlet, did you know about daddy's mistress in Mobile, some chick by the name of Ginny?"

She is silent for a moment. Then Laura Lynne hears her take a deep breath and sigh it out. "So, the rumors are true. I suspected there was someone. He started going to Mobile for 'business' quite a bit after you left. I was at Ole Miss, but when I came home, I knew something was not right. At the time, I just figured it was normal marriage and family stuff. You know, you, me, and Tripp were out of the house by then. It was just Momma and Daddy, little Avery. But, over the years, I realized he was gone an awful lot to Mobile, much to Momma's frustration. There were rumors around town, of course, but there is always gossip of some sort, so I just ignored it."

"Well, apparently, Daddy and this woman had an arrangement as well as an affair. According to Uncle Gabe, our father has been paying a monthly stipend up until his death. Uncle Gabe has been paying it the last five years."

"Wait, he pays her? How much? Why?"

"I did not ask how much, but he pays her monthly from an account set up separate from the trust. That is really all I know. But Scarlet, I agree. Doesn't it sound fishy? I was wondering about blackmail."

"God, let's hope not. What a mess. Listen, I just don't have the bandwidth for this today. This tooth is wretched."

"Have you heard anything from Momma?"

"No, honestly, this cracked tooth has been taking all my time and energy. Plus, to be honest, I don't talk to Momma unless I have to. It's just joy-sucking." Laura Lynne is surprised by Scarlet. She had no idea she felt this way about their mother. Over the years, she has been the one to deal with their parents without complaint.

"Well, maybe it's smarter not to poke the bear. You take care of yourself. I will go to Mobile and see what is what."

"Call me on your ride home from Mobile. I want to hear all about Daddy's side gig. Sorry, Laura Lynne, my mouth is killing me. Talk to you later." She hangs up. Laura Lynne glances at her phone, shaking her head and wondering what is going on with her sister.

Chapter 14

Spring 1986

Saturday morning dawns bright. Laura Lynne is up early and attempts to arouse Avery. He is a slug this morning. "Meet me downstairs. I want to grab some tea. You want anything?"

Sitting at the side of his bed, rubbing his eyes, he mumbles, "Coffee, lots of coffee."

Melanie is already up and dressed, sitting on the front porch drinking coffee. Resigned, Laura Lynne joins her, pouring hot water over a tea bag before sitting down.

"Good morning," Laura Lynne says.

Melanie nods, looking tired. "Your father told me about your discussion last night. I think it's for the best, you staying here. Finishing up your senior year. It would be hard for you to return. Besides, you seem very happy here. I think it was a good decision for you to come to Aunt Eileen's." Melanie dabs her lips with a napkin, and Laura Lynne is shocked into silence. "Now that that is out of the way, we can enjoy the rest of the weekend. What do you have planned for us today?"

And just like that, Laura Lynne's future is planned. Laura Lynne realizes her mother never wanted her to come back home and is relieved she had no intention of returning. She slams down her mug, "Seriously? You think I want to spend time with you? No, that is not going to happen. I am spending the day with Avery." Laura Lynne gets up from the table, grabbing her mug. With the utmost care, Laura Lynne walks to the coffee pot and pours a mug for Avery, "Please have Avery meet me at the barn."

"Laura Lynne! You stop this immediately! What in the world is wrong with you?" Laura Lynne stops in her tracks, turning around. Years of training kick right back in. Melanie is standing, looking impervious. "I have no idea what your issue is, young lady." She sits back down, picking up the newspaper. "You are getting just what you wanted."

"I wanted you to fight for me. I wanted you to be my mother." Laura Lynne feels the tears well up and hears a rushing sound in her ears. She turns on her heel and heads off the porch before her mother can respond.

Avery runs up beside her, "You left without me!" He takes the coffee mug from her hand, waiting for her response. When none is forthcoming, he continues, "Come on, Laura Lynne, don't be mad. This is early for me!" And he nudges Laura Lynne with his shoulder, gently blowing on his coffee. As he looks over the rim, he notices the tears running down her cheeks. "Whoo, wow, okay, what is going on?" Laura Lynne says nothing and just keeps walking. "No, stop, Laura Lynne, what happened?" He pulls her over to a grove of trees, pulling her close for a hug. "Don't you think it's time you tell me why you are here? I have heard rumors, but I want to hear it from you. I am old enough. Laura Lynne, I would never tell your secrets."

This is the most serious Laura Lynne has ever seen Avery. He is so gentle. He is going to be a wonderful man one day. Laura Lynne puts her head on his shoulder and weeps. He pats and rubs her back, saying nothing, just making shushing sounds and saying, "It's gonna be ok."

Finally, her weeping subsides. Keeping her head on his shoulder, her face against his chest, Laura Lynne whispers, "I was sent here because Momma and Daddy think I am lying about something important." Her breath shuddering in, Laura Lynne says emphatically, "I did not lie. I am not lying! They just won't believe me." Avery is quiet. His hand stills while she is talking. He picks up his soothing strokes and sighs.

"Okay, so, you weren't pregnant? I am not an uncle?" Avery gently pushes Laura Lynne away from him and looks into her eyes. He hands her a handkerchief from his back pocket. Well trained, our Avery. Laura Lynne shakes her head no while wiping her eyes. "That is the rumor going around town." Laura Lynne sighs and puts her head back on his shoulder. "So, what happened with Daddy last night? He came upstairs late; I heard him. He was obviously drunk."

"He wants me to come home and stay, but Momma doesn't want me there. He still accused me of lying; it's all just a mess!" Laura Lynne pulls away from Avery and starts to walk, blowing her nose. "Then this morning, Momma agrees with me, best if I stay here." She turns red eyes at Avery. "She didn't even fight for me or act like she wanted me."

"Yeah, not surprised by that. Momma has been all but shunned by her friends at the country club. She was even voted out as Chairperson of the DAR. Those old biddies are having a fine time knocking Momma down off her high horse. She has been sitting on it for a long time. They see a chance to knock her off, and they are taking it. You know that is all Momma cares about, maintaining her spot in society."

"And the Beauregard name." She looks over at him with new eyes. "Has it been awful for you too?"

"Not awful. Most of the focus has been on Tripp's senior year, but I have been in a few fights."

"You have been in fights?" Laura Lynne says, surprised. Avery is the clown. Tripp, Laura Lynne could see, not Avery.

"Have to stand up for my sister. Not gonna let anyone talk ugly about you, Laura Lynne."

Laura Lynne wraps her arm around her baby brother as they two continue to walk. "You believe me, don't you? That I am not lying, right? For a while, I thought I was as crazy as Aunt Augustine."

"Hell no." He puts his arm around her, walking arm and arm to the barn. "Just wish whatever happened didn't. It's been mighty weird around the house since you left."

"Weird how?"

"Momma and Daddy haven't shared a room since you left. Things are not good between them. Lots of heated 'discussions' when they think I can't hear them. Daddy has been getting a lot of flak from the Hugers, too. I know farm business is down. Some deal he and Mr. Huger were planning is on hold. Causing a lot of stress between them."

"I am sorry you are getting the brunt of this." Laura Lynne leans her head on his shoulder.

"Nothing to it, Sissy. I just keep up the family clown act, and they are none the wiser."

"So, it is all just an act? Why?"

"Easier, really. Tripp is the superstar, and I am good with that. Being charming and funny takes the pressure off. Our parents don't expect much from me. I prefer it that way."

"Very clever. Wish I had thought of that."

"You do it in your own way, Laura Lynne. You don't compete with Scarlet in what she is good at. You focus on what you are good at. It's really the same thing. No need to compete with your siblings."

"You should be a psychologist." He looks at her funny and then smiles.

"Actually, I would love that. Watching people and figuring out why they do what they do is fascinating to me."

"Be sure to talk to Dr. Mabel about it before you leave. She has a PhD." Laura Lynne kisses Avery on the cheek. "I love you, Avery. I hate what our parents are doing to us."

"Me too. Just four more years. I just have to make it four more years."

"Come on, enough with the serious talk. Let's see what Ham is up to."

The two siblings play on the farm for the rest of the day, first with the animals and then on the four-wheelers. Laura Lynne takes Avery to the garage with all the toys, and he is in heaven. Martha makes them a picnic lunch, which Laura Lynne straps to the back of the four-wheeler. They receive stern warnings from Aunt Eileen and safety instructions from Ben. Laura Lynne and Avery have never had a day, just the two of them. They have a blast together, covering at least 100 acres before eating a lunch of bologna sandwiches, potato salad, deviled eggs, and Moon Pies, all washed down with Diet Pepsi. The two laugh and cut up, giggling as they sit by the stream, shoes off, feet dangling in the water.

"Wait, I think I hear the ranch horn! Avery, stop splashing me! Listen!" As silence descends, Laura Lynne hears the distinct sound of the horn Martha uses to call in the ranch hands. Since today is not an official workday, Laura Lynne suspects it is for her and Avery.

"Come on! I think we are being called home."

"It's kind of early for supper. Wonder why?"

"No telling, but I bet donuts to dollars y'all are headed back to Tea Olive."

The two arrive, wet and sweaty from their day in the sun. Their mother and father are standing on the porch, dressed to leave. And sure enough, their father confirms Laura Lynne's suspicion, "Avery, business has come up at the farm, and we need to head back home sooner than expected. Need to go clean up and pack. We need to get to the airport.

"Come on, Avery, I will help you pack."

The two siblings walk up the stairs and around their parents. Laura Lynne refuses to meet their eyes. She would not give them the satisfaction of seeing her disappointment.

Avery shakes his head, "Wow, I never thought I would be disappointed in my parents. But today, I am."

"Welcome to the club. But by this point, nothing they do surprises me anymore." Looking over at Avery, Laura Lynne smiles as they climb the stairs. "Don't be a stranger, okay? Call me when you can, and I will do the same. And don't worry about me, I am fine. Honestly, after today, I realize I feel more sorry for you than for me."

"I think I do, too."

Laura Lynne packs Avery's things while he takes a quick shower. She's surprised all over again about how much he has grown up this past year. Before leaving his room, Avery pulls Laura Lynne in for one last brotherly hug, kissing the top of her head, his eyes bright with tears. "I wish you were coming with me."

Laura Lynne squeezes him tight, "Come on."

The two descend the stairs and Laura Lynne walks over to her Aunt Eileen, placing an arm around her waist and laying her head on her shoulder. Eileen absently kisses her head and rubs her shoulder. Not willing to allow her parents to leave without at least one finely honed knife to the heart, Laura Lynne says to her father, "I hope the business at Tea Olive is not too serious. I don't want you to worry about me while I am here. Aunt Eileen and Ben have turned into superior parents. I couldn't ask for better."

Sawyer halts in midstride, her mother hissing, "That is spiteful. I expect better from you."

Laura Lynne rolls her eyes, like she cares what her mother expects of her anymore. "I learned from the best Momma, the *very* best." With that, Laura Lynne leaves the porch and heads to her room, letting the tears that are left fall on her pillow and on Scout. Eileen comes to her room a few minutes later. "Want to talk about it?"

"There is really not much to say. You know all of it. Are you really okay with me staying here?"

Eileen sits down at Laura Lynne's desk chair, absently rubbing Scout as she nudges her hand, "Baby girl, never doubt it. You are my precious gift."

"Avery and I had fun. And it feels good to have a plan for the next year." Laura Lynne closes her eyes and buries her face in her pillow. "I am exhausted.

Hanging out with Avery is like chasing after a kid-sized Ham! But thanks for all this. I know it's a lot."

"Your Momma is a *lot*, truer words! Have a nice evening. Church tomorrow, but otherwise the day is yours. You got everything you need for your first full day as a working girl on Monday?"

"Yep, all good. Good night."

Chapter 15

Present Day

The drive to Mobile is about 120 miles. Laura Lynne figures she can make the drive in two hours. Victoria is packing a lunch for Laura Lynne, giving her the hairy eyeball as she eats her leftover grilled cheese from Cheese Louise! for breakfast. "Okay, what is wrong? Why are you giving me the same look your grandmother used on us kids when we tracked in something smelly from the fields?"

"Hmmph, paying good money for something I can make right here! If you want a fancy grilled cheese sandwich for lunch, all you have to do is ask!" Laura Lynne has offended Victoria by eating restaurant food in her kitchen. Whoops. Laura Lynne walks over to the other side of the kitchen island, giving her a quick squeeze. Victoria is no more than 5 feet tall, tiny but formidable.

"I know you can! Just got busy is all yesterday, forgot to ask. I am going back tomorrow, and I was planning to ask if you could make both Miss Wright and me lunch. I would sure appreciate it." She is appeased but still hands Laura Lynne her lunch cooler and Yeti filled with unsweetened iced tea with more force than necessary. "Thanks, Victoria. I plan to be home well before supper."

The drive is without incident. Gabe had provided Laura Lynne with the woman's address, along with her name: Virginia Phillips. Plugging in the coordinates to her GPS, Laura Lynne uses the time in the car to make phone calls. She calls Avery, Gray, and Ashley to update them on the current situation. The closer she gets to Mobile, the more her nerves start to sing. She decides to stop at a gas station about ten minutes away from her destination. Freshening up and grabbing one last Diet Coke, Laura Lynne walks to her car, praying the entire time. With nothing left to do but drive, Laura Lynne arrives at the address. She parks on the street and looks at the modest-style ranch sitting on a half-acre lot. Now what?

Deciding the best course of action is to go up to the front door and knock, Laura Lynne gets out of the car before losing her nerve. After a few minutes, giving Laura Lynne time to look around the well-manicured lawn, the door opens. A staggeringly beautiful woman in her late 60s is standing in the doorway, a look of inquiry on her face. "Yes, can I help you?"

Laura Lynne stutters, "I…I'm sorry, forgive me! Are you Virginia Phillips? Ginny?"

She looks at Laura Lynne again and recognition dawns. "Laura Lynne…Atkins now, right? Well, I have been waiting on this day for quite some time. Come on in." She opens the glass storm door and steps aside. "And, yes, I am Ginny."

"You know who I am?"

"Yes, your father and I talked about you, well, all his children at length over the years. I have been following you most recently through your website and blog. I read your book, too. It's quite good."

Laura Lynne is still standing on the stoop. "Please come in, Laura Lynne. We have a lot to discuss. Unless you prefer to stand on the step?" She is smiling.

Laura Lynne is thrown by her ease and acknowledgment of her appearance, but she follows her inside. Her home is as gracious as she is. Laura Lynne steps into the cool, noticing the large brick wall and modern sculpture dominating the entrance. Ginny ushers her to the left, around the wall, and into the main living quarters. The entire back of the home is glass with a garden view.

"Your home is lovely."

"Thank you. The designer of the home used Usonian-type features. It's L-shaped to highlight the backyard garden. This way to the terrace. Can I get you a drink?"

"No, thank you."

"If you change your mind, let me know. I just sat down when I heard you knocking at the front door." She walks out on the terrace, and Laura Lynne feels like she has entered into Mr. Miyagi's Japanese garden from the *Karate Kid* movie. Laura Lynne said as much. Ginny laughs, "You aren't far off! I wanted something just like that, inspired by nature. It seemed to fit the house." She sits down at the wrought iron table, where she has a glass of ice water and lemon wrapped in a colorful napkin. "I am pretty sure you are not here to discuss my home and garden, though, to be truthful, I can talk about it all day long! It has become my passion since your father died."

Laura Lynne sits across from her, staring intently. Not exactly the third-rate hussy, chain-smoking, vodka-loving trailer trash Laura Lynne pictured on her drive down. Not flinching from Laura Lynne's rude appraisal, Ginny asks, "How did you find out about me?"

"Avery mentioned he thought he might have accidentally met you at a diner when he was on one of his trips with Daddy. When I followed up with Uncle Gabe, he told me what he knew about you and the monthly stipend."

"Avery is a smart boy. I told your Daddy I thought he figured out we were more than acquaintances. It was purely a coincidence, though your Daddy and I had been seeing each other for a while by then. I was working a shift at the law firm and had come to the diner for some take out, and there they were. Could have swallowed my tongue, but your Daddy, he just introduced us and acted like I was a business acquaintance."

"The law firm? I thought you were an escort." Glancing down at her hands, Laura Lynne apologizes, "I am sorry, that is a very rude question."

"Yes, it is rude, but no less the truth. I was an escort. That is how your father and I met."

"Here is another rude question. How did you become an escort? Or not how necessarily, but why?"

"Why does anyone turn to prostitution? Poverty mostly. I was raised rough. Prostitution was one way out. I was pretty enough and smart enough to be what was referred to as a high-end call girl. Believe it or not, my mother was the one who got me started with escort services. I was 15 my first time but looked much older. She didn't want me turning tricks on the corner like she had done most of my life." Hard to believe, looking at her today, that her life had been anything other than refined. "Now, a question of my own." She looks at Laura Lynne with sea-green eyes, piercing. "What brings you here now, Laura Lynne?"

"A corpse."

"Well, that is intriguing. Tell me more."

"I'd rather not. What I want to know is do you know anything about it?"

"Why do you think I would?"

Laura Lynne shrugs. "I know about the monthly stipend. My father is generous, certainly, but no way would he pay you every month because he loves you. It is blackmail money." Laura Lynne leans across the table. "Why, Ginny, are you blackmailing my family? What do you know?"

"Well, you are a smart one. And the truth? I know plenty." The sheen of sophistication begins to slide. Ginny from the streets is emerging. "Time for you to go," Ginny stands up from the table. Laura Lynne doesn't budge.

"Not until you tell me what you know."

"Why would I tell you? I have a good thing going. It is not harming anyone. Your family has plenty of money. And plenty of secrets. I know all about yours, well, yours and Dr. Butler's."

Laura Lynne feels the earth shift, not expecting her father to betray her confidences to anyone, much less one of his mistresses. Noticing the smirk on Ginny's face, thinking she had scored a hit, Laura Lynne countered. "You think that scares me?"

"Yep, scared you whiter than you already are."

Smiling broadly, Laura Lynne counters, "Hmm, how little you know. It is the topic of my next book, due for publication this summer. Try again."

"Liar."

"You can blab it to the far reaches of the earth for all I care. Probably increase book sales. Don't forget who you are talking to, lady. I am the black sheep of the family. I couldn't care less what happens to our reputation. Mine was shattered years ago. Big deal. Momma and Uncle Gabe, they only have a few years left. They can weather the storm."

"*Get out of my house!*" Ginny screams, spittle flying and pointing her finger toward the door.

Laura Lynne slowly gets up from the chair. "Fine, but the money stops flowing today. You will never get another dime from our family. Ever." Walking toward the sliding glass door, Laura Lynne continues, "Don't worry, I will see myself out."

"You do that, little miss high and mighty! Acting like you own the place with your haughty ways. You will regret this decision. I have enough information to bury you and your family."

"You very well may, and then, more than likely, you have nothing. My guess is you are all smoke and mirrors. Just like this façade of a life you live."

"Really, well, before you go, it might surprise you to know that maid of yours? Pearl? Well, who do you think fathered that daughter of hers? Half white, isn't she?"

Laura Lynne pauses. "So?"

"Who do you think her daddy is?"

"I have no idea. Who do you think her father is?"

"I know who it is. Don't you wish you did?"

"Lady, you are an idiot. I am not playing this game. If you have all this information, sharing with me one tidbit of it might persuade me to keep up the payments."

Ginny takes the bait, "Well, the next master of the house, of course, your big brother, Tripp, I believe y'all call him."

A smile breaks across Laura Lynne's face, causing Ginny to hurl her drink at Laura Lynne's head. Ginny continues, "You think that is funny? You think I am lying?"

Easily dodging the glass, Laura Lynne shakes her head, smiling and laughing, "Neither! I think it is delightful! Victoria is a wonderful girl! I would be thrilled to have her as a niece."

"You think your Momma would be as thrilled?"

"No, absolutely not, but as I said before, she can weather the storm. She is made of sterner stuff than that, I can assure you." Turning to walk out of the house, Laura Lynne continues, "Don't throw another glass at me again, or I will put you on your fake manicured ass." And as if just realizing she had something more to say, Laura Lynne snaps her fingers, "One word of advice: you are no adversary for this generation of Beauregards. We don't scare as easily of scandal. In fact, I personally appreciate it. Drives up book sales."

Laura Lynne cannot get out of the house fast enough but leaves the situation with one parting shot given over her shoulder at the shaking woman on the front stoop, "If you talk to my family, approach my mother, reach out to my Uncle Gabe, or so much as breathe near one of our children, I will use every means at my disposal to destroy you."

"This isn't over, not by a long shot."

Under her breath, Laura Lynne whispers, "Well, it's done for today." Quickly opening her car door and sliding behind the wheel, Laura Lynne drives down the street but not before looking out her window at her father's mistress. She is shooting Laura Lynne the bird.

It takes Laura Lynne about twenty minutes before her heart rate slows down and the bile in the back of her throat disappears. She glances at her phone. There are multiple missed calls from Scarlet. She calls her back. Scarlet picks up on the first ring.

"Laura Lynne, are you okay? I have been kicking myself all day for not going down there with you. It wasn't smart for you to go alone."

"Not going to disagree with you. I am fine, but that is one first-class bitch."

"Why? What happened?"

Laura Lynne fills her in on the details, minus the comments about Dr. Butler. Scarlet hangs on to every word. "Well, do you think it's true? Do you think Tripp is Victoria's father?"

"I don't see how. Both were off to college by then. I guess it could have happened during a holiday break. It seems far-fetched to me. The two are close, but we were all close. We need to ask, though."

"Are you upset Scarlet. Would it bother you?" Laura Lynne asks.

"The only thing that would bother me is if he is Victoria's father, he has played no part in her or Pearl's life. So, to answer your question, no. It might, however, send Momma to the grave. Not so much because of crossing color lines, but more of Tripp fraternizing with the help. It would cause him to fall off that very high pedestal she has him on. Not to mention the fun her 'friends' will have needling her about it."

"Daddy got himself messed up in something, Scarlet. This woman, she knows something. I don't know about what, but we need to figure it out."

"I agree. Listen, I need to run. I am glad you are okay. I promise I won't let you keep doing everything by yourself. It's just, well, things around here are tense for me right now."

"Scarlet, what is going on? What can I do to help? You haven't seemed yourself."

Scarlet turns defensive. "How would you know Laura Lynne? You don't know me any more than I know you. It is not like you have been around for the last 40 years."

"Wow, that is harsh, even for you, Scarlet. The queen of mean but fine. I will butt out of your business but don't act like nobody cares for you or is willing to help. All you have to do is ask. Have a good rest of the day." Laura Lynne hangs up the phone and shakes her head, wishing her relationship with her older sister were anything but what it was.

Laura Lynne makes the decision not to go to Tea Olive, she is just not ready to face her Uncle Gabe after the run in with Ginny. Though a good shower with some clean-smelling soap might help with the sleezy feeling Laura Lynne has embedded in her skin. She parks in the same spot she did yesterday, in front of the Gazette. Grabbing her computer bag and lunch box, thank you Victoria. Laura Lynne walks into the front entrance of the newspaper office. The tinkle of the bell alerts Mary of her arrival.

Mary is at the counter, working a microfiche scanner with a pad of legal paper sitting next to her. "Oh, Laura Lynne! Hi! I didn't expect you today. Did your meeting go well this morning?"

"It was very enlightening. I hope you don't mind me coming in today. I wanted some time to get my thoughts together, and this seemed a good place to do it."

"Of course not. You are welcome anytime." She waves her hand as if it's a silly question.

"What are you doing?"

Mary takes her glasses off her nose and looks a bit chagrined. "I am butting in Laura Lynne. After yesterday, I thought maybe I could help with the research. So, I set up another microfiche scanner, there are several of them available, and started scanning articles using the same guidelines you are using. I decided to work my way backward and started in 1990. I hope you don't mind."

"Mind? Mary, thank you! I can use all the help I can get at this point. It might be pointless, but at least we are doing something."

Mary nods in agreement, "I also talked to the librarian at Venice High. Spring Break ends this week, so she said she would bring the yearbooks by as soon as she has the opportunity."

"Wonderful. Thank you so much. You really don't mind helping?"

"This is the most fun I have had in ages. Besides, I love your Uncle Gabe. He has been a good friend to my mother and me over the years. If I can help, I want to." And with that, she turns back to her viewfinder. "I haven't found much of anything yet, and no missing children either."

"Okay. Mary, just out of curiosity, if you see any articles about Dr. Kenneth Butler, can you make a note of them? And a photograph for the files?"

"Of course. Any particular reason why?"

"Just a feeling. Not sure, but I think it is worth following up on."

Sitting down at her desk, Laura Lynne takes out her legal pad and begins to write down notes from her interaction with the notorious Ginny. If she is to be believed, and Tripp is Victoria's father, then that would make Victoria around 36 or 37. It is perfectly plausible, but instinctually, Laura Lynne doubts its validity. The scenario does not ring true, not from what Laura Lynne knows about her brother and Pearl. Some other questions occurred to Laura Lynne on the drive in, like who is the actual owner of the deed of Ginny's house? What escort service was Ginny employed at in 1986? She seemed prepared for Laura Lynne's visit, not like it was a surprise. How would she know Laura Lynne was coming? Who would have alerted her? What trailer park did this woman come from? Who are her people? She mentioned a law firm. Which one? And what, if anything, does this have to do with Mr. Dead Doe?

Laura Lynne writes all this down, along with her conversation and impressions of Ginny from the Streets. She is reviewing her notes when Mary gently knocks on the door and sticks her head in. "Laura Lynne, it's 5:00, time to lock up!"

"Is it that late? I got caught up. Did you find anything interesting?"

"The only thing of note was really a tragedy. Did you hear about the car accident that killed the four senior high school students in 1990? It was just a few weeks before graduation. I had put that memory aside, but I remember those kids. The three boys were from Moseley, and then one girl, Sarah Jane Pirkle, who attended Venice High. It would have been Avery's graduating class."

"I do remember hearing about that. I was in college at the time, but Avery called me, crying and frantic. The boys were all friends of his. Drunk driving, wasn't it?"

"Some things you tuck away and try to forget about. That spring is one of them. Those boys had the world at their fingertips, Sarah Jane too. She was valedictorian of her class and had a full-ride academic scholarship to Ole Miss. Bright and beautiful, snuffed out over drinking. Anyway, I went ahead and marked the article and took pictures of the scanner. Sent everything to the email address you gave me."

"I think I need to start a 'parking lot items' file. I ran into a thought today, too, that has nothing to do with Dead Doe…"

Mary interrupts, "What is dead dough?"

"Dead Doe is the name I gave the corpse found at Tea Olive. I was tired of referring to it as 'the corpse.'"

Laughing, Mary says, "Oh, Dead Doe! I thought you were talking about batter of some kind! I just couldn't imagine what bread dough had to do with anything!"

"No! No! Forgive my horrible sense of humor. It is morbid, I know. Just trying to gain some levity. Today has been a pretty rough one."

Still smiling, Mary waves off her concern, "No, I get it. Dead Doe it is."

"So, a parking lot list for all the side stories we keep uncovering, not directly related to Dead Doe, but that piques our interest. A tickler file of sorts. It seems like a lot happened in the early years I was gone, especially in my family. It's time I quit hiding from it and face it."

"Not to be punny, Laura Lynne, but some skeletons are better left in the ground. Be careful. Family secrets are sometimes best kept buried, especially in a family as prominent as yours. People could get hurt."

Laura Lynne grimaces. "Plenty of people have already been hurt, but I appreciate the warning. Listen, could you do me a favor?"

"Sure, what's up?"

Laura Lynne hands Mary her lunchbox, still full from the morning. "Do you mind taking this home and eating it for supper? Victoria made it for me, and if I bring it back uneaten, she will be offended. I already made her mad eating my leftovers from Cheese Louise this morning."

"Are you kidding? Absolutely, no problem at all."

"Don't worry about lunch tomorrow. I will have Victoria make enough for both of us. Maybe I can get back on her good side."

Laura Lynne waits next to Mary as she locks the front door. The two part company in the parking lot.

Pulling through the front gates of Tea Olive, Laura Lynne is greeted by the sight of her Uncle Gabe overseeing the digging of a very large mud hole. John and Liam are shoveling. Gabe is on his knees, pointing and gesturing. Laura Lynne honks her horn, waving as she drives by. Uncle Gabe glances her way, absently waving back, immersed in his project. Parking her car, Laura Lynne decides to see what the men are up to. She slowly walks through the budding gardens so lovingly maintained by her uncle.

As she approaches, Laura Lynne calls out, "You know Mississippi Mud Pie is not actually made with mud, right? What are y'all doin'?"

"We, young lady, are attempting to lay the pipes for the irrigation system and its messy work. Men's work! It is going to be fabulous when it's finished, but getting there is proving a challenge." Uncle

Gabe looks up from his handiwork. "And how was your day, Laura Lynne? Productive?"

Laura Lynne rolls her eyes and shakes her head. "I think 'interesting' is a better word."

"I can't wait to hear about it, but first, the pipes. Please tell Victoria I am going to be late for supper. In fact, no need to fuss; a sandwich is fine." Laura Lynne rolls her eyes again. He knows better. It's half an hour before supper time. The entire meal is made and waiting to be eaten.

"I will let her know, but it won't be a sandwich. Y'all be careful, and Uncle Gabe? You be careful! There will be no broken body parts. We have enough on our plate!" Uncle Gabe waves Laura Lynne away, frustrated with her mothering.

"Off with you, woman! Stop your fussing! Been playing in the dirt since before you were born. I know what I am about. Come on young Liam, stop your lazing about. John, I think we should attach a riser to that fitting. See if that works." Laura Lynne watches them work for a few minutes before she heads back to the house. She is ready for a shower and a cold drink.

"Victoria!" Laura Lynne heads to the kitchen refrigerator, intent on fixing a drink. The kitchen is alive with wonderful smells and something amazing appears to be in the oven.

"M'am?" Victoria pokes her head out of the pantry.

"Oh, there you are! Sorry, we are running late today, but Uncle Gabe is still playing in the dirt, and

I want to catch a quick shower before supper. I don't want you to have to hang around. If you just show me what we are having, I will make sure Uncle Gabe is fed and the kitchen cleaned up."

"Well, I figured Mr. Gabe might get caught up with his fancy irrigation system, so I made a tomato pie and a fresh salad for supper. The pie is out of the oven in about ten minutes. It needs to sit for another ten before you cut it, or you just get a watery mess. Otherwise, just put dressing on the salad when y'all are ready to sit down."

Laura Lynne finds herself staring at Victoria's features, trying to see if the Cooper chin or the Beauregard nose is present.

"Is everything okay, ma'am?"

Shaking herself, Laura Lynne grins sheepishly, "Sorry, long day. I figured you would be irritated. I should have called you earlier."

Victoria fans herself with her dishcloth, "Before you came to stay, it was just Mr. Gabe and the occasional visitor, or John, to keep him company. He prefers a less formal supper than Mrs. Beauregard, so this is nothing new. Breakfast is a different story! He wakes up hungry and likes a farmer's breakfast. If this suits you, I will just head out after I take the pie out."

"It suits perfectly. Thank you." It's on the tip of Laura Lynne's tongue to ask her how old she is, but it would be rude and inappropriate. She sighs and opens the fridge. Two teas, labeled one sweet and the other LL, are perched on the shelf. It's amazing how such a small thing has such a big impact. That small gesture filled Laura Lynne's heart, her eyes swimming with tears. "Thank you for remembering the tea. I sure appreciate it."

Laura Lynne holds the refrigerator door open, letting the emotions of the day overwhelm her as she stares at the tea pitcher. She feels the gentle hand of Victoria on her arm, soothing.

"You sure you're okay, Miss Laura Lynne? Momma will be back tomorrow, but I have a pretty good ear if you want to share."

Leaning her head back and taking a deep breath of air, the tears overflowing, Laura Lynne says, "I had an incredibly awful day today, just the worst. And then I come here, home, to a pitcher of tea made especially for me. It just hit me hard right then. Queenie used to do the same thing for all of us. Mark the food she made special for us. Our favorites."

"I know, she told me. I didn't mean to make you sad."

"You didn't." Laura Lynne releases the doors and turns to Victoria, giving her a big hug. "You made me nostalgic. There is a difference." Taking a step back, Laura Lynne swipes at her eyes and nose, then reaches for the tea pitcher.

"No ma'am. You go wash those nasty hands. Don't you go rifling through my refrigerator all germy! I will pour the tea!"

Laughing, Laura Lynne gives Victoria a grateful smile and walks to the kitchen sink, washing her hands and splashing her face. Victoria puts the glass of tea on the counter. "Go on now, get your shower. You will feel better."

"I am going to do just that. Thank you, Victoria."

Laura Lynne stays in her bedroom, waiting for Gabe to come in from the garden. She texts Gray and Savannah but is just not ready to talk to anyone before she talks to her uncle. Looking out the window, Laura Lynne sees the three men heading toward the house. They must be done for the day. Laura Lynne slips on some shoes and checks her reflection in the mirror. Not bad considering. The two meet in the kitchen.

"Did you get the plumbing worked out?"

"We did. We certainly did. And I am starving. Do you mind making a plate for me? I need to clean up a bit before I eat. I am covered in mud."

"Of course. I will wait for you."

Laura Lynne busies herself tossing the salad, cutting the pie, and arranging the plates of food. She pours a glass of wine for her uncle and refills her tea glass. By the time she is done, Gabe is back fresh from a shower. "That looks mighty fine, Laura Lynne. Let's just eat here at the island. No need to make a fuss. Besides, I want to hear about your day."

"You are not going to like what I learned."

With a sigh, Gabe picks up his glass of wine and takes a swallow. "I am sure I won't, but I doubt I will be surprised."

Laura Lynne sits on the barstool next to her uncle. "She is one ugly piece of work, Uncle Gabe, nasty, through and through. She knows something. I don't know what. But that stipend? You were right. It is blackmail money."

Digging into his tomato pie, he chews thoughtfully. Laura Lynne does the same. She hasn't eaten since breakfast. She is starving. "Worried that was the case. Tell me the whole story."

Laura Lynne relates the events of the day, her impressions, and Ginny's accusations about Tripp. She does not tell him about Ginny's references to Dr. Butler. Laying his fork down, Gabe picks up his wine glass and takes a sip. "Tripp Victoria's father? Now that is interesting. I guess it is possible, but I don't think so."

"I thought the same. I think I need to ask Pearl. I think she will tell me, but regardless, she needs to know if her family could be a part of the fallout." Laura Lynne looks at her uncle. "You don't seem too upset about all this. I thought you would be scandalized."

"Scandalized? No, that would be Melanie. I am more concerned about what she hasn't told us. And where she is getting her information. I find it hard to believe your father would divulge such family secrets to this woman. But she knows something.

We know that. Otherwise, your father would not have paid her."

Getting up from the stool, Gabe picks up his plate and takes it to the sink. "Finish up your meal, Laura Lynne, and meet me in the study. I want a brandy and my recliner."

"Yes, sir."

As Laura Lynne finishes up, she hears jazz coming from the study. The nostalgia hits her once again, her mind flashing back to the evenings of her childhood. Why is remembering the good times so much harder than the bad ones? Wiping her eyes for what seems the hundredth time that day, Laura Lynne joins her uncle in the study. He is sitting in his wingback leather chair, his feet propped on the matching ottoman, cradling his Old Kentucky.

Laura Lynne sits across from him with a feeling of overwhelming love. She has lost so many opportunities over the years to share tomato pie and the day with her uncle. And now, at 73, there are not too many more opportunities.

"Uncle Gabe, why didn't you ever get married? I know you dated and had a few long-term relationships, but you never married. Why not?"

He raises an eyebrow at Laura Lynne. "Where did that come from? Well, the simple truth is that the love of my life married another. It would not have been fair to marry someone else, someone who did not have my heart. To me or to her."

"Really? Do I know her? Is she still married?"

"Laura Lynne, some things are not your business. This is one of those things. It does not matter. It was many years ago. We both had very exceptional lives, separate but still well-lived lives."

"You're right. None of my business. I'm sorry. I was just curious. You are such a wonderful uncle. I know you would have made a wonderful husband and father if you had chosen that route." Clearing her throat, Laura Lynne barrels on, "I have another question that is really none of my business, but I want to ask you if you don't mind?"

"Well, by all means, you can ask. Won't promise I will answer, though."

Nodding, Laura Lynne just blurts it out, "Uncle Gabe, did Poppy Cooper abuse you?"

He is silent for so long that Laura Lynne begins to backtrack, "I'm sorry. I crossed a line…"

Gazing over Laura Lynne's head as if peering into the past, Gabe begins to talk, "Abuse. Such a small word for the punishment he inflicted on me. Nearly killed me a couple of times. Broke my arm once. He was a mean drunk, a real son of a bitch." Laura Lynne has never heard her uncle cuss before. "But he only hit me, never my mother or sisters. Just me. And I was glad of it." His eyes lose the faraway look as he focuses on Laura Lynne. "How did you find out? It's been a well-kept secret."

"Maybe not as well as you thought, Uncle Gabe. Apparently, Mary Wright's mother, Edith, suspected it all along. She intimated her grandparents believed it to be the case as well. She mentioned it to me in passing. I don't think she meant to tell me, but she did."

"Edith Trumble, yes, of course. Well, I did come to school bruised and battered. Hard to hide a black eye or a busted lip. The tale I told, of course, was that I fell down the stairs or ran into a tree. Not exactly lies. I just eliminated the fact that my father was the reason those things happened." He clears his throat.

"What made him stop? Or did he?"

"The beatings stopped when I was 12 years old. I remember it vividly. My gentle, sweet, dear mother packed our bags. Packed up my sisters and me and left Tea Olive without a word to Daddy. She gave him an ultimatum. It was the booze, or it was family, but he could no longer have both. We went to her parents' house and stayed for six weeks or so. I found out later that she had divorce papers drawn up. She was not going to let him hurt me again. The broken arm was the catalyst. Still can't smell whiskey without thinking of some of his beatings."

Uncle Gabe puts his glass down on the table beside him. Places his feet on the floor and leans forward in his chair. "I find myself very tired now, Laura Lynne. I think I am going to head up to bed." He stands up and walks over to where I am seated. "You don't think less of me, do you?"

The tears overflow. "How could I think less of you? All that you endured. You are still one of the best men I know. I am so proud that you are my uncle."

Laura Lynne stands up, and Gabe pulls her in for a tight, fierce embrace. He is crying, too.

"We are a sorry lot, Laura Lynne, you and I! Crying over spilled milk. Mop up the tears, and let's go to bed. Sunrise comes early." The two walk up the stairs together, arm in arm. "I love you, baby girl."

"Oh, Uncle Gabe. I love you, too. Good night."

"Good night."

Chapter 16

Laura Lynne's sleep is fitful. Her head is filled with images of Gabe's childhood and trailer park trash. Between blackmail and battery, rest is not in the equation. Giving up on sleep, Laura Lynne slips on a pair of jeans and a flannel shirt before taking a walk out to the river. There is something soothing about gazing at the water as it rushes by, and she needs soothing. Not to mention, the walk will do her good before sitting in front of the microfiche film projector all day.

Banging out the back screen door, Laura Lynne hears Pearl calling to her from the barn. "Laura Lynne! You're up and out early this morning. Headed to the dock?"

"I am. Didn't sleep well last night. Would you care to join me?" Pearl hesitates. "Come on, Pearl, it will be fun. The house isn't even up yet. Besides, I want to talk to you about my, well, let's say, experience yesterday. We haven't had much time together."

"Okay, let me put down my purse and get these strawberries into the kitchen. Give me a minute. I need to change my shoes too."

"No rush, I will wait outside." Laura Lynne heads out the door and waits while Pearl gets herself together. She tries to plan out how to ask her about Tripp. Pearl clomps down the stairs in her boots. Laura Lynne lets out a belly laugh at Pearl's outfit. Along with the muddy work boots, Pearl has on a pretty sundress and pearls. "That is lovely, Pearl."

"I didn't know I was going to be traipsing through the fields when I got dressed this morning! I would have chosen a different outfit, like overalls." She smiles. "Come on, let's go."

The two friends set off to the dock, along the well-worn path they used to skip and play along when they were children. "Pearl, I really don't know how to go about telling you all this. I am embarrassed, and I don't want to offend. And you have every right to know because, well, it could have an impact on you and, well, Victoria."

"Best just tell me."

"Ok, you are right." Holding her hand like she did when they were children, Laura Lynne continues to talk. "So my trip to Mobile yesterday was to see my father's mistress. A woman by the name of Virginia Phillips, she goes by Ginny." Laura Lynne glances at Pearl, "From the look on your face, I can tell you have heard the name before." Squeezing her hand Laura Lynne continues, "A nasty bit of work that woman."

"What does this have to do with me? And Victoria?"

The two women have reached the dock. Laura Lynne sits down on the bench, motioning for Pearl to join her. "Well, there is really no easy way to say it. This woman claims Tripp is Victoria's father. So, I am wondering, is he?"

A huge grin comes over her face. Pearl clutches her sides and doubles over, a huge belly laugh escaping.

"Oh Lord! How I wish! No, Victoria's biological father is white, but he is not Tripp."

"You are sure? There is not the slightest chance. Because honestly, when she told me, I threw back at her how happy I would be to have her as a niece."

Wiping her eyes and containing her laughter, Pearl sits up straight and looks Laura Lynne in the eye. "I swear to you, Tripp is not her father. If he were here, he would tell you the same. Whatever this nasty Ginny woman insinuated, she is lying to you. I have no idea who is feeding her this information, but it does not sound like something your father would tell her. Family business is private. He would not share his secrets with a stranger."

"I thought the same. Later… when I calmed down to think about it."

"Ok, now that we have cleared the air, tell me all about her. I am dying to hear your impressions."

Laura Lynne described her time with her father's mistress. Giggling through the glass throwing and the spittle. "I am telling you, Pearl! It was like she knew I was coming! She acted surprised to see me, but it felt fake. Everything was too perfect."

"And we know she is a liar. Watch your back, Laura Lynne. I don't trust this situation."

"Me either." Reaching out and holding Pearl's hand, Laura Lynne asks, "Can I be so rude as to ask who Victoria's father is? It is absolutely none of my business, but I am curious now."

With a sigh, Pearl pats Laura Lynne's hand. "I don't visit that time in my life much. He was a mistake. A mistake I made when I was at college at Rust. It doesn't matter now. Besides, Victoria has been an amazing gift to me."

"Understood. A lot of life happened after I left, didn't it?"

"Things certainly were never the same. It was as if something that summer shifted, and all the good, the laughter, the love just disappeared. Feels like now, maybe it is starting to come back."

"I sure hope so, Pearl. I do hope so." Laying her head on her friend's shoulder, Laura Lynne speaks softly, "I love you, Pearl. Thank you for being my friend."

"I love you too, baby girl. Don't stay away again for so long."

"I won't. I promise."

As the two amble back to The Residence, Pearl and Laura Lynne swing their joined hands between them, and Pearl asks, "So, what are the plans for today?"

"Back to town, doing some research at the Gazette. Hope to hear from Uncle Gabe's new lawyer, a guy named McElhanney, regarding the coroner's report. Last we heard, we should know something early next week. Waiting is the hardest. Uncle Gabe's court date is still pending as well, though McElhanney feels confident he can have it thrown out. At least, that is what he is telling us. Hope he is right. That would be one less worry."

"It is all gonna work out. Always does."

"Enough about me! How is Queenie doing? I have missed you around here the last few days."

"Truth is, she is not doing well. Not sure how long it will be before it is her turn to meet Jesus. Her dementia is the most difficult part. She remembers me and Malcolm but hardly anyone else. Her mind is scattered, and it makes her afraid. She had a bad spell this week: lots of anxiety and shuffling about. I am wondering if it has anything to do with the dead man. I mentioned it to her, and she hasn't been right since."

Laura Lynne stops and looks at Pearl, "You think she might know something?"

Shrugging, Pearl keeps walking, "If she does, not sure how we would know. I have asked some pointed questions, but she just mumbles and gets restless. It has made for a rough week."

"Would you mind if I came over? Spoke with her? I want to see her anyway. Thank her for all the letters she sent me over the years. Did you know she sent one to me every week for two years straight? Until I graduated high school."

"No, I didn't know. But I am not surprised. Your leaving was like losing one of her own children. It weighed heavy on her. But feel free to come over and visit. She would love to see you. Just don't have too many expectations."

The two women hug and part company, Laura Lynne walking up the back porch steps and Pearl to the kitchen and her daughter, minus the work boots, of course. Laura Lynne hears Victoria admonishing her mother for her tardiness. Laura Lynne smiles. Maybe Pearl is right. Maybe some of the goodness is coming back.

Laura Lynne hears the main house phone ring and rushes to the study to answer, shouting, "I've got it, Pearl!"

"Hello?" The line is scratchy. There is a great deal of static and a delay. Laura Lynne hears herself echoing on the receiver. "Hello? Tripp, is that you?"

Waiting for the delay to catch up, Laura Lynne hears a voice she has not heard in too many years to count. "Laura Lynne, just listen. There is a dddd-elay, so i-- hard to ---alk. I got your mmmm-essage but have n- information -n what is --pening. Do I need to ccccome to Tea -live?"

Laura Lynne does not hesitate. "Yes Tripp, you need to come home!" Laura Lynne is shouting into the phone, trying to overcome the static.

"I w-- be t--e as soo- as I c--! It's go-- to t--- time. May-- a coup-- of -eeks." The line goes dead. Laura Lynne puts down the receiver and looks to the doorway where Gabe is standing, dressed for the day in his overalls.

"Was that Tripp? Did you tell him to come home?"

"Yes, sir. I did. He said it might take him a few weeks. I think. The delay was brutal. He would be here as soon as he could."

"Good, it is time." He lowers his voice, "Did you ask him about Victoria?"

"No sir, but I did ask Pearl. She swears to me Tripp is not her father. After she finished laughing."

"Well, that solves one riddle, doesn't it? But it is a puzzle, isn't it? Why would she lie about something we could so easily check?"

"I have no idea, but Tripp coming home is good news. And Victoria is making you pancakes with strawberries and cream."

"That is good news. I hope there is bacon with it", he mutters as he walks toward the dining room.

Laura Lynne fishes her cell phone out of her back pocket. The cell service is at times sketchy at The Residence, mostly because Gabe has not upgraded any of the systems. He all but uses dial up on the computer. Laura Lynne starts a text group with Avery and Scarlet, letting them know Tripp has called and would be arriving at Tea Plantation, though not sure when. After receiving two thumbs up, Laura Lynne heads to the kitchen to get her lunch box for two. Victoria is piling pancakes and bacon on a plate for her Uncle Gabe.

"Thanks for the meal, Victoria. I will be home for supper."

"No breakfast for you? There is plenty."

"It looks fabulous, but I think I will grab a banana instead. I am not generally a breakfast person." At this, Laura Lynne receives a disapproving frown. Laura Lynne hides her smile. Victoria looks just like Queenie. "Please let my uncle know I am heading into town."

"Yes ma'am. I packed you a Yeti of tea. It is in the refrigerator. Have a good day, Miss Laura Lynne." She smiles as she takes breakfast to Gabe, pushing through the swinging door.

Laura Lynne parks in what has become her regular parking space in front of the Gazette. Mary is waiting for her when she opens the front door, a stack of yearbooks piled on the desk. "Hey Laura Lynne, you just missed Kathleen. She dropped off the yearbooks we requested. I was just getting ready to start thumbing through them."

"Wow, that was quick! I am sorry I didn't get to meet her, thank her personally. Maybe a thank you note?"

"I am sure she would appreciate it, Laura Lynne. But it is not necessary."

"No, I was raised better than that," she says as she makes her way behind the front desk to the office she is occupying. Scarlet wants to help, maybe she would be willing to write and send thank you notes. She was always good at that kind of thing. Sending off a quick text, Scarlet sends a thumbs up. Laura Lynne gets an email address and sends Kathleen's name. As she considers, she adds several others,

Grady Cunningham, Beth Ann Bodeen, Gerald and Ace Lally, and as an afterthought, Virginia Phillips.

Laura Lynne's phone pings, it is a text from Scarlet, 'Talk to Pearl?'

Laura Lynne replies, "yes, answer is no."

Scarlet sends back, "see, she is a liar."

Laura Lynne laughs and gets back to work. She opens up the next box of microfiche from 1981.

Two hours later Mary walks through the office door holding a yearbook and talking excitedly. She says, "I think I found her! It's hard to tell, but I think that is her in the background of this picture of the lunchroom! She is not listed in the class pictures, but look! This is the 1980 yearbook. She's the right age, and she's an Asian girl." Laura Lynne blinks twice to refocus and look at the picture. Mary is right. There is an Asian girl with bangs who looks 15 or 16, dressed in jeans and a sweatshirt.

Laura responds, "She's not in a class photo or individual? Is there a name listed next to the photo?"

"No, nothing. We could always ask Ron Adams. He might remember the story, maybe know her name. He and I talk, so I could ask him."

Laura Lynne leans back and looks at her, "You talk? Really?"

She slaps at Laura Lynne's shoulder. "Yes! We are friends. Have been for years. Nothing more than that."

"Do you want it to be more than that?" This is the first time Laura Lynne has ever seen Mary flustered. Her cheeks flush pink, and she won't meet Laura Lynne's eye.

"That is none of your business, Laura Lynne! Now, do you want me to call him or not?" She has a hand on her hip, defiant.

"By all means, ask him. And while you are at it, ask if he remembers any more teenagers with similar stories. I have been looking at 1982 and nothing yet." Mary looks at Laura Lynne with curiosity but says nothing. She just nods as she heads back out the door.

Fifteen minutes later, Laura Lynne's office phone is blinking. She picks up. It's Mary with an update on Ron Adams. "He remembers the story but not a name. He is checking his notepads, but that could take a while. He has kept all his notes and papers for the last 40 years stored in boxes. He did mention there was one more scenario, like the Railroad Girl. This girl was African American, though. He was going to check. See if he could find the information. He said he would call me back."

"Thanks, Mary. Did you enjoy your chat?" Mary hangs up the phone without replying. Laura Lynne laughs; this is fun.

An hour later, Laura Lynne looks at another article on a missing girl. The article is buried on the back page and is no more than six sentences. It is written by True Schuler, and the title reads, "Parents of Local Negro Teenager Claim She is Missing,

Parents Worried." From the article, Laura Lynne senses the sheriff's office and True Schuler don't seem very concerned. "Hey, Mary?" Laura Lynne hollers across the room, "Think I found another possibility. And True Schuler, isn't that Hope Schuler's grandmother?" The Schuler family are all named after different virtues, sort of like everyone being named after a flower or using the same first letter. "She's got to be dead by now. Good Lord, in 1980, she was probably close to 80 herself. She worked at the Gazette?"

"Well, I don't rightly know as I was not working here then. But True is long dead, and so are most of her children, if not all of them. Should be some grandchildren around and about, though. I know them from my English class. Let me see the article." She comes to the desk and leans over Laura Lynne, spectacles perched on her nose. "Sounds like something True would write. Her prejudice all but jumps off the page. See how she uses her words in the title to bestow her opinion about the matter? I can assure you, if the parents had been white, it would have read something like "Upstanding Citizens and Parents Terrified as They Search for Missing Teenage Daughter." It would not be buried on the back page either."

Mary stands next to the desk, arms crossed, peering over her spectacles. "You mind telling me about your special interest in these missing girls?"

Laura Lynne looks at her lap, then, with a sigh, lifts her head. "It's personal, Mary. But these girls, let me just say I can relate. And now, I can't let it drop."

"Okay, well, I am a willing participant in the search. Whatever I can do to help. I will call Ron; give him the specific date."

Laura Lynne takes a picture, notes the microfiche catalog information, and sends it via email to Ashley for conversion. "What time is it? I need a break. I think I am going to go sit outside for a bit." Laura Lynne looks at the clock. It is after noon. No wonder she is hungry and thirsty. "Oh, I have our lunches from Victoria! I almost forgot!" Laura Lynne digs into her bag and brings out the lunch cooler. "I am going to take mine outside, find someplace to sit down, and people-watch. Want to join me?"

"No, but thanks. I think I will keep at it for a while. I am hooked now. I want to keep looking through the yearbooks. See if I can spot the girl in any other photos, maybe with a name. If I could figure out what grade she was in, some sort of identifier, it might narrow the search. I know "fun" is not the right word to use, but I am having fun with the puzzle of it all." Laura Lynne stands up and heads to the door. "There is a picnic table behind the building. It was used for the Gazette smoking crowd. It's a nice place to sit and have a break."

"Thanks, I think I will."

Mary follows Laura Lynne up to the front desk. She watches as Laura Lynne unloads the sandwich and sides. There is even a mason jar of sweet tea for

Mary. What a nice touch. "Be sure to thank Victoria for me, Laura Lynne. Two homemade meals for this spinster is a treat." Mary sits at the desk, pretty as a picture in her coordinating pink outfit. "Sweetheart, if you ever want to talk about, well, anything, you can trust me."

"I know, and really, I appreciate it. I came to terms with my situation a long time ago. Angry at myself for allowing my parent's decisions to keep me away for so long."

"Yes, well, distance from the situation always helps, so don't beat yourself up about it. Time does give you perspective and maybe some wisdom. And forgiveness does not mean forgetting, just moving forward. But I, for one, am glad you are back. You have been away for far too long, in my opinion."

Sitting at the picnic table, she opens her sandwich bag and takes a swig of tea. Laura Lynne has to agree with Mary, at least about forgiving and not forgetting. Once her parents left River Oaks in the spring of 1986, Laura Lynne did not lay eyes on either of them until Beau was born.

Chapter 17

Winter 1998

Laura Lynne is relieved, sitting in her hospital bed, little Beau in the hospital bassinet sound asleep. He has taken to the breast much easier than his big sister, but then again, Laura Lynne is a calmer mother this time around. Beau was born via C-section, but that was fine, so was Savannah. Though navigating a two-year-old and a newborn while healing may prove challenging. Her husband Jimmy had done well. He hated the whole hospital deal, but he manned up and was by Laura Lynne's side the entire time. Savannah had stayed with Jimmy's parents. She was so excited to be a big sister. It was a nice entry into the world for little Beau. He was hard fought for, and Laura Lynne was so glad her part in the whole experience was complete. "Job well done, little Momma!" Laura Lynne thought to herself. Nobody else had said it, so Laura Lynne did it to herself, but that is nothing new. Jimmy and Jimmy's progeny were all doted on. Laura Lynne is basically ignored. So, when Jimmy asked if she minded him going home with his parents and Savannah for a shower and some real food, Laura Lynne readily agreed. She wanted some alone time with her son.

He is such a long little guy. His eyes are dark, not light like his sister's. They are like Laura Lynne's father. In fact, little Beau is all Beauregard. Sometimes, Laura Lynne misses being able to pick up the phone and call her father to share the news, but for the most part, Laura Lynne manages the pangs of regret. Calling Aunt Eileen has alleviated a lot of the pain. She packs for a two-week post-partum visit, much to Jimmy's chagrin. Laura Lynne asked her to let Scarlet and her brothers know. A bouquet of gorgeous flowers arrived earlier with a note from the three of them. Scarlet's doing, Laura Lynne was certain. Nobody knew Beau's name yet, though, not even Jimmy. Savannah was all Jimmy's idea and a good one. Laura Lynne loved the name. But this time, Laura Lynne would choose. And, she knew, if it was a boy, it would be Beauregard Cooper.

The situation with Jimmy and his parents is becoming untenable. The three regularly teamed up against Laura Lynne, overriding her parenting and undermining her authority. Laura Lynne felt every move she made as a mother was met with criticism. It is not unusual for Jimmy to call his mom to get her opinion, as opposed to trusting Laura Lynne's ability to mother her own children. So this, this was going to be Laura Lynne's decision, and no amount of ugliness was going to change it. This little man would be a Beauregard. He already looked like one.

Laura Lynne slides the bassinet a little closer. She decides there is no harm in holding him. She is on bed rest for another 12 hours, but it is simple enough to reach in and pull him out. Laura Lynne snuggles him against her chest and smells the top of his little head. She talks to him, telling him stories about growing up on Tea Olive, regaling him with all things Cooper and Beauregard. He sleeps through it all. He is such a snuggle bug.

There is a gentle tapping at the door. The nurse is in for a check on both the baby and mother. She is pleased with the results. "You have some company. It's after visiting hours, but if you like, I can show him in."

"Who is it?" It is nearly 10 PM. Aunt Eileen would not be in until the next day.

"He says he is your father. Sawyer Beauregard? He said it was up to you if you wanted him to meet the baby."

Laura Lynne looks at the nurse in surprise. "My daddy or my brother? They are both Sawyers."

"He said he was your father. I can tell him you are not up to it if you prefer not to see him."

"No, no, it's okay. You can send him back." Although both her parents attended her high school and college graduation, she refused to see them then. But tonight, with her hormones fluctuating and her heart full, she wanted her dad to meet his namesake.

She nodded and left, wheeling the blood pressure machine out as she went. "Call me if you need me."

"Thanks, Jane, you have been lovely." She smiles and shuts the door halfway. Laura Lynne waits. She stares at the door, not sure how she feels. Her heart beating fast, and as if little Beau senses her restlessness, he begins to rouse. "Shhhh, shhh,

Momma's got you, sweet boy." Laura Lynne gently rubs his little back and kisses his head. He soothes immediately, settling back in against her chest. The door opens fully and in walks her father, flowers in hand.

"Hi, baby girl." He is as handsome as ever. At 60, his hair is more white than black, and his always robust, athletic frame has begun to sag. He has tears in his eyes.

"Hi, Daddy. Want to meet your grandson?" He nods, walking forward and setting the flowers on the side table. He uses the sanitizer and places his big hand on Beau's back. Leaning down, he kisses Laura Lynne on the head.

"How are you feeling? Things go okay? He looks like a fine strapping little man, Laura Lynne. May I hold him?" When Laura Lynne nods, he gently picks Beau up. Little Beau opens his eyes, staring at his grandfather. "Well, looky there; he has the Beauregard eyes. Hello, young fella. I am your Poppy." Daddy snuggles him in the crook of his arm and sits in the chair beside the bed. "Now tell me how you are doing. Eileen tells me you had to have another c-section."

"Yes, two c-sections for me. I'm just not shaped right to deliver naturally. They wouldn't even let me try either time. But I am fine."

"You do good work. What have you decided to name this young fellow? Or have you decided?" He is staring at Beau, just enamored.

"Yes, I have a name: Beauregard Cooper Smith. I plan to call him Beau."

Laura Lynne sees the tears slide down her father's cheeks. "It is a fine name. And it fits him perfectly. He is a Beauregard through and through. Looks just like me and your brothers." Finally, Sawyer looks at Laura Lynne, the tears unchecked. "It is a great honor—one your momma and I don't deserve."

Laura Lynne is crying, too. Little Beau is oblivious to the drama unfolding, content in his Poppy's arms. "It's not about you and Momma, Daddy. This is about me. I need something of myself, my roots, in my life. I was just sitting here thinking how I was going to stand firm on this one thing. I was not going to compromise my heritage anymore. Been doing that for too long. I have lost myself somewhere in this marriage. Hoping little Beau will help me find her again."

"Have things been bad, Laura Lynne?" He takes the handkerchief out of his pocket and wipes his face.

"They aren't bad. They are just not what I had hoped or what I dreamed about when we got married."

"Jimmy's job didn't work out?"

"Can we not talk about this, Daddy? I want to enjoy being a new mom. I don't want to discuss my marriage with you. Notice I am not asking you about Momma."

"Fair enough." The two are quiet, staring at Beau with obvious delight. Sawyer whispers, "Do you forgive your old man for his poor choices, Laura Lynne? I am ashamed by your momma and my behavior back then. I have no excuse. And, even after all these years, I don't know what happened that summer. Would you at least share that with me? It would help to know who you were protecting. If it wasn't Buck, who was it? I promise I won't get mad. I *need* to know. I want to understand." He is gently rubbing Beau's back, has his cheek on his little head, his dark eyes gazing over at his youngest daughter.

Laura Lynne sighs. Maybe he is right. Maybe it is time to trust him with the truth. Even as a mother now herself, she cannot understand or condone her parent's actions. Laura Lynne makes the decision. After 15 years, it is time to clear the air. Perhaps then, they can move forward as a family. "Honestly, Daddy, I am not sure you will believe me, even now, even all this time later. I have never lied to you, not in all these years." He starts to interrupt, but Laura Lynne holds up her hand. "*Never*. If you can accept that, then perhaps you are ready for the rest of the story. I have only recently been able to piece it together. At least, I think I have." He looks confused and wary. "Hand me Beau, Daddy. Let me call for the nurse. I don't want him to hear what I have to say. We will do this, clear the air. But understand me clearly when I say this changes nothing."

Laura Lynne rings the nurse. She pops in. "Jane, can you take little Beau to the nursery for a bit? I have a little time before his next feeding."

"Of course, Mrs. Smith." She gently places Beau in the wheeled plastic bassinet and starts for the door. "Can I get you anything else? Something for pain?"

"No, I am good. Thank you, Jane."

Laura Lynne scoots over in the bed, patting the bed for her Daddy to sit down next to her. "Do you remember that summer I was doing an internship at the hospital?" He nods. "I think the man who hurt me was Dr. Ken Butler."

His gaze hardening, he takes Laura Lynne's hand in his and squeezes, hard. Clearing his throat and swallowing the retort Laura Lynne knows is at the tip of his tongue, he murmurs, "Go on."

"It was during the summer of my sophomore year. I was dating a med student, Wyatt Donovan. He was doing a rotation in the emergency room and relaying the crazy things he saw come through the door. One story was about a girl, a college student who had been beaten and raped. She remembered nothing, not any of it. The only thing she remembered was taking a drink one of the frat brothers brought her. Next thing she remembered was waking in the hospital. From Wyatt's calculations, she was out of it for around three hours. Wyatt told me that incidents like this were on the rise. The drinks were being laced with Rohypnal. You might know them as roofies." Sawyer gives a terse nod. Laura Lynne continues, "It really freaked me out. I ended up having a full-blown panic attack. Anyway, once I calmed down and could think about the situation and what he said, it all made sense to me."

Laura Lynne looks at her father, her eyes intent, almost pleading. Laura Lynne says, "I am almost 100% certain Dr. Butler laced my Diet Coke with some drug, maybe Rohypnal. While I was drugged, he did terrible things to me. It never made sense that his niece and nephew were not there when I arrived or that it was hours before Momma showed up or was called. It only makes sense if his plan all along was to rape me."

Laura Lynne wipes at the tears running down her cheeks. "Do you believe me?"

Kissing her hands and standing up to pace, Sawyer says, "I don't recall you spending time with Dr. Butler other than at the hospital. You babysat for him? Were alone with him?"

"Yes, twice. Well, once with his niece and nephew, and then the second time when they were not there."

Nodding, he continues to pace. "Have you told anyone else?"

"Aunt Eileen, and well, Jimmy knows enough to be careful with Savannah. I told Dr. Mabel what I suspected but not *who* I suspected. I still keep tabs on Dr. Butler. I don't want him near me or my family."

"Nor do I." He comes back to the bed and sits down, wrapping his arms fiercely around me. "I swear to you, as I live and breathe, I will keep her safe. Where is the bastard now?"

Laura Lynne does not like the tone of his voice: flat and determined. Deadly. She is not dumb enough to think her father would not take a few boys to Boston and kill the man. Pulling back and looking at him, she realizes he is planning just that. "Daddy, don't do anything stupid."

"Not stupid, just something I should have done a long time ago. I should have defended my daughter. Just because I failed at that so miserably does not mean I won't defend my granddaughter."

Frantically clutching at his shirt, Laura Lynne starts talking. Her words are laced with panic. "You will not do *anything*, you hear me? This is my story! My life! I get to decide what happens to the man who did this to me! You have no right! You lost that right years ago when you refused to believe me in the first place!"

He pulls Laura Lynne close to his chest, his touch light and soothing on her back. "Shh, shhh! Okay, okay, calm down." He rocks her back and forth until her breathing slows. Her hands release his shirt.

Leaning back, she wipes her face and nose with her top sheet. "Daddy, you will tell no one. Not even Momma. Promise me."

"Baby girl, I promise I won't kill the man, but Melanie deserves to know the truth. She needs to understand the mistake we made. She loves you no matter what you might think."

"You know nothing! She forced me to go to his house. I didn't want to babysit. I told her it made me uncomfortable. She shamed me into it. She can't accept my truth because to do so would be to admit her own guilt. It would kill her."

The realization dawns across Sawyer's face. A missing puzzle piece falls into place. *"That's it. That is who you have been protecting all this time. It's not the person who hurt you, who did this, this, this thing. It's your momma. You are protecting your momma."* His eyes are sad. He rubs both his hands down his face. "God, what a mess. What a mess I have made of all this."

Laura Lynne is watching him carefully. "I didn't start out protecting Momma, but once I thought I figured it out, it didn't make sense to tell. I was in college; what would it have changed? Seemed smarter to just keep on as things were. Besides, Scarlet was getting married. Tripp was off to the military and the war. Avery was still in high school and dealing with all his friends dying in that car accident. What difference did it make?"

"You are still my child. Those are just excuses. You know not one of you is more important than the other to us."

Laura Lynne laughs, short and hard. "You can sell that story to someone else. I am not buying." Shaking her head with chagrin, Laura Lynne continues, "And it's simply not true. You don't send a frightened 15-year-old to her aunt's if they are 'important to you.' Give me a break." Rolling her eyes, Laura Lynne says what she has held in her heart for too long, "I disappointed you. I shamed the Beauregard name, though I did nothing wrong. I was the sacrificial lamb. It was me, or it was you. You chose yourself, and so did Momma."

"Is that really how you feel? We sacrificed you?"

"Don't look so worried, Daddy. I have come to terms with my situation. And who and what my family are, at least who you and Momma are. I have forgiven you. But, as I said earlier, this changes nothing."

"You are wrong. This changes everything."

"No, no, it doesn't. Only for you because now you know the truth, my truth."

There is a tap at the door. Jane is back with Beau. "Laura Lynne? Little man here is hungry."

Smiling, Laura Lynne lifts up her arms, adjusting her smock, she discreetly puts Beau to her breast. His cries immediately cease. "There you go, little man. Momma's got you."

Chapter 18

Present Day

Laura Lynne's phone is buzzing on the table with a text from Grace that reads, "call me."

Laura Lynne smiles and calls her immediately. "Hi, Grace! Got your message. What's up?"

"That was fast, Laura Lynne. I thought you might be busy. I didn't want to interrupt. But I am so glad you called because you are joining Charlie and me for dinner tomorrow night at the Club." Laura Lynne stares at the phone. She has not been to the Country Club since Buck gave her that first kiss.

"That is really sweet, Grace, but I don't think that is a good idea. Like a really bad idea."

"Laura Lynne, you are going to come as our guest. We won't even put your name on the list, so nobody will know. You don't want to arrive on Sunday for church without having dealt with the vipers ahead of time. And I have the perfect plan. It's the annual Spring Formal! All the regular set will be there, along with many of those who want to be. Money raised this year is for refurbishing the Memorial clock and courtyard, so it's for a good cause. You may as well get it over with, and I need a friend. Charlie will be busy doing board work, and I will be left to fend for myself. Be a friend!"

"A formal? I don't have anything to wear to a formal Grace! I didn't bring that type of clothes. At best, I have a suit. And I don't think I am ready to face the Country Club crowd."

"Now, don't you be a coward, Laura Lynne. You have a chance to put all those gossipmongers out of business. You showing up will shut them up. They think you are hiding something. I would tell you to bring Mr. Gabe too, but I think that might be a little much."

"Won't Scarlet and Buck be there? She can handle it." She was quiet for a moment like she was trying to think of a response.

"Honey, Scarlet and Buck haven't been a part of the club for years. Scarlet has come to the occasional meal with your Momma, but she stopped doing that awhile back."

"What? Why? Scarlet and Buck, that is totally their thing. I was certain they were involved and active, especially with the boys. Didn't they do Cotillion?"

"Oh, the boys did Cotillion. Your Momma saw to that. I don't want to gossip about your sister. I think it's just best if you ask her." She changes her tone and gets bubbly again. "You cannot lay this at your sister's feet. You are here, and you are coming. Where are you now?"

"What? I am at the Gazette I am doing research."

"Research? Great, you can put it aside for a while and go shopping with me. I know just the place. It's right in town, so I will swing by and get you in an hour. Love you, mean it. See you shortly!" She hangs up. Laura Lynne has forgotten how bossy Grace can be. As if she can read Laura Lynne's thoughts, a text from Grace comes across her phone reading, "Yes, I am still bossy, and yes, I am always right. Be ready at 2, I will come get you." Laura Lynne shrugs and picks up her sandwich. Victoria has outdone herself with a pimento cheese and fried green tomato sandwich. Taking a big bite, Laura Lynne resolves herself to attend. Grace is not going to allow her not too. Laura Lynne takes another bite, wishing Gray could be her escort.

Cleaning up, Laura Lynne returns to the Gazette. Mary is on her perch at the front desk, munching her sandwich. Today she is in a peach-colored outfit, matching pants, shirt, cardigan, and pearls. It off-sets her white hair. "Oh, Victoria outdid herself on this one. I haven't had a fried green tomato in ages! Is this homemade pimento cheese?"

"It is good, isn't it? I have no idea, but considering its Victoria, she probably milked the cow and curdled the cheese and grew the tomatoes. Listen, Grace just called and invited me to the Spring Formal tomorrow evening, and I have nothing to wear. She is going to be here in an hour to take me shopping." Laura Lynne shakes her head. "I have no idea how I got roped into this, but I guess I am going."

"Good for you! Meet them head-on. Should be a lot of fun." She puts her glasses down her nose and peers over the top of them, "However, you look like you would rather not be going."

Laura Lynne turns around and jumps up on the counter, sitting next to Mary. "That's the thing, Mary. I haven't been there since I was 15. I don't even know who is in the Country Club set anymore. Grace even told me that Scarlet and Buck aren't regular members! I doubt anyone will even remember me, and honestly, maybe that is for the best."

"Laura Lynne, who are you trying to kid? You are a Beauregard. Of course, they know who you are. As far as who are still members, it's all the same people, just a different generation. I imagine Grace will tell you all about them, prep you before you get there. It's really a smart thing to do, make church on Sunday easier."

"Now you sound like Grace. I know y'all are right, but honestly, I don't plan to be here but for a few more weeks. Living through the gossip seems the simpler tact."

"Easier for you, not the ones you leave behind." She turns from Laura Lynne, going back to her sandwich and her notes.

"Wait a minute. What don't I know? Is this about Scarlet?"

"I only know rumors and gossip. I have never spoken to any of the Hugers. Just ask Scarlet." She turns back to her food.

"No, wait, I am asking you. Scarlet would probably never tell me anyway. What don't I know? You told me about Uncle Gabe. Thank you for that, by the way. I am asking you to tell me about Scarlet. I will talk to her, just like I did Uncle Gabe."

"You talked to him? Did you tell him it was me? Or more, Momma?"

"I did, and he confirmed it all. Told me the entire story. He was not mad. It was good for us both to hear it. Made me love him all the more. Mary, I swear, he is not upset with you or your mother."

"I am glad. I made myself sick with worry when I let that slip." She takes a deep breath. "Listen, I wish you would just talk to Scarlet, but I will tell you what I know. There has been some financial trouble. When the boys were at Moseley, tuition was not paid for quite a while. In fact, I know the school threatened to kick them out if it was not paid in full. I was told by the school secretary that Mrs. Beauregard, Melanie, came in and wrote a check. Paid it all. The secretary was then instructed to have the tuition statements sent to her at Tea Olive. A few weeks later, Buck's parents sold their property and lived in a little townhouse until they died a few years back."

"What in the world happened?"

"No idea, and honestly, that is all I know. It was not my place to ask. That's been, what, ten years ago or so. Your daddy was still alive."

"Thanks." Laura Lynne hops off the counter and walks around the desks to the back office. Laura Lynne has 45 minutes until she meets Grace and decides to spend it doing some research on the

Huger Estate, Merriwether Plantation. In the archives of The Gazette, Laura Lynne locates an article from February 2009 regarding the sale of Meriwether to an outside developer. The developer, a group called Overpass Development Partners has plans to construct a series of subdivisions in varying range of prices. This will include apartments and townhomes, parks, swimming pools, and even a golf course. The sale of the property amount is undisclosed.

In a follow-up article dated February 2011, the property remains undeveloped and is embroiled in litigation with local landowners over the water rights and, more specifically, the legality of the sale. Laura Lynne finds nothing more after that article, but the reporter for both articles is none other than Mary's main man, Ron Adams. Laura Lynne glances at the computer clock. It's almost 2:00. She sends one last email to Ashley requesting she send the box of letters Queenie wrote in the mail courier with strict instructions to overnight them. She wants no chance of losing them; it would break her heart. Laura Lynne then shuts everything down and cleans up her desk.

"Mary, I am calling it a day, actually a weekend. I will be back on Monday if that still works. And I will bring lunch."

She smiles. "Can't wait. You and Miss Grace have fun. This will all be here when you get back."

Laura Lynne walks over and gives her a hug. "Thanks, Mary. You have been great. I can't imagine doing all this without you."

"Listen, you just keep bringing me Victoria's sandwiches. That one today was great. Put poor *Cheese Louise!* to shame! Now scoot. Go buy yourself a pretty dress."

Laura Lynne heads out the door and sees Grace pulling in next to her car on the side street. She finishes parking the car and gets out. "Timed it just perfectly. We will walk from here. It's only a few blocks."

"Let me put my stuff in the trunk. I don't want to lug this with me." Laura Lynne looks at Grace. She looks like she just walked out of a Southern Living magazine. Laura Lynne looks at herself. "Are you sure about this, Grace? I dressed for work. I don't have the right undergarments on or shoes." Laura Lynne is wearing her typical capris and sleeveless blouse, untucked at the waist, and slide-on flat sandals. Her hair is pulled into a high bun. Laura Lynne read on social media that a high bun pulls facial skin tighter, giving an instant facelift. She likes to think it is working.

Grace waves her hand in front of Laura Lynne like she is shooing away a pesky fly. "You are fine. You look great! I wish I had your arms and shoulders so I could wear sleeveless shirts. Too much flapping going on under these chicken wings. Put your stuff away, and come on! Daylight is burning!"

"Where are you taking me?"

"Do you remember Rachele White from Moseley? She would have been a few grades higher than us. She was the head cheerleader, homecoming queen, super smart, pretty, and sweet. You would think she would have been a snob, but she wasn't. Well, she is Rachele Humphrey now, and she owns and operates Strasse Boutique. She started it about ten years ago. She got bored being a housewife. She has two daughters and a son, all are as fabulous as she is, and all either attending or graduates of Moseley." The two women have walked eight blocks down Main Street. Grace makes a right and then points across the street. "See that alley? Called Canal Alley. It's been updated and renovated, thanks to Rachele and her little shop. Come on, you will see."

They walk down the sidewalk to the crosswalk, which has been laid with brick and is a pedestrian path. The alley looks like a scene from Italy. Its narrow street is paved with stone, and there are hanging baskets with flowers overflowing. Laura Lynne sees a men's shop, a gelato shop, a cigar store, and a wine bar on their way to Strasse. "Isn't this great? Venice, Mississippi's little slice of Italy! See that store on the right, with the boarded windows? It was leased, and renovations are supposed to start soon. And guess what is going in there?"

"A pizza shop?" Laura Lynne giggles.

Grace stares at her. "How did you know?"

"You can't have Italy without pizza!" Laura Lynne laughs and then turns serious. "Hey, you're a real estate agent, right? What can you tell me about the sale of Merriwether?"

"Oh, God. What a mess. It's a long story. Can we wait until after we see Rachele? She is expecting us."

"Now, I am really intrigued, but sure. It can wait."

The boutique is fabulous. It has patchouli-scented air, art on the walls, and designer everything. Rachele is in the back with, well, it must be one of her daughters as they look just alike. She walks over. "Laura Lynne Beauregard! It's so good to see you. I heard Venice's most famous author was in town. How are you? And your Uncle Gabe, poor man, it's all just so ridiculous." Laura Lynne starts to answer, but she just keeps waving her hand at her daughter. "Samantha, you come over here right this second and meet Miss Laura Lynne. Laura Lynne, my daughter Samantha."

Samantha is as beautiful as her mother was when she was at Moseley Hall. If Laura Lynne could not pinpoint her when she first laid eyes on her, once she saw Samantha, she immediately placed her. "It's nice to meet you, Samantha."

"Ma'am. I really enjoyed your book." Samantha's voice has a lovely drawl, her manners impeccable.

"You read my book?"

"I did, and I would love to talk to you about it more sometime. Maybe you can come and talk to the English class at school. That would be cool."

"I would love, too." Laura Lynne is captivated.

"It's really nice to meet you." She turns to her mother. "Momma, I have to go back to school." She looks at Laura Lynne. "I am in the school play, and practice is every day after school. I am sorry to meet you and go, but opening night is just a week away!"

"Of course, perhaps I will come and see it. What's the play? "

"*Beauty and the Beast*. If you are really interested, I will make sure Momma has tickets for you at the will call. I would love to have you there! Sorry, gotta run. Thanks, Momma! Bye, Miss Grace."

She dances out the front door, all energy and cheer. "She is fabulous, Rachele. Is she Belle?"

Rachele smiles and nods. "She is and my baby. If you would like to see the play, it would make Samantha's day. She has talked non-stop about you since you arrived. She thinks you are very daring and brave. I think she wants to do theater, art, writing, or something very artsy. She just hasn't been ready to tell me yet."

"I can't believe a 16-year-old read my book. It has a lot of adult themes."

"When she found out you were here, she asked me if she could read it. I gave her my copy. She is smart, has an active mind. Plus, we could have some conversations about being a female, a Southern female in a patriarchal system. It gave her food for thought."

Laura Lynne is floored and humbled. "It did all that?"

Rachele laughed. "It did. Come on upstairs, let's see what kind of dresses we have for you. I have this gorgeous dark peach dress that just came in. I think would be fabulous with your coloring."

Laura Lynne thinks, "Peach?" Turning to Rachele, she says, "I was thinking more navy or black."

"No, Grace gave me the lowdown on what the plan is for the evening. Right Grace?"

She nods. "I did. Rachele knows what we need. In fact, Rachele will be there with Hugh as well. She knows what she is doing. Let her do it, Laura Lynne."

Thirty minutes later Laura Lynne is gazing at her reflection in the mirror as Grace stands beside her with a big smile on her face. Then she catches Laura Lynne's eye, and her smile turns to frustration. "Darn it. Laura Lynne, we should have gotten to do this together in high school!"

"I know." Laura Lynne agrees. "I know! I was thinking the same thing. I feel like I was robbed of this moment with you 40 years ago, and now, somehow, we got it back. Thank you for making me go to this thing I don't want to do."

She hugs Laura Lynne from behind. "What are friends for? Love you. I have missed you! Glad you are home."

Laura Lynne and Grace walk out the door loaded down with boxes and bags. The price at the register was steep but worth every penny to have this experience with Grace. Grace says, "Come on, let's find someplace to sit down. I will tell you about Merriwether while we celebrate. Not every day that my bestest friend in the whole universe comes home!"

The two decide on gelato and sit down at a table outside overlooking the "canal." They place their order, and Grace takes a sip of her water. Grace begins, "Merriwether. Well, honestly, I thought you would know more than I do."

"I should; I agree. But truthfully, Scarlet and I rarely talk. And when we do, it is always about our parents or Uncle Gabe. I don't even know much about my nephews, really."

"I figured you must have had a falling out. I am sorry to hear it. Don't know what I would do without Grady around to pester me all the time."

"I love that the two of you are so close, Grace. I wish it were true with me and Scarlet, even with my brothers. Truthfully, we all live very separate lives. The family just seemed to fall apart over the years. The more I am home, the more I realize I am not the only one whose life is not as our parents planned."

Laura Lynne and Grace wait while the waitress delivers their gooey confections and refills their ice water. Laura Lynne continues, "Enough about me. Tell me what you know. I am not going to lie. I am shocked the Hugers sold the estate."

"From what I gather, there was not much choice. But the sale to the developer was done behind closed doors. Buck and his parents, as they were alive at the time, did not offer the opportunity to purchase the property to any of the neighboring farms. I know for certain my parents would have jumped at the chance, not to mention your own family." Grace scoops up her strawberry gelato, rolling her eyes in ecstasy. "I really shouldn't be eating this today. I have a dress to get into tomorrow."

"Give me a break! You are as tiny as ever. Eat and talk. I can't wait to hear the rest."

"There is not much to tell. Nobody knows why the land was sold. Some suspect gambling debts, others poor business decisions, drugs, or the Dixie Mafia, but those are all just random guesses. Once the estate was gone, Buck and Scarlet disappeared from the social circuit. In fact, it has been years," she closes her eyes, pondering, "around 10, in fact, since I saw him. Probably would not recognize him if I did."

"And Scarlet? What about her?"

"Oh, I see her occasionally around town. I know she visits with Miss Melanie and Mr. Gabe on a regular basis, but she keeps to herself. She does come to the Tea Olive Chapel for Easter and Christmas, and she is always well put together. She is awfully thin and has this air of tiredness around her." Pointing her spoon at Laura Lynne, she punctuates the comment, "That last is just my impression. She could be perfectly normal, just menopause or some other horrible mid-life woman's issues."

"What about the litigation? I saw something about it in the newspaper article."

"Mmmm, yes." Nodding and putting the last of the gelato in her mouth, she licks her lips. "That was the brainchild of my daddy and yours. The plan for the development would seriously impact the flow of water to the neighboring farms. And, as we know, crops don't grow without a reliable water source. The idea was to sue the developer over water rights and tie them up in litigation for as long as possible in an attempt to delay the construction. At least until they had a better idea. As the work was pro bono, Gerald Lally willingly accepted the case. The group of plantation owners paid litigation costs minus the attorney fees."

"At first, the developers fought bitterly. Lally had his hands full for about two years. During those two years, the developers were building. If you go there now, you will see some of the infrastructure for the neighborhoods. When the injunction was approved, the developers turned tail and ran. Nobody has heard from them since."

"Wow...just wow." Laura Lynne flops back in her chair, licking her spoon. "That is crazy."

Nodding, Grace signals for the check, handing the waitress her credit card. "You get the next one," Grace says before Laura Lynne could object.
"Finish up, Laura Lynne. I need to get home. The boys will be waiting."

Laura Lynne sits up and downs the rest of her peach gelato. "I still want to hear about your son and Charlie."

Signing the check, Grace smiles. "I will tell you about them on the walk back to the car. Shouldn't take long, though Trey has himself a sweet little girl I think might become my daughter-in-law."

The two women get up from the chairs, picking up Laura Lynne's bags. Laughing and talking, Grace regales her with stories of her family. And asks endless questions about Laura Lynne's husband and children. As Laura Lynne is loading her car, she looks over at Grace. "Grace, do you think you could do me a favor? But I need to keep it private."

"Sure, honey. What is it?"

"If I give you an address, can you do a deep dive on the property? Who owns it, for how long, anything about the house."

"I can, yes. You want to tell me whose property I am researching?"

"Not yet. But depending on what you find, maybe."

"Sure, shouldn't be too hard to do. Just text me the address." Grace comes to the car and gives her a hug. "I will send the car over to pick you up tomorrow night. Be ready at the door at 6:30. Oh, and wear some of your mother's fabulous jewelry!"

"I can…" Laura Lynne closes her mouth when Grace looks at her without saying a word. "You know, I had forgotten what a pain in the ass you can be."

Laughing, Grace heads to her car, leaving Laura Lynne shaking her head. "Steel magnolia, Laura Lynne, a steel magnolia!"

Once in the car, Laura Lynne calls Savannah and tells her all about the dress. Laura Lynne texts her a picture of the dress and then calls to share the details. The two have a wonderful time talking about the shop, Grace, Rachele, and the formal. "Wish you were here to go with me."

"Mom, I would look like a whale! But I do wish I could people-watch. Send me pictures so I can put names to faces." Laura Lynne is dazzled by how smart her daughter is. Why has she not thought to do the same? It is exactly what she needs to do. Start putting together a file with pictures of the locals, details and descriptions. If nothing comes of it, Laura Lynne could always use it as a basis for her next novel.

"Love you, sweet girl. I am back now, gotta run."

Laura Lynne hangs up and gets out of the car. She pops the trunk and hauls her bounty into the house and up to her room. She needs to ask Gabe about her Momma's jewelry. The good stuff would be here. Melanie would never take it to the assisted living facility. Maybe the pearl drop earrings would work. They are Cooper family heirlooms and date back to pre-Civil War. They were given by the founder of Tea Olive, Ezekiel Lynne Cooper, to his oldest daughter, Francesca, on her wedding day.

Every Cooper daughter has the opportunity to wear them on her wedding day. They pass from the oldest living female Cooper each generation. Scarlet is meant to inherit when Melanie dies. Laura Lynne sighs, thinking there are too many emotions rolled up into those earrings. She did not wear them when she married Jimmy, but Aunt Eileen couriered them to her when she married Gray. She cried when she saw them. There is bound to be another option.

Laura Lynne's phone begins to light up like a Christmas tree. First Gray, then Ashley, next Savannah, and then Beau. "What in the world?" Laura Lynne picks up her phone and calls Gray. "Hey baby, got your text. What is going on?"

"Well, you made the news. One of your local stations did a segment on Tea Olive, including your current circumstances. Appears they plan to do a series about your family. They are even interviewing some of the locals to get their perspectives. Who in the world is Natalie Johnson? She had some rather unsavory comments about you."

"I only met her for like two seconds at the coffee shop! What could she possibly have to say?"

"Basically, the rumor is you went off in 1985 to have a child, and most of the town suspect the dead guy is the kid's father or some such nonsense. Honestly, I was not paying as close attention as I should have. I wanted to give you a heads up."

"Thanks, baby. Guess I need to call Ashley. The kids texted me too. Savannah sent a few hashtags. I guess that means it is all over social media." Laura Lynne sits on her window seat, gazing out over the gardens. "We knew it would happen. But I did not think it would warrant a television series."

"Has all the elements of a good story. Deep South, small town, prominent family, and a dead body. Ever consider making it into a book? Not to be crass, just seems smart."

"I am not gonna lie; it has definitely crossed my mind. Today, I had Mary start a tickler file. A way to file away stories that might be of interest later but not relevant to Dead Doe. And before you ask who that is, it is my nickname for the corpse." Laura Lynne enjoys Gray's snort before continuing, "I think, in the back of my mind, I have been thinking the same thing."

"What else did you do today?"

"Well, I bought a very expensive dress and all the stuff that goes with it. Don't be shocked when you see the bill. Grace is making me attend the Spring Formal at the Club. And that should be really fun now that the Beauregards are a media sensation."

"Wait! No way you are doing this alone. When is it?"

"It is tomorrow night, Gray. I would love for you to be here. I just don't see how to make that happen. Besides, I won't be alone. Grace and Charlie will be there. Grace will be by my side all night. I will be well chaperoned."

"Are you sure, baby? Maybe it's best to cancel. No harm in it. You won't be there long."

"I have thought about it, but Mary said something to me today, and I think I have to be there. Made me realize Scarlet has been carrying the Beauregard burden on her shoulders for too long. As Mary said, it would be easier for me to ignore but harder on those left behind. I really need to do what I can while I am here."

"You know best, babe. Follow your heart."

"I need to go, Gray. My phone has been alerting for the past 30 minutes. I need to call Ashley." Laura Lynne stands from her window seat, heading to her desk. "Oh, speaking of Ashley. I asked her to courier Queenie's letters to me. Can you have Marguerite get them out? They are locked in my desk. She has the key."

"Sure, baby. Love you."

"Love you more than that."

Laughing, Laura Lynne hangs up and immediately dials Ashley. She spends the next hour discussing the series. Apparently, the local news channel, Alive 5 News, reached out for an interview. Ashley turned them down but recommended that Laura Lynne have Gabe's lawyer draw up a statement. Once done, Laura Lynne texts Scarlet and Avery the news. The three siblings have a group call and agree to silence for the time being. Scarlet would contact Mr. McElhaney and make arrangements. Worn out and ready for some food, Laura Lynne makes her way to the kitchen to scrounge for scraps. It is nearly 8 PM.

In the kitchen is a note from Victoria. There is a plate for her in the refrigerator with heating instructions and a side salad. Looks like roasted vegetables and some kind of fabulous seasoning. The mud room door opens, and Uncle Gabe walks in wearing his customary overalls and socks. He looks tired and happy. "You look pleased with yourself."

"Oh, I am. Finally got that contrary water pipe issue fixed, and it turned out better than expected! Girl, what are you doing standing over the sink eating? We got plenty of tables and chairs in this house."

Laura Lynne swallows a forkful. "Hungry, it's been a busy day. Go get cleaned up, and I will heat up your supper. Victoria left you a plate too." Laura Lynne opens the refrigerator, "Looks like a pork chop, potatoes, and roasted vegetables."

"There should be some fresh rosemary bread somewhere too. She was making it when I came in for lunch. I won't be but a minute. Join me at the kitchen table." He gives Laura Lynne the eye. Eating like a field hand is not approved of in the Residence.

"Yes, sir."

Uncle Gabe is clean and dressed in khakis and a golf shirt—his idea of casual. "I got it all done, Uncle Gabe. Pour yourself a drink, and let's sit out on the back porch. It's a nice enough night."

Uncle and niece sit down to a relaxed supper. The roasted vegetables and potatoes are excellent. It's quiet between the two. No need for small talk. Each is comfortable with the other. After dinner, during clean up, Laura Lynne broaches the subject of the family jewels.

"Uncle Gabe, do you mind if I wear some of the family jewelry tomorrow night? Grace convinced me to go to this Spring Formal at the Club. You wouldn't want to come with me, would you?" Laura Lynne gives her uncle the side eye as she loads the dishwasher.

"Not on your life. Listen, I didn't want to mention it during dinner, but Gerald came by. Apparently, Alive 5 ran an 'investigative report' on our family. Not much investigation from what I gather, more rumor and supposition. He and McElhanney are crafting a statement for the family in response."

Laura Lynne shakes her head. She should have known her uncle would be on top of the situation. He might be old, but he is still sharp as a tack.

"I should have known you would be on top of it. My phone has been buzzing for the last two hours with updates. It is all over social media. I hope it dies a quick death, but I think it's best we be prepared. I need to go. If I don't, it will look like the family has something to hide."

Gabe gently rubs Laura Lynne's back and kisses her head as he moves out of the kitchen. "There's my brave girl. You know how to access the vault. Feel free to take what you think is appropriate. I am going to the study for a nightcap if you need me."

"Yes, sir. I love you, Uncle Gabe."

"I love you, baby girl."

Laura Lynne finishes loading the dishes and runs the dishwasher. Then, with the delight she used to feel as a young girl, she heads to the vault. The monstrosity is a carryover from the Civil War. It was built as a hideout for the family and is no less than six feet tall and 10 ten feet deep. In the 1950s, Poppy Cooper had a steel vault installed to house what he deemed family relics. For the most part, it is home to the family's guns, jewelry, silver, and papers that date back to the original deed for the land. It is a treasure trove of family history.

Laura Lynne opens the first drawer of jewelry and immediately spots her Grandmother Birdie's favorite piece, a sapphire and diamond art deco necklace from Tiffany's. The earrings are housed in a matching light blue box. Deciding it is fate, Laura Lynne looks no further and removes the gorgeous pieces from the vault. They will work perfectly with her peach dress.

As she heads up to her room, dragging her feet with exhaustion, Laura Lynne allows the emotions to flow. The return to The Residence has been bittersweet. To Laura Lynne's surprise, the sweet has outweighed the bitter. Clasping her Grandma Birdie's jewelry to her breast, she thinks about all the wonderful memories she has of growing up in this house. Holidays were the best. The house was alive with parties and entertainment, her parents hosting countless social functions. Now, they're distant memories, mere whispers in the stairwell of her childhood home.

Chapter 19

Laura Lynne wakes up later than her usual 5 AM, having slept through the night for the first time since her arrival to Mississippi. Still brain foggy, she rolls out of bed and heads to the bathroom to splash cold water on her face. Shaking out the cobwebs, Laura Lynne hears a tap on her door before it swings open. Pearl walks through the door with a tea setting and a teacup of steaming Earl Grey. With a smile and a giggle, Laura Lynne heads to the bedroom.

"What is all this, Pearl?"

"I thought you might need some pampering this morning."

"Pampering? Why?" Laura Lynne picks up the teacup and saucer and takes a sip before the realization hits. "Oh, right. The Docuseries on Dead Doe. How could I possibly forget?" Looking over at Pearl, she asks, "Did you watch it?"

"I surely did. Not one of the people interviewed has been here more than a skinny minute! Acting like they are personal friends of yours and Mr. Gabe! Idiots!"

For the first time, realizing Pearl and her family could be a part of the saga, Laura Lynne puts down her teacup with a clunk. "Pearl, you and your family weren't mentioned, were you? I had not even thought about that."

Pearl shakes her head. "Not yet, but I am sure at some point over the upcoming episodes, we will be mentioned. Hard not to include my family, considering we have been together for generations."

"Oh, Pearl. I am so sorry. I just never considered."

Patting Laura Lynne's hand, she continues, "Not to worry, baby girl. Whatever comes, comes. Everybody in the family agrees at this point to just lie low. If more is needed, then we will deal with it then. But for now, we will watch and wait." She gestures to the breakfast tray. "Anyway, I wanted to tell you myself."

"I am glad you did."

"Can I do anything for you today? Mr. Gabe tells me you are going to the gala this evening. If you want, I can do your hair for you. I still have a hand at it."

"I would love that! You really don't mind?"

"No. Show me the dress. Then, I can make a hair plan." For the next 20 minutes, the two women fuss and drool over the outfit and Tiffany jewelry. Finally, Pearl takes her leave. "I will be back at 3 to do your hair. Don't wash it. Does better if it is dirty."

As soon as Pearl leaves, Laura Lynne takes her tea to her computer and fires it up. She really needs to do some actual work. After updating her blog, she reviews her emails and then starts laying out an idea for a possible novel. Her conversation with Gray has her mind spinning with a Truman Capote-style book. It would be fun to write and interesting. A text comes over her phone from Ashley. She has sent Queenie's letter via special delivery. They will arrive today at about 4 PM.

Laura Lynne works through the morning, stopping once to refuel with a Diet Coke. The alarm on her phone startles her from her writing. It is 2:00, and time to start getting ready for the evening's gala. Laura Lynne loathes to stop, but she promised Grace, and she has this fabulous dress to wear. She runs the water in the tub and grabs the book she bought at Wheelbarrow Books. Nothing more soothing than a tub bath and a good book.

As she was reading about the Choctaw Indians, the original settlers of Mississippi she hears her Uncle Gabe's over the intercom, "Laura Lynne! A special delivery has arrived for you. You need to come down and get it."

Laura Lynne makes her way out of the tub, dripping wet and standing in a towel. She presses the button in her room. "Just put it on the entry table, Uncle Gabe. I will get it later."

"Laura Lynne, it won't fit. Please come down and take care of this." What in the world did Ashley send? It's just a box of letters.

"Give me a minute." Laura Lynne opens the bureau and throws on her customary gray sweatshirt and pajama bottoms. She heads downstairs, muttering the whole way, "Uncle Gabe, what is the big deal…" Her voice trails off. In the foyer, big as life is Gray, holding Queenie's box of letters. She stops midway down. He is grinning, tickled to death with himself.

"I told you I was missing my woman, so I am here to claim her." Laura Lynne hurries down the stairs and into his arms. He sweeps her up and holds her close, burying his head in her neck. Lord, he smells good. She has missed this man. Laura Lynne pulls back and kisses him soundly on the mouth. Then slaps him in the arm.

"What are you doing here? I am so glad you are here, but why are you here? You met my Uncle Gabe?"

"I did. He and I are going to finish watching the Master's while you get all dolled up. Listen, honey, I missed you. I didn't want you to go to this shindig alone. Ashley and Lenny agreed to handle things at the hacienda. I rearranged some work stuff. Then the amazing Ashley met me at the airport with my tuxedo and the box of letters. She had a flight booked to Biloxi and the rental car ready for me. She even told me she had reached out to Grace and made arrangements for me to join you tonight."

Laura Lynne hugs him again. "I am so glad."

Gray hands Laura Lynne the box of letters. "We need to get the amazing Ashley a raise. That girl is a wonder. I need to unload the car. Do you mind making me an egg sandwich? All I have had to eat are peanuts and some gum. I am half starved."
Laura Lynne kisses him again.

"On the way. Uncle Gabe can show you my room. Thanks for coming. Makes me so happy."

"You make me so happy. Mr. Gabe, this woman is my blessing. I tell her every day, but I don't think she believes me yet." With that, he heads out the front door and starts unloading the car.

"He sure makes an impression. Looks like maybe you found a good one this time. I never really cared for Jimmy."

"Now you tell me! Yes, he is a keeper. I am going to make him a snack. Would you like me to get something together for you?"

"No, I am good. Got some pretzels a bit earlier. Go on ahead and get him something to eat."

Laura Lynne heads to the kitchen, so delighted and relieved. She did marry a keeper this time. All of a sudden, she is looking forward to tonight. She gets the egg sandwich together and hears the current two main men in her life discussing golf and being delighted with each other. Laura Lynne gives Gray his sandwich. Uncle Gabe has already seen to his drink. "You good? I've got to finish getting ready."

"I am great, honey. Go get all gussied up. Won't take me 30 minutes to shower and put on the monkey suit. Gonna sit here with your uncle for a while." Laura Lynne leans over, and they kiss. He pats her butt as she heads out the door. Laura Lynne laughs, reveling in her love for this man.

Laura Lynne takes the time to finish her preparations and then settles into her window seat to await Pearl. Pulling up a blanket and propping her head on a pillow, Laura Lynne falls asleep.

"Laura Lynne! Laura Lynne! Wake up, girl! You need to get ready for the evening."

Laura Lynne rolls her head over to the side and opens her eyes, gazing at Pearl with her hands on her hips. She smiles. "I love you, Pearl."

"That must be some dream you were having! I love you too. Listen, is that big 'ol guy that just barreled into my kitchen Gray, by any chance? Miss Grace said you might be having a surprise visitor."

"It is. You talked to Grace?"

"She called. Said she has been texting you for the last hour with no response. Wanted to make sure you were okay. She was worried about you." Pearl walks over to the door when she hears Gray bounding up the stairs. "He sure makes a ruckus. Sounds like your brothers."

"He is definitely as big as one of them." Laura Lynne gets up from the window seat and performs a few yoga stretches. "Man, I must be more tired than I thought."

Gray appears in the doorway and walks in, headed for the bathroom. "And exactly where do you think you are going, Mr. Gray?" Pearl asks, hands on her hips.

"Ma'am?"

"No need to ma'am me. I am Pearl. You don't think you are getting ready in here, do you?

"Ummm, no?"

"You go use Mr. Tripp's bedroom to get ready. Us girls need our space." Pearl turns toward Laura Lynne. She drops her gaze and bites her lip. Without turning around, Pearl demands, "You still in here, Mr. Gray?"

"No, ma'am."

Laughing, Laura Lynne finally intervenes. "Gray, love. Tripp's bedroom is two doors down. The one with all the trophies. Looks like a mausoleum with all the statuary. You can't miss it."

Gray makes a 180 and heads down the hall. "Holy cow! It's like a shrine in here. You are taking your life into your own hands now, Miss Pearl. I am liable to break something in here."

"Get on with your own self!" She looks at Laura Lynne. "Is he always like this? He takes up a lot of space, doesn't he? What a personality. Why does he call me Miss Pearl? He knows better than that, doesn't he?"

"It's a sign of respect, but he is also teasing you. He knows how much you mean to me. Come on, let's figure out something with this hair. Thanks for doing this. All of a sudden, there seems to be a lot going on. I am slightly overwhelmed." She squeezes Laura Lynne's shoulder and pushes her into a chair.

"I brought some hairpins and plenty of hairspray."

Over the next hour, Pearl fusses and pins, curls and sprays Laura Lynne's hair into submission. Laura Lynne does her makeup, choosing subtle and neutral with a shiny lip. She doesn't want to take away from the drama of the dress, though her hair is a masterpiece. Pearl has done an updo, soft and loose, with curls framing her face.

She helps Laura Lynne into her dress. "Put your shoes on first, Laura Lynne, and then step into the dress. Hold on to the bed frame to keep yourself steady." Pearl zips her up and secures the bodice, saying, "My work here is done. You look beautiful. I am going to check on Gabe and then head out for the evening." Gathering her pins, Pearl stops in the doorway. "Have a lovely evening. Chin up, Laura Lynne. Those women do not know your story. Don't let them judge you. You are a Cooper and a Beauregard. That's double the steel in your spine."

"Don't you make me cry, Pearl! I don't have time for ruined make-up! I love you too."

"God, Laura Lynne, you look stunning." Gray is standing in the doorway, handsome as ever, in his tuxedo. Gray loves clothes, particularly shirts and shoes. For his birthday last year, Laura Lynne got him a tuxedo and all the trimmings. He loves it. Tonight, he is classic. He is wearing a black vest, black tie, white handkerchief, pearl buttons, and his dad's red cuff links. Much to his dismay and Laura Lynne's delight, Gray's hair is more gray than black, and he is sporting a goatee. Her silver-haired fox.

"You're not so bad yourself, Mr. Atkins. I just need to add my jewelry. I don't plan to bring my purse. Do you see a reason I might need one?"

"Can't think of one. How are you holding up?" Laura Lynne puts in her earrings and hands Gray the necklace.

Laura Lynne asks, "Can you help me with that? There is a latch on it somewhere, probably hidden in the filigree. I can't find it." He pulls up his snap glasses. They hang around his neck and snap together at the bridge piece, attaching with magnets. "I was okay. Now, I am nervous. I think the dress is a bit much. There is nothing subtle about this outfit."

"Here, got it." He holds the necklace open, then hooks it around my neck. "Perfect. And you are gorgeous. Let's go knock 'em dead."

Laura Lynne looks at him. He is revved. He loves this kind of thing. He is so good at it. Laura Lynne has often teased him about his glad-handing, as good as any politician. "Ok, *Mr. Governor*. I am ready. Not sure Venice Country Club is ready for us though." Gray cocks his arm at the elbow, and Laura Lynne holds on as he escorts her down the stairs and out the front door. Uncle Gabe waits at the door, dressed in his tuxedo.

"Uncle Gabe? Are you going with us?"

"Can't let you young people have all the fun. Besides, you said something earlier, and it made me realize it is time to make a statement. Hiding is not an option. It is just not in our genes. We fight. We face trouble head-on. And we do it together." Looking over his shoulder at Gray, Gabe gives him a wink, "Come on, young man, let's blow this popsicle stand."

Laura Lynne walks out the door first, and waiting at the bottom of the stairs is the car Grace sent. It is a 1940s Rolls Royce. Gray lets out a low whistle. "How about that?"

The driver opens the car doors and steps back. Laura Lynne and Gray take the back seat. Gabe insists on sitting up front with the driver. "This is sure one nice ride. And look here, a bar, and it's fully stocked."

Laura Lynne says, "There is a note from Grace that says, 'Gray, glad you could make it! Enjoy a drink; you are going to need it! Laura Lynne, the bar is stocked with TopoChico and limes. Love Grace and Charlie.' Well, isn't that nice?" Gray already has a vodka and tonic poured with a lime. Laura Lynne says, "Just make mine with the tonic and lime, its fine."

He hands Laura Lynne her drink and picks up his own. "To true love, second chances, and God's blessings." They clink glasses and take a sip. Gray settles in and grabs my knee, "I could get used to this and The Residence. God, that place is gorgeous."

"Mr. Gabe, you want a cocktail?"

"No, son. I am good. I will get something at the club." Gabe turns around in the seat. "I am glad you like our home, but truthfully, you haven't even seen it yet. How about I take you on a tour after church tomorrow?" He looks at his niece. "That okay with you, Laura Lynne?"

"That actually works great. I made plans with Pearl to see Queenie around 2." Nodding, Gabe turns back to face forward as they enter the clubs' gates. "And here we are. Doesn't take long to get anywhere in Venice," Laura Lynne says.

Gray quickly finishes his drink as the driver opens the doors. The three are escorted along a red carpet to the entrance. As each couple walks in, their name is announced by the country club's usher. Gabe pulls out a card and hands it to Gray. Gabe says, "Just give this to the usher when you get to the doorway. Laura Lynne knows what to do." Grinning, Gabe straightens his tie and hands his card to the usher. He says, "Mr. Gabriel Lynne Cooper of Tea Olive Plantation. Son of Dean Nathaniel Cooper and Judith Frances Ravenel Cooper. Representing one of the six founding families."

As if one body, the ballroom turns to watch as Gabe walks down the stairs, ramrod straight and every inch the gentleman. Before he reaches the bottom, Gray and Laura Lynne hand their card over and are announced. "Mr. Grayson Lee Atkins and Mrs. Laura Lynne Cooper Beauregard Atkins. Mrs. Atkins is the daughter of Sawyer Ashley Beauregard II and Melanie Louise Cooper

Beauregard. Representing two of the six founding families."

There is a hush over the crowd as everyone stares at Gabe, then gazes at Laura Lynne and Gray as they come down the stairs. Laura Lynne has a smile pasted on her face, and Gray squeezes her hand between the crook of his elbow in gentle reassurance. Grace and Charlie sashay over to the base of the stairs to greet the three guests.

Grace leans in to whisper, "You did great."

Charlie shakes Gray's hand as Gabe introduces the two men. The three head to the bar while Grace and Laura Lynne make their way over to Rachele.

"Your Uncle Gabe is like a returning soldier from the war. Look at the line trying to shake his hand and get close to him. I am so glad he decided to come tonight. Your uncle is well-loved around here." Rachele leans in for a brief hug. "You look great. Love the jewelry. Miss Birdie's right?"

Laura Lynne nods. "I was shocked to see him standing at the front door dressed for the evening. But you are right. It is good he came. Do you think I need to intervene?"

Rachele replies, "No, but you need to go stand next to him. United front and all that. Come on, Grace and I will stand with you. Hugh is already over there. Seems he and Gray have hit it off."

The three women work their way across the floor to the men, sidling up next to them. In the end, a sort of greeting line forms. As Laura Lynne looks at

Grace and Rachele, she realizes between them, they represent four of the five founding families. It seemed every member wanted a chance to greet them and give Gabe their support and warm wishes. Finally, the usher announces dinner, and the group is escorted to the Founder's table. Laura Lynne asks, "Is anyone here representing the Monroe family?"

"No, thank goodness. It would be a bit awkward considering Chandler and Silas seem hell- bent on prosecuting your uncle," Rachele replies.

"I figured Maureen would come out of spite. And to gloat over the current Cooper conundrum," says Grace. Maureen is Silas's sister and has a particular hatred for the Cooper family. She would spread rumors and gossip at the expense of the Cooper's in her younger years.

The dinner is lively and uneventful. Gabe is the center of attention. He is telling tales about the club, growing up in the 50s, and stories about each of the founder's families. All to the delight of the guests at his table. Because tonight, Gabe is the guest of honor.

"You good, honey?" Gray leans over close to Laura Lynne and whispers in her ear.

"Better than good. I am so glad I came. Uncle Gabe, too. How about you?"

"You know me; I love to fellowship. Been invited dove hunting in the fall at Charlie and Grace's place and turkey hunting next weekend if we are still in town. After dinner, we men apparently head to the gaming tables, drink bourbon, smoke cigars, and play cards. You good with that?"

"Just don't stay in there all night. I want a dance or two, and I don't want to miss the bidding for the auction. I heard there was some good stuff up this year. I think we need to contribute to such a good cause."

"Be sure to explain the Founder's table to me later. I am guessing this has something to do with your family's prominence around here?"

Nodding Laura Lynne whispers, "Yes. I promise I will explain everything later."

The usher announces the end of the dinner portion of the evening. The men escape to their man cave. The women head to the sitting rooms to freshen up and use the facilities. There is a practical reason for this intermission. The dining area and ballroom need to be 'flipped' and prepared for the dancing and auction.

Grace and Rachele excuse themselves to oversee the changeover. They have been by Laura Lynne's side all evening and no domineering chaperone could have done a better job at warding off potential suitors than the two of them. "Why don't you come with us?" says Rachele.

Laura Lynne replies, "No, I am fine. I think I will take a stroll on the veranda. I could use a little fresh air. I am fine. But I appreciate y'all. This is the most relaxed and happy I have seen Uncle Gabe since I got back."

"If you are sure…" Grace sounds uncomfortable leaving Laura Lynne.

"I am fine! Stop worrying!" Laura Lynne heads out the door to the veranda. She hears the unmistakable voice of her husband. She heads in that general direction. Spotting Laura Lynne, Gray excuses himself from the group.

"Hello, Mrs. Atkins," Gray says with a sexy grin. He has a cigar and a bourbon and looks every inch the Southern gentleman.

"Hello, Mr. Atkins." Laura Lynne gives him a deep kiss. "You have no idea how sexy I find you tonight. I may just have to get you naked when we get back to The Residence." Laura Lynne snuggles up close as he puts his arms gently around her. "Don't you put a burn hole in my dress with that cigar, Grayson Lee Atkins."

"Yes, ma'am." Gray kisses her deeply. "Definitely doing naked." Laura Lynne laughs and kisses his neck as I take a step backward. "I love you, woman."

The couple sways back and forth in the cool air and night sky of Southern Mississippi. Eventually, Laura Lynne disentangles herself. "How is Uncle Gabe holding up?"

"Seems to be fine. Having a grand time. He knows to let me know if he wants to leave. I left him with his cronies in the library sipping his Old Kentucky."

"Okay, see you back in the ballroom? I need to go freshen up." Looking down at her dress, Laura Lynne giggles. "It might take me a while to figure out exactly how to use the ladies' room in this get-up."

The two engage in one last passionate kiss. Gray pats Laura Lynne's butt as she turns away. "Definitely naked time tonight."

Laughing and feeling loved, Laura Lynne makes her way to the women's rooms.

"Never thought I would see the likes of you back here. That takes some balls considering the circumstances around your departure," says a voice from behind the stone column on the porch. "Real nice romantic guy you got there, Laura Lynne. Y'all put on quite the performance."

Laura Lynne pulls up short. She recognizes the voice. Laura Lynne replies, "Well, you thought wrong." She walks toward the column. "You know as well as anybody Beauregards are Tea Olive. We always end up coming back home." She looks at the man leaning against the column. He is overweight, bald, and smoking an unfiltered cigarette. "How are you this evening, Sheriff Westerman?"

"Hummph, these shindigs. The wife likes to come and spend money on the fancy stuff." He takes a puff of cigarette, exhaling slowly. "Not me. No, I prefer to watch the people. Keep tabs on the folks of Venice."

"That is surprising," says Laura Lynne. "I would think you would be enjoying your retirement. I am sorry you lost the last election. I am sure it was a surprise. You were sheriff, what 25 years?"

He smiles. "Try 38 years. I spent most of those years cleaning up after folks. You would be surprised what kind of dirty laundry some of these old families would pay good money not to have aired out in public." He flicks out his cigarette and uses his shoe to slowly grind it out. He lifts his gaze. "Folks like your family, Laura Lynne."

"Are you threatening me?"

He gives a mirthless laugh. "No need for threats." He walks over, grabs her arm and pulls her up against the column. He puts his face in hers. She can smell his smoky breath. His eyes are hard. Laura Lynne struggles against his grip, and he simply twists her arm behind her until it feels as if it will break. "Keep wiggling and it will break."

Laura Lynne goes completely still, staring into his eyes, unflinching. "Let go of me!"

He releases her arm, but not before pressing his obese body against her, forcing her against the column. She can barely breathe and can't move. Against her will, Laura Lynne begins to tremble. He feels it and grins widely, displaying his tobacco-stained teeth. "Hush your pretty little mouth." Bubba leans next to her ear and whispers, "You don't want to stir up any old memories, Laura Lynne. Best to let sleeping dogs lie."

"I don't know what you are talking about," Laura Lynne wheezes out, her vision beginning to darken.

He pulls back slightly, allowing Laura Lynne to take a gasp of air. She fills her lungs with much-needed oxygen. A door opens, and Laura Lynne hears someone walk out on the terrace; she opens her mouth to scream. Bubba quickly puts his hand over her mouth, shoving the back of her head into the column. Her ears ring as he pulls in close to her ear and whispers harshly, "Keep your fucking mouth shut."

He suddenly releases her and stands tall, brushing his tuxedo off and rebuttoning his jacket. As he walks away, he issues one last warning, "I'm watching you."

Laura Lynne is left with her back pressed up against the column, gasping for air. Her mind is whirling. What is he talking about? Keep quiet about what? Or who? Dead Doe? Dr. Butler? She wants to find Gray and tell him what happened, then decides against it. It is not the time or the place. As her mind clears, she goes from terrified to angry. She looks around the column where she has remained well hidden. Seeing a few guests have made it to the terrace, Laura Lynne composes herself before walking across the wooden decking to the women's lounge. She is not going to let Bubba Westerman ruin her night.

She takes one last breath before opening the door. And walks straight into the Mean Girls club led by none other than the notorious Natalie. Laura Lynne glances around and, not recognizing any of the faces, nods and attempts to exit with grace and dignity. Which she thought she had mastered well until Natalie decides to engage. Laura Lynne does not have the bandwidth for this high-school drama right now.

"Laura Lynne! Where are you rushing off to? We were just discussing last night's show. Care to join in?"

Taking a deep breath and schooling herself not to let herself be baited by this horrible woman, Laura Lynne pauses. She attempts to gather her wits about her, gently rubbing her arm where Bubba had twisted it painfully. "I am sorry, I am slightly confused. You act as if you know me, though we have never even been introduced?"

Natalie walks toward Laura Lynne, her hand extended. "My apologies. I am sure you are right. I am Natalie Johnson."

Looking at Natalie's hand with disdain, Laura Lynne nods, keeping her hands lightly clasped in front of her waist. "I am going to assume from the heavy Boston accent you are not from around here, so I will forgive you for your rudeness in using my first name, Mrs. Johnson. In the future, please refer to me as Mrs. Atkins." Snapping her fingers, Laura Lynne continues, "Actually, don't refer to me or my family ever again." Laura Lynne smiles as she looks around the room, she knows she is out of line with her anger, but she cannot stop herself. Several of the women have their phones out, videoing the events.

"As far as last evening's show, I have no comment. Our family attorney will be issuing a statement. And contacting any and all persons involved in what he refers to as 'defamation and slander.'" Looking straight at Natalie, Laura Lynne says, "I understand your name is on the list." She holds out her hands. "I have no idea what you have against me or my family. Please excuse me, ladies."

"Who the hell does she think she is?" asks Natalie, knowing Laura Lynne is still within earshot.

Laura Lynne turns around slowly, back to Natalie and her friends. Between nasty Natalie and the nastier Bubba Westerman, Laura Lynne has had enough of this nonsense. She gathers herself to her full height and slants her chin, looking as much like her mother as ever before. She says in her most Southern, cultured voice, "I am Laura Lynne Cooper Beauregard Smith Atkins. And as I was told just this evening, that means I have double the steel in my spine. Go lay your traps for some other poor, unsuspecting soul. Your venom doesn't work on me."

Laura Lynne exits the room and nearly runs over Grace and Rachele having obviously been alerted to the situation. "Laura Lynne! Are you okay?" asks Grace. "We couldn't find you anywhere."

Laura Lynne replies, "Yes! I just desperately need to pee. Rachele, can you help me with this dress?"

"Sure, sweetheart. Come on. You're not upset, are you?" Rachele steers her toward the little used bathroom near the club's locker rooms.

"By Mean Girls? Hell no. You do remember who my momma is, right?" Laura Lynne plants a fake smile on her face. She refuses to succumb to Bubba's intimidation. And she doesn't want Grace or Rachele to know what happened on that terrace.

Laughing, Rachele and Laura Lynne manage to use the facilities with minimal fuss. When they come out, Grace is waiting. She is holding her cell phone up. "Looks like you already hit the social platforms. You gave quite the performance."

"Oh God, really? I am so glad I didn't hit that woman. Do y'all have any clue what her bone is with me?"

"Come on, let's go find a place to sit. I texted Charlie and sent him the video. He is having Natalie and her husband escorted off the premises."

"What? That is just going to make things worse. Just let her be."

Grace looks steely-eyed at Laura Lynne. "Those women surrounded you and prevented you from exiting. Not only is that illegal, but it is also downright dangerous. We can't have that at the club. Besides, Natalie isn't even a member. She is simply a guest."

The women find a quiet corner upstairs in the Ladies' bridge room. The three plop down in all their finery. They slip off their shoes and curl their feet under them as they sit on the overstuffed chairs. With one last final text, Grace starts to giggle. "God, Laura Lynne. You did really good."

Leaning toward the phone, Rachele says, "Let me see! I haven't had a chance to look yet. Laura Lynne was all fired up about peeing."

Grace hands over her phone, and Rachele plays the video, Laura Lynne cringing the entire time. "My momma is going to kill me."

Rachele says, "The fact that you are worried about your momma at a time like this speaks volumes. My momma always scared the shit out of me too. Grace, you had it easy. Mrs. Cunningham is a sweetheart."

"Hmmph, to *you,* maybe! I was raised same as y'all," says Grace.

"Okay, spill. What is this Natalie's deal?" asks Laura Lynne.

"Honestly, I am not sure why she has you in her sights this minute. Easy prey, I guess. She and her husband waltzed into town about 20 years ago. He is actually a pretty decent guy. Vice President of Grant construction. Natalie, she just rubs everyone the wrong way. Acts like she is something she is not. She's new money who wants to be old money. Carpetbagger type," explains Rachele.

Grace's phone pings, and she glances at the text. "Okay, girls, we are being summoned. Laura Lynne, seems like your uncle is ready to call it a night. And, apparently, Hugh and Charlie are having a hard time keeping Gray from barging up the stairs to check on you."

"Thank y'all. Other than the last 30 minutes, I had a really great time." Standing, giving Grace and Rachele a brief hug, Laura Lynne and her friends head down the stairs. Their three husbands greet them with hugs, kisses, and comments. Everyone is talking over each other, discussing Laura Lynne's debut on TikTok. Apparently, she is a reel now. As they make their way through the crowd to get Uncle Gabe, Laura Lynne is stopped repeatedly by club members expressing their support.

Gray puts pressure on Laura Lynne's waist and steers her to the ballroom. The music is playing; it is not a DJ but a live band. "Quite the shindig. Come on, Laura Lynne, dance with me. Let's show them we aren't hiding, enjoy ourselves." He takes her hand and kisses it. Then, he walks her onto the dance floor. It's a slow song, so he holds her close. They aren't very good dancers, but they don't care. Gray says, "You okay? I can see your mind whirling."

Laura Lynne smiles up at him. "Yes, I am. I expected to be vilified and gossiped about when I came back. It's a bit surprising that the source is somebody I met for five seconds at the coffee shop."

"Not so surprising. Mean Girl seems like a social climber. She has not been able to break into society because she wasn't born into the right family. So, she tries a different way, by dividing and conquering or sowing seeds of doubt. The class system is alive and well in Venice. You and your family are one of the chosen few. The rest have to hustle to find a place."

"I know, I know. It's wrong. But so is publicly attacking me and then posting it on Tik Tok!"

"It is." Gray is rubbing her back. "Just giving you another perspective. Must be hard to break into a small town like this. Cliques are formed before birth. Now tell me about the Founders Table."

"It was something the women created when the country club was first opened. The men who started the club were all from prominent families. There are five families who are considered the founders of Venice: the Coopers, the Beauregards, the Cunninghams, the Hugers, and the Monroes. To acknowledge their importance, the Founder's Table is delegated to the five families, one representative per family."

Gray adds with a nod, "Except in your case, where you are both a Cooper and a Beauregard. And what about Scarlet? She occupies three seats?"

"Yep, once she married Buck. But the founders are also the voting members of the board. There are no board members outside the original six families."

Gray is quiet a moment, contemplating. "So y'all could easily sway the vote, with a 50% stake. Doesn't seem fair."

Laura Lynne snuggles against Gray's chest as the music plays, "I don't know. You can ask Uncle Gabe. He has been on the board for years. That is one thing I have very little knowledge about."

"Speak of the devil." Gray stops dancing and takes a step back.

"Excuse me Gray, but I would like to dance with my niece." Gabe has his forearm resting on the small of his back. He has his right hand extended.

Releasing Laura Lynne and bowing slightly, Gray replies, "Of course."

Smiling, Uncle Gabe holds out his arms and Laura Lynne walks right into them. Gabe is a phenomenal dancer. He is much better than the swaying she and Gray were doing earlier. The band breaks into a waltz and the two glide around the floor. Those long-ago steps Laura Lynne learned in Mrs. Witherspoon's class are remembered. The dance floor is filled with couples. Gabe expertly maneuvers her around the floor, smiling and laughing. Guiding her through the steps until ending with a flourish and a bow as Laura Lynne curtsies in front of him. Everyone not on the dance floor applauds as the band moves into their next selection.

"A grand way to finish the evening. Come on Laura Lynne. I am ready to go home."

"Yes, sir. Me too. Thank you for that dance. It was wonderful."

"It truly was."

Gabe escorts Laura Lynne off the dance floor. Out of the corner of her eye, she sees Bubba Westerman staring at her from the edge of the dance floor. A shiver runs up her spine. Gabe hands Laura Lynne off to Gray and Gray says, "I have the car out front. That dance was the perfect end to the evening. Let's go." Then he whispers, "Time to get my woman naked." Shaking off the trepidation she feels, Laura Lynne smiles and gives a soft laugh. It certainly is.

Chapter 20

Laura Lynne scoots over in the bed to spoon her husband. Gray knows the signal and automatically turns on his side to wrap his arm and leg around her. They have perfected this pose over the years. He keeps her warm, and she protects his bad knee. After all the standing and dancing last night, Laura Lynne imagines today will include ibuprofen and ice packs.

Gray nuzzles her neck and kisses the back of her head. He is slow to wake up. The two are the complete opposites in the morning. Laura Lynne's eyes pop open, and her brain activates. Gray needs about 30 minutes and several large coffees before he is human. Laura Lynne pats his hand and snuggles back against him before disentangling herself. The clock shows 7:30. Church service starts at 11:00, so there is time for tea and coffee on the porch. Glancing over at her husband, Laura Lynne sees he has fallen back to sleep. Laura Lynne puts on her sweater and thick socks over her pajamas and heads downstairs to start the coffee pot and tea kettle.

Laura Lynne has the coffee brewing and pours hot water over her tea bag when her husband makes his entrance. "Good morning, baby. You sleep good?" He comes over to her and puts his arms around her body. His hands slide down the back of her pajama bottoms, and he squeezes her cheeks. He loves to play with her butt in the kitchen, anybody's kitchen. Laura Lynne just sinks into his chest and stands there snuggled up with her man while the coffee brews. As soon as there is enough for a mug, Gray kisses her head and wastes no time filling the cup.

"Come to the front porch. I like to sit there in the mornings and watch Tea Olive wake up." They head outside and sit on the settee. Gray puts his left leg on the ottoman and rubs his knee. "Bothering you?" Laura Lynne asks.

"Not too much. Thought it would be worse. Plane ride won't help, but it's so much better since I had the PRP treatments. I have another appointment in a couple of weeks for my third injection. I am kinda lookin' forward to it." Gray had started Plasma Replacement for his knee, basically a stem cell injection to rejuvenate the cartilage and add some cushion to the knee joint. The doctor thinks he is too young for knee replacements, so this helps in the meantime. Gray has had some pretty good success. "This is an awfully nice setup y'all got here. I didn't get to see much of it yesterday."

"I had forgotten how much I loved it here. I wanted to broach the subject with you about returning now and again. Check on Momma and Uncle Gabe. Help out Scarlet, but also just for myself. It feels like it is time to put my past behind me and move forward."

"Whatever makes you happy, Laura Lynne, you know I don't care. If you want to start making regular trips here, then we just add it to the schedule." The two sit in companionable silence and sip their drinks. "You know, it occurs to me that you have set up the hacienda to be like The Residence. Was that intentional?"

"I hadn't really thought of it that way. I guess you are right. When I think about home, I think about here. Maybe subconsciously, as I was creating our home, I put in the same components. Does it bother you?"

"No." He reaches over and puts his arm around Laura Lynne. "I love our little life. We are blessed."

"Mind if I join you?" Uncle Gabe is heading outside with his coffee and is already dressed for church.

"No sir, have a seat. Just telling Laura Lynne how great this place is. I have never seen anything quite like it before." Gray comes from the mountains of Tennessee.

It's the perfect segue for Uncle Gabe to tell Gray all about the history of Tea Olive. He regals Gray with stories of indigo, cotton, war, land deals, and the various questionable practices of the Cooper clan. After an hour, Laura Lynne excuses herself and heads upstairs for a shower. Gray comes up about 20 minutes later with an egg sandwich and another mug of coffee. "Your Uncle Gabe is a character. We could have spent another two hours out there. You done in the shower?"

Laura Lynne scoots out the bathroom door and heads to her vanity. "It's all yours." She loves having him with her and that he loves her Uncle Gabe. "I hate that you are leaving today, but I am so glad you came."

Kissing her on the head as he climbs into the shower, Gray replies, "I am glad I came too. One thing for you to talk about this place. It is a whole other deal to actually experience it." He climbs into the shower, still talking, "Listen, I know you don't want to hear this, but your kids deserve this place. It is their heritage, and it's not fair you are keeping them from it."

"I know you are right. Maybe soon."

Sticking his head from behind the curtain, Gray gives her a look that conveys his displeasure with her answer. Laura Lynne rolls her eyes. "I know, I know." She turns and walks out of the bathroom. Then she turns back around. "Listen Gray, something happened last night that I don't want to talk about. I need you to trust me to deal with it."

Laura Lynne waits impatiently as Gray finishes his shower and then grabs a towel. He wraps it around his hips and looks at Laura Lynne with serious eyes. "I need more details."

"I know. You deserve them, but I don't want to go into it. Besides, there is nothing to do. I handled the situation."

"What *situation*, Laura Lynne? There was another one? Other than with Natalie?" Gray is unflinching in his appraisal of her face.

Laura Lynne meets his gaze. This is one man she does not fear. "There was, out on the terrace after I left you."

Gray is quiet as he towels off, thinking through his words, "And you don't want to tell me who it was or what it was about?"

Laura Lynne shakes her head. "No, I want you to trust me to handle the situation."

Gray pulls on his underwear when he gets done, putting his hands on his hips. "And I want you to trust me enough to tell me."

Laura Lynne walks up to him and places her hands on his chest. She can feel the tense muscles and his valiant attempt to remain calm. "I know. And I do, truly. This is just something I want to handle my own way. On my own. Please."

He walks around her and out of the bathroom. She follows, toweling off and getting dressed. Gray walks over to the window and looks out over the gardens. "This is not how a marriage works, Laura Lynne. Well, not how I want ours to work. No secrets." He turns around and faces her. "I don't like it, at all. You would tell me if you were in danger?"

Laura Lynne hesitates, then replies carefully, "I would tell you if there was immediate danger, yes."

Gray's hands go on his hips again. "So there is potential danger. Don't play word games with me, Laura Lynne. We are better than that."

"Don't get angry. I wasn't going to even mention it because I knew you would take it wrong! It took me a lot to even tell you. You know we have baggage from our previous relationships, stuff we have to muddle through. We have given each other permission to do that, even when it hurt the other one. I am asking for a chance to handle this myself. I don't want you to solve my problem for me."

With these words, Gray's stance relaxes slightly. "Sweetheart, I am not Jimmy. I know you are capable of handling anything on your own." He walks over to stand in front of her. "But until you figure that out for yourself, we are going to keep running into this same obstacle." He let out a sigh, still frustrated and bent out of shape. "Come on. We are going to be late."

Laura Lynne wears a summer dress, sandals, and her pearls. Not quite Birdie's Tiffany sapphires, but it's pretty enough. Gray puts on gray dress slacks and a white button-down with an open neck. He slips on a dark blue jacket.

Laura Lynne looks at him. "No bowtie?"

"Uncle Gabe said I didn't have to. Do you want me to put one on?" Laura Lynne shakes her head.

"Gray, please don't be mad at me."

Gray looks at her with sad eyes, "I'm not mad, just disappointed. You do what you think is right. I do trust you. I just wish you trusted me."

Uncle Gabe and Laura Lynne wait on the front porch for Gray to pull around in the rental car. "I really like him, Laura Lynne. Seems like a good man. Never did care much for the first one."

"You know, that would have been good to know *before* I married him. Daddy told me the same thing."

"Not like we got to meet him before you called to tell us you eloped. Water under the bridge. You got two beautiful children, and Jimmy made you strong in ways you didn't know you could be." He ushers her down the stairs. "Laura Lynne, you have to start looking at the hard times as a blessing instead of a curse. God placed those challenges in your life to make you more like Him."

Laura Lynne glances at him as he opens the car door. "You doing the sermon this morning?"

He chuckles. "No, Laura Lynne, I leave the preachin' to those holier than me. That's just common sense I'm spoutin.' You're smart enough to know that." He slides into the back seat after he ensures Laura Lynne is safely ensconced in the front seat.

Then, Gabe asks, "Laura Lynne, tell me about that Natalie person?"

Laura Lynne cringes in the front seat; she had hoped the information had not made it to her uncle. He continues, "Thought I didn't know about that? I knew as soon as it happened. Mrs. Cunningham came straight to the library and told us the entire story. She said you handled yourself well. Would have made Melanie proud."

"I am not sure about that, Uncle Gabe. Honestly, I know very little about her." Laura Lynne relays what Grace and Rachele told her last night. Gray added his two cents.

"Husband works for Grant, does he? Hummph," says Gabe.

"Uncle Gabe, what are you planning?" asks Laura Lynne.

"Curtis Grant and I go way back. Think I will give him a call this afternoon. Better yet, probably see him at church this morning."

With a sigh, Laura Lynne resolves herself to keep quiet. Her uncle is going to do what he thinks is best to protect the family. Hope it doesn't cost Natalie's husband his job.

Church is as Laura Lynne remembers it. Not much has changed. New pastor, same congregation, though the attendance seemed sparse. Lot of the same people from last night were there, including Grace and Charlie. Grace looks exhausted. "You recovered?"

"Shoot, it will take me a week! Charlie is meeting some buddies to golf after church, and I will have a few hours to rest this afternoon. But I am basking in the glory of last night's success. We made $70,000 toward the renovation project. That is $20,000 more than our goal. However, I am done hosting this event for a few years. In fact, I think next year it is time for a Beauregard to step in."

"Tap Scarlet." Laura Lynne easily and without compunction throws Scarlet under the bus. "It's certainly not going to be me! I will happily attend, but organizing an event like last night takes skill, a skill set I don't possess."

"Shoot! You just don't want to deal with the politics. Don't blame you. Every year, it seems to get worse." She looks over her shoulder, and Charlie is at the door waving for Grace to come on. "Gotta run, Charlie is chomping at the bit to get to the course. Let's do coffee at Magnolia Café this week! I will text you!"

Laura Lynne nods and turns to Gray. "Ready? Let's go home."

Riding home, Laura Lynne receives a text from Pearl telling her not to bother coming over. Queenie is having one of her bad days. "Well, shoot! Y'all mind if I join you on your ride around the farm? Queenie is having a bad day, so Pearl asked me to try another time."

"Plenty of room on the side-by-side."

Lunch on the back porch consisted of leftovers from the week: tomato pie, vegetables, pimento cheese, rosemary bread, and ham. Gray and Laura Lynne clean up while Gabe retrieves the side-by-side. He pulls up to the door outside the mud room, where he waits for his niece and Gray to get on some mud boots. Gabe calls out, "Come on aboard, my latest toy! John convinced me I needed to stop riding the tractors around for transportation. He was right. Call her Jolene."

Laughing, Laura Lynne asks, "Why Jolene?"

Shrugging his shoulders, Gabe replies, "Just feel like I am cheatin' on my tractors with a new girl."

"I am sure Dolly Parton would approve."

With a wink and gear shift change, the three are off across the fields. The plantation is set up with four main fields plus the acreage that includes The Residence and the surrounding gardens. Each field is divided into smaller fields. The main crop has been and will remain cotton, at least while Gabe is alive. John and Malcolm would like to diversify the crops and include organic sweet potatoes.

"Just not ready for that type of transition. Maybe when you young folks take over the trust, you can make less conservative decisions."

Gray looks quizzically at Laura Lynne, "Take over the trust?"

Looking over his shoulder at Laura Lynne, Gabe is quizzical. "Yep. When I die, the trust executorship will go to Laura Lynne's older brother, Sawyer. At least, that is the current situation and tradition. The trust is split equally among the oldest living relatives to care for and invest in for the next generation. In truth, the trust is simply a way to keep Tea Olive productive and lucrative and the Coopers in a solid financial position."

"Okay, so it's just the plantation?"

"Lord, no! We have partial ownership in most of the businesses on Main Street in Venice. We also have stocks, bonds, and real estate. Rentals mostly. Plus, we have property in addition to the 2,000 acres of

Tea Olive." Gabe is driving and talking excitedly to Gray, "I am most excited about this property about 40 miles north of here. Want to turn it into a hunting camp with a lodge. Something for the corporate folks who want a hunting and fishing experience."

"Wow, sounds wonderful," says Gray.

Laura Lynne is stunned. She had no idea the trust had grown to such large proportions. As a 1/6 owner, well 1/5 now as Scarlet withdrew her money upon her marriage, Laura Lynne is a woman of considerable wealth. Her intention has always been to leave it alone, and then when Savannah and Beau were old enough, they could decide for themselves regarding the family trust.

Gabe stops the side-by-side in front of the shack near Mill Road. Laura Lynne had to look around a few times to make sure she was in the right location. When she left, the shack was exactly that—a shanty of sorts with a few rooms that held fishing gear. Not any longer. The shack is now a cabin, completely renovated.

"Is this the fishing shack?" Laura Lynne asks.

"It used to be. John lives here now. Completely renovated the place on his own. Come on, let's see if he is home. I would like Gray to meet him before he leaves."

Climbing out of Jolene, Gabe heads to the front door. Gray takes his time helping Laura Lynne out of the side-by-side. Gray says, "Sounds like you and

I need to talk. Just how much is this trust worth? Are we talking 100,000s or more like millions?"

"I honestly don't know. I never intended to touch it. My plan has always been to leave it for the children. But I would guess it is more like millions."

The door opens, and John stands in the doorway looking nothing less than like an ad for Southern Living's hunting and fishing edition. He is a ruggedly handsome man. John says, "Good afternoon, Mr. Gabe. Come on in. I was hoping y'all would come by today."

Gray leans over to Laura Lynne and whispers, "We will talk later."

The cabin has been updated and decorated to include a fully equipped kitchen, two bathrooms, a master bedroom, and living space. While showing off his home, John explains, "All told, I have about 1,400 square feet. Plenty of room for me. The only thing missing is a dog."

"You did all this work yourself?" Laura Lynne is running her hands along the concrete countertops in the kitchen.

"Yes, ma'am." John smiles. "I like to work with my hands. Not much for television, so plenty of time in the evenings to work on projects. My next one is the fishing dock. Would you like to see it?"

Nodding, they follow John out to the dock. John continues, "Unfortunately, it's completely rotten. I need to start with the pillars and work my way up. Wet work, so it has to wait for warmer weather."

For the next 30 minutes, the men discuss the pros and cons of dock-building materials. Laura Lynne sits in one of the Adirondack chairs and closes her eyes, allowing the sun's heat to soothe her.

"Sweetheart, you awake?" Gray gently places his hand on Laura Lynne's shoulder. She opens her eyes and smiles. "Listen, John has invited me to stay and fish awhile. Your Uncle Gabe is going to head back to The Residence. You want to stay here or go back with him?"

"I'll go back. You two bond. Besides, I know how much you love to drown a worm."

"You sure?"

"Absolutely. Just text me when you are done. I will come get you. Stay as long as you want. I will pack your bag. I think it's good y'all get to know each other."

Laura Lynne stands and hugs Gray. The two hold tight and sway side to side. Gray kisses her head, then her lips. "I love you, even though I am still angry with you."

"I love you, too." Untangling, Laura Lynne walks over to John and rubs her hand along his back in sisterly affection. "Thanks. The place is great. You have done wonders." She smiles, turns, and sees her Uncle Gabe in the doorway, ready to make his escape. The weariness around his eyes is visible. "Come on, Uncle Gabe, let's go back."

Arm in arm the two head through the cabin to the front door. Laura Lynne says, "John seems like a good man."

"In the two years he has been here, he has been nothing but an answered prayer. He came with excellent references, but even if he hadn't, I would have taken a chance on him. There is something about him, an innate goodness. He cares. Like you said, a very good man."

Gabe gets into the side-by-side with a sigh.

Laura Lynne asks, "You okay, Uncle Gabe? You look tired."

He gives a mirthless laugh. "I am tired! It is hard dealing with a dead man, lawyers, a plantation, business, and then keeping up with you young folks at the country club! I want a nap."

"Okay, while you take your nap and Gray is fishing, I think I will go into town and visit Momma. I probably need to tell her what is going on. My guess is she has already heard about it, though."

"No doubt she has. She will have defended you."

"No, she would have defended the Beauregard name."

"Isn't that the same thing?" Gabe stops the side-by-side, shifting it into park. He looks at Laura Lynne. "Let me set you straight on one thing, Laura Lynne. First, I have never agreed with your mother and father on their treatment of you. *Ever.* I will not defend them. I do not defend them. However, what you have to get clear in your head is the Beauregard and Cooper names matter. And they matter to more than just you. They represent something greater than yourself. Own it. You are a Beauregard. You are a Cooper. Claiming different just makes you sound petty. Now, do you want to tell me what is up between you and your beau? He seems a bit put out by you."

Hanging her head, Laura Lynne feels a rush of tears. She sniffs and lifts her head, letting her see he hit his mark. "Well, that hurt my feelings. Mostly because I know you are right. And, no, I don't want to talk to you about Gray." Laura Lynne makes her way out of the side by side. She wipes her eyes and nose with the back of her hand. "Can we talk about this more later? I want to see Gray off, and I need to see momma."

Kissing her forehead and handing her a handkerchief to wipe her eyes, Gabe nods in agreement. "I know you know to be kind to Melanie. I don't like her any more than you do, but I love her. We have to remember the love. That goes for your Gray, too." He takes a step back. "Take the Cadillac. Keys are in the glove box."

Laura Lynne gives a little wave as she heads to the barn and Gabe back to the house. She picks up her phone and dials Scarlet. Scarlet picks up on the second ring.

"Well, if it isn't the little troublemaker herself! Girl! You are all over social media." Scarlet is laughing and slightly out of breath. In a sing-song voice,

Scarlet starts repeating Laura Lynne's put-downs from the night before, *"I am Laura Lynne Cooper Beauregard Smith Atkins. And as I was told just this evening, that means I have double the steel in my spine."* Laughing harder, Scarlet continues, *"Go lay your traps for some other poor unsuspecting soul. Your venom doesn't work on me."*

"Oh God, you already heard."

"Already heard. Honey, I have pictures that were sent to me last night! By the way, your dress is beautiful."

"What are you doing? You sound out of breath. And why weren't you at church this morning?"

"Well, I am kneading dough. I am making some cookies and bread to go with the thank-you notes. I plan to hand deliver them tomorrow. Will you be at the Gazette tomorrow? I can bring some by, maybe help you out a bit."

"Yes, that is my plan. Right now, I am headed to see Momma. I don't want to go, but I don't think I can avoid it."

"No, you need to go." She is rolling dough and whacking the pin while she talks. "She will be furious when she hears about Natalie. This is not our first run-in with her." Whack! "She's like super, uber bitch! Why doesn't she just go away and give us all a much-needed break?" Whack!

"Scarlet!"

"Well, you were thinking it. I just said it." Now Laura Lynne hears what sounds like kneading. "Did you have fun? By the way, your Gray is a good-looking man. All the women were impressed with him. My sources tell me he is friendly and easy to talk too. I am sorry I did not get to meet him."

"Me too. His visit was a surprise and a lovely respite from the real world." Laura Lynne takes a deep breath and slowly lets it out, like air released from a tire. "Fun? Not sure that is the right word. It was very enlightening. Uncle Gabe was the evening's darling. He charmed everyone. It was my first time sitting at the founders' table. I wish you had been there with me." Laura Lynne tries another tact to see if she can pump some information from her sister.

"Those days are done for me, Laura Lynne. I haven't been to the club in a coon's age."

"But why Scarlet? The club was always your thing. You and Buck used to be all about the club, didn't you? Queenie even wrote me y'all had taken Momma and Daddy's spot for a while on the council."

"I did, but not anymore. Handed it back. Momma and Uncle Gabe do it now. Honestly, not sure who goes, if anyone. You might ask Uncle Gabe. I just don't care anymore. Got other things I am dealing with here at home. The club is no longer my problem." Whack!

Laura Lynne pulls up to the entrance to the assisted living facility. "I'm here. I gotta run. But Scarlet, this discussion is not over! Have fun killing your dough." Laura Lynne pulls into a space and parks the car.

"Not killing it. Just knocking it into submission. Chin up, baby girl. Don't let Momma push you around." She hangs up. Laura Lynne realizes as she disconnects that Scarlet never told her why she was not at church.

Laura Lynne checks in at the facility's front entrance. The front desk clerk, Ruth, points Laura Lynne in the direction of her mother's room. The door is open, and Laura Lynne looks in. "Momma?" Getting no answer, Laura Lynne walks in and sees her mother has decorated her room as she had The Residence. She has oil paintings capturing life in coastal Mississippi, including the watercolor from the state's most iconic artist, Walter Anderson. There are a couple of blown glass bowls in rose hues, and a sculpture of a magnolia blossom artfully designed in stone and marble. Laura Lynne recognizes the furniture from her grandparents' rooms. The room is elegant, regal. Set up in the corner is a half-completed puzzle. Laura Lynne walks over to the table, picks up one of the pieces, and attaches it.

"You always were a good at puzzles."

"Not as good as you." Laura Lynne turns around and says, "Hi Momma." Laura Lynne can sense the tension in herself as well as her mother. She looks at her mom, refusing to walk over and make the first move. She knows she will not get an apology after their last meeting, but she holds out hope this time will be different. A hope that soon fizzles.

Laura Lynne realizes this is the first time since she was 15 she has been alone in a room with her mother. Melanie clears her throat and pulls the tails of her cover up together over her slacks and blouse. She sits down in her wingback chair and motions for Laura Lynne to sit in the other one. "Does your visit today have anything to do with the debacle at the clubs formal last night? If so, I know all about it! The biddies here couldn't wait to tell me." She pauses and looks at me. "But, I want to hear it from you."

"I don't know why I even expected an apology."

Melanie says nothing, she just waits for Laura Lynne to fill the silence. With a sigh, Laura Lynne acquiesces. Some things never change.

Laura Lynne tells her the story of last night's gala, leaving out her run-in with Bubba Westerman. "I know this Melanie character. She and Scarlet have had a few run-ins over the years."

"Scarlet said the same thing. Any reason she has us in her sights?"

"More than likely because I blocked her bid to join the country club."

"Well, that would do it! Why?"

"She and her husband interviewed with the board. His name is Brad, I think. Nice enough man. They met the qualifications, and all seemed to be in line.

They were new to town, and the Grant family have been good friends to us over the years. Anyway, in reviewing their resume, I recognized there was, shall we say, an inconsistency."

"She lied? About what?"

"She said she attended Boston University and was a Kappa Delta legacy. She wasn't. In fact, neither her mother, grandmother, nor great-grandmother on either side were in the sorority. Natalie was in school on a scholarship which is perfectly commendable. There was no reason to lie."

Her grandmother Birdie was a KD, her mother a KD, and Scarlet a KD. Laura Lynne refused to join a sorority at all, much less become a KD. She wanted nothing to do with her mother or her legacy. But in her mother's eyes, the sorority was sacred. Second only to Jesus himself.

"I told the board my concerns. Maureen fought bitterly to bring them on board. In the end, we voted and chose not to accept them as candidates. That was probably 15 or so years ago. I imagine Maureen informed them of why they were not accepted. That would be my guess anyway."

"Are she and Maureen friends?"

"I have no idea. I don't associate with either of them."

"You know I have never asked Momma, but why the bitter feelings between our two families? I realize you rejected Sal, but that was a lifetime ago."

"You have the story wrong, Laura Lynne. I never rejected Sal. My parents did. And I have no idea why." She settles back in her chair. "In those days, marriages were meant to align families to create stronger dynasties. Sal's parents and mine were dear friends for years. I always knew I was intended to marry Sal. But something happened to sour the relationship between our parents. Your father was their next choice."

"You have no idea why?"

She was quiet for a long minute. "I do believe I know why, but it is just supposition. And I am grateful Momma and Daddy made the choice they did for me. Sawyer was a much better match for me." A gentle smile plays across her lips, making her look almost young.

Ready to change the subject, Laura Lynne pulls her phone out of her pocket. "I have a video of the Natalie incident. Want to watch?"

"How gauche Laura Lynne! But yes, of course, I want to watch." As the video plays, Melanie cannot help but comment, "What is the poor girl wearing? She looks like an eggplant. Well, bless her heart."

When it is over, Melanie pats Laura Lynne's leg. "Well, you didn't punch her, so that was good."

Laughing, Laura Lynne continued the tale. "When it was over and I walked out, I nearly ran over Rachele Humphries. he asked me if I was all right. I said, 'Because of the mean girls? Please. You do know who my mother is, right?' All I could think about was how you would have handled the situation. You do a marvelous put down."

The hand on Laura Lynne's leg stills, and Melanie gazes at Laura Lynne intently. Laura Lynne stops laughing and gets to her feet, holding her mother's hand. "Momma, are you okay? What is it?"

"You paid me a compliment."

"What?"

"You said something nice about me. To me. It just surprised me."

"Momma, I basically said you were good at being a bitch."

Instead of reprimanding Laura Lynne for her language, Melanie replies, "We all have our gifts." Patting Laura Lynne's leg again, she points to her phone. "Now show me some more of the pictures from the formal."

Laura Lynne spends the next hour talking about the country club members, Grace, Gray, Savannah, and Beau. Melanie is interested and intent, giving Laura Lynne background and insight into the social circle of Venice society. It is a most enjoyable time.

Eventually, Laura Lynne interrupts the chatter, "Momma, I need to go. Gray is leaving for the airport soon, and I don't want to miss him. But thank you. I am not going to lie. I did not want to come and see you today. I dreaded the conversation. Instead, I find myself sorry to see the hour go so quickly."

"Laura Lynne, before you go, I want to caution you. Be careful who you trust. And whatever you do, protect the family legacy. At all costs. You understand?"

"Uncle Gabe said the same thing before I left today."

"He is a good brother to me. Heed his advice if not my own. Goodbye, Laura Lynne. I hope you visit again soon."

"Goodbye, Momma." As Laura Lynne leaves, her head is filled with a jumble of thoughts, and her heart is filled with…something new, something other than hurt. It is filled with…hope.

Chapter 21

Laura Lynne has a hard time sleeping. When she returned home yesterday afternoon, it had been nothing less than a whirlwind of activity. She saw Gray off to the airport. He was still angry at her. Well, more hurt. She hated to end the weekend with them on the outs, but she was not ready to confide in anyone about Bubba Westerman. She was still trying to work it out for herself. She would need to make this right. And she would, she just needed time.

Gray is barely down the driveway when her phone began ringing. It was Savannah. Laura Lynne spent the next two hours talking to her daughter. She wanted all the details of the evening and was mortified her mother was a TikTok star but also secretly pleased. Ashley called. Then Avery. Uncle Gabe wanted to know about her conversation with Melanie. Then Gray called after he had safely arrived home. Their conversation was stilted and formal. It was nearly 10 PM before Laura Lynne finally silenced the phone after sending a "good night" text to everyone. Her mind wouldn't relax enough to let her sleep.

 After a night of tossing and turning, she gives up and gets up. It's 5:30 AM. She puts on her sweatshirt and woolly socks and heads to the kitchen for some tea. Mug in hand, Laura Lynne goes outside, careful not to slam the back door. The moon is bright, so there is no need for a flashlight. The longer Laura Lynne stays in Tea Olive, the more she goes back to that long-ago summer. The nights spent out on the dock, playing in the fields, roaming, no place in mind but her body and brain restless. That is how she feels today. Her brain is restless like something is getting ready to happen. She arrives at the dock and sits down, dangling her feet. The tide is high, the moon is full, the current is swift, and the air is warm. She closes her eyes and just breathes it all in. Home, it feels like home.

***

Mary is waiting for Laura Lynne when she arrives at the Gazette. She gives Laura Lynne a hug. "You good? You had quite the weekend."

"If you could help me unload the car? Gray brought Queenie's letters to me this weekend." She hands Mary her coveted box of letters. Throwing the computer bag over her shoulder, she picks up a picnic basket of food. "Victoria insisted on packing us a massive lunch. I think she is worried I didn't eat this weekend without her there to cook." Laura Lynne shuts the trunk. Mary holds open the office door. On the counter are the school yearbooks. They are laid out with the pages marked.

Mary says, "You weren't the only one busy this weekend. I went through the yearbooks. Had some luck. Ron was able to locate his notes, and he has two names for us. I marked them in the yearbook: Anna Nguyen and Felicia Manigault. Not certain of Anna's age, but Felicia was a freshman the year her abduction occurred." She looks at me. "I think we can call these abductions at this point."

"Felicia Manigault. I recognize that name."

"You should. The Manigaults have been in Venice for generations. Felicia's father was a professor at the community college for years. He taught engineering. Good people."

"I did not get that from the article," Laura Lynne says.

Mary gives Laura Lynne the side-eye. She goes to the yearbook and points to one of the pages. "This is her during freshman year. She is not in any of the later yearbooks. Not certain, but Ron thought she was homeschooled by her parents." Mary hands Laura Lynne a piece of paper. "This is the address of her parents. They still live here." Laura Lynne takes the paper and looks at the address. It's on the south side of town in one of the more affluent neighborhoods.

"Thanks, you have been busy."

"Not all of us get to kick our heels up at the country club all weekend." Mary sits on her stool and gets her coffee. "Grab some tea in the back. I brought you a kettle and tea bags. There is also a mug. Then come sit next to me and tell me all about your run-in with the infamous Natalie."

"Maybe later, Mary. I want to get started. I bet you know as much as I do."

"Seems you made quite an impression." She turns back to her counter as Laura Lynne heads to her office.

Her phone rings, and it's the sheriff's department. She picks up, "Hello?"

"Laura Lynne? It's Grady Cunningham. Did I catch you at a good time?"

"Can you give me just a second? I just got to the Gazette. I want to put my stuff down."

"You're in town? Listen, let me just come over to you. I will be there in five." He disconnects. Maybe he heard something from the coroner's office.

Five minutes later, Grady comes through the front door. He says his pleasantries to Mary and heads back to Laura Lynne's office. He shuts the door and pulls up a chair. "Just got this in from the coroner's office. Thought you might be interested."

"What does it say?"

"Unfortunately, not a lot. Age 55-65, Caucasian male, approximately 6'1", blunt force trauma to the head. Cause of death appears to be suffocation. The hyoid bone is fractured. Been dead approximately 30 years. They have submitted dental records, but no hits yet." He hands Laura Lynne the report, and she starts reading it. "You can have that copy. It's just preliminary but thought you would want to know." He leans forward. "Any ideas about who this might be?"

Laura Lynne is shaking her head. "No, but I wasn't here then, either. Would have been 1989, 1990." Laura Lynne looks up. "Did you check the data bases for any possible missing person that fits this description?"

"We are running it. Lots of missing persons, but none have hit all the right notes yet." He stands up to leave. "I need to get back but wanted you to see this as soon as I had them."

"Wait, Grady, can you sit down for a moment? Or come back when you have some time?" He sits back down.

"What can I do for you, Laura Lynne?"

"It's of a personal nature, not related to the case, but well, maybe related to me. I don't want to get into why, but I have two names of girls who were abducted in the early 80s. I have their names and newspaper articles related to them. I am wondering what you can tell me about them and if there are any more?"

He tilts his head. "This have to do with why you left in 1985?"

"Maybe, I am not sure yet." Laura looks at him with pleading eyes. "I don't want anyone to know. I am trusting you and only you. Is it possible to look into and not raise any suspicions?"

"It's a small town with lots of loose lips and tongues wagging. But I can snoop around some." Laura Lynne writes down the names and gives him the paper. He looks at Laura Lynne and smiles. "Saw you Saturday night. Sorry I didn't get to say hello and introduce you to my wife."

"It was busy! Why didn't you sit at the Founders' Table with us? Would have loved for you to meet Gray."

"That's more Grace and Charlie's thing. Me, I am just a good ol' boy deputy sheriff. Don't care to be in the spotlight. Makes my job more difficult." He stands up. "Anything else?"

"Well, now that you mention it. Let me tell you about Ginny Johnson." Laura Lynne briefly discusses her connection with the family, minus the blackmail. Grady is not surprised. Her father's exploits with other women is not a secret.

"I can run a check on her. Have a buddy in Mobile. He is discreet. May even pay her a visit myself."

"If you do, be aware she is cunning. Beautiful and cunning. Don't get sucked in by her the way my father did." She shakes her head and rolls her eyes. "You good with me sharing this information with my brothers and sister?" He nods. "Okay, I am also sending a copy to our attorney."

"The attorney of record will get one. The investigation is ongoing."

"Thanks, Grady. I know you don't have to do this, but I sure do appreciate the help." Laura Lynne mentally adds him to the list for Scarlet to send a thank you. Grady takes his leave. Laura Lynne fires up the microfiche and starts by finishing 1981. She moves through the rest quickly, looking specifically for two things: abducted girls and a white male aged 60. Laura Lynne gets up to refill her mug. As she passes Mary, Mary continues to scan articles and take notes. Mary stops when Laura Lynne sidles up next to her. Leaning back, she stretches her neck from side to side and gets off her stool.

Mary asks, "Any way we can narrow down the search a bit? It's fun to relive old memories, but I have no idea what I am looking for other than missing girls. And I haven't found any more at this point."

"Hold that thought." Laura Lynne retrieves the coroner's report and hands it to Mary. Mary looks at it and realizes she needs her glasses. She starts hunting for them. "They are on top of your head," Laura Lynne remarks, and Mary sighs.

"Can't find the things half the time. I refuse to get a chain. Make me look like an old woman." Today, Mary's outfit is head-to-toe white: dress, cardigan, and pearls. She looks like an egret. "What is this?"

"The coroner's report. It's just preliminary. What it does tell us is the victim is a white male, 55-65, around 6"1'. I was thinking we could change our search parameters to be focused on males around this age during those years. Missing persons, persons of interest, I am not sure." Laura Lynne looks at her. "For personal reasons, I would like to keep track of the abducted girls too."

"I wondered why we were focusing on those two girls. About the same age as you when you were sent to your Aunt Eileen's. That have anything to do with it?"

"I am not ready to share. Maybe at some point, but not yet. I am not ready yet."

Mary pats Laura Lynne's arm and takes her hand gently in hers. "I have been a schoolteacher for close to 40 years. Nothing you tell me will surprise me." Laura Lynne opens her mouth to make a denial, but Mary pats her hand again. "Shhh, I am not asking you to tell me. Just telling you nothing you say will change my opinion of you, Laura Lynne."

The door opens, the little bell jingling above the door. Scarlet comes through with a box of boxes. She is dressed in a long-sleeve navy blue blouse, white jeans, pearl earrings, and sandals "Hi! Hate to break up the party!" She puts the box on the counter and unloads a cute navy blue box with a gold ribbon. She opens the box and inside are beautiful cookies, mini bread loaves, and miniature cupcakes. She hands Laura Lynne a thank you card. It is white with gold piping, and in a navy blue script is written, "The Beauregard Family" and under that, "Tea Olive Plantation. Flip over the card." On the back of the card is a list of all the items in the box, including Laura Lynne's favorite, red velvet cupcakes.

"This is gorgeous! My Lord, Scarlet! When I asked for a thank you note, I thought of a boxed card at the store with maybe a scripted "B" on the front." Laura Lynne looks up at her with awe. "You did all this?"

"It was fun. Besides, we need to make a statement like you did at the club. It's a statement dress." She picks up the box and holds it out. "Go ahead, try them. It's one thing to look good; it's another to taste good." Mary and Laura Lynne each take an option. Laura Lynne chooses the red velvet cupcake, and Mary tries the banana split bread. They look at each other and open their mouths. They pop the treats in. In unison, the women close their eyes and savor the taste. Laura Lynne gives her two thumbs up.

"God, that is good, Scarlet. Is that dark chocolate in the bread?" Mary is looking in the box for another choice.

Scarlet nods her head. "That is a recipe from Buck's aunt. The red velvet is Queenie's recipe. The rest are some I am playing with. There is a sweet tea cookie I am particularly fond of." She reaches in the box, pulls out a cookie, breaks it in half, and splits it between Mary and Laura Lynne.

"I had no idea I have a sister that bakes like an angel." Laura Lynne picks up the coroner's report and turns toward her office, waving Scarlet back. "Before you make your deliveries, do you have a minute? Want to share some of the new information I just got from Grady. And, if you have an extra box in there, a thank you to him is also appropriate."

"Sure, I have several more." She walks behind Laura Lynne to the office. "Want me to shut the door?"

"No need unless it makes you more comfortable. Mary has been a huge help, and she knows most of what is going on." Laura Lynne pulls out her phone and dials Avery's phone number." Let me see if I can get Avery on speaker, so I only have to do this once."

Avery picks up on the second ring. "Hey, Sissy, what's new? Heard about the Natalie incident. You good?" Laura Lynne rolls her eyes. Lord, how news travels.

"Good Lord, even you know? I am fine! I have some news. Scarlet is here with me." The two exchange greetings. "Grady Cunningham came in this morning with the preliminary coroner's report. There is not much additional information, but maybe it will mean more to one of you." Laura Lynne reads them the report and then hands it to Scarlet. Laura Lynne recounts the rest of the conversation she had with Grady.

Scarlet shakes her head. "Nothing I can think of, especially around that time. I was off to Ole Miss most of that time. Avery, you were here then. Anything?"

"No, nothing." The siblings talk a few more minutes about the police investigation and notifying the attorney. Scarlet agrees to handle it when she delivers her thank you notes and baked goods.

Laura Lynne says, "Avery, you should see these thank yous. I will send you a picture. And the desserts Scarlet made are divine." Scarlet is blushing. Her head is down and tilted a bit to the side. When she moves, Laura Lynne spots a bruise on her neck. Laura Lynne reaches over and pulls down her collar to look. Scarlet glances at her and slaps her hand away. Her eyes dart to Laura Lynne and she looks wary, then mad.

Avery hangs up. Laura Lynne looks at Scarlet. She is already up and heading to the door. Laura Lynne calls out, "What happened? Why do you have a bruise on your neck?"

"Just a kitchen injury! Ran into the shelf on the door of the pantry when I was baking. No big deal."

Laura Lynne gets up from the desk, hands crossed over her chest. "I know better than that, Scarlet. Who hurt you?"

"You have lost your fool mind, Laura Lynne. Nobody hurt me. I told you I ran into a shelf and that is exactly what happened. Now drop it." She turns at the door and pastes on a smile for Laura Lynne. "I am off to make the deliveries. I have several more ready when needed. Just send me the list." She turns away, then turns back. "I think I will give Grady the box for…." Scarlet is at a loss for words.

"I call her Ginny from the Streets."

Scarlet clears her throat, "Yes, well, *her*. Let him hand deliver it. Save me the trouble of mailing it."

"Did you add the appropriate amount of poison?" Scarlet rolls her eyes and heads off. Laura Lynne calls after her, "I'm not going to drop it!" Laura Lynne hears Scarlet and Mary talking briefly before the chime above the door dings, signaling Scarlet's exit.

Laura Lynne sits up straight, another missing girl in 1982. This time in nearby Wisteria. She is 14 years old, white, and attends the local high school.

Parents say she never returned home from school. Both parents work shift work at the local textile mill. No name is listed. Laura Lynne continues to scroll until she finds the follow-up article. The girl is found two days later. She is disheveled, dirty, and walking aimlessly down Route 24. There are no names mentioned in the second article either. Laura Lynne does not recognize the reporter's name, Judy Washburn.

Laura Lynne walks into the main office to tell Mary. Mary is eating at her desk, scrolling the microfiche. Laura Lynne says, "I found another one." Mary looks up from her screen as Laura Lynne continues, "Another abducted girl. This time in Wisteria in 1982. That is three now. Each about the same time each year, spring. She was 14. Found two days later stumbling toward home. No names."

"This is sounding less and less like a coincidence."

"I know. I think maybe we need to cross-reference the time frame with local events, like maybe festivals, tournaments, church functions, state fair." Laura Lynne taps her forehead with the heel of her hand. "I don't really have a clear idea, but might be some type of timeline."

"Do you want me to stop my scanning and start creating a timeline? I am not getting anywhere today. I made it to 1988, but nothing is popping up."

"You know, that might really be helpful. A timeline of everything we have gathered of interest, maybe look at it as a whole." Laura Lynne's phone rings.

It's McElhanney. "I need to get this. Be right back." Laura Lynne heads around the corner and out the front door. "Hello?"

"Laura Lynne, it's Ernest McElhanney. I have Scarlet in my office. She is fattening me up with her wonderful cookies. I shared with her my thoughts on the coroner's report and based on the lack of physical evidence. I plan to submit a petition to drop the charges." Laura Lynne hears rustling in the background. "There is nothing for them to suggest, other than the location of the body, that your Uncle Gabe was involved. I have already spoken with him, and he agrees, but he wants y'alls thoughts before we proceed."

"Absolutely! This is good news. Scarlet?"

"I already said the same," Scarlet chimes in.

McElhenney continues, "Now, let me caution both of you. This does not stop the investigation. Future charges could still occur based on the investigation."

Laura Lynne says, "Understood. I say we move forward. Scarlet?"

"Agreed," Scarlet responds.

"Great, I will get this done today. Should know something by the end of the day tomorrow. I have already put our name in for the docket. We will appear before Judge Watson," says McElhanney.

"Wait, what about Judge Monroe?" asks Laura Lynne.

"No, this does not fall in his circuit. Besides, I think we could argue prejudice if we ever did end up with him presiding. I have been working on that angle since I learned of the grievances between the two families. But, for now, we can keep that in our back pocket," reassures McElhanney.

"Wonderful. Anything else we should know?" asks Laura Lynne.

McElhanney hesitates and then dives in, "Well, I was not planning to mention this, but since I have both of you on the phone, Laura Lynne, the run-in you had with Natalie. Gabe and I discussed a way to potentially shut her down. Or at least scare her enough to stop her continued discussion of you and your family to the press."

"I am all ears," says Laura Lynne.

"The footage of your exchange is all over social media. I think we can figure out who was in the room and then file charges. Maybe not slander, but more perhaps false imprisonment." Laura Lynne starts to speak, but McElhanney cuts her off, "Before you say anything I know the term sounds like kidnapping. But it can also be used in this situation if we approach it as an intentional torte claim. Thoughts?"

"I don't know what that even means," replies Laura Lynne.

McElhenney explains, "It's a personal injury claim. Basically, it is when someone intentionally meant to harm another individual. In this case, we would claim Natalie set out to intentionally cause harm to Laura Lynne specifically, but also the Beauregard name."

Laura Lynne sighs and says, "What do you think, Scarlet?"

"I don't think we have a choice. Laura Lynne, if we don't hit this head on, it could get much worse. And Ernest is right. We need to try to shut this down. If it only impacted you, I might feel differently. But Natalie has been a problem for me and Momma for 20 years," Scarlet says.

Laura Lynne concedes, "Okay. I am fine then. Whatever we think is best for the family and the situation."

"Great. I have already drawn up the letter. Scarlet, do you think you can put names to the women in the video?" McElhanney asks.

The three finish the call. Laura Lynne feels light and carefree as if a weight has been lifted. Dead Doe is still an issue, but her uncle being removed from the crosshairs feels like progress. Laura Lynne texts Gray and then Avery the news. Laura Lynne tells Mary the good news before grabbing her lunch and tea. "I am going to take a break out at the picnic tables. Little celebration." Mary nods and pulls out her ruler. When Laura Lynne said timeline, Mary took her literally. Once a schoolteacher, always a schoolteacher.

The rest of the afternoon passes quickly. Laura Lynne scrolls through 1983 and 1984. She locates two more girls. This is no mere coincidence. She ditches her efforts to locate Dead Doe and devotes all her attention to searching exclusively for abducted girls. She rapidly scrolls through 1985, 1986, and 1987. One more girl fits the pattern. There are few identifiers. A teenaged girl is really all the article said. Each article has a different reporter assigned. There is one in Venice, one in Wisteria, and one in the neighboring town of Castille. Laura Lynne then checks the dates of the abductions, the day of the week, and the season. There is no pattern she can identify. Stymied, she picks up her notes and shows Mary.

Mary takes one look at the information and says, "You have to call Grady and tell him what you found."

Laura Lynne nods in agreement. "I think instead of calling him, I need to go and see him. I want to sleep on it. Let the information settle." Laura Lynne looks at the timeline Mary is working on. "No girls found after 1986? You didn't see any when you scanned those years?

"No, but maybe we need to check out the Wisteria and Castille newspapers." She looks at the information Laura Lynne has in her notes. "These reporters were probably string reporters or worked for those newspapers. Might be worth a try."

"Can you reach out and see if we can get the microfiche? If they can pull it out of storage, I can run and pick it up."

"You okay if I share this information with Ronnie? He has more contacts than I do. He might be able to probe around without stirring up too many questions. Maybe hint at a book he is working on. It would at least be more credible."

Laura Lynne shakes her head. "I think we keep this between you and me for now. The fewer people involved, the better. If you don't have any luck, then we can pull your Ronnie in." She looks her in the eyes. "I don't know what we have here or even if we have anything. The less we divulge for now, I think, the better."

Mary nods. "Okay, but you can trust Ronnie. He can keep a confidence."

"I don't doubt that. I just need to digest this a bit more. Honestly, it feels a bit overwhelming. I mean, it's not like I am a trained investigator. If the deputies didn't see it all those years ago, it's probably nothing."

Mary snorts. "You are kidding, right? Before this young whipper snapper, what's his name? The new sheriff? Anyway, doesn't matter. Before he came on to the scene, Bubba Westerman was the sheriff for decades. It's no secret he was well-paid to let certain matters slide. Could be this was one of them." She returns to her timeline. "Or, more than likely, he was just too lazy or ignorant to put the pieces together."

Everything in Laura Lynne sets off an alarm bell at Mary's words. Laura Lynne remembers Bubba's threats at the gala. "Let sleeping dogs lie." What if this is the sleeping dog? What if Bubba Westerman was a part of things, and he knew all along?

"Laura Lynne? You okay? You sorta zoned out there for a moment." Mary asks, concern lacing her words.

"What? Oh, I'm fine. It's just getting late. Time to wrap it up for the day and head home. Thank you for all your help today."

She wants to call Gray and talk to him about what she has found. And tell him about the Bubba incident. She should have told him in the first place. She kicks herself for falling into old habits. She knows Gray is not Jimmy. He would never treat her like a child, as if she is unable to think for herself. That was Jimmy's way, not Gray's. She owed him an apology and she needs someone who knows her story to help her plan. Before she talks to Grady, she wants her husband's full support. This could have a large impact on the entire family. The decision is not one to take lightly.

Laura Lynne decides to go to the family cemetery before heading back to The Residence. It is quiet there—a safe place to talk. She drives through the Magnolia Café on her way out of town. She thought maybe a hot tea would settle her nerves. She parks in front of the chapel and calls Gray. He picks up on the first ring.

"Hey baby, was getting worried. You doing good?"

"Yes, surprisingly good. Be much better when Uncle Gabe has the charges dropped, and The

Residence is no longer collateral. But I do feel like a burden has been lifted." Taking a deep breath and getting out of the car into the fresh air, Laura Lynne continues, "But God has placed another burden on my shoulders."

"He has a way of doing that. What's got you bothered?"

Laura Lynne hears rustling in the background. "If now is not good, we can talk later."

"No, it's good. Just sitting at a bar with the guys. We won't be heading out to dinner for another hour. Just walking outside where its quiet." Laura Lynne hears him walking through the lobby and out the sliding front doors. He greets everyone as he walks out. "Okay, I am out front on a bench, and there's nobody around. What's going on?"

Taking a deep breath, Laura Lynne blurts out a summary of all the things she's thinking, "Okay, well, you know those girls I was telling you about. The ones from the newspaper articles where they were abducted for a day or two and then found with no recollection of events but obviously abused in some way?" He mutters an agreement. "Well, I have now found a total of six girls over a seven-year period. All young teenagers." He is silent. "Gray, I think maybe the same thing that happened to me happened to these girls."

"And why do you think this?"

"It is nothing more than a hunch. It just seems too coincidental. All the same age as me and with no memory of anything. I am taking a leap here because I don't have solid proof, but I am guessing they were all sexually assaulted." Laura Lynne begins pacing. Laura Lynne begins pacing. "I thought maybe I could talk to one of the girl's parents. They still live here. See what they might know. But if I do that, I could just cause more pain." Laura Lynne takes a deep breath. "I don't want to stir up the past on a hunch." Laura Lynne is pacing faster now. "Maybe I could talk to Dr. Goldbug, though I am not sure he is alive." She makes it to the gravestones and then turns back around, pacing. "Here's the thing. I want to tell Grady my story."

Gray is quiet for a moment. "It's your story to tell, Laura Lynne." Then he continues, "But what is on my heart is also telling your children." He is quiet for a moment. "I think it's time."

"I don't want them to know, Gray."

"It is not fair to them, honey, and besides, it may be that you have no choice."

"I don't want to talk about them yet. I need to know what you think about Grady." Laura Lynne's voice tells Gray to back off. This is not territory she is willing to cover yet.

"I have no issues with you telling your story. It's yours to share or not. The trauma you had as a child is what made you the woman I love." He barrels on, "But I also think Savannah and Beau deserve the truth from you. Maybe not right this second. But if you are planning to share this with Grady, there is a chance it will leak. It would be awful if they read this story in the news or on some blog, or worse over a television broadcast." Laura Lynne is silent. She stops walking. "They are old enough to understand. And, baby, times are different than they were when we were kids. Shame and blame are not for the victim." Laura Lynne swallows. The fear clutches at her throat.

"This conversation is making me not want to talk to Grady."

"I know it does, but you are braver than that." His tone goes from serious to soft and practical. "You are right though. Let's not worry about the kids today. Talk to Grady, see if he uncovers anything first or if he thinks that it's just a coincidence of some sort." Laura Lynne hears him pacing as well. "It would probably be smarter to meet him outside of the sheriff's office. Probably some pretty big ears there."

He is right. Venice is a small town. Lots of ears to hear things. Grady said the same thing that very morning. "Good idea, okay. So, no qualms about me talking to Grady? You think it's the right thing?"

"I absolutely do. Worse if you said nothing and it turned out to be something. I know you well enough to know you couldn't live with yourself. It would eat you up inside." He's right; he knows her very well.

"I love you." Laura Lynne takes a deep breath, then barrels on. "Gray, I am so sorry." He is quiet. "I want to tell you what happened on the terrace, but I also want you to not be angry." Silence greets her request. "So, here it goes. I was threatened to keep my mouth shut and not stir up old memories by a man who used to be sheriff here. His name is Bubba Westerman."

With deadly calm, Gray replies, "And how did he threaten you?"

She hesitates, "This is what I didn't want to tell you." She takes a moment then honors her commitment to herself and her husband by being truthful. "He twisted my arm behind my back, hard. Then he leaned up against me, pressing me into the porch column." She quickly continues, "But he didn't hurt me so much as threaten me. At the time I wasn't sure what he meant by "letting sleeping dogs lie," but I think he meant my story from that summer."

Gray is quiet. The silence is deafening. Laura Lynne knows her husband well enough to realize he is processing what he told her and he is not pleased. "This man, this Bubba guy, lays hands on you, threatens the woman I love, the one I would protect at all costs, and you don't tell me? How do you think that makes me feel, Laura Lynne?"

"Horrible. I know. I was wrong, I just didn't want to ruin the night. And I *do* know you would protect me at all costs and that scared me, too. I didn't want you to defend me, I wanted to defend myself."

He lets out a long sigh. "Laura Lynne, when are you going to learn it's not you *or* me? It's you *and* me.

Together, baby. Whatever dragon there is to slay, whatever nasty Bubba Westerman doles out we face it *together*."

Laura Lynne replies, "I know you are right. Absolutely. I messed up. But I promise I have learned my lesson. I won't hide anything from you again. I swear."

Gray lets out a harsh laugh, "Now that's a damn lie. You try to protect me as much as I do you." His voice is back to even tones, much to Laura Lynne's relief. "But I know you will try. How concerned should I be about this sheriff?"

"I honestly don't know. I got the sense it was all threats. He would be a fool to come after me or my family. I think I need to tell Uncle Gabe, but otherwise I say we keep it close to our vest. I honestly don't know."

He is quiet while he contemplates, "I am going to talk to your uncle. Then, I think you need to consider telling Grady. And I think I need to be there. I don't like this one bit."

"Gray. Please. Let me do this one thing. I need to prove to myself I am not a scared teenager anymore." She rushes on. "I promise, it has nothing to do with me trusting you. I want to do this for myself, by myself. Please."

He is silent so long Laura Lynne wonders if he is still on the phone. Finally, he gives a deep sigh, "Okay. I am trusting you to keep your sweet butt safe, Laura Lynne. If anything were to happen to you I would never forgive myself."

"I know. Thank you. I love you, Gray."

He laughs. "You damn well better! I love you too. And more than that." He makes Laura Lynne laugh. "Proud of you, baby. Keep me posted. And I mean that. I want to know what is going on. No more secrets."

"No more secrets."

The two hang up, and Laura Lynne sits on the bench. Laura Lynne texts Grace and asks her to have Grady call her on her personal phone. No questions. The phone rings within moments.

"Hey, Laura Lynne, what's up?" Grady answers.

"Sorry to call you on your personal phone, but I hoped you and I could meet somewhere fairly private and talk." Laura Lynne takes a deep breath. "I have some things to say to you that are personal and may sound crazy. I prefer not to do that at the sheriff's department." He is quiet for a moment, thinking.

"What about my Momma and Daddy's? We could meet there, take a walk around Cotton Mill, and you could tell me what's on your mind. Does that sound good?" Laura Lynne agrees. "What time works for you? Either early or late for me. I could meet you around 8 AM before my shift starts. If that is too early, then maybe tomorrow evening, around 7 PM? I would do earlier, but Josie has a softball game after school."

"No, no, 8 AM sounds good." Laura Lynne hesitates. "Grady, thanks for this. And for not asking a bunch of questions."

"Laura Lynne, Grace would skin my hide if I was anything but kind to her oldest friend! I have some information for you as well. Information best not shared over the phone. This works for me too."

"Thanks anyway. I will see you then." They hang up, and Laura Lynne heads back to her car. The sun is beginning to set.

Chapter 22

Sleep is fleeting again. Laura Lynne is anxious to meet Grady and talk to him. Laura Lynne rises early and makes tea and a pot of coffee. She scrounges around in the refrigerator and spots half of an avocado. Taking her avocado toast and tea to the front porch, Laura Lynne watches the day begin.

Her phone pings. It is a text from Savannah— a bump picture. Today, she is six months along. Laura Lynne sends back a picture of her avocado toast and tea mug using the gardens of Tea Olive as a backdrop.

Savannah quickly replies, "OMG! Is that Tea Olive? When do I get to come for a visit?"

Laura Lynne smiles and texts back, "Soon. Got to do a few things but will call later today to make a plan." Savannah attaches a heart emoji.

Gabe comes out to the front porch. He has his overalls on and is carrying a cup of coffee. "Care if I join you?" Laura Lynne shakes her head, her mouth full of toast. "Thanks for the coffee." She swallows.

"My pleasure. Thought today you deserved a cup. What time is the hearing? I will join you."

"This McElhanney fellow is supposed to call sometime this morning with an update. Once I know, you will know. But honestly, you don't have to come."

"No, I will be there. Scarlet too." He starts to object. Laura Lynne holds up her hand and shakes her head. "No need to argue. We are going to be there. *But* no matter how Momma insists, I will keep her out of the courtroom." Laura Lynne holds out her hand for a shake. "Deal?" He clasps her hand.

"That is a deal…and fair."

Laura Lynne hears Victoria coming in the back door. She gets up from her seat and picks up her dishes. "I am going over to Grace's parents this morning for a visit. Then, heading into town. I will probably be at the Gazette or the café, but either way, I will be near the courthouse. Have McElhenney call with the details." Laura Lynne kisses the top of Uncle Gabe's head on the way inside. She moves quickly so he doesn't ask her about the Cunningham visit.

At 7:30, Laura Lynne loads the car for the day. She honks the horn at John and Liam on my way down the drive and arrives at Cotton Mill in less than 10 minutes. Laura Lynne smiles as she drives by the acres of cotton fields with their green shoots beginning to sprout. Every spare inch of land is seeded except the acre surrounding the house. Laura Lynne feels a catch in her throat as the house comes into view. Her throat clogs with the memories of the wonderful times she and Grace spent together.

Laura Lynne determinedly pulls around to the back and there is Grady, leaning against his sheriff's vehicle. "Hey, Grady, thanks for meeting me. Where's your deputy suit?" Laura Lynne walks to the trunk and pulls out her mud boots. She slides her sandaled foot into the boot.

"Since this is not official, I thought we would both be more comfortable if I opted for jeans." The screen door opens, and there stands Mrs. Cunningham.

"I know you are not here to see me, but I wanted to say welcome. Glad you made it around. You need anything? I have coffee, tea, water, juice?" Laura Lynne looks at Grady. He has a coffee mug in hand.

"Hot tea would be lovely."

"Coming right up!"

She watches her disappear inside the house and says to Grady, "I love your momma."

He smiles as he watches her bustle out with a mug in hand, tea bag already steeping. "Me too."

"Thank you, Mrs. Cunningham." Laura Lynne smiles as she leans over and kisses her cheek. She gets a whiff of the tea and it is Earl Grey. Surprised, Laura Lynne asks, "How did you know Earl Grey is my favorite?"

She giggles and winks. "I have my sources." Laura Lynne looks at Grady.

"Don't look at me! Momma has people all over town give her information about everything. I could never get away with anything as a kid. It's why I went into law enforcement. Seems like the best option to keep Momma out of my business."

"Humph. I still keep my ear to the ground about you and your offspring! Never too old for mothering!" And she turns around and heads back into the house. Gray takes Laura Lynne's arm and steers her around the cars.

"Let's walk toward the creek. It's nice out there. You can talk as we go. I want to hear what you have to say before I tell you what I learned."

Laura Lynne tells him about the additional abductions she and Mary found. He nods his head, contemplating. Then she takes a big breath. "The reason this is of interest to me is because I cannot shake the feeling this is what happened to me. Or at least something similar that summer in 1985." She stops and looks at him. He does not look surprised. "You're not surprised?"

"No. I figured maybe the two were connected."

"Well, there is more to the story. And it's very private. Only a handful of people know what actually happened to me that summer, and two of them are dead. Some of my conclusions are based on supposition, but it all just makes sense to me." Laura Lynne tells Grady about Dr. Kenneth Butler, the babysitting, the STIs she contracted, the lack of memory, the realization in college that she was probably drugged, everything. She stops talking and looks at him. "Am I crazy?"

"If I had not looked at the files of the two names you gave me yesterday, I would have said it was a far stretch. But after all you told me, I think it's at least possible." She stops and leans against the fence post. She is more than a little stunned. By the time she finally fell asleep last night, she had convinced herself she was making things up.

"Why is that? What did you learn?"

"Both of the girls contracted gonorrhea, chlamydia, and HPV. They were both sexually abused and had no recollection of the events." He takes a sip of coffee. "There were lab results from Dr. Goldburg in the charts."

"Dr. Goldburg saw these girls? Both of them?" He nods. "When I was talking with Gray about this last night, I mentioned he might be someone to follow up with. Is he even alive?"

"Yes, he's alive. Pushing 90 by now. I think he and my parents were at Moseley around the same time, which means he was also with your parents." He sips his coffee thoughtfully. "Before we start asking any more questions, let me see if I can find out about these additional cases you located. Let me run this through our database too. Maybe see if I can get a hit. We may find more of a similar nature." He looks at Laura Lynne over the rim of his coffee cup and takes another sip. "What do you know about Dr. Kenneth Butler?"

Laura Lynne looks into her now cold mug of tea and then shifts her gaze out over the field. "Not much. He married sometime after I left in 1985, that Christmas. He moved shortly after that and lives in Boston. He works in the pathology lab." Laura Lynne turns her gaze to him. "He's still married and has one adopted daughter. She is married with children of her own. There are no pending articles against his medical license. I have no idea about litigation, but nothing I could find by simple Google searches." She turns her gaze back to the fields and sips her tepid tea. "I never wanted him to know I was looking. In truth, I have no evidence. I only have conjecture."

He nods. "There is a lot of that, but I am not one for coincidences. I am curious, though, if all these girls were contracting STDs, why didn't Dr. Butler get treated?"

"Could be he didn't know he had it. Not everyone has symptoms." She clears her throat. "I was checked because I did have symptoms."

Grady nods. "What are your plans for today?"

"I am meeting Grace for coffee this morning. At some point today, Uncle Gabe is supposed to go before the judge and get the charges dismissed. I want to be in the courtroom when that happens. Scarlet plans to attend as well. Other than that, I will be at the Gazette with Mary looking through files. I still have Queenie's letters to review. She wrote me all the time I was away, well, at least, until she couldn't anymore. They are like a time capsule of information about the town and the people in it." She pushes herself off the fence post, and the two start walking again. "Oh, and I have Mary creating a timeline, just a way to see what we have as a whole. I thought it could help me keep my facts straight. As part of the timeline, we planned to look at festivals, conferences, or fairs that might happen each year at the same time during our timeframe."

"That's probably a shot in the dark. At this point, we are not certain how many abductions may have occurred."

"I'm sure you're right. I have no idea what I am doing; just trying to do something." Laura Lynne fiddles with the tea bag string. "After all these years, I almost feel like maybe I could know the truth. Really know what happened to me, by whom, and why? I mean, why me? Why these girls? What did we have in common, if anything." Laura Lynne pauses to look once more over the fields of cotton. "If you think about it too much, it will make you crazy."

Grady pats her back softly as they meander back to the house. "Laura Lynne, why now? What made you decide to come forward? To tell me?"

Laura Lynne sighs. "Feels like the right time. My kids are grown, and I have nothing to fear anymore. And I am done protecting and hiding my truth. Momma can't hurt me again. If there are others, then I am not alone. It's a sisterhood of sorts. A horrible sorority, for certain, but it makes me feel more secure." She looks over at him. "And then there's Gray. He is my rock. He loves me. He knows all about me, and still, he loves me. He is not going to stop simply because this comes out into the open. It's a nice feeling, unconditional love." She turns toward him. "It's not something I have had much of through the years. Makes me safe and secure, strong."

"May I ask who knows everything you have told me? Does Miss Melanie know?"

"Momma? No, I couldn't tell her. Not sure she would believe me. Besides, she would feel terrible guilt. No need for that when I am not certain. Aunt Eileen, Daddy, Gray, and now you. That's it.

"I will do my best to keep this confidential. But Laura Lynne, there is a possibility others will find out."

"Yes, I know. Gray and I discussed the same last night. We agreed I needed to do this thing. I will tell my children. I will call them today and arrange a time to meet with them. I don't want to do this over the phone." Grady and Laura Lynne start heading back toward the house.

They walk the rest of the way in silence. Both thinking about the next steps. Then, Grady lets out a long sigh and stops walking. He grabs Laura Lynne's hand and stops her forward motion. "Laura Lynne, if this proves to be true, it's going to shake the foundations of this town. Not to mention Wisteria and Castille." He takes a deep breath, "The ramifications are huge."

"I know. I know. What do you think has been churning in my head for the past two weeks? That first article on the missing girl just turned my world upside down. The similarities with me, then another girl and another. If what I am thinking is true, it breaks my heart."

"Say it. What are you thinking?"

"Dr. Kenneth Butler is a pedophile. A serial rapist of children: number unknown. I am one of his victims."

Grady nods in affirmation. "I am thinking the exact same thing. God, I hope we are wrong."

Laura Lynne looks at him. "I don't. I hope we nail the bastard."

They arrive at the cars. Laura Lynne pulls off her work boots. Gray opens her car door so she can slide in. "Tell your momma I will be by for a real visit soon." She turns toward the wheel. "Thank you again, Grady."

"No, thank you. You are one of the bravest people I know. What you have gone through…I just can't even imagine. That you trusted me enough to tell me is humbling."

"I am not worried." She gives him a cheeky grin. "I know your sister. She will skin you alive if you break that trust."

"Truer words!" Grady chuckles and slams the door. Laura Lynne rolls down her window, and Grady continues, "Keep me posted. Use my personal phone for now. Nothing in writing via email or text. If we need to talk, I will come to the Gazette."

"Got it!" She waves and puts the car in reverse, makes a Y-turn, and heads down the driveway. She looks in the rearview mirror and sees Grady standing in the driveway. He has a mug in both hands and watches as she drives away. Laura Lynne honks her horn twice and waves out the window. Grady nods his head, lifts his mug, and walks toward the screen porch.

Heading toward town, Laura Lynne allows the wind to blow through her hair. The tears roll down her cheeks in relief and fear. It is time to tell her children. They need to understand Laura Lynne's love/hate relationship with Tea Olive—the place of her best and worst memories. Laura Lynne pulls into her parking place at the Gazette and wipes her eyes. Squaring her shoulders, she takes a deep breath. It is time to get to work.

Mary is not at the counter. Laura Lynne glances around the Gazette offices and notices the door to the upstairs offices is propped open. She calls up the stairs. "Mary? Are you up there?"

"Yes! I will be down shortly."

Laura Lynne heads to her office and fires up her laptop. Checking her emails, she sees several from Ashley and one from Scarlet. She opens the one from Scarlet. It's the pictures from the country club formal with names listed under each of the photos. She has also added tidbits about people she knew more about. This is great. Laura Lynne sends her a reply email thanking her for the assistance. She gets an immediate reply back, asking if there is more she could do. Laura Lynne looks at the box with the letters from Queenie. Laura Lynne replies,

"Interested in going through Queenie's letters? See if there is anything that stands out? I can bring them to the courthouse." She gets a smiley face emoji as a response.

Laura Lynne hears Mary coming down the stairs as she heads out to meet Grace for coffee. "I am going to meet Grace for coffee. All good?"

"Yes." Mary scurries back to her perch behind the counter. Today, she is in a tie-die dress and cardigan. "This is for spirit week. Every year, the kids do a 60s theme day. This is my contribution to Make Love, Not War." She smiles. "Before I forget. I was able to talk to the Wisteria and Castille newspapers. They are pulling their microfiche for us. It can be picked up tomorrow afternoon."

"Wonderful. Oh, and before I forget to tell you, I spoke to Grady about the abducted girls." Mary perks up as Laura Lynne continues, "Off the record. He is going to do a little gentle probing. Pull the files and see what he sees. Which reminds me." Laura Lynne snaps her fingers. "I was going to print off the articles from my files so I can get them to him. Can you help me remember to do that when I get back?"

Mary is busily writing on her ever-present sticky notepad. She pulls it off, goes to Laura Lynne's office door, and sticks it on there. Laura Lynne laughs on her way out the door.

The walk to Magnolia Café is lovely. It's still early enough that the humidity has not fully set in. Traffic is light. The sun is shining in a cloudless blue sky.

The atmosphere seems to reflect Laura Lynne's good mood. She rounds the corner to the café and sees Grace walking from the other direction. She is dressed in a summer skirt and white top. Her hair pulled back in a low ponytail. She has on sandals and pearls to finish the look. "Hey, beautiful!" Laura Lynne calls out, "You look like a teenager. I love your outfit!" Grace does a little twirl and then gives Laura Lynne a hug.

"Have you recovered from Saturday night? No more mean girl antics?"

"Not a peep. It might be because Uncle Gabe's defense lawyer sent all the mean girls an even meaner letter."

"Really?" Well, isn't that just special?" The two link arms and head inside to the counter. "Charlie had a talk with Brad concerning his wife's antics, and I personally spoke with the Notorious Natalie." The way she said that made Laura Lynne think sharp instruments and threats may have been involved.

"Let's order. I can't wait to hear more."

To Laura Lynne's disappointment, there is no Amanda today. Maude takes their order. "Y'all be careful. They're awfully hot." The ladies smile as they walk away.

Laura Lynne starts, "Okay, what have you been up to?"

"Charlie and I spent Sunday talking through the events of Saturday night. Unfortunately, it's not the first time we have had guests of members behave in ways that spoil the atmosphere for the members." Grace blows on her coffee. "There have been complaints made to the board regarding golfers, pool guests, and now at the annual formal. We called an emergency meeting and decided to enact as a temporary measure to suspend guests of members for the time being. This includes meetings, dinner, golf, bridge club. The list goes on and on." Grace sips coffee. "Then, last evening, Charlie and I went to Natalie's to explain the consequences of her behaviors for her and her friends."

"Isn't that going to hurt the club financially?"

Grace shakes her head. "We don't think so. The club members have been staying away more and more because the non-members are taking over all the tee times and seating in the dining room. Besides, it's just a moratorium of sorts. It won't be forever. We need to enact some bylaws regarding guest relations."

"So, how did Mean Girl Natalie take it?"

"On the chin. Got to give her props. She took her lumps. I don't think she would be half bad if she wasn't trying so hard." Laura Lynne nods and tells her Gray's observation regarding Venice's caste system. "He's right, but it doesn't discount the bad behavior."

"Just so you are not doing this on my account." Laura Lynne blows on her tea before taking a sip.

"As little as I am here, Natalie has no bearing on my life."

"Well, when you are here, I want it to be comfortable for you to come to the club!

And for all the paying guests." She blows the hair out of her eyes. "We are a boorish, entitled lot, and we want to keep it that way." Laura Lynne laughs at the truth of those words.

"Oh, big news I wanted to share with you. Talking about Natalie made me remember. I went to see Momma yesterday, and it wasn't terrible." Laura Lynne recounts the hour she spent with Melanie. "Were you aware of the sorority inconsistency?"

"No. I wasn't on the board then, though. Momma and Daddy were still filling our spots. I could ask."

"What I found intriguing was Momma's comment about Maureen Monroe being upset with the verdict. The way Momma was acting, I think she felt it was way out of line for the situation. Made me wonder what connection Natalie may have with Maureen."

Laura Lynne's phone buzzes. It's a text from Scarlet. "Courthouse at 1:00 PM." Laura Lynne looks back at Grace and says, "It looks like we might have some good news for Uncle Gabe today. We have a hearing to dismiss the charges for lack of evidence this afternoon. I hope it works."

"You need a friend? Happy to come sit with you and show support."

"Thanks, Grace. I mean it. I have missed having you as a friend. Scarlet and I will be there. That is enough. Uncle Gabe didn't even want us there. I compromised by telling him I wouldn't bring Momma if we could go. He latched on to that like a drowning man to a life raft." Laura Lynne pushes back her chair and moves to stand up. Grace does the same while gathering her purse.

"Listen, before I go. Rachele wanted to remind you of the school play. She will have a ticket for you at will call on opening night. She hopes you can make it and see Samantha. Sounds like Samantha was quite taken by you."

"Wonderful! I will do my best to be there." The friends hug. "I enjoyed our hen party. Next time, we need to invite Rachele to join us." Grace goes out the way she came in, but Laura Lynne decides to visit the bookstore before heading back to her microfiche. Diane is in the back, ringing up a customer. Laura Lynne calls out, "Missed Mandy this morning at the coffee shop."

Diane glances over. "Laura Lynne, good to see you!" She nods at her customer. "I think maybe y'all know each other, but let me re-introduce you. Laura Lynne, this is Candace Westerman. Candace, Laura Lynne Atkins."

"Bubba Westerman's daughter? Sure Candy!" says Laura Lynne. "It's been ages, but I remember you trailing around behind your big sister when we were younger. How is Honey?" Candy looks just like her name, sweet. Interesting, since she was a menace in high school. Serious mean girl issues.

"That's me," Candace replies. She takes her bag from Diane. "Honey is good. Loves being a grandma." She looks at Laura Lynne with a sparkle in her eye. "In fact, you could say hello to her yourself Wednesday night at book club. Why don't you join us? It would be great to have you there. We are doing your book next month, and you can give us a preview. Maybe sign some copies."

Diane adds her push. "What a great idea! We meet here, well, at the café at 8 PM. It's a bit late, but we wait until everything closes. We serve charcuterie, bread, wine, coffee, and discuss the book."

"I may not have read the book. What is it?" Laura Lynne says as she feels like she has been set up. She wonders how long they have been planning this ambush.

"We are reading, or re-reading, *To Kill a Mockingbird*. We like the Southern classics." Candy replies and winks at Diane. Yes, it's official. Laura Lynne has been set up. "Can you make it? The women would love it, and so would we."

"You two are not at all subtle! How long have you been planning to ask me?" They both laugh. "All right, all right, ya'll have convinced me, but it's been years since I read Harper Lee. Don't expect any grand contributions to the book discussion."

Candy and Diane are grinning from ear to ear. "Great! See you then!" Candy says as she heads out the front door. She is already on her phone texting.

Laura Lynne looks at Diane. "You two do this often? Ambush the clientele?"

Diane smirks. "I was going to ask you for a book signing, but this seemed more appropriate." She walks from behind the register and leans her back against the counter. "If you don't want to come, I completely understand. I can tell them you are tied up with Mr. Gabe."

"No, no, I said I would be here, so I will. Besides, it will be good to see Honey. We were not close friends, but everyone knew Honey. Her daddy being the sheriff for so long, she was a good friend to have." Laura Lynne starts to wander over to the books. There is something special about new books. "Where is Mandy today?"

"Oh, she is a part of the play this week. She is in charge of the set designs, so the crush is on for opening night. Haven't seen her all weekend! Be glad when this one is over. You should come. It's *Beauty and the Beast*.

"Rachele got me a ticket for opening night. My plan is to attend, but we will see how the week unfolds." Laura Lynne shuts the book she is scanning. "I really need to go. I just didn't want to get back to reality quite yet. A bookstore is a nice place to hide."

Diane smiles and starts back to the register as the door jingles. "Hang around as long as you like." Laura Lynne wanders through the stacks of books. She is humbled that her book is on one of the shelves. Really a dream come true. Laura Lynne waves goodbye to Diane and opens the front door to come face-to-face with Natalie. Natalie is as shocked to see Laura Lynne as Laura Lynne is to see her. She recovers quickly, pastes on a smile.

"Mrs. Atkins, it's good to see you. I was hoping to catch up with you sometime to apologize for my behavior the other night. Things got out of hand. I think I had too much to drink! No excuses, mind you! But my lips are just looser after a few glasses of wine." She is starting to fluster as Laura Lynne stares at her. She clears her throat, looking over Laura Lynne's shoulder. "No hard feelings, I hope?"

Remembering what Gray told her and feeling guilty about being involved in her ostracization from the club, Laura Lynne smiles warmly and takes her hand. "It's Laura Lynne, please. And certainly, no hard feelings on my end." Laura Lynne steps to the side, attempting to get around her. Natalie doesn't let her.

"Really? You're not mad?" Natalie asks suspiciously.

"No, I am not. Listen, Natalie, I understand what it is to be on the outside looking in and wanting what someone else has so badly you would do about anything to get it." Laura Lynne looks at Natalie.

"You will catch more flies with honey than vinegar. You might try being kind. Mean is not working for you."

"You sound like Brad. That letter your attorney sent to me and the others made everyone take notice."

"I'm glad. Just because I am not mad does not mean I approve of your behavior. And the Beauregards will do whatever is necessary to protect their legacy. You knew that going in."

"I did. I guess I thought you would be the weak link. You aren't, though. In fact, I think you were right. You do have double the steel in your backbone."

"Thank you. I take that as a compliment." Before turning to leave, Laura Lynne extends one more piece of advice. "Your Brad sounds like a smart guy. You might try listening to him. And stop listening to Maureen Monroe."

And that is when Laura Lynne sees she is right to assume there is a connection between the two. Natalie cannot hide her surprise at Laura Lynne's comment. She tries to cover her slip. "I'm sure I don't know what you mean."

"And I'm sure you do." Laura Lynne starts down the sidewalk. Damn! She hates when her own words come back to haunt her. She needs to catch this fly, not piss it off. "Hey, Natalie. I am coming to book club here on Wednesday. Why don't you join me? It's *To Kill a Mockingbird*." Natalie stares blankly at Laura Lynne, surprised at the invitation. "Well, think about it. 8 o'clock."

Laura Lynne has done her good deed for the day. Gray will be proud of her. She hopes he is right and didn't just invite a wolf into a flock of sheep. Laura Lynne decides not to worry about it. She probably won't even show up.

At 1:00 on the dot, Scarlet and Laura Lynne are sitting behind their Uncle Gabe at the defendant's table. Chandler Monroe is at the prosecutor's table. Judge Abernathy comes through the doors and everyone stands. He sits, and everyone follows suit except Gerald McElhanney, Gabe's attorney. McElhanney requests a dismissal of all charges against Gabriel Cooper. To Scarlet and Laura Lynne's surprise, the DA sitting next to Chandler agrees there is not enough evidence to hold him. Then, the judge dismisses the case. It is over in 15 minutes. Laura Lynne looks at Scarlet and asks, "That's it?" Scarlet is smiling. Uncle Gabe is shaking Gerald's hand. Laura Lynne leans over the bench and hugs Gabe before shaking Gerald's hand. It's over. At least for now.

Mr. McElhanney excuses himself, walks over to Chandler Monroe, and shakes his hand. He returns and tells the family he will call later. The bond is revoked, and McElhanney will handle the details. He has to run to his next appearance.

Mr. Monroe walks slowly over to Gabe and holds out his hand. "Mr. Cooper, glad this all worked out for you. Please know it wasn't personal."

Gabe shakes his hand and says, "We both know better than that, son. Tell your daddy I asked after him. Him and your momma. Hope they are doing well." Chandler nods and heads out of the courthouse.

"Well! That's over! At least for now." Laura Lynne says and looks at Scarlet and Uncle Gabe. "Can I interest you both in a celebratory ice cream? I know this place over on Canal Street."

"You two girls go ahead. = John is waiting for me in the parking lot. I just want to go home, put all this behind me." He gives them a hug. "My flowers are calling me." He shuffles down the center aisle. He looks tired today.

As he walks away, Scarlet leans over to Laura Lynne. "I don't know. I think this has been harder on him than he is letting on. He is so old. Not sure how long he is going to be with us. Momma too." She links arms with her sister. "I will go by the assisted living place and tell Momma *after* we have our ice cream. Your treat."

"Absolutely!" The two sisters chat as they make their way over the streets. Both are happy to be thinking about something other than their uncle's arrest. "Oh, we need to let the family know!" Laura Lynne pulls out her phone and sends a group text informing everyone of the dismissal. Lots of fun emojis come across the screen. Laura Lynne shares her screen with Scarlet. Laughing and smiling, Laura Lynne realizes this is the best walk she has ever had with Scarlet.

There is a line at the shop that gives the women a chance to peruse the selection. They both decide on the lemon lavender sorbet. Scarlet chooses an outdoor table near the canal. "Okay, Laura Lynne, tell me what you expect me to do with Queenie's letters. What am I looking for?"

"Oh shoot! I left them at the Gazette! I got a little behind in my schedule today." She told her about book club and her run in with Natalie. "Why don't you join us?"

"No, not for me. You are the reader in the family." That is not true. Scarlet loved literature. She graduated from Ole Miss with a BA in Literature and a minor in Art History.

"Scarlet, what has happened? Why are you hiding at your house?" Laura Lynne takes a scoop of sorbet. It's delicious. Laura Lynne immediately realizes she asked the wrong question. Scarlet's entire demeanor changes. She is suddenly cold and defensive.

"I am not hiding. I simply am not interested in joining a silly club full of gossipy women."

"I'm sorry! I asked the wrong question. I didn't mean to upset you." Laura Lynne looks closely at her. She is visibly shaking. "Scarlet, you are shaking! I didn't mean anything by it. I was just surprised! It's all good." Laura Lynne starts to plead. "We were having such a good time. I don't want to ruin it. What can I do to fix it?"

Staring into the water of the canal, Scarlet quietly answers, "You can't fix me, Laura Lynne." She brings herself back to the present moment and eats a scoop of ice cream. "Silly, it's not you, it's me. You just touched a nerve, that's all." She changes the subject. "Now, tell me about Queenie's letters."

Willing to change the subject, Laura Lynne barrels on. "Well, I am not sure exactly what I am looking for. Anything that might relate to Dead Doe." Then Laura Lynne decides to confide in Scarlet, at least a little. "And if there is any reference to missing or abducted girls that were later found." This catches her attention.

"What are you talking about? What abducted girls? Here, in Venice?" Laura Lynne nods. She tells her about the articles she found in newspaper archives. "And why is this important? What does it have to do with Dead Doe? I don't see the correlation."

"There isn't one. It's personal."

Scarlet looks at Laura Lynne. She reaches across the table and places her hand on Laura Lynne's. Laura Lynne turns her palm over and squeezes.

"Personal how?"

"I think you know."

Nodding in agreement, she squeezes Laura Lynne's hand back. She looks calmly into Laura Lynne's eyes as if a missing puzzle piece has been found. She removes her hand and picks up her spoon. "Okay, how many letters are we talking about?"

"Several hundred. She wrote to me regularly for years." Laura Lynne is mindlessly stirring her ice cream. "She also wrote to me about you and Buck. Your wedding. She told me how lovely it was. I am sorry I couldn't make it, but I just couldn't come here."

"It was for the best. It would have been awkward for both of us." Scarlet finishes up her ice cream. "That was good. I guess I need to face the beast and head to see Momma." She is fishing through her purse to find her keys. "How about I meet you at the Gazette, and I will get the letters."

"Sounds good." Laura Lynne does not finish her sorbet. Something profound is happening between her and her sister.

The two ladies part company. Laura Lynne strolls down Main Street, her mind on her conversation with Scarlet. Something is not right with her sister. She is happy and helpful one minute and defensive the next. It is as if she is hiding or ashamed.

Scarlet is already at the office when Laura Lynne arrives. She is standing next to Mary with her hands on her hips. She is looking at the timeline Mary has been working on. "What is all this, Laura Lynne?"

Laura Lynne comes around from the front of the counter. "I really don't know. I have no idea what we are looking at. Could be something. Could be nothing." Laura Lynne stands next to her and looks at all the marked dates. Mary has been meticulous in her work. "I did talk to Grady about the six girls. He is doing a search to see if there are more. Then we can go from there. We haven't found anything useful about middle-aged white men, though."

Mary scoots off her perch. "I am going to grab a cup of coffee from the pot. Y'all want anything?" The two sisters shake their heads.

When Mary leaves, Scarlet takes Laura Lynne's hand. Using her index finger, she glides along the timeline, stopping in July 1985. She looks at Laura Lynne with compassion and understanding and says, "Am I right? Should you have a marker too?"

Quietly and with difficulty, Laura Lynne replies, "Yes. Yes, I think so." Hanging her head, she whispers, "Please don't tell anyone."

Scarlet lifts her chin and looks at her as a mother would a child. "Thank you for telling me. You can trust me. We are sisters first."

Laura Lynne raises her hands and clasps her sister's cheeks. "I hope one day you can trust me too."

Mary breaks up the scene when she returns with her coffee. "Oh, I am sorry. I am just, uh, leaving," she stammers and walks backward, realizing she has entered a poignant moment between sisters.

The sisters smile at each other. Laura Lynne says, "No need. We are done. Waterworks avoided." Laura Lynne turns practical. "Give me a minute, Scarlet. The letters are in my office."

Laura Lynne returns with the box. "Here you go, Scarlet. It's a treasure trove. Please take care of them. They mean a lot to me." Laura Lynne hands over the box. "And thanks for taking this on."

"Now, I am intrigued," replies Scarlet. Mary and Laura Lynne look at each other and laugh.

Mary chimes in, "Welcome to the club. It's like an addiction." She presses the button on the microfiche to move the film forward. "Come join us any time. There is plenty of room here. Besides, I like the company."

"Thanks, but I work better from home." She readjusts the box and moves to the other side of the counter. Laura Lynne follows her to open the door and walks her to her car. "Bye, Mary!" Scarlet calls.

"Don't be a stranger!" Mary replies, "And bring cake!"

Laura Lynne escorts Scarlet to her car. Scarlet pops the trunk and puts the letters inside. Slamming the trunk closed, Scarlet leans her back against it and crosses her arms. "Those girls, those six girls, they remind you of what happened to you. Am I right?"

"Yes. Is it that obvious?"

"Not to anyone outside of family. And I only know what Tripp told me." Laura Lynne is silent. "I hope one day you feel comfortable enough to tell me what happened. Because it didn't just happen to you. It messed up the whole family."

"I know that now. I didn't then, but I know that now."

Scarlet nods and gets into her car. She shuts the door and gives a nod as she pulls out. Laura Lynne watches her and thinks, "I am obviously not the only one in this family who needs healing."

Laura Lynne returns to her office and the microfiche. She finds nothing of value. She copies the articles and puts them in an envelope trying to decide how best to get them to Grady. She could text Grace and have her do it, but then the circle widens. Laura Lynne is not comfortable with that. Mary pops her head in the door. The tie dye outfit is Laura Lynne's favorite so far. "Just heard from Wisteria and Castille called earlier. They both have the microfiche pulled and ready for pick up tomorrow. Are you able to get them? It's going to take most of the day."

"I would love to do that! I could use a break." Laura Lynne glances at the envelope and then looks at Mary. "Listen, Mary, would you be interested in some clandestine work?"

"Like a spy?" She lights up like a chandelier.

"Well, maybe a little bit. I need to get these articles to Grady without anyone suspecting they are from me. He has stuff for me too. Would you be willing to be our courier?"

"Ooohhh, I would love to! Besides, I go by and see Beth Ann Bodeen all the time. She and I do bingo together on Tuesday nights." She holds out her hand. "Hand them over. I will go by after work."

"Great! I will text him and let him know so he is there." Laura Lynne hands the envelope to Mary. Laura Lynne's phone pings. "That's Grady. He is quick. Maybe he can teach Beau. Laura Lynne smiles. "He says he has something for you too. Whatever it is, just hold on to it until tomorrow. I will get it from you when I get back from my trip."

"Okay, got it. This is getting more and more interesting and fun." Laura Lynne laughs. Mary is so thrilled to be asked. She turns back to Laura Lynne as she heads to the door. "I forgot to ask! What happened with Mr. Gabe?"

"They dismissed the charges. At least for now. We are taking it as a win."

"That is excellent news. That Chandler Monroe is a class A jerk!"

"Mary, I am out. I will see you tomorrow afternoon." Laura Lynne goes to the door and starts to open it when a thought occurs to her. "Do you mind if I camp out here until 8 PM tomorrow? I got sucked into the book club deal by Candy and Diane."

"Shouldn't be a problem. There is a door in the back that automatically locks when you walk out. I quit setting the alarm a long time ago. There is nothing here to steal. Anyway, it doesn't work right half the time."

"Thanks for everything."

"Are you kidding? Thank you. Most fun I have ever had."

Chapter 23

Everyone is in a celebratory mood when Laura Lynne arrives back to Tea Olive. Pearl and Victoria are busy making some of Gabe's favorite dishes. The kitchen is alive with laughter, music, and the banging of pots and pans. Gabe has invited everyone to dinner to celebrate the dismissal of the charges. Victoria, Pearl, Laura Lynne, Gabe, John, Liam and Malcolm sit around the dining room table. Watching Gabe at the head of the table telling stories of Tea Olive and his mother Birdie, Laura Lynne smiles at the transformation in her uncle. It is as if the years fell away and he is a younger man, presiding at the head of his table. Everyone enjoys the light-hearted banter after weeks of worry.

After dinner, Laura Lynne sent everyone on their way while she cleaned up the kitchen. Victoria and Pearl did not complain and took their leave with Malcolm. John and Liam stayed for a while. John played a game of chess with Gabe while Liam read one of Gabe's recommended readings. Liam is quite smart and a straight-A student. By 8:00, Liam announced his intention to leave as he planned to bike back home before dark. Before Laura Lynne could protest, John told Liam to put his bike in his truck. He would get him home. It was evident this was a normal occurrence. John is more of a father figure to Liam than a boss or mentor.

Laura Lynne went to the back porch to wave them off and then pulled out her phone. "Uncle Gabe, I am going to call my children. I might be a bit."

She walked toward the oak tree as she texted the children telling them she was calling so please pick up. Laura Lynne calls Savannah first and she picks up on the first ring. She then conference calls Beau and he too picks up on the first ring.

"Hi Loves. Thanks for answering." She clears her throat. "I have a story to tell you, but I want to do it face to face." She rushes on. "And it's pretty bad. It is also very personal to me. But you are old enough to hear it now. And I need to speak with you before my story possibly becomes public knowledge. You need to hear it from me first."

There is silence for a moment before Savannah asks, "Mom, are you asking us to come to Mississippi?"

"I am. The story began here, so it needs to end here. Ashley will book the tickets, or if you prefer, you can do it, and I will reimburse you. And I have one more ask…"

Beau interrupts. "Wait! We are coming to Tea Olive? No way. Wait until I tell Claire. Mom, we will be there. When do you want us?"

Laura Lynne continues, "I do want you to come to Tea Olive and stay here with me and Uncle Gabe. But this first time, Beau, I am going to ask that just you and Savannah come alone. Not bring Claire or Chris. I know it is a lot to ask."

Savannah chimes in, "If that is what you need from us, we can do it. Besides, I think this first time should be just the three of us. Right, Beau?"

"Fine by me. When do you want us there?"

"As soon as you clear your calendars. I was hoping for this weekend. That only gives you two days to prepare, though."

"I already sent an email to my boss. She is good. I can be there." The ever-efficient Savannah is already in plan mode. "Beau, I sent an email to Ashley with my travel plans. Do you need me to send yours?" The next few minutes are spent ironing out the details. By the time Laura Lynne hangs up, it is decided the two will arrive on Friday and drive to Tea Olive from the airport together.

Laura Lynne cannot decide if she is thrilled or scared to death.

The next morning, Laura Lynne pulls into the parking lot of the Wisteria Chronicle. They are expecting her, and the boxes of microfiche are efficiently loaded into her trunk. The Castille Telegraph office is not as efficient as the Wisteria Chronicle, and Laura Lynne spends the next two hours locating the microfiche at the library and then checking it out. She is hot and frustrated when she finally gets in the car for the drive back to Venice.

Mary meets Laura Lynne at the front door of the Gazette. She is holding an envelope from Grady. "He found four more victims that meet the parameters of the previous victims. Names, dates, and files. He gave me copies and told me not to share with anyone." She is excited and nervous. "I have been on pins and needles waiting for you to get here."

Laura Lynne opens the manila envelope as she walks into the offices, letting the door close behind her. Mary locks the door, saying, "Just in case."

The contents of the envelope spilled onto the counter. It contains copies of police records on all ten of the girls. There is a police report with the missing person's information, some medical records, and a few pages of notes from the record. Mary starts piecing it together. She organizes the pages into ten separate piles. There is a note from Grady that reads, "I have to elevate this. Okay?"

Laura Lynne takes a deep breath and pulls out her phone, texting her reply, "Okay."

"What do you think will happen now?"

"I really don't know. Maybe call in the State Police." Laura Lynne shrugs her shoulders. "Honestly, your guess is as good as mine."

"I want to put these new girls on the timeline and see if a pattern emerges."

Laura Lynne's phone pings with Gray's response. "Meet you at the Gazette after closing. I will use the backdoor." Laura Lynne relays the text to Mary.

She nods. "I'm just going to head out like normal and lock up. No need to make people suspicious." She looks over at Laura Lynne. "You may want to move your car closer to Wheelbarrow Books."

"Wheelbarrow Books? Wh- Oh damn, that's right! The book club is tonight. Oh God, maybe I should cancel."

"I disagree. You should go. Nothing you can do tonight anyway." She takes out her ruler and pencil and begins drawing on the timeline. "Go get the microfiche out of the car. It's going to melt in this heat." Laura Lynne looks at her, wondering why she can't make her brain work. Like a robot, Laura Lynne unlocks the front door and goes to her car. As she is unloading her boxes, a thought occurs to her.

"Hey, Mary, where did the girls come from on the additional four cases?"

"Hmmm, let me look. Three from Wisteria and one from Castille." She tilts her head, gazing at the timeline. "He stayed in the same three counties. I wonder why?"

"Mary!" Laura Lynne hurries over to the counter and drops her boxes. "Help me!" Laura Lynne frantically goes through the files. "On the medical records. Who is the doctor?"

Laura Lynne's heart rate shoots up; her breathing is rapid and shallow. She begins to sweat as Mary and her put together the laboratory slips. At the top of each form is the ordering physician, Dr. Sydney Goldburg.

"The labs are from different laboratories, but the doctor is the same on all the results. Dr. Sydney Goldburg." Oh God, Laura Lynne's mind is screaming. He knew. He knew.

"And all the girls are positive for gonorrhea, chlamydia, and HPV?"

Mary checks the records. "Yes."

Mary plops down on her stool. She hands Laura Lynne the lab sheets. "He knew Mary. He had to have known. That son of a bitch. Why didn't he tell someone?"

"Are we sure he didn't? Maybe he did. Maybe Bubba just didn't follow up. Maybe they had something on Dr. Goldbug and held it over his head or, or maybe…"

"Or maybe he is in on it! I don't know, but no way did he not put two and two together. No wonder he acted that way with me…" Laura Lynne shuts her mouth. Laura Lynne slaps a hand over her mouth and stops pacing. She looks at Mary.

Mary is calm and unruffled. "I thought maybe this happened to you too. You went to Dr. Goldbug?" Laura Lynne nods. Her eyes begin to water, and the nausea begins to well up her throat.

"He could have stopped this then. Told Momma the truth. Instead, he had me thinking I was a lunatic! Crazy like my great aunt! I went to a psychiatrist because he told my parents I was *Lying*! He *knew*!" She sobs, "Oh God, I am going to get sick."

Laura Lynne runs to the bathroom and slams the door shut. She throws up, emptying everything in her stomach until nothing is left but the dry heaves. The betrayal is real. She trusted him, and he had betrayed her.

Laura Lynne closes the commode lid and sits down. She blows her nose and wipes her eyes. Mary knocks softly on the door. "Laura Lynne, are you all right, honey? You want me to call anybody?"

"No. I am fine. Just give me a minute to wash up." Laura Lynne leans over the sink and rinses her mouth with some water. Splashes her face. She looks in the mirror. "I am a mess."

Mary is standing at the door waiting patiently when Laura Lynne walks out of the bathroom. "You want to talk about it?"

"Not really. You know most of it." Mary goes to the little refrigerator she keeps under the counter, pulls out a Diet Coke, pops the top, and hands it to Laura Lynne. She takes a sip, and it burns her raw throat on the way down, just like it did that night at Dr. Butler's house. Laura Lynne looks at the can and feels for the first time as if she has come full circle.

"I'm okay, really. It's just like this puzzle I have been putting together had all these missing pieces. Forty years later, I am finally finding the pieces, one at a time. It's causing the picture to shift. To look different than I thought it would." She takes another sip. "My kids are coming this weekend. I am going to tell them." She looks at Mary for understanding. "I want them to hear it from me before it gets splashed in the papers or goes to trial." She looks at her soda can and rubs the condensation with her fingertip as it drips from the can. "Even if it doesn't, they deserve to know the truth."

The two women sit at the front counter quietly. Laura Lynne looks at the timeline and the boxes scattered across the counter. She gazes at the ten stacks of paper. Each stack depicts a victim. Laura Lynne asks, "What are the dates, Mary? I never asked." She looks at the timeline again, though she already knows the answer.

"They span from 1980-1985. The last one in spring of that year."

"No. The last one would be the summer of 1985. July 13th. That's me."

"Honey, are you sure you want to add that right now? Why don't you wait until you talk to Grady." Laura Lynne nods. Maybe she is right. Laura Lynne's mind is still foggy. Mary purses her lips. "I wonder what happened that they stopped so abruptly?" She flips around to her computer. "At least, we think they do. Maybe he moved?"

"He actually got married and moved away around the holidays of 1985. Probably need to check Boston and see if they have any hits that have similar characteristics." Laura Lynne gets up off the stool. Mary is staring at her with wide eyes. "You know who, I mean, don't you?" asks Laura Lynne.

"Only because I have his wedding noted from 1985 in my notes. It was splashed all over the paper. Quite the social event in Boston. Her people are well-heeled. Some of the locals were invited, interviewed, that kind of thing," replies Mary.

This piques Laura Lynne's interest. "Who? Can you go back to your notes or the article? I bet Dr. Goldbug is one of the attendees." Laura Lynne looks over Mary's shoulder as Mary pulls up her notes.

Mary rustles through the pages of her notes and says, "I didn't make a note of the attendees. I need to go back to the microfiche and scan it again. I do have the frame noted." She reads off the information to Laura Lynne. Laura Lynne goes to her office to hunt through the boxes for the correct film.

"Found it!" shouts Laura Lynne as she puts the film in and scans to the proper frame. She starts reading, and Mary comes to look over her shoulder. "I was right! Read this."

"Attendees from Venice include Dr. Goldbug with his lovely wife Barbara and Sheriff Bradford "Bubba" Westerman with his lovely wife Matilda "Tilly." Invited but unable to attend were Judge and Mrs. Silas Monroe."

"I am texting Grady right now. I don't care if somebody sees him. I need him to see what we found." Laura Lynne breathes heavily. "It all makes a weird kind of sense, doesn't it? If all of them were in some type of 'ring' to cover it all up."

"You need to calm down." Mary points to the time on the computer screen. "It is nearly 5 now. Let's just stick to the plan. We don't know what we have found, if anything." Mary stands up straight and puts her hands on Laura Lynne's shoulders. "Breathe deep, sweetheart." She pats her shoulder gently before walking to the office door. "I am going to clean up the counter and put everything away. Then, I am going to wait a bit until Grady gets here. I don't want to leave you alone."

Laura Lynne hates to admit it, but she is grateful for Mary's soothing presence. Mary is dressed today in a light blue matching outfit. She looks like a blue tulip. "Thank you, Mary. I don't want to be alone right now." Laura Lynne puts her head on the desk. "This is a lot to take in."

Pulling it together, Laura Lynne decides the next best course of action is collating the victim's files Grady gave her with the information she and Mary collected. Pulling up the files on her computer, she downloads and print off a copy. Laura Lynne collects the papers from the printer. She walks to the front counter. "Want to help me organize the victim's folders? I thought we should add our research to the files."

The two ladies work quietly arranging the information. Mary quietly says, "I think we should make a second copy. One for you to keep safe."

"Really great idea. We wouldn't want to get anything misplaced."

"All three of these men are still alive and still highly connected. They were able to keep it hidden for nearly 50 years. They have children and families to protect."

Laura Lynne shakes her head. "Trying not to freak out here."

Laura Lynne's phone pings. Grady will arrive shortly. Laura Lynne goes to the back door and opens it, watching as he comes around the corner.

"Hi Grady. It is good to see you." She ushers him in. He looks excited and grim all at the same time. "Mary, I have him," Laura Lynne calls to the front door. She looks at Grady, "Tell her you will make sure I get to Book Club safely." He looks at Laura Lynne strangely. "Just do it!"

"I'll take care of her, Miss Mary! And make sure she gets to book club safe!" Grady replies.

"See that you do young man! Good night!" The door tinkles as it closes.

"Come on. Have a seat. We have a lot to talk about." Laura Lynne hands him the ten files she and Mary have been working on.

"This is everything I have so far. Can you tell me what you know?"

Grady sits in one of the office chairs and lets out a huge sigh before putting his elbows on his knees and steepling his fingers. "You uncovered something here Laura Lynne." He drops his hands and begins rubbing the tops of his thighs. "I discreetly called my connection. His name is Mason. We hunt at the club together in Wisteria. I trust him implicitly."

He keeps rubbing his thighs. "I asked if he was familiar with the cases of the girls we had located." He shook his head. "He was not aware of them. Told me he would check. Then I took a gamble. I don't know anyone at Castille, just acquaintances, but no real people I can trust. I asked Mason if he knew of a trusted source at Castille. Turns out he does."

He leans back in his chair and looks at the ceiling. He then turns his gaze to Laura Lynne. "He called me and asked to meet me at this country road between our towns. I knew then he was concerned about what he had found." He sighs. "Anyway, I met him. He gave me the files I requested, then he told me to be careful. Told me he had gotten wind that this was swept under the rug by some pretty powerful people. He could not name names, but he pointed to one name on the file." He looks at Laura Lynne, and in unison they say. "Dr. Goldbug."

"So, you already figured it out?"

"That part? Yes, but I still don't understand how he got the girls from Wisteria and Castille."

Grady holds up his hands. "I have no idea."

"Is that all the information you have?"

"Why?" He sits up straight in his chair. "Do you have something else?"

"Maybe. I am not sure what I have." Laura Lynne gets up. "Follow me. I want to show you the timeline Mary put together with all the information we have so far." She turns on the light over the front counter. "Look at the dates of the abductions. There are ten in all. Well, eleven if you count mine. Range in dates from 1980-1985. Then they stop. My rape would be the last event. So summer of 1985."

Grady nods as Laura Lynne continues, "If you add in what I know, which is Dr. Butler is involved. What happened that winter?" Laura Lynne points to the next timeline point. "Dr. Butler got married and moved to Boston." Grady gets very still, looking intently at the timeline. "We might want to consider expanding the search to the Boston area. Let's see if there are similar cases there."

Laura Lynne turns on her heel. "Hold on a second." She goes back to her office and grabs the file before sitting it on the counter. She thumbs through the pages until she finds the article about the wedding. She pulls it out and hands it to Grady. "Look who was invited to the wedding in Boston. It would have been big news. His bride was related to the Kennedys. It would have been on page 6 of all the high society news. Dr. Goldbug, Bubba Westerman, and Judge Silas Monroe." Laura Lynne sits on Mary's stool. "Those big enough names for you?"

Grady's mouth opens, then closes. He closes his eyes, opens them, and looks at Laura Lynne.

Grady softly says, "Laura Lynne, I have to call the sheriff." Laura Lynne shakes her head to say no, but Grady continues, "I have too. He's a good guy. He can be trusted." He squats so he is eye to eye with his sister's best friend. "I am asking you to trust me with this. He is at the office right now. I can have him come down here, and we can explain everything to him." Laura Lynne is unconvinced. "I know he comes off like Barney Fife. He is shy, but he's super smart. We were lucky to get him from Philadelphia."

"That's where he's from? I couldn't place the accent." Laura Lynne stands up. "Can we call Gray first?"

"No. We are not using our cell phones. Besides, we both know what he is going to say. He already said it when he told you to bring it to me. It's time for the truth to come out." He takes Laura Lynne's hands and forces her to stop pacing. "Laura Lynne, its time. Trust me."

"Okay. But you had better be right, or I am telling Grace."

He laughs and smiles. "Well, we can't have that. She can be a mean little thing." He pulls out his phone and sends a quick text to the sheriff. It pings back within moments. He looks up at Laura Lynne. "He's on the way."

"What did you text?"

"I asked him if he was interested in a slice of pecan pie. He said yes. I told him to come to the Gazette." Laura Lynne stares at him blankly. "Pecan Pie is code for 'this is a 911. I need you now.' Police don't trust phones, even encrypted ones."

Five minutes later, there is a tap on the back door. Grady escorts the sheriff, talking quietly as they make their way to the front counter. "I believe you two have already met."

"Ma'am." The sheriff takes off his hat and holds it in his hands. "I am afraid I was a bit star-struck the last time we met. Not too often we get a famous author in town. I bumble through social stuff." He shakes his head. "I assure you I am very good at my job."

Laura Lynne stares daggers at him. "I hope so. I'm not going to lie. I would prefer to work exclusively with Grady, but he trusts you. Against my better judgment, I am going to do the same. Don't let me down."

"Yes, ma'am." He looks at Grady. "What do you have?"

Grady takes him through the entire story. Jerry walks over to look at the timeline. Grady pauses. Jerry signals for him to continue, but Grady says, "I think this next part should come from Laura Lynne."

Laura Lynne begins, "This is the first time I have told a stranger this story, Sheriff. I don't do this easily. I think there are at least three men involved in the abductions and cover-ups. Possibly a fourth." Laura Lynne tells him about the wedding article and her suspicions about the other three men. "The reason I think this is true is because I believe Dr. Kenneth Butler perpetrated my rape when I was 15. I am the 11th victim." Laura Lynne tells him the rest: her suspicion that she was drugged and the piecing together of my trauma over the years. "It's the only thing that makes any sense, at least to me."

"You did this all on your own?"

"Well, no. I had two other people helping me. Mary and Ashley. You know Mary. Ashley is my assistant. She doesn't know what she is doing exactly. She is helping with the IT piece and conversion of the microfiche." Laura Lynne stands next to the men. "Only a handful of people know what I think happened to me that night of July 13, 1985. I told my daddy, my Aunt Eileen, my husband, Grady, and now you. I never even told my therapist, though I should have." Laura Lynne shakes her head, "Anyway, of those five, two are now dead, so there are only three people who know what I think I know." Laura Lynne looks from one to the other. "Mary probably knows most of it. She is no idiot." Laura Lynne takes a deep breath in and lets out a long, slow exhale. "So, what do you think?"

The sheriff quietly looks at Laura Lynne with gentle and concerned eyes. "I think, Miss Laura Lynne, it's time we seek out some justice for you and these other girls." He starts to walk to the timeline. "Just too many coincidences. I don't like coincidences. And, not to get into specifics, I would not be at all surprised if Bubba was either in on the whole thing or, at the very least, helped to cover it all up."

Jerry turns around and props himself against the counter. "Grady, you and I need to call in the state boys. I think it best if we take everything to them. Too many loose lips at the station. We will call tomorrow. Maybe we can see them on Friday." He looks at Laura Lynne and Grady. "I would like to pay a visit to Dr. Goldbug, but I don't want to play my hand." He shakes his head. "No, let's check the Boston database first. Laura Lynne, can you and Mary go through the microfiche from the other news outlets? Just focusing on 1980-1985? I would like to add the articles to the file."

"I can, well, we can." Laura Lynne is suddenly cold. She rubs her arms up and down with her hands, attempting to generate some heat. "What happens once you hand this over to the state police? What should I expect?"

"They have to believe it's credible. I don't think that should be a problem. Once they agree to take on the case, the investigation proceeds. They will send detectives who will more than likely be SVU. The investigation will include interviews of the victims." He looks at Laura Lynne with concern. "That means you too. There is no way around it. You are the piece that ties it all together."

Suddenly, no longer chilled, Laura Lynne is fierce. She stands up straight and squares her shoulders. Her hands are clenched into fists. "I am ready."

"It won't be able to stay a secret," Grady warns.

"I know. I have spoken to my husband. My children will be here on Friday. I will tell them when they come in. The truth is it's a part of who I am. I am no longer ashamed. Shame and blame have kept me silent all these years. I can't be quiet any longer." Laura Lynne smiles grimly. "Besides, I really want to take down this monster."

The three discuss strategy until 7:45. Laura Lynne excuses herself to freshen up before her book club meeting. Returning to the front office, Laura Lynne sees Jerry has confiscated the timeline and all the files. "I am going to take these with me. I am going straight home and have a gun safe that they will fit in. I don't want to take any chances."

Laura Lynne knew it would happen. She was glad she had the second file. "Tomorrow afternoon, I will have Mary bring copies by the office of anything we find in the Wisteria and Castille newspapers. Doubt it will be much."

Jerry attempts to reassure Laura Lynne, "You are doing the right thing. Thank you for trusting me. I know it's hard."

"I don't trust you. I trust Grady. Don't let either of us down."

"I will do my best not too." And that is the best he could do. There are no guarantees. She nods and thanks him as he takes the files and heads out of the office to his cruiser. Grady escorts Laura Lynne out the back door, turning off lights as they head out. The night air feels like a warm hug. Laura Lynne takes a deep inhale and a full, open-mouthed exhale.

"Not too sure how articulate I will be at this book club meeting. At least it's a book I know."

"My wife will be there. You will finally get to meet her. Don't be surprised if she asks you for your autograph." He chuckles and shakes his head. "She loves your book. She wouldn't appreciate me telling you, but she stopped drinking after she read it. Realized she had indulged too much in the 'Mommy Drinking' culture, and it was starting to be a problem." Laura Lynne pops the trunk on her car as they get closer.

"Don't worry. I won't mention it. You would be shocked how many people tell me the same thing. It's not a problem until it is. And when it is, it can ruin your entire world." Grady helps her load her trunk with all her bags. She turns to Grady one last time. "Thank you again. I would be lying if I didn't tell you I was scared to death. What if they didn't do anything, and it's all just conjecture on my part and really I am as crazy as my Great Aunt Augustine?"

He laughs. "You're not crazy. Or if you are, so am I." He shuts the trunk lid. "You gonna be okay getting home? I can follow you afterward. I don't mind."

"No need for all that." Laura Lynne leans over and gives him a big hug. "You turned out okay for a bratty little brother of my best friend." They both laugh.

"Grady Cunningham, are you hugging on another woman?" Laura Lynne tenses up and pulls back. Grady holds on tighter.

"I most certainly am Mrs. Cunningham. Why don't you come over here and do something about it?" He is laughing. He releases Laura Lynne and introduces his wife, "Laura Lynne, meet my wife, Priscilla, though we call her Prissa." He steps back and wraps his arm around the most petite woman Laura Lynne has ever seen. Doesn't top out at 5'0 and is maybe

100 pounds soaking wet. She reminds Laura Lynne of a teacup poodle. "Prissa, Laura Lynne Atkins."

Prissa smiles and gives her a hug. "I have been wanting to meet you! Grady and Grace have told me all about you. I am sorry I missed you at the club formal. I wanted to thank you for writing your book. It's been really inspiring." Laura Lynne nods, and Prissa is talking faster than Laura Lynne can understand her. Grady winks at her over his wife's head.

"I asked Prissa to meet me here. She is going to ride with you to Wheelbarrow Books." Prissa hands Grady her keys. "Thanks, sweetheart. I will pick you up when it's over. Just send me a text." With that, he gives Prissa a kiss that makes Laura Lynne blush before he heads over to the Pontiac.

"Come on, Laura Lynne. Time to have some charcuterie and red velvet cake." Prissa slides into the passenger seat. "Our book club has the best snacks."

It turns out Prissa is right. Their book club does have amazing food. And lots of wine. Diane has the bookstore and the café doors open, so everyone is milling about with appetizers and a glass of wine. Diane greets Laura Lynne and begins introducing her to the ladies as everyone gathers around. One of the newcomers leans over to whisper in Diane's ear. Diane looks at Laura Lynne and then excuses herself to pop back to the bookstore. Laura Lynne excuses herself to the food table. After her vomiting episode this afternoon, she is hesitant to dive into anything too odd. Cheese and crackers seem like just the thing.

Diane makes her way over to Laura Lynne and whispers, "There is someone here to see you? She says you invited her this evening?" Laura Lynne looks at her blankly for a moment. Diane leans in. "It's Natalie."

"Oh, yes! I did invite her! I completely forgot. Where is she?" She pulls Laura Lynne through the café toward the bookstore.

"She's hiding in the reference aisle." Diane pulls Laura Lynne around. "Are you sure you want her here?" She looks at her with concern and not a bit of angst.

"Yes, I do. Let's give her a chance, okay? I will tell you about it later, but let me go get her." Diane starts off as Laura Lynne continues, "Go back to your guests. We will be in momentarily." Laura Lynne heads to the reference section with cheese and crackers in hand. "Natalie? Natalie?" Laura Lynne spots her. "What are you doing back here?"

She looks terrified, and then she gets defensive. In that split second, Laura Lynne figures her out. She holds up her hand. "Don't say what you are about to say. It's going to be ugly. And it's going to be ugly because you are scared. And when you get scared, you lash out and demean others to make them scared of you, and then y'all can be scared together." Natalie looks at Laura Lynne. "Am I right?"

"I don't know…maybe. I was all confident about coming here. Then I get here and see all the women and how comfortable they are with each other. They all grew up together. I just don't fit in, and I try, I do, but …" and here come the tears, "but mean is just easier."

"Don't you cry, Natalie! Then I will start crying, and Diane is going to regret she invited me." Laura Lynne gives Natalie a hug. It's like hugging an ironing board. "You're right. It's scary being vulnerable. Try writing a book about your struggles with alcohol!" Laura Lynne leans back. "But you are wrong about one thing. Most of these women did not 'grow up together.' Perfect example is Diane."

Laura Lynne takes a bite of cheese and cracker before offering one to Natalie. "So, what do you think? Hide in the reference section until you can make your escape or make nice with the book club ladies?"

"Are you sure you are being nice to me, or am I about to walk into the lion's den?"

"I guess you will have to find out for yourself." With that, Laura Lynne takes her leave. Natalie can follow, or she can go home. Laura Lynne has done her best. Laura Lynne hears Natalie's heels hitting the brick as she follows. Laura Lynne smiles as she enters the café and catches Prissa with her eye, giving her a wink.

Getting the hint, Prissa prances over to the two women, all teacup poodle-like. "Come over here and sit with me. I just can't take my eyes off that purse! It's Gucci, right?" Natalie latches on to Prissa and lets her take her to her seat. The chatter resumes.

Diane claps her hands to signal it's time to get to the business of book discussion. "Let the April meeting of Between the Covers Book Club begin. Candy, I think you chose the book, so you can start the meeting." Laura Lynne sits back and relaxes. This is just what she needed after the day she had. The women are very articulate. They have a lot to say about Maudie, Atticus, Boo, Scout, the trial, race relations, and gender politics. Nothing is off limits, and the discussion ranges from passionate to resigned.

After an hour, Diane begins to wrap it up. "Great discussion ladies, as always. Next month's book is Laura Lynne's *Bluebird Diaries*. I warned her when she agreed to come y'all might have some questions. Laura Lynne, do you mind?"

"Not at all!" Laura Lynne leans forward and grabs the water bottle Diane brought her. "And, I must say, if you are as animated and passionate about *Bluebird* as you were tonight, I expect an invitation for next month's meeting." Everyone laughs, "Candy, why don't you start?""

"Why did you choose Quit Lit?"

"Shoo, y'all just jump right into the heart of it, don't you?" Laura Lynne sits up straighter. "Okay, best answer. Because I quit drinking, and the process was the second toughest thing I have ever done.

Don't ask about the toughest thing I have ever done! That's my next book!" And the questions come one after the other.

After 30 minutes, Laura Lynne throws up her hands. "That's it, ladies! I am plumb wore out! Diane, I am handing it back to you." The ladies clap, and Diane thanks everyone for coming.

"Okay, ladies, I have ordered the book for those of you who requested it. They will be in by tomorrow afternoon. I will text details."

The ladies start getting up, still chatting. Several go and talk to Natalie. Prissa comes and sits next to Laura Lynne. "That was nice of you." She nods at Natalie. "Your momma would have annihilated her."

"Well, I absolutely did that the first time I came against her. Then, my husband pointed out a few things that made me think maybe I needed to think differently." She smiles. "Not that I don't want to be my mother at times. But my husband makes me see the good in people, even in the Natalies of the world." Laura Lynne whispers to her, "Balances out the bitch in me."

"Nah, you're just a good person." Prissa gets up. "It was nice to meet you, Laura Lynne. You going to be okay getting home? I don't mind having Grady follow you."

Laura Lynne looks at her curiously. "What did he tell you?"

"Absolutely nothing. I swear. But he and I have been married for 30 years. I know when something is up. Him walking you to your car and hugging you? Having me meet you at the Gazette? He's worried about you."

"He is a good man." Laura Lynne brushes off her pants and straightens her waistband. "I am fine, but thanks." Laura Lynne gives Prissa a smile and gently squeezes her arm. She takes her dirty dishes to the table for cleanup."Diane, thank you. I'm heading home. Great night, and love the name of the club!"

"I am glad you made it. You livened things up a bit. Be careful driving home." Laura Lynne gives her the thumbs-up sign. Several of the women chat with her as they walk to their cars, waving and wishing everyone a good evening. Laura Lynne sits in the driver's seat and closes her eyes. t has been the world's longest day.

Chapter 24

Laura Lynne gets out of bed and glances at her phone. It is 4AM. Early even for her. Sleep is elusive which has become her new normal. She walks over to the window seat and pulls a blanket around her as she sits in her nook. She had enjoyed her evening with the women of Between the Covers. She smiles at the name. Laura Lynne enjoys hanging out with women, though she doesn't do it very often. She loves the drama, the gossip, and the emotions women bring to every discussion, every aspect of their lives. However, it is very draining and so as a rule, Laura Lynne avoids groups of women. She prefers one on one relationships. But she had such a good time last night she cleared her calendar to attend next month's book club meeting.

She needs to talk to her Uncle Gabe. They have been on opposing schedules the last few days. Last night, he was in bed when she returned from town. Thinking she might catch him this morning, Laura Lynne throws on some sweats before going to the kitchen. As she puts the kettle on for tea, Laura Lynne contemplates the ramifications of yesterday's decisions. Some consequences she can foresee; others are not as clear. She consoles herself with the knowledge she did her best to shield those who would be hurt by her story. She shrugs her shoulders. She cannot in good conscience remain silent any longer.

"Who are you shrugging your shoulders at, baby girl?" says Gabe.

Laura Lynne lets out an unladylike squeal and grabs her chest. "Uncle Gabe! You scared me to death."

"Mind putting that knife down, Laura Lynne? What has you so jumpy?"

Laura Lynne looks at her hand, and she realizes she grabbed a knife from the butcher block when she turned around. "Guess I am. Had a hard time sleeping."

"Pour me a mug of that tea your always making and tell me what's on your mind."

Laura Lynne makes a second mug for her uncle. He takes a sip and grimaces. Laura Lynne smiles and leans against the counter.

"Spill it, Laura Lynne. You have been up all night, pacing like a caged lion. Up early today. You were gone for the last several days and your children are coming tomorrow. Something is going on and I want you to tell me what it is."

"It's a long story. Do you want to sit in your study?" asks Laura Lynne.

"No, I want to hear it now. I am comfortable enough."

Laura Lynne clears her throat contemplating how to begin. "Remember how I told you I was working with Mary reviewing the Gazette archives? Trying to do some research on Dead Doe?" He nods. Laura Lynne explains to her uncle about the girls who were abducted, missing for a few days, only to return disheveled and with no memory. "By the time I finished the microfiche yesterday, we found a total of ten girls from 1980-1985 who fit the description." She stares into her mug. "Eleven if you count me."

Gabe says nothing as he waits for the rest of the story. Laura Lynne lays out the events of the night she babysat for Dr. Butler and the events that led to her being sent to Eileen's. Laura Lynne finishes her tale, waiting on Gabe to process the information. Finally, he looks at her, his eyes filled with compassion and strength.

"So, you believe Dr. Butler raped you? And these other girls?"

"Well, yes, but there is more to it than that, Uncle Gabe. I think there were several prominent Venice people involved. I cannot tell you who we think they are or why." Laura Lynne looks at her uncle. He is staring into his full mug of tea. "Did you suspect Uncle Gabe? What happened to me?"

"It could only be a few situations warranting your parents' behavior. Not that anything deserves displacement from your home. Eileen and I talked over the years. She said enough for me to understand the situation but never disclosed the truth. I am wondering, though, if Eileen knew your suspicions about Dr. Butler. I find it hard to believe he would still be living had she known."

"I didn't piece it together until years later. But, yes, I eventually told her. I even told Daddy once Beau was born. It's all speculation. I have no proof. I have a lot of coincidences and suspicions. I want you to know I told the sheriff and Grady. They are taking it to the state police. If they warrant it deserves to be investigated, then it's all going to be out in the open. It could get bad, especially if our supposition ends up being true." Laura Lynne paces to the window and looks out. "It's why I called the kids down. I need to tell them what I told you. I don't want them to be blindsided or think I hid something from them."

"I think that is wise. Don't worry about me. You take care of yourself." He gets up from the stool and stands beside Laura Lynne at the window. "You plan to tell Melanie and the rest of the family?"

"No, not yet. The fewer people who know, the better. Once I know for certain an arrest is being made or it's been leaked to the press, then I will. But if nothing comes of it, it's better to just keep it to ourselves. Nobody needs to know except me."

He hugs Laura Lynne tight. He wraps his arms around her and pets her hair. The two sway back and forth. "I am so sorry. I am just so very proud of you." She relaxes into his hold and absorbs his strength and his acceptance. They stand like that for a few minutes and then separate. "I love you, baby girl."

"I love you too. Now, can we talk about something else? Tell me about the garden."

"Only if you make me some coffee. This tea is nasty. Why does it taste good when it's iced but tastes like tree bark when it's hot?"

"Could be the two pounds of sugar Victoria puts in it to take the bitter away." She opens the cabinet beside the sink and pulls out the coffee maker. "I thought you were on coffee restriction."

"I am an old man, Laura Lynne. If I want a cup of coffee, I am going to have one."

"I can't argue with that." She rummages for the coffee filters and the coffee. "I can't find the coffee or the filters."

"Victoria hides them from me. She thinks if she is clever enough, I won't make it myself." He points to the cabinet above the refrigerator. "Try in there." She walks over and, standing on tiptoes, opens the doors. There it is, just waiting patiently for them to find it. "Told you."

As the two wait for the coffee to brew, Laura Lynne decides to ask her uncle about the Huger place. "Uncle Gabe, what can you tell me about Buck's old place? Heard it was sold off to some developer. I drove by, and it looks like nothing is happening." Laura Lynne pours the tea out of Gabe's mug, rinses the cup, and refills it with coffee, black and hot. Gabe smiles as he takes it from her hand.

"They sold it some years back and made a bunch of money. Some of the local farmers, including me, filed to stop the development. We hired an attorney, and so far, so good." He sips his coffee and sighs. "Why do you ask?"

"No reason, really. I was just surprised the Hugers would sell the land. It's been in the family for generations. Or, if he was planning to sell it, why they didn't offer it to a local first?" She picks up her tea. "Come on, let's go sit on the porch and watch the sunrise."

Uncle Gabe nods. "I asked Scarlet the same thing. Would have loved to expand Tea Olive to its original 4,000 acres. Adding the Huger plantation would have been a real boon. Would have taken a lot of capital."

"Yes, I guess it would have. Water under the bridge now." Laura Lynne sits in the rocking chair and slowly begins to rock back and forth. "I love it here, Uncle Gabe. I didn't realize how much until I came back. Regretting that I did not come back sooner."

"No, don't do that. Never regret what might have been, or what you didn't do, or even what you did do. One thing I have learned, or more the wisdom I have gained, is the good Lord has a plan for you. His plan was to make you strong enough to face your past. It just took some time, that's all."

Once the sun comes up over the horizon, Gabe is ready to start the day. "Enough chitter chatter! It is time to get movin'! You headed into town today?"

"I am. But today is my last day. I am going to pack it all in and close up shop. It's time for me to start thinking about heading home for a while. Get on with life. I want to spend the weekend with the kids and show them Tea Olive. While they are here, I want to do a ceremony for Aunt Eileen. I need to spread her ashes like she always wanted." His eyes tear up.

"That's nice, real nice."

"Hopefully, we will know something about the other thing sometime next week. Oh, I almost forgot! I am going to opening night of the show tonight at Moseley Hall! They are doing *Beauty and the Beast*. I promised Rachele's daughter, Samantha, I would come and watch her play Belle."

"You know you can stay as long as you like, Laura Lynne. I love having you here. It's been nice having some company."

"Thank you, Uncle Gabe, but my life is in New Mexico now. But I promise I will visit and have holidays here with you. I won't be a stranger anymore. And, if all goes well, Tripp should be arriving sometime soon. He can keep you company."

"Hmmph. He hasn't been home since Sawyer died. I'd like to talk to him. He needs to be updated on the trust, the farm, the businesses. There is a lot going on, especially right now. Be good to see him." Laura Lynne gathers the mugs and kisses Gabe on the head.

"You're a good girl, Laura Lynne." Laura Lynne does not reply. She just lets the tears fall.

Mary is waiting impatiently when Laura Lynne gets to the Gazette. "Where have you been? I am dying to know how it went last night."

"Okay, okay. Give me a minute. I have been up since 4 AM, and it's been a whirlwind." She puts all her bags on the front counter. Mary looks fresh in a pale yellow dress and matching cardigan, pearl earrings, pearl necklace, and pearl-rimmed reading glasses. Today, she looks like a daffodil.

Laura Lynne plops in the chair next to Mary and gives her a run down on yesterday's meetings with Grady and the sheriff. Mary nods approvingly. Then, Laura Lynne regales her with tales of the book club and encourages her to join in the fun. Mary shakes her head no.

"I have my own book club, The Nerd Herd. It's a group of all the retired teachers and librarians. We have a grand time. If I went to another book club, I would feel like I was cheating on them." She giggles. "Last month, we started the *50 Shades of Gray Trilogy*." Laura Lynne stares at her. She can only imagine the discussion.

"On a serious note. Today is my last day at the Gazette," says Laura Lynne. "I need to get back to my life. With Uncle Gabe off the hook for Dead Doe and Grady and Jerry taking the lead on the abducted girls, there is really nothing more for me to do here." Mary nods her agreement.

"I understand completely. It's time for you to go and live your life. But don't you be a stranger! I have loved getting to know you as an adult! These last couple of weeks have added a spark to my life I didn't realize was missing." She pats Laura Lynne's hands. "I am not gonna lie. I will miss seeing you every day."

"I have a proposition for you. Not sure how it will work, but thought it might be appealing. You would be helping me, *and* you could earn a bit of extra money."

"Go on. I am intrigued." Mary leans in.

"Would you be interested in helping me with research? A large part of writing is having the appropriate research, and my story, well, it needs to be written. I need to finish my next *Bluebird* book first, but this will follow it. Nobody knows more about it than you. With you being local and well respected, I think it might just be a win-win."

Mary is visibly excited. She starts bouncing in her chair. "I would love it! Kind of like a second career. Plus, I can do a lot of it while I am here. The days do get long when you sit at that counter with nothing more to do than read a book."

"So, you'll do it?" Laura Lynne holds out her hand for a handshake. Mary giggles as she takes it. They do an exaggerated shake. "I will send Ashley the details. She handles all the fine print. If you have questions, she is the person to ask." Laura Lynne points to the microfiche machine. "For now, let's start scanning the newspaper for the articles about the abducted girls."

As suspected, the articles on the missing girls found in the Wisteria and Castille archives were the same as the Gazette. The articles were shared between the papers, a common practice in small town newspapers. But there was one that hit the front page of the Wisteria Chronicle in 1985: victim number ten. The article states she did not arrive home from school. Her family was middle class and white. Her father owned the Feed and Seed store. There is a small snippet about her coming home, and the article states she had run away but was home safe now. "Mary, come look at this."

Mary comes into the office and reads over her shoulder. "We know for certain this is victim 10. I remember her father from the store. Buy my cat food there." Adjusting her spectacles, Mary continues. "I am thinking they were hiding the truth. Maybe trying to keep her reputation intact. Better she be a runaway then a rape victim."

"I agree. The story is a cover up. Good for her."

Laura Lynne sends the article to Ashley. "That's the end of them for me. I am through 1985. How are things going for you? Need me to scan some for you?"

"Goodness, no! I have been done for the last hour. I just kept going to see if anything interesting pops up. I forwarded everything to Ashley. She should have it all."

"Let's have lunch. By then, Ashley will have the paperwork done. We can print off two copies, and you can take the information to Grady." Laura Lynne smiles at her. "If you are comfortable with me manning the front desk."

Mary just laughs. "Come on, let's eat on the picnic table out back. I will put a sign on the door. It's normally what I do when I am here alone and want a breath of fresh air."

Laura Lynne and Mary have a lovely meal of hummus wraps and veggies with a side of strawberries. For dessert, they have a macaroon. Mary says, "I am sure going to miss Victoria's lunches. I wonder if I could order a week's worth from her, sort of a side hustle."

"You could ask. She cooks an amazing amount of food each week. Adding an additional mouth would probably not be a big issue. Just don't try to steal her away from Tea Olive. Uncle Gabe would perish if Victoria was not there to cook his meals. He and Pearl are what keep him going and staying in that big house all alone."

Mary laughed. "Steal her? No chance of that. But I do think I will ask. Get tired of canned soup and sandwiches."

"Let me go print the paperwork, so you can deliver to the sheriff's office." Laura Lynne leaves Mary to clean up the picnic table. While the printer is running, Laura Lynne starts packing her bags. She has accumulated quite a bit of stuff during her ten days at the Gazette. Laura Lynne also sends a quick text to Scarlet asking to talk. She replies she is not available today. Laura Lynne shakes off the feeling Scarlet is avoiding her for some reason. She has not been seen or heard from since Gabe's court date.

Laura Lynne takes the printouts to Mary who folds them and puts them in an envelope. The two ladies walk out the front door together. "Be back shortly."

Mary walks down the street stopping to talk and wave as she passes people on the street. Laura

Lynne clears out the rest of her office, which requires her to make several trips to her car. She does a bit of housekeeping. She organizes the microfiche. Mary has still not returned. She has been gone for nearly an hour. Having nothing else to do, Laura Lynne sits behind the desk and waits.

The door swings open and in rushes a breathless and energized Mary. "Laura Lynne, it's happening today!"

"What is happening today?"

"The state police! Apparently, the sheriff contacted a friend of his over in state and whatever he said triggered an immediate response. They want to meet with him and Grady *today*. He held them off until I came by, but they are on their way to meet them right now. I was to tell you to be prepared for them to come by Tea Olive later today or tomorrow morning."

"What do you think set them off? I mean the abductions are close to 40 years old. Doesn't seem like it warrants this type of reaction."

"You and I are starting to think alike. This is why I am a bit late. I hung around the water cooler to see what type of information I could gather from Beth Ann. She let it slip that she was asked to find some files from Bubba's tenure."

Mary leans in to whisper, "She thinks they found something on the old sheriff."

"Or maybe a connection. Did she tell you which files?" Laura Lynne starts to pace the office. "That has to be why the strong reaction to the abductions. Another cog in the wheel." Laura Lynne stops pacing and looks at Mary. "Makes our theory more credible."

"I didn't want to pry or look like I was digging. That's all the information I have." She pushes Laura Lynne out the door. "Get your stuff together and head on to Tea Olive. You need to let your Uncle Gabe know what's going on before police show up at his front door again." She shepherds Laura Lynne out to the car. "Be careful, Laura Lynne. Keep me posted, and I will do the same."

Laura Lynne arrives at The Residence to see John, Liam, and Uncle Gabe in the front gardens. They have done so much work. The base for the water fountain is laid. The stone paths are complete. And there are new plants, trees, and bushes freshly planted.

Laura Lynne rolls down the passenger window as she drives by. "Looks really good y'all!" She waves as she drives to the house.

Laura Lynne unloads the trunk and immediately spots the copied file of the abducted girls. Removing it, Laura Lynne takes it immediately into the house and to the vault. Opening the door, she looks around and decides to store the four-inch thick file under the boxes of ammunition. She locks the safe behind her and takes a deep breath. Everything is beginning to feel real. The surreal feeling of the last few days is dissipating. Laura Lynne acknowledges to herself that who she is right this minute is not who she will ever be again. Her world is going to change, hopefully for the better. But it will change.

Laura Lynne empties out the contents of her car. She is suddenly exhausted. Walking to the back porch, she sees her book on the ghosts of Venice and decides to lie down on the lounge and read for a bit. She gets a throw from the basket and covers her legs as she stretches out. She opens her book and starts to read.

"Laura Lynne, Laura Lynne? Wake up sleepy head!" She opens her eyes. Pearl is shaking her leg. "You been asleep for three hours! Don't you have a show to see tonight?" Laura Lynne sits up and looks around, groggy as Pearl says, "Must have needed it. I let you sleep as long as I could." Laura Lynne shakes her head to clear the cobwebs before spotting the tea next to her. She takes a big gulp.

"Lord, what time is it, Pearl?"

"It's a little after 5. The school play starts at 6. I checked the website. Mr. Gabe mentioned it to Victoria and me over breakfast this morning. I didn't want you to be late." She puts her hand on Laura Lynne's forehead to check for a fever. "You feelin' all right?"

"I am fine. I just haven't been sleeping very well." Laura Lynne asks curiously, "Anybody stop by while I was sleeping?" Pearl shakes her head in the negative. "Hmmm, I thought Grady might come by." Laura Lynne throws off the cover and stands to her feet. "I need to get ready."

"You want me to make you something to eat before you go?"

"No, no, I had a late lunch with Mary. I think I am good. I will get something this evening." Laura Lynne picks up her phone and checks the messages. There is one from Grady that says, "Can't wait to see you tonight at Cotton Mill. Party starts at 8 PM." Laura Lynne turns to Pearl and says, "Looks like there is an afterparty at Cotton Mill. That will be nice." Pearl just gives her the hairy eyeball. Laura Lynne is a terrible liar.

Laura Lynne takes a shower that lasts longer than time permitted. The water feels wonderful and does the trick to revitalize the drooping Laura Lynne. She dresses in black slacks and a pink top. She twists her hair into a high bun and adds a touch of makeup, pearls, and strappy sandals. She looks in the mirror and mutters, "Closest thing to theater clothes I have. Will have to do." Checking the time, Laura Lynne rushes down the stairs and rushes by Pearl, calling out, "Tell Uncle Gabe I'll be late tonight. If he needs me, I'll be at the Cunninghams!" She waves as she hops in the car and barrels down the driveway. She honks the horn at the boys as they head in from their work in the gardens.

Laura Lynne makes it to Moseley Hall a few minutes before the opening scene. She picks up her ticket at will call and makes her way to the front of the house. Rachele lifts her hand in greeting, and Laura Lynne says, "How did I get so lucky with family seating?"

Rachele gives her a brief hug before taking her seat. "I had hoped Momma would be able to make it, but she is not feeling well tonight. I exchanged your ticket for this one. I am so glad you made it!"

"Me too." The lights flash. It's time to begin.

The curtain comes up, and the show begins. Samantha is the star of the show as Belle. The other actors try their best, but Samantha has a gift. Laura Lynne notes Mandy's work on the set design. The whimsical view of Belle's village is spectacular. Laura Lynne joins the crowd in a standing ovation as the curtain closes. The applause for Samantha's rendition of Belle is thunderous. Laura Lynne leans over to Rachele, jabbing her with an elbow. "She is a star."

Rachele has tears streaming down her cheeks unchecked "I know. She wants to audition for Juilliard. I think I have to let her."

As Laura Lynne makes her way out into the aisle, a friendly teacup poodle in the form of Prissa comes up alongside her. "Laura Lynne, don't forget to join us tonight at Cotton Mill. Mr. and Mrs. Cunningham are so excited you have time to come by for a visit!" She winks as she heads up the aisle.

"Thanks, Prissa. I am on my way!" Laura Lynne replies. She looks at Rachele and says, "I have been trying to see them since I got here, and it's been so busy. But I want to see Sam first and tell her how wonderful she was. I am so glad y'all invited me." They make it to the lobby. "I haven't been to Moseley since my sophomore year." Laura Lynne looks around the lobby. "Doesn't seem to have changed much." There is a hush and then a round of applause. The cast enters the lobby.

Rachele takes Laura Lynne's hand, and they plow their way through the crowd to Samantha. Rachele looks at her daughter and opens her arms, and Samantha just walks into them. They are crying and laughing together. It's beautiful to see. Hugh joins in the hug. His baby girl is all grown up. Everyone gives their congratulations and praise. Laura Lynne joins in the accolades before turning to take her leave.

Before getting to the door, Laura Lynne spots Mandy along the wall, standing amongst the guests.

"Mandy, the set is fabulous! I love the whimsy!" Laura Lynne leans over and hugs her neck.

"Thanks." Mandy looks around. "Set design is not as important as the performance." She seems upset and disappointed that no one is acknowledging all her hard work.

Laura Lynne takes her hands. "Look at me." Mandy is looking at her feet, and Laura Lynne uses her finger to pull up her chin. "Look at me, Amanda." She meets her eyes, and Laura Lynne smiles. "That is absolutely not true. You create the scene. Without your vision and your understanding of the characters, it's just actors up there doing lines." She cups her cheeks. "You create the magic. You paint the scene. Very few people can do what you did."

"Really?" She doesn't look convinced.

"Really." Laura Lynne drops her hands and steps back. "I have a gift with a pen, but I suck with a paintbrush." Laura Lynne smiles, and Mandy grins.

"Thanks, Miss Laura Lynne. I guess I need to go and tell Sam what a great job she did."

"I think that would be nice and absolutely the right thing." She watches as Mandy goes over to Samantha. She taps her on the shoulder, and Samantha squeals, grabbing her in a big hug. Laura Lynne smiles at the two girls and is delighted to see Samantha introducing Mandy to the onslaught of well-wishers. Samantha is a fine young lady.

Laura Lynne leaves the lobby and walks toward her car. The parking lot is deserted. Everyone is still hanging out in the lobby. Then, Laura Lynne hears someone calling her name. As she turns around, she comes face to face with Bubba Westerman. Laura Lynne freezes and forces herself to smile. She attempts to act nonchalantly. "Sheriff! What are you doing here?" He spits in the grass. He has a wad of tobacco tucked in his front lip.

"The teapot is my granddaughter, Candy's youngest. Try to make it to all the grandkids stuff. Didn't get to do too much of that with my own daughters." He spits again. "How you enjoyin' your return home? Been awhile, huh? Hear you been going to the Gazette ever'day. Spendin' time with the retired schoolteacher, Mary Wright." He looks at her with piercing, beady eyes. "What y'all doin' in there ever'day Lookin' for somethin' special?"

Laura Lynne clears her throat. "Just doing research for a book. But today is my last day. I cleared out this afternoon. It's time for me to head back home to my husband now that Uncle Gabe has been cleared." Laura Lynne starts walking backward in an attempt to create space between them. "Don't worry, Sheriff. I got your message loud and clear at the gala."

"Hmmph. When you leavin'?" He spits again. Laura Lynne is pretty sure he is aiming for her sandaled foot.

"Early next week." Laura Lynne stops her backward retreat. "I find it curious you are so fascinated with my schedule. Why do you care? What about me worries you?"

He clears his throat and spits again. This time she has to sidestep or risk his wad of nastiness hitting her bare feet. His aim is intentional. "Just keeping tabs on the comings and goings of the people in my town." He turns away. "You have a safe trip back to New Mexico, Laura Lynne." He takes his hand out of his pocket and gives a little wave. "And give my regards to Mary."

Laura Lynne hurries to her car and gets in. She calls Grace, who picks up on the second ring. "Grace, just listen to me. Call Grady and tell him I am running late. Tell him Bubba Westerman caught me in the parking lot at Moseley Hall."

"What? What's wrong, Laura Lynne? You sound scared."

"I am not scared! I am *pissed*! That southern fried fat bastard just tried to intimidate me *again* and now I am *mad*! Just tell him, please!"

"Okay! Okay! What do you mean again? Let me text him. Just stay on the line with me."

"Text him and then call him. Listen, I will explain everything later. Oh, and tell him to send somebody to check on Mary Wright. He sort of threatened her too." She hangs up and forces herself not to hightail it out of the parking lot. No way he knows he rattled her. Laura Lynne suspects he is still watching her.

Laura Lynne's phone lights up. It's a number she doesn't recognize. It's local. With trepidation, Laura Lynne answers, half suspecting Bubba Westerman to be on the other end. "Hello?"

"Hi, Laura Lynne! It's Prissa. Just making sure you remember how to get to Cotton Mill. I forgot to ask when I saw you in the theater. I should have had you follow me." Grady is having her call, but Laura Lynne is sure he is standing next to her.

"Prissa. Glad you called. I am sorry I am running a little late. I am on the way. I just got tied up for a few minutes. I should get there in the next ten minutes or so."

"Great! We will see you then." As she hangs up, she starts to calm down. She refuses to succumb to Bubba Westerman's scare tactics. She enters the gates to Cotton Mill, and a sense of relief floods her body. She parks in front of the house, and Mr. and Mrs. Cunningham come out the front door.

"Hello, Laura Lynne. So glad you could make it."

She makes her way up the front stairs, feeling like she is being watched. Mrs. Cunningham opens her arms, and Laura Lynne steps in for a hug.

"You all right, Laura Lynne?" Mrs. Cunningham whispers in her ear.

"Yes," she whispers back, "Just got spooked."

"Grady is waiting for you out back." Mrs. Cunningham steps back. Mr. Cunningham puts his hand on the small of Laura Lynne's back, pushing her in front of him while Mrs. Cunningham holds her hand. Mrs. Cunningham says, "We are just going to put on a little show in case anyone is watching." Laura Lynne squeezes Mrs. Cunningham's hand. She squeezes back and releases Laura Lynne to go through the door first. Both Cunninghams are putting themselves between her and whatever may be lurking in the dark. She nearly cries with the sweetness of the gesture.

Grady motions her out the backdoor, keeping a finger over his lips in a gesture of silence. Once outside, he whispers harshly, "What in the hell happened?"

"You tell me! I thought this was supposed to be kept a secret! You have a leak in that office, or Bubba has friends at the state police." Laura Lynne has her hands on her hips, and her chin juts out in defiance.

"Let's take this away from the house. We need to walk toward the back of the farm out toward the mill." He looks at her feet. "You need better shoes." He snaps his fingers. "Hold on. Prissa has a pair."

"Grady, are you serious? Your wife is the size of a teakettle poodle! Her feet are half the size of mine! Get me a pair of your dad's mud boots." He is back in a matter of moments. Laura Lynne hastily slides her sandaled foot in. "Okay, let's get going." The two start walking. Grady has a flashlight, but he has not turned it on.

"Tell me what happened," Grady says.

Laura Lynne relays the events in the parking lot word for word. The conversation is embedded in her brain. "And, Grady, I should have told you, but Bubba threatened me at the gala. He told me to let sleeping dogs lie, or a similar metaphor. Sorry I didn't mention it." Laura Lynne keeps talking. "Did you send someone to check on Mary?"

"Yes, she is fine. She packed a bag and headed over to spend the night at Ron Adams." He looks over his shoulder, glancing at Laura Lynne. "Did you know they were dating?"

"I suspected."

"He said he would look out for her. I sent Grace, so nobody from the department. I also told my dad enough that he is going to Tea Olive to check on your uncle."

Panic fills Laura Lynne. "Why? What do you know?"

"Nothing. Calm down. But if Bubba and his cronies are going to stoop to intimidation, they may try your family. Now, tell me what happened at the gala."

Laura Lynne nods. Grady is right. "I will, but first, call your daddy and tell him there is a farm hand named John who lives on the property. You know that old fishing shack we used to play in as kids? Near Mill Pond Road? He lives there now." She stares at the ground, trying to make sure she does not fall on her face in the huge work boots. "He knows how to use a gun. I think he is ex-military. He will watch out for Uncle Gabe if you let him know."

Grady takes out his phone and calls his father. He picks it up in one ring and relays the information to his dad. "And Pops, take the river. Be discreet." He hangs up. "Said he will handle it and let us know if anything is going on. Now, quit stalling and tell me about the gala."

Laura Lynne relays the events on the back veranda of the club. Grady grunts his disapproval but does not chastise Laura Lynne for her failure to disclose this information to him.

Finally, Grady turns on the flashlight and lights up the path. "Come on, we are almost there." Laura Lynne can hear the water from the brook flowing across the rocks. She and Grace played there for hours growing up. Grady walks in front of her and pulls out his gun. He keeps it to the side of his leg.

"Grady, why the gun?"

"Listen, Laura Lynne. I don't trust anyone anymore. I would rather be prepared. Jerry is supposed to meet us out here with the agents from the state police. They have some questions for you."

"I have some questions for them too."

Grady whistles and receives a whistle back. Laura Lynne rolls her eyes. Boys never grow up. Jerry comes out from around the mill house, saying, "Don't shoot. It's me." He also has his gun drawn but at his side, just like Grady. "I have two special agents with me." He walks toward Laura Lynne. "Thanks for coming and dealing with all the espionage. This is bigger than we knew when we talked yesterday."

"You don't know the half of it."

"What? What happened?" Jerry asks as he looks at Grady and takes Laura Lynne by the arm to escort her to the mill.

Grady answers, "She had a run-in with Bubba Westerman in the school parking lot after the play. Some veiled threats. She's fine, just a bit rattled."

Laura Lynne shakes her arm loose. "She is standing right here and can answer for herself."

The three enter the mill and blink at the bright lights. From outside, it appears pitch dark. It takes a moment for their eyes to adjust. Standing against the far wall are two agents dressed in khakis and golf shirts. They, too, are armed, but their weapons are holstered. The older of the two steps forward.

"Laura Lynne?" The agent says look at her. Laura Lynne looks over at Grady. He catches her signal and stands between her and the agent. The agent continues, "I am Special Agent Mark Shingle. This is my partner, Special Agent Derrick Johnson. "We are from the FBI." Laura Lynne looks to Grady as he shrugs his shoulders.

"Can I see some identification, please?" Laura Lynne asks. They nod and pull out their badges. Laura Lynne has no idea what she is looking at, but she acts like she does. "Thank you."

Putting their badges away, the two men pull up chairs. Agent Shingle starts speaking again. "Do you mind if we all sit down? This may take some time. We have been waiting for you Laura Lynne, for a long time."

"Waiting for me?" Laura Lynne asks, taking a seat in an empty chair.

"Or someone like you," says Agent Shingle. "Someone who can put the key players of an investigation we have been running for the last 30-plus years together."

"I am very confused. Can we start over?" Laura Lynne looks to Grady. "What are they saying?"

Grady explains, "They are saying you are the hammer they are going to use to nail the lid on a coffin of some very bad men."

"I am a hammer?" She looks over at Agent Shingle. "How am I a hammer?"

"We received an anonymous tip in the late 80s that some girls were being hurt, and someone needed to check it out," says Agent Shingles, "The only identifier was a female, and the phone number was traced back to a public phone on the south side of this town. We had nothing to go on, but an investigation was started. It ended up being a cold case." Agent Shingle pauses a moment.

He continues, "Over the years, there had been rumors of corruption in the Venice sheriff's office. Not terribly surprising for small-town Mississippi. The good ol' boy network is alive and well in small towns. Especially in the backwoods of Mississippi."

Agent Shingle looks at Agent Johnson and continues, "It's Derrick and my job to investigate these claims." His gaze swings back to her. "Our line of work is forensic accounting, misuse of funds, bribes, those types of crimes. Sexual assault is not generally under our prevue. However, when investigating Venice, we located the original file from the anonymous tip. Some of the interviews in the files had the same names we were looking at. This piqued our interest. Without going into more detail, let's just say this is much bigger than Venice County."

Agent Johnson takes over, "Sheriff Bubba Westerman is one of those names. We haven't moved on this yet because we think he is a fairly small fish in a much bigger pond. Then yesterday, we got a call from Jerry's buddy in the state police department about an interesting situation that has been uncovered in Venice, Mississippi, involving sexual crimes of underage girls. The officer gave us three names." Derrick looks at Laura Lynne. "Two of the names we, too, uncovered. But we have no proof. We didn't have the third name, Dr. Kenneth Butler."

"What about Judge Silas Monroe?" asks Laura Lynne.

"Why do you ask?" asks Agent Shingle.

Laura Lynne replies, "He was invited to Dr. Butler's wedding. He didn't attend, but the other two did. It just seemed suspicious."

Agent Jonhson and Agent Shingle look at each other. Agent Johnson answers, "We have not currently linked him to the investigation."

"Currently? So, you are looking?" Laura Lynne asks.

"Not at this. Not from the crimes you uncovered," Agent Johnson says.

"You didn't know about the abducted girls?" Laura Lynne questions.

Agent Johnson shakes his head. "We didn't know about them until recently. Their cases were never filed through the proper channels. Plus, this was before everything went to computers. Easy to hide evidence. That is exactly what we think Bubba Westerman did in this instance."

Agent Shingle says, "We couldn't put it together until we learned about you. Laura Lynne, I need you to tell us what happened to you in 1985 that makes you think these men are involved in a conspiracy."

Laura Lynne shakes her head. "I am not ready to tell you my story. Let it suffice to say my experience was similar enough to the other girls that I know I am the 11th victim. My rape date was July 13, 1985. And I have reason to believe my rapist was Dr. Kenneth Butler."

"We need details," says Agent Shingle.

"I'm sorry. You are not going to get them. Not tonight. But I have no reason to lie. I can file a complaint, but the statute of limitations is long past the deadline." She looks between the two men. "You are just going to have to take my word on this."

"Would you be willing to testify in a court of law?" asks Agent Johnson.

"If it came to that, yes." Laura Lynne stands from her chair and begins to pace. "My hesitation is simply that I have not told my children or my siblings or even my mother. They have a right to know before it becomes available for public consumption."

Grady cuts in, "Laura Lynne, this can't wait. Bubba Westerman already confronted you in the parking lot."

"Wait. What? What happened?" asks Agent Johnson. The agents also stand up. Grady relays the incident, and the agents nod.

Agent Johnson explains, "He is still connected. Somebody is talking to him. I don't think he knows what we have, though. He's fishing."

"Listen, I need to call my boss. I want to arrest these men tonight. I don't want them to get scared and run. We are too close," says Agent Shingle.

Laura Lynne asks, "Is it really this urgent? I mean, these men are old now, in their 80s. Dr. Butler is the youngest, but he has to be pushing 70. Do you really think they care at this point? They will die before they end up in jail." Everyone gets silent and looks at Laura Lynne. "Wait, what am I missing?" Laura Lynne looks at Grady as she clutches her shirt collar. Her throat begins closing. "Grady?"

He walks over to Laura Lynne. Taking her hands from her throat, he rubs them with his thumb. "Laura Lynne." His voice is serious and low. She stops fidgeting and meets his eyes. "It's still happening." Grady rubs her hands. "Remember I told you I would check Boston for similar incidents? They have quite a few that seem to match."

"Oh God, oh God. How many?" Laura Lynne sinks into the chair.

"We don't know yet," Grady says as he sits down in front of her. "And you are right. These men are too old to be doing this anymore. But somebody is. We have traced money back to Venice. We believe these men still have their hand in the game."

Agent Shingle comes back into the building. "Listen, we have to go. The director has given us the go-ahead. I have the arrest warrants."

"What about Dr. Butler?"

"Local boys are picking him up. We are coordinating with them."

Jerry has been quiet this entire time. He leans on a post in the mill house. "Grady, you take Laura Lynne back to Tea Olive. Keep her safe. I recommend we coordinate our efforts and pick up these two men at the same time." He points his finger at himself. "I will get Dr.Goldbug. He shouldn't give me much of an issue." Then he points at the agents. "Bubba's going to be a challenge. Don't see him coming quietly." He looks at Grady. "Grady, thoughts?"

"Agreed," confirms Grady.

Laura Lynne clears her throat and raises her hand. "I am safe at Tea Olive as long as John is there. He knows how to handle a weapon. He will watch out for my uncle and me."

"You sure?" asks Grady.

Laura Lynne nods.

"Okay, it is settled," says Jerry. "Grady and Derrick will get Dr. Goldbug. Mark and I will get Bubba. I want to be a part of that arrest if you boys don't mind." He looks from one to the other. "I don't trust pulling in anybody else. Not after the run-in Laura Lynne had in the parking lot."

Agent Johnson holds up his phone. "I just got the search warrants. Let's go."

Grady and Agent Jonhson surround Laura Lynne with an unspoken agreement. One takes point, and the other swings in behind. "Grady? I have a thought. I think you could turn Dr. Goldbug. He's their weak link," says Laura Lynne.

"What makes you think that?" asks Agent Johnson.

"Just a gut feeling,"

The trio arrives at the Cunningham's main residence. Laura Lynne takes off her boots and goes inside. The Cunninghams are waiting. Mr. Cunningham holds up his hand before Laura Lynne can even ask. He is armed. "Your uncle is fine. John is guarding the house. Anything you can tell us?"

Laura Lynne sighs. "Only that it's going to be all over in the next couple of hours. Grady is going to make the arrests as we speak."

"Come on, honey," Mrs. Cunningham speaks up. "Let's see Laura Lynne off like she's been visiting with us for the past hour." They go to the front door and open it. Mr. Cunningham props his rifle at the door within arm's reach. They give hugs all around. The Cunninghams stay close. "Don't be a stranger!"

Laura Lynne waves and gets in her car. As she turns right onto the road, she sees Grady driving his daddy's Cadillac. He flashes his lights, and Laura Lynne flashes back. She drives straight to Tea Olive.

Gabe is standing at the mud room door waiting on her. He is holding his rifle.

"Laura Lynne, you okay?" Gabe asks.

"Yes, I'm fine. Everything good here?"

"Just fine. John is watching the house. Come on in, sweetheart. I have the kettle on for some hot tea."

Laura Lynne sends a quick text to Grady, "safe."

"Tea sounds lovely," she says.

As they walk into the kitchen, Gabe lifts his gun. "There are two more of these. One at the back door. The other is on the entrance table. You remember how to use them?" Laura Lynne nods. You don't grow up on a farm and not know how to handle a rifle.

Gabe places the rifle on the island and fills a mug with hot water, soaking a tea bag. "What can you tell me?"

"Looks like everything will either be over or just starting in the next few minutes." She takes a sip of tea and closes her eyes. "They are making arrests and have obtained search warrants. Seems my story is the catalyst they were waiting for." She leans back against the counter. "It's all very surreal, you know? I have been living with this fear that no one would believe me if I accused the man who I believe assaulted me. Now, not only am I believed, but I'm helping put away the bad guys."

"Cunningham came over and said you had been approached in the parking lot of the school by

Bubba Westerman. You were safe but rattled. What did he say to you?"

"He just wanted me to know that he was watching me. He knew about me going to the Gazette. He wanted to know what I was poking around in. When I was leaving. He didn't touch me." Laura Lynne wrinkles her nose. "He aimed his tobacco spit at my foot!"

Staring at his gun, Gabe says with a wry smile, "Want me to go shoot him for you?" Then his face turning serious, he asks Laura Lynne, "Is he one of the arrests happening tonight?"

"I am probably not meant to tell you, but I think you know the answer to that, right enough."

"Not at all surprised. Surprised it took so long. A more crooked sheriff never existed. He was on your father's payroll until he died." Laura Lynne looks over at him, not sure what he is telling her. "Thought you should know as it might come out in all this mess."

"He ever been on yours?"

"No. He came around once or twice when he was still sheriff. He realized quickly enough I was not interested in his style of law. And, well, I threatened him, so that helped." He walks to the window and looks out. "Once he was no longer in office, it was no longer an issue."

"Threatened him? With what?"

"Doesn't matter. It worked." He holds up his hand. "You have your secrets, and I have mine."

Laura Lynne's phone pings. It is Grady. Apparently, there is no more need for subterfuge. The message says, "Arrests complete. On the way to the sheriff's office."

Laura Lynne asks her Uncle Gabe, "You want to come sit in the study with me? I need to call Gray and tell him what is going on. You may as well hear it at the same time."

"Sure, can't wait." Gabe leaves the rifle in the kitchen. In the study, he opens a desk drawer and pulls out a pistol. Gabe places it on the side table and takes a seat in the leather recliner. Laura Lynne places her phone on the end table and calls Gray on speaker phone.

"What's up beautiful?" Gray answers right away.

Laura Lynne updates him on the events of the last 24 hours. Gray does not take it well. "Laura Lynne, I am on the way right now. You stay put!"

Laura Lynne rolls her eyes and looks at her uncle. He just shrugs his shoulders, suggesting that Laura Lynne was the one that married him. What is he supposed to do?

Laura Lynne tries to calm her husband down, "Gray, there is no need! It is all over now. Believe me, if I had any idea this would happen, I would have asked you to come."

He is silent.

"Gray," Laura Lynne continues, "Uncle Gabe is sitting right here with a pistol on the side table and three rifles posted at each door. And John is outside watching the house."

Gabe finally chimes in. "Gray, don't you worry. I won't let anything happen to Laura Lynne."

The tears begin streaming down her face. She did it. She stood up in her power and embraced her past. She is no longer ashamed, regardless of the outcome. "Gray." Her voice cracks with obvious tears.

"Baby? What is it? You're breaking my heart."

"No, no, it's good." Laura Lynne wipes at her eyes. "I did it. I faced the monster, and it feels really good."

"You sure the hell did! You're my wife! You slay dragons! And you capture hearts, baby. You sure did get mine. I love you so much. And I am proud of you!"

The two talk for a few more minutes. Laura Lynne relays her travel plans, with her return date on Monday. "Now that this is over, it's time to get back to our life."

"I miss you, sweetheart." Gray raises his voice, "Mr. Gabe, you still there?"

"I'm here. Listening to you two love birds," says Gabe.

"Thank you for keeping her safe for me. I owe you one."

"No, son. I owe you. I can see you love her and take good care of her. She deserves it." He shakes his head. "Never did care for that first one." Laura Lynne laughs. You got to love family.

"Okay! Enough," Laura Lynne cuts in. "I am hanging up! I love you, you big lug! I will see you on Monday."

"Count on it. Keep me posted. Love you more!" Laura Lynne rolls her eyes and disconnects.

She walks over to the back porch and calls out into the dark. "John? You out there?"

He whistles. What is it with men and their whistle signal? It sounds like it's coming from the azalea bushes next to the old barn currently being used as a garage and storage shed. "It's over! You can go back to your place now if you want!"

John comes out from the azaleas. He is dressed in fatigues and combat boots. "Thank you, Miss Laura Lynne. But I plan to keep watch for the night. It will make me feel better." Laura Lynne gives him her "mother eye."

"Did my husband text you? Ask you to keep watch?" He gives Laura Lynne a slow grin. Laura Lynne notices again his rugged good looks, now enhanced by the fatigues and gun.

"No, ma'am. No text."

"Okay, but I am taking myself and Uncle Gabe to bed. You do what you think is best. Thank you for everything. For tonight, for looking after my uncle,

The Residence, all of it." She turns around and heads to the house. Then it hits her. "He called you, didn't he?" She hears John's low laugh as he walks back to his post.

Laura Lynne returns to the study. Gabe is in his chair with his pistol next to him. But now he is sipping his bourbon. "Laura Lynne, I have to be honest with you. I found the file. The one in the vault." He looks at her over the rim of his glass. "It wasn't intentional. I was getting the guns and ammunition out of the vault. I wanted you to know. I read it. Well, enough of it to know who got arrested tonight."

"It's okay. I am glad that you know. I planned to tell you at some point anyway. You already knew most of it." Laura Lynne squats in front of her beloved uncle. "Don't let it worry you. More concerned about the grapevine tomorrow. It will probably get pretty ugly."

"I don't think it will be as bad as you believe. Plenty of good people in this town will see what I see—a beautiful, brave warrior."

"You think so? I don't." Getting up from her squat, Laura Lynne picks up the pistol and places it back in the desk drawer. "Alcohol and guns don't mix, Uncle Gabe. Besides, I think we can put the guns away. John is going to keep watch over us tonight. He and Gray have worked something out."

He nods and looks sad. "I won't be long. Gonna sip this bourbon and then head up." Laura Lynne kisses him on top of the head.

"Love you, Uncle Gabe. Good night." He doesn't respond. He just gazes into his glass of bourbon. "You okay, Uncle Gabe?"

He shakes himself aware. "What? Yes, yes, I am fine. Just a lot to take in, you know? I have known those two men my whole life. It makes me sad they hurt you and all those other girls."

"I know. They fooled a lot of people. Beau and Savannah will make you feel better tomorrow. They should be here around noon. I can't wait to show them Tea Olive for the first time. I know they will love it as much as I do. Would love for you to join us."

"I wouldn't miss it. Love you, Laura Lynne."

Chapter 25

Laura Lynne enters the kitchen the next morning to find Pearl and Victoria in deep discussion. Laura Lynne chimes in, "Grapevine working overtime this morning?"

Pearl gives a very unladylike snort. "Your ears must be burning! The arrests of Bubba and Dr. Goldbug are the talk of the town. Everyone thinks you had something to do with it. Care to confirm?"

"No. I plead the fifth," Laura Lynne replies. "I prefer to focus on my two beautiful children coming to see me for the very first time at my childhood home. I am going to embrace the joy of the moment." Laura Lynne looks outside the window. "Where is Uncle Gabe? He was up pretty late last night."

"He's already outside and working in the garden. The fountain came yesterday. He is anxious to get it installed for Eileen's memorial," Pearl says.

"Oh, how wonderful! And sweet. I don't know what he is going to do without that project to keep him busy," says Laura Lynne.

"Plenty to do around here, Laura Lynne. He will just choose another piece of dirt to make into a garden," Pearl says.

Laura Lynne laughs at the accuracy of this statement. "Are the rooms ready for my children? Anything you need me to do?"

Victoria nods, "You can review the menu with me and make sure I have chosen appropriate dishes. I am not sure what Savannah and Beau like to eat."

Laura Lynne looks at the list of potential meals. "I am happy to say neither are very picky, but Beau has never liked a tomato. He will eat ketchup, tomato sauce, and even tomato soup, but not a fresh tomato. And both of them eat meat, so you don't have to plan a vegetarian menu. That should make things a bit easier."

After handing the list back to Victoria, she remembers, "Oh, Pearl, I meant to ask. What is that wonderful lavender and lemon sugar scrub and lotion I found in the bathroom last night? I really loved it but didn't see a label. It's in a mason jar?"

"Oh, that's Scarlet's gift to the house every Christmas. She makes a different scent each year. The lavender and lemon is last year's scent. I think it's one of her best," explains Pearl.

"Really?" Laura Lynne says with surprise, "I had no idea. Do we have any to put in the kid's bathroom? They love stuff like that, all about the smells."

"If we have any, it's in the pantry. Look next to the laundry and dish detergent. She makes those too," says Pearl.

Scarlet makes laundry and dish detergent. And bakes like a wizard?

The kitchen pantry is large, and the shelves are carefully stocked with supplies. There is an entire wall dedicated to dishes. It's a veritable history of the house. Pearl follows Laura Lynne. Laura Lynne smirks. "Worried I might touch something? Move it out of place?"

"Yes."

Laura Lynne laughs as Pearl hands her the scrub and lotion. "Thanks, Pearl. They will love it."

Pearl gives Laura Lynne a quick hug. "I am so glad they are coming. I finally get to meet them. They are going to love it here."

"I certainly hope so."

At 12:30, Laura Lynne is standing on the porch watching her children drive slowly up the entrance in a convertible. Beau is driving. "They are here, Pearl! Uncle Gabe!" Both come up behind her, as excited as Laura Lynne to greet her beautiful children.

"Mom! This is The Residence? My God, it's Tara from *Gone with the Wind*!" Savannah rolls out of the front seat and hugs her mother.

Laura Lynne laughs. "Not quite, but it's stunning, isn't it?" Beau comes around the front of the car and gives her a side hug.

"Hi, Mom. Nice digs."

"Come on, I want you to say hi to Uncle Gabe and meet Pearl." Laura Lynne links arms with her children and walks up the front stairs. Savannah hugs Uncle Gabe, and Beau shakes his hand. Laura Lynne continues with introductions, "Y'all, this is Pearl. She is one of my oldest and dearest friends."

Laura Lynne looks at Pearl. She has tears in her eyes. "Pearl, my children. Savannah Lynne and Beauregard Cooper." That does it; the water wells break loose.

Pearl opens her arms for a group hug.

"Lordy, y'all are beautiful. Cooper through and through! Especially you Mr. Beauregard! Look just like your Uncle Tripp when he was a young man." She turns around. Y'all go on inside. Take your Uncle Gabe. Victoria has set up the back porch for a light meal and drinks." She gently pushes everyone forward. "John and I will get the bags and park the car." She looks at Beau. "Keys?"

Not knowing what else to do, he hands them over. "Yes, ma'am."

The kids ooh and ahh their way to the back porch, absorbing the house while Uncle Gabe gives them a tour of the downstairs. He shows them his latest project, and Laura Lynne watches from a distance. Beau is dressed in khakis and a button-down with his ever-present Sperry shoes. Savannah has on a cute maternity dress, holding her bump as she listens to Uncle Gabe discuss the fountain and the gardens. She crosses her legs, and Laura Lynne gets the signal. She comes to stand behind her daughter and says, "Uncle Gabe, let's let the kids freshen up and have a bite to eat. We can show them the fountain and gardens after our meal."

"Of course, of course. I do get caught up, don't I?" Gabe responds.

Laura Lynne shows Savannah to the powder room. Savannah instantly falls in love with the rich patterned wallpaper and antique fixtures. Uncle Gabe escorted Beau out to the porch. They are pouring drinks and settling in with the cheese and charcuterie. Laura Lynne's heart is full. She realizes just how badly she wanted to share her home with them. Hopefully, what she needs to tell them will make them proud and not embarrassed.

Savannah comes out of the bathroom, rolling her eyes. "Beau came around to pick me up in that convertible, and I just about died." She wraps her arm around Laura Lynne's waist. The two walk arm-in-arm to the porch. "He does realize I am pregnant, right? I made him put up the top about 15 minutes down the road when I had to find a gas station and pee again!" Laura Lynne just laughs as she lays her cheek on top of Savannah's head.

Once the charcuterie board is demolished, Victoria brings out soup and sandwiches. It is a festive meal, each enjoying the company. Gabe pushes back from the table. "I am going to let y'all have some private time with your Momma." He looks at both Savannah and Beau. "I expect you both to be kind when you hear what she has to tell you." He gives a slight bow and heads to his study.

The children look expectantly at their mother. She clears her throat. "Y'all up for a walk to the river? I could use the walk while we talk. I have a lot to say, and I would rather do it out in the wide-open spaces." She gets up from the table. "You two may want to change into something more comfortable. If you don't have mud shoes, there are plenty in the mud room located off the kitchen." The kids get up, and Beau gives a mighty stretch.

"Can we get some of that sweet tea to go?" Beau asks.

"Sure. Savannah, how about water for you?" Laura Lynne asks. Savannah nods and rubs her belly. Laura Lynne continues, "I will meet y'all out back when you are ready." She walks through the kitchen doors, the kids following at her heels. "Pearl will show you your rooms. She has probably already unpacked your bags and set you up." They look at their mother quizzically. They have never had anyone unpack their bags before. "It's a Southern thing. Or at least a Tea Olive thing. Just go with it."

Victoria has the tea and water waiting. She has been no further than a whisper away the entire meal. "Victoria, the meal was perfect. Thank you for all the effort."

She smiles. "It was easy. Glad they liked it. Tonight will be the star, though. I have been working on the grits all morning."

"Queenie will be proud." Laura Lynne picks up the drinks. "I'd like to invite John and Liam to join us, but I think I need to see how this afternoon goes with Beau and Savannah."

"It's gonna go great. They are fine young people. They have good manners. You raised them well, Miss Laura Lynne." She shoos her out of the kitchen. "Now, scat! I can't have you distracting me while I am trying to cook!" She waves a kitchen towel at Laura Lynne and then throws it over her shoulder. Once again, she reminds Laura Lynne of Queenie. She can't help but smile.

"I'm going! I'm going!" Laura Lynne exits the kitchen through the mud room. She waits at the beginning of the path. Savannah and Beau arrive together. Savannah stayed in her sun dress, but Beau switched to shorts and a t-shirt. Both are sporting shoes from the mud room. Laura Lynne hands them their drinks, and she starts to walk and talk.

"First, thank you both for coming down here. I know it was an inconvenience, and you have been really great about not asking why I needed you here." She takes a breath and sighs it out. "But I wanted you to hear this from me personally. Then you can ask me any questions you might have." Laura Lynne gazes at her children. "Nothing is off limits, you understand?"

"Mom, what is it? Did you murder somebody? Is there a brother or sister we don't know about? Are you a polygamist?" Savannah asks in rapid fire. Laura Lynne realizes at that moment that she has made things worse by waiting. They have been stewing for days about the visit. It was wrong of her.

"No! No, I am sorry! I am just now realizing I may have made things worse than they actually are!" Her breath hitches, and she slows her pace. "I just never wanted to tell you this, so it's a bit difficult for me.

It's just a hard story and one I have not even shared with your father."

Savannah and Beau look concerned as their mother continues, "I guess the best place to start is the summer of 1985. I was 15 and had an internship at the hospital. I was pretty excited because it was a paying job. I was saving for a car. It was a beat-up BMW with a million miles on it. Daddy told me I could have it if I could pay for it. The job was the first step." She tells them everything, from the babysitting gig to the visit with Dr. Goldbug. She tells them everything in detail, from her sophomore year until the previous day. The story takes two hours. The children listen without interruption. When Laura Lynne finally finishes, the three are sitting on the dock with their legs dangling.

"Mom, why didn't you ever tell us?" Savannah asks. "I don't know. I just didn't see where it made much of a difference. I couldn't prove it. Plus, I was ashamed." Laura Lynne looks out over the river and the marsh. There are three egrets standing in the pluff mud holding watch. "But I have pretty solid proof now. I am no longer ashamed. It's time to put all this behind me. I just couldn't do it as long as I didn't know for certain." She looks over at them. They are sitting one on each side of her. "I am still not 100% positive. Nobody has confessed. But yesterday, three of the men we think are involved were arrested." She pats each of their legs. "That is why I needed to tell you. There is a good chance my name will be in the newspaper, and the facts of the case will be public knowledge. I didn't want you to hear my story from anyone but me."

Beau looks at Laura Lynne and smiles. "I am glad you aren't dying. Or I have an older brother you never told me about."

"Might be easier than the nasty things that could be written about me, not to mention the Beauregards and Coopers. You don't realize how prominent your lineage is in this town." Laura Lynne looks back over the marsh. One of the egrets lifts his wings, drying himself off. "Lots of secret deals and unsavory characters in our family tree. Uncle Gabe alluded to some of them earlier. Plenty of people want to see us knocked down a rung or two. This might give them that opportunity."

"Let 'em try. We have been through a lot worse," reassures Beau. Laura Lynne knows Beau is thinking about the divorce from his father and the subsequent years of obstacles and challenges the three faced and overcame. "Are we going to meet your Momma this weekend?"

"I don't know. Do you want to?" Laura Lynne hangs her head. "She doesn't know the full story. I haven't been able to find the words to tell her." She lifts up her chin and squares her shoulders. "She may still not believe me. But if you want to meet her, I can bring her here." Savannah puts her head on Laura Lynne's shoulder. "I don't want us to go to town this weekend. There will be a ton of gossip."

"No, Mom. We are going. Tomorrow," Savannah says sternly, "We are going to have coffee at the Magnolia Café. You are done hiding." She holds Laura Lynne's hand with hers. "Beau and I want to be seen with our very brave Mom."

Laura Lynne sighs. They still don't understand. "I don't think you understand just how powerful these men are and the influence they have on this town. It could get very ugly. And honestly, I just don't want to face ugly right now. I want you to enjoy Tea Olive. I want you to fall in love with The Residence."

"Just so you know, we are not ashamed of you, Mom," says Savannah.

"That is so good to hear, sweetie. You have no idea." Laura Lynne looks at Beau. "How about you, Beau? Are you embarrassed by your mother?"

"Hell no! But I sure don't understand your parents. I can't imagine you ever throwing us out like that. I think the punishment is worse than the crime. It makes sense now why you never wanted to come back here." His legs are so long his boots are grazing the water in the river.

"Watch your mouth, young man!" Laura Lynne starts to get up from the dock. "But thank you for understanding. Your grandparents? Well, they are a product of their time. I try to believe they were doing what they thought best. It backfired for certain. Momma and Daddy lost a lot by taking the stance they did." Laura Lynne puts out her hand to help Savannah to her feet. Her baby bump keeps her off-center. "But so did you. You never got to grow up at The Residence. It really is a magical place."

"They lost more mom. They lost you…and us." Savannah rubs her belly. "Maybe it's because I am getting ready to be a mom myself, but I don't understand how anybody could treat their child the way they treated you. I am glad you have forgiven her. I plan to hold my forgiveness for a later judgment."

They collect their drink bottles and start heading back to the house. They take a detour to the live oak tree with the swing. Beau helps Savannah onto the wooden board base. She holds on to the ropes, and he gently pushes her. Beau asks, "How many acres are there, Mom?"

"Now, about 2,000. At its height, Tea Olive was closer to 4,000 acres. Over the generations, land was sold off or given in marriage. I know it was Uncle Gabe's and Aunt Eileen's dream to expand it back as close to that as they could."

"Really, why?" Beau asks.

Laura Lynne does a slow circle and looks around. "Maybe by the end of the weekend, you can answer that yourself." She stands next to Beau. "Preserve it for the next generations mostly." She clears her throat. "I am not sure y'all know, but Aunt Eileen made me executor of River Oaks. Uncle Gabe handles most of it. But she encouraged me to sell River Oaks and use the money to buy up land here if the opportunity presented itself. What do y'all think? You have as much of a stake in the decision as I do."

"How is that?" Savannah has put her feet down to stop the swing. Beau helps her off, teasing her about her ungainly dismount.

"Well, when Daddy died, Uncle Gabe inherited The Residence. The land is held in trust for my mother, Tripp, Scarlet, Avery, and me. The same will happen to the next generation. Tripp will inherit The Residence and continue to oversee the land use and business dealings. Anything that has to do with the trust. Up until now, I have kept my money in the trust. I just never wanted to touch it. I guess in my heart I knew I would be back one day. I was not ready to sever the connection. Avery did the same thing. Tripp is not given the choice."

"What about Aunt Scarlet?" Savannah asks.

"She took her money out or at least part of her money when she married."

They are both quiet. Laura Lynne knows the question swirling in their heads. "You want to know why I never pulled any out. Why I chose to do things on my own, right? Even when we could have desperately used the funds."

Savannah shakes her head. "No, I know why you didn't, Mom. Pride. You wanted to make it without your parents' help. You needed to prove it to yourself and to them." She hugs Laura Lynne from behind. "I feel the same way. Chris and I talk about making it on our own and not relying on our parents."

"Beau?" Laura Lynne asks, looking at her son.

"Did Dad know about the trust?" He has his hands in his pockets. He is so good-looking, tall, and strong. All Beauregard genes. Pearl is right. He looks like Tripp.

"No, I never told him," answers Laura Lynne.

"Why not, Mom? Seems to me he had a right to know," says Beau.

"Beau…" Savannah starts to chastise her little brother.

"No, it's okay", Laura Lynne interrupts, "I said earlier no questions were off limits." Laura Lynne looks at Beau. "I didn't tell him because I know he would have pressured me to take the money out." Laura Lynne shrugs her shoulders. "The money. The trust. It's my inheritance, and I wanted it for you. If I had pulled it out all those years ago, it would more than likely be gone." She shrugs again. "I don't know if I made the right decision or not, Beau, but the one I made was to preserve the trust for you and your children."

"What exactly is involved in the trust?" Beau asks.

"Honestly, I am not certain. Right now, Uncle Gabe is running everything. But he is getting old, and that is not going to work for much longer. Tripp is coming home for a while; at least, I think he is. It's his responsibility to work with Uncle Gabe to understand all that is in the trust domain, including the property, the house, River Oaks, stocks, businesses, and bonds. River Oaks converted to the trust on Aunt Eileen's death, though the final decisions with the property and home are mine alone."

She links arms with both her children. "But I want your input. This decision will affect you and your children and their children." She starts to walk down the path. "If we can do it right, it's quite a legacy we could leave behind." She starts to skip and pull them along. They join reluctantly. "It's a wonderful dream."

"Wait!" Beau stops and stares at his mother. His financial brain is at work. "Momma, how much money are we talking about here? Property, stocks, bonds, businesses…that is a lot of capital."

Laughing and skipping again, Laura says, "I have no idea. But you are right. It is a lot of money."

"Millions?" guesses Beau.

"Yes. I am sure Uncle Gabe could give you a better idea. The wealth is not liquid. It is in the land. And the land will never be sold."

Beau grabs her hand and starts skipping ecstatically down the path. They get to the house breathless and silly. Savannah's skipping is more like fast walking, but she keeps up. Pearl comes to the back door. "What is this ruckus going on, Laura Lynne? Thought there was a wild pack of river dogs at the back door!" They look at her and burst out laughing.

"God, Pearl, you look like your Momma! And Victoria shooed me out of the kitchen just like Queenie used to! I swear it's like I am a kid in trouble again." She gasps for air. "She would be so proud!"

"Get on with you, Laura Lynne. Miss Savannah, you get in here and put your feet up. Get those muddy boots off first. Beau, get yourself cleaned up before supper now, you hear? We do supper at 6 sharp!" Pearl heads back into the house, and the screen door slams shut behind her. Laura Lynne and her children look at each other and start laughing.

"Well, you heard her. It's best not to argue," says Laura Lynne.

"I think I love her," Beau says.

"Me too," agrees Savannah.

Laura Lynne smiles. "Her mother was the same way. Queenie. She was my Pearl when I was a teenager. You knew she loved you because she fussed after you."

"Does this mean Pearl loves us?" Savannah asks.

"Absolutely! I love you too." Laura Lynne turns serious. "Are y'all good? It was a lot to take in today. Listen, if after you think on it for a while, you want to talk some more about it, then let's do it. We have two days to sort through the emotions and feelings."

"I'm good," Savannah says. Beau nods in agreement.

"Mom, is it okay to tell Chris and Claire? I think they have a right to know," Savannah says.

"Of course. I don't want you two to keep secrets from your spouses. Though I prefer, for now, y'all keep it amongst the six of us. At least until we understand how this is going to pan out."

Laura Lynne and her children head in the house. Savannah goes to the back porch, Beau to his room, and Laura Lynne to the front porch. Laura Lynne calls Gray, and he picks up on the first ring.

"Hey, sweetheart. I have been dying to hear how it went."

"Surprisingly well. It was a two-hour telling. And we even got into the trust and how that worked. Discussed their legacy and the decisions we needed to make about River Oaks."

"Wow, you did cover a lot of territory."

Gray and Laura Lynne talk for another half an hour about the kids, the future, Eileen's memorial, and her return trip. "Any word from Grady or the Sheriff?"

"Not yet. I have a ton of texts from a lot of people, but none from them. I am going to hold off calling anyone back as long as I can. I hope to hear something soon, but I'm not counting on it."

"Okay. You good otherwise?"

"I am. You doing anything exciting this weekend?"

"Golfing with the boys is all, so keep me posted. I want to know what is happening." He waits a beat. "I miss you like hell. Plan to get naked when I see you Monday."

"It's a deal. Love you!"

"And I love you more than that." He disconnects as he gives her kissing noises.

Chapter 26

Laura Lynne wakes up the next morning with a feeling of peace and contentment. It has been so long since she has felt this way. She feels as if a tremendous burden has been lifted. She slips on her sweatshirt and wooly socks to make tea in the kitchen. She meets Savannah on the stairs. "Hi, Mom. I heard you get up. I hope you don't mind if I join you."

"Of course not. I love it. Did you not sleep well?"

"No, I slept great. I just wake up early these days." She pats her tummy. "I think God is just preparing me for when the little man gets here."

Holding hands, mother and daughter go to the kitchen. Laura Lynne prepares tea as the two chat. Laura Lynne hands Savannah her mug. "Come on. Let's sit on the front porch and watch the sunrise. It's beautiful in the mornings."

"I think it must be beautiful all the time. It's no wonder you never talked about Tea Olive Mom. It must have broken your heart to leave."

"It did, and it took some of my soul with it. There were many days when my soul cried for home." She takes a deep breath. "I don't think I realized just how much until I came back." Laura Lynne sits and pats the seat next to her. Savannah sits down. "But I have had a good life, Savannah. Your dad and I had a good marriage for a lot of years. We made beautiful children, and you both turned out so good, even with the awful years of the divorce." She takes a sip of tea. "Gray, the book, coming back to Tea Olive, it's just the icing on the cake."

"Chris and I talked for a long time last night. I told him the gist of why I am here. We are in agreement that whatever you need to do to finish this journey you are on, we support you 100%." She looks down at her tea. "He said something else too, mom. He said he loved me more, knowing I came from such strong stock. And we needed to have a girl next because I need a strong daughter of my own." Her eyes tear up. She swipes at them. "Stupid hormones."

"Not stupid." Laura Lynne lays her cheek on top of her daughter's head. "You did good with Chris, sweetheart. He's a good man. He will be an amazing father."

"I know."

Laura Lynne's phone buzzes. It's Grady. He has some news and wants to come by this morning. Laura Lynne replies, "I am up, so whenever."

Laura Lynne turns to Savannah, "That was Grady. The sheriff's deputy. He has some news. He is on the way over now. Sweetheart, do you mind waking up your brother and Uncle Gabe? I want us to hear whatever he has to say as a family."

"Sure, Momma. And you might want to change your clothes. No need looking like a homeless person."

Laura Lynne looks at the sweatshirt she is wearing. It has worn so thin at the shoulders and elbows it is see-through. "What? I love this sweatshirt! I bought it the day I found out I was pregnant with you. It is one of my favorites."

"You tell that same story every time you wear it."

"Okay, I will change. After I get the coffee going. We may all need a cup."

Twenty minutes later, Grady is at the door. Everyone is dressed for the day. Beau even took a quick shower. He rings the doorbell, and Laura Lynne sighs in delight. The chimes sound like church bells.

Laura Lynne looks at her Uncle Gabe. Grady has never used the doorbell in his life. Gabe says, "This must be official business. Beau, come with me."

Laura Lynne watches as her robust son walks next to his great uncle. Gabe is all quiet dignity. Her son is youth and vitality.

She hears Gabe introduce the two men and say, "Come on in the kitchen, Grady. Laura Lynne is serving coffee."

Grady sighs. "Been up all night. It sounds great." Laura Lynne pours him a mug and hands it to him. "Laura Lynne, perhaps you would like to talk in private first?"

She shakes her head. "No. Everybody here knows the whole story. At least as much as I can remember. It's good that they hear the rest from you."

He nods and looks at his coffee. He takes a sip. Savannah and Laura Lynne stand behind the island. Beau leans against the cabinets, and Uncle Gabe sits on a stool across the island, waiting for the news.

Grady begins, "Doctor Goldbug killed himself last night."

Uncle Gabe hits the island hard with his hand and mutters, "That son of a bitch!"

Laura Lynne jumps at the noise and spills her tea, heedless of the burning or the mess she has made. Beau walks over and stands next to his mother. Savannah takes a step closer to Laura Lynne. They create a united front.

Grady continues, "He gave a full confession. Told us the entire story. He said he had been waiting years for someone to figure it out. In his suicide note, he commented that he could die now in peace knowing the truth was coming to light." He shakes his head. "Apparently, he began to suspect there was a sexual predator after the second girl's examination. The information he received from the girls was almost identical in nature. He brought his findings to Bubba. Bubba blackmailed him into silence. Apparently, Dr. Goldbug had a significant drug problem. Somehow, Bubba knew. Though Dr. Goldbug did not know how or from whom."

Grady takes a sip of coffee. "When another girl was raped, Bubba made sure the child was seen by Dr. Goldbug. He says it wasn't until years later he realized it had to be Dr. Kenneth Butler. Once he moved away, there were no more girls. Bubba did continue to blackmail him through the years, though. He has been at his beck and call this entire time."

"How did he kill himself?" Uncle Gabe is still miffed.

"Shot himself in the mouth," Grady responds.

"How did he have access to a gun?" Beau asks.

"He was released to his home after his confession. He is an old, frail man with a bunch of health needs. We can't handle that in our jail. We sent a deputy to guard the house. He also has an around-the-clock caregiver." He shook his head. "That man went into his study, something he does every evening, and sat at his desk. His caregiver was in the room the whole time." Grady is exhausted; he looks beat, his face showing his anger. "He took out a gun from under his desk and shot himself in the mouth. That poor woman was sitting on the couch crocheting when he did it. I doubt she will ever be the same."

"Did he leave a note?" Beau asks.

"He left two. There was a note on the desk that gave directions to a storage unit where he kept all his old records and files from his medical practice. In it are all the files from the girls he treated, along with his letter of confession, everything he knows. It is dated and signed 12/31/1999." Grady sighs. "There is also a file of the others, mostly women, he treated for Bubba as part of the blackmail."

"How many girls, Grady? I found 11 if you include me," says Laura Lynne.

"Your file is among the ones found. There are 21 total." Grady shakes his head. "Many of the girls are minorities, lower socioeconomic status, broken families. They never reported the crime. Not that I blame them. The department was run by a bunch of prejudiced rednecks back then. It wouldn't have done them any good."

"What are you going to do next?" Laura Lynne asks.

"We still have Bubba," says Grady, "So far, he is not talking. He is also not going anywhere. We have him locked up here for now, but we have plans to move him to Jackson. The plan is to extradite Dr. Butler. Currently, he is being held in Boston for similar cases."

Grady looks at all the faces around the island. He settles on Laura Lynne and reaches across the island to grasp Laura Lynne's hands. "There is a lot more to this, Laura Lynne. A network of some sort. Lots of layers. There is a greater conspiracy. Bubba is just not smart enough to be the mastermind. He is following orders. We don't know whose orders."

Savannah finally speaks, "A conspiracy? What type of conspiracy, like sex trafficking?"

Grady nods and pushes himself upright, releasing Laura Lynne's hands. "Among other things." He shrugs his shoulders. "Drugs, gambling, real estate, money laundering. We have some leads. We are going to start tracking them down. We believe your mother's case is only the beginning."

Laura Lynne slowly puts her mug down as her children press into her, showing their support. "But for me, for the abductions, my part is over?"

Grady nods. "Yes, well, you may be asked for a deposition or even need to be at the trial. But for the foreseeable future, your part is done."

Laura Lynne allows the tears to fall. "Thank you, Jesus."

"You put the pieces together, Laura Lynne," assures Grady.

"Are you going to notify those girls that their rapist is now off the streets? They deserve to know. No, no, they *need* to know," Laura Lynne insists.

"We will make sure that gets done. I promise." Grady starts backing out toward the kitchen door. "Thanks for the coffee, but I really need to get going. There is still a lot to do."

Laura Lynne takes the handkerchief offered to her by Beau and wipes her tears. She smiles as she hands it back. She pats Savannah's hand as she disengages and walks around the island to Grady. She hugs him and whispers in his ear, "Thank you."

"Just doing my duty, ma'am." Grady rubs her head and steps back. "Can you walk me out, Laura Lynne?"

"Happy to." Laura Lynne walks with him to the front porch. "What's on your mind, Grady? What didn't you want the others to hear?"

He signals for Laura Lynne to walk down the stairs to his squad car. "Do you remember I told you I was going to go and visit your father's mistress in Mobile?" She nods. "She wasn't there. The place was deserted. I have not had time to do anything more, but thought you would want to know."

"Thank you for telling me. I asked Grace to run the address through her real estate platforms. See what she could come up with. I will follow up with her. Let Tripp know."

"You heard from Tripp? How is he?"

"Well, I feel better knowing he is not staying in touch with one of his best friends either! We thought it was just us!" Laura Lynne grins. "He is supposed to be coming here. I called him when all this broke with Dead Doe."

He opens the driver's door and slides behind the wheel. "Gonna miss having you around, Laura Lynne. You sure do liven things up!" He shuts the door and rolls down the window. "When are you headed out?"

"Monday afternoon. It's time to get back to my life." She smiles at him. "Think I am going to make this visit into a book, and you will have a starring role! Think I might call your character Stubing!"

"Stubing?! Good Lord, the Love Boat Captain?" He shakes his head, laughing. "I don't want to know why that name came to your head." He grins and puts the car in drive. "I look forward to reading it. I expect a signed copy!" She laughs and waves as he heads out the drive.

Laura Lynne turns toward the house. Savannah and Beau are on the porch, watching and waiting. "Momma, what was that all about?" asks Savannah.

"Nothing that concerns you, I am happy to report." She starts heading up the stairs. "But there is some financial stuff I need to relay to Tripp; let him follow up with it." She puts her arms around her babies' waists. "Come on. I am starving. Let's go make a farmhand's breakfast!"

To Gabe's delight, Laura Lynne and her children began making breakfast. Beau mans the griddle. There is laughter and banter as they discuss Grady's visit. The foursome convenes on the back porch for the meal, where Gabe tells story after story to his great-niece and -nephew. He regals them with the colorful ancestors that litter their heritage. Savannah records the stories with her phone. Gabe's memory is remarkable, though Laura Lynne knows he is embellishing the telling.

"I knew about the slave cabins on the property, but talking about owning slaves makes it more real…and uncomfortable." Savannah is appalled.

"Yes, everyone did back then. Some of your ancestors were better owners than others. Pearl's family was originally owned by the Coopers before they were given their freedom. Your great-grandmother Birdie ensured the property Queenie now lives on was deeded to the Jacksons before her death." He clears his throat. "I would show you the slave quarters, but they are still cordoned off with the police tape."

Savannah waves her hand. "No, no, it's fine."

"There are many parts to our family history that are uncomfortable, I know. It is better you hear them from me and your momma than from the papers or other people." He pushes his chair back. "It's up to us to do better moving forward. Nothing illegal under my watch or of questionable ethics. We do the best we can to right the wrongs of the previous generations and to better the community we live in. We serve because God has placed us in a position of stewardship. We must take care of the land, the family, the community. It is our duty." He waves the rest of the family along. "Go get cleaned up. Let's go see Tea Olive the way it is meant to be seen. We will take the side-by-side."

Savannah looks at her mother.

Laura Lynne reassures her, "It's a redneck golf cart. You should be fairly comfortable."

The rest of the day is spent checking the fields, riding to the river, and covering a large part of the 2,000 acres. Beau and Gabe sat in the front, talking about everything from cultivation to hunting and fishing. Gabe is an excellent and patient instructor. Laura Lynne had forgotten until he mentioned it, but Gabe taught classes at the local community college for many years. Listening to the conversation, Laura Lynne begins to realize there is a lot more to running Tea Olive and its assets than she knew. It seems Gabe has his finger in a lot of pies, including the businesses in town. He has been smart enough to see the transformation of downtown coming and has capitalized on its revitalization efforts.

"We have a stake in Wheelbarrow Books and the Magnolia Café?" Savannah asks.

"Yes!" Gabe shouts over his shoulder as the family drives across the cotton field. "I also have invested in the Tuber Bed and Breakfast, a couple of antique stores, and my favorite, the pizza shop on Canal Street."

Laura Lynne had no idea. The day turned into a lovely evening. Victoria stopped by to make sure they had plenty for supper and to prepare some light snacks for Eileen's celebration the next day. Savannah sits at the kitchen island, and Victoria puts her to work. She mixes, stirs, chops, and even ices the red velvet cake. Laura Lynne stands at the kitchen doorway, listening to their banter and conversation. It sounds just like she and Pearl once did. Savannah is flush with exertion and happiness.

Beau spends the bulk of his time with Gabe. They discuss business. The farm, stock market, mutual funds, the trust, all things business and financial. Gabe loves it. He takes out his books and fires up his computer to show Beau the spreadsheets and the plans he has for the future.

With the children content, Laura Lynne decides to take an hour and go speak with her mother. It was time for Laura Lynne to tell her story. Laura Lynne rises from her seat in the study.

"Beau, you good here with Uncle Gabe? I need to go and see my mother."

Uncle Gabe looks over at his niece from his computer screen. "Wondered when you would talk to her."

"Yes, well I have put it off long enough. I need to invite her to Aunt Eileen's celebration anyway, so I can kill two birds with one stone."

"Mom, I can come with you. Savannah too," says Beau.

"No, I appreciate it, but this is between my mother and me. I have to do it alone." She walks toward the kitchen. "But if I am not back by supper then send in the troops!" Savannah has the same reaction as Beau when Laura Lynne tells her of her errand.

"No, I need to do this my own way, and I have to do it alone." She hugs her daughter's sweet little self from behind and kisses the top of her head. "But thanks!"

On the drive to the assisted living facility, the peace Laura Lynne has cultivated all day begins to fracture. She has no idea how she is going to tell her mother her story. There is no guarantee her mother will even listen.

Upon her arrival, Laura Lynne is directed to the solarium as she is informed by the pert receptionist, Pam. "Mrs. Beauregard is taking sun in the back garden."

Her mother sits alone on a black bench in the broiling hot sun with a sweater over her shoulders. Laura Lynne walks down the paved path to her bench and sits beside her.

"Hello, Mother."

"Laura Lynne."

So, this is the way it's going to be. "Mother, I wanted you to know Savannah and Beau are here this weekend. We are hosting a celebration for Aunt Eileen tomorrow afternoon at 2:00 PM. I would like you to be there and to meet the children."

"I would like to meet the children." She still has not looked at her daughter. Laura Lynne is talking to the side of her head. Laura Lynne is not deterred by her mother's seeming lack of interest.

"I am sure you are wondering why they are here. Let me just go ahead and tell you I invited them here. I needed to tell them something in person." She takes a deep breath. "I needed to tell them about the summer of 1985."

This gets her mother's attention. "Oh, Laura Lynne, why must you harp about something that happened 40 years ago? It was a bad time; now, it's over. You have had other bad times, and you don't harp about those."

Laura Lynne bites her tongue and sits quietly. Maybe she just doesn't tell her? There is no reason for her to know the entire story, at least right now. But that is the coward's way out. Laura Lynne is no longer 15. "Last night, Dr. Kenneth Butler was arrested. He was arrested because of me."

Melanie says nothing.

Laura Lynne continues, "Dr. Goldbug was also arrested. He confessed his part as an accomplice in Dr. Butler's sexual abuse." Her mother is silent, but Laura Lynne can tell she is listening. "He killed himself last night. He left behind a suicide note. In the note are directions to a warehouse where he stored the records of Dr. Butler's victims. My medical record is among them."

Taking a deep breath, Laura Lynne explains, "I never lied to you, Mother. Dr. Butler raped me the night he called you to pick me up because I was vomiting. He is the one who gave me gonorrhea, chlamydia, and genital warts. He drugged me and did things to me while I was unconscious. And to make it worse, Dr. Goldbug knew about it. That day in his office, he knew I was telling the truth."

Melanie remains silent. She remains still as a statue. Laura Lynne can see her mother is beginning to understand what she is saying to her. Her breathing is escalating.

Laura Lynne explains the rest of the story, "I wasn't the only one. He did the same, or worse, to 20 other girls here in Mississippi. He has been doing the same in Massachusetts. He and Bubba Westerman were also arrested yesterday. It seems Bubba Westerman covered up the sexual abuse and blackmailed Dr. Goldbug for his silence. Dr. Butler paid him handsomely for his service."

The two sit in silence. Her mother's breathing evens out. She never acknowledges Laura Lynne's story.

After ten minutes, Laura Lynne gets up. "I will send Beau and Savannah to pick you up tomorrow at 1:30. Please be ready." Laura Lynne walks away realizing to receive validation from her mother would be for her mother to admit she was wrong. That probably will never happen. But it didn't matter. Laura Lynne realizes this whole time that she only needed validation from herself. What an amazingly wonderful feeling!

"Excuse me." Laura Lynne walks up to the nurse's station. "Can someone please see to my mother, Mrs. Beauregard? It's probably time to come in from the sun."

Laura Lynne calls Grace as she leaves. She picks up on the first ring and asks, "What in the world is going on? I got a terse response from Grady that he was busy, but you were fine. I don't even know what that means. Were you not fine? And did you hear about Dr. Goldbug and Bubba Westerman?"

"Yes, yes I know." Laura Lynne spends the next ten minutes replaying the last several days. "Grace, listen. Why don't you, Charlie, and Trey come for supper tonight? I know it's short notice, but I want you to meet my children, and I want to meet Trey. Maybe 6:30 PM? Not sure what it will be, maybe pizza."

Grace does not hesitate. "We will be there. I will bring the meal. I already have stuff out for dinner:

steaks, potatoes, and a salad. Charlie can man the grill. It will be fun. Plus, I want the scoop."

Laura Lynne pulls around to the back of The Residence. Both Savannah and Beau come off the back porch with drinks in hand. "Were y'all waiting on me?"

Savannah responds, "Kind of, but more just enjoying cocktail hour with Uncle Gabe. Victoria left for Queenie's 30 minutes ago. She told me to tell you she would be back tomorrow at 1:00 to get things set up."

"There was no need for that. I think you and I could manage," says Laura Lynne.

Savannah laughs. "She said you would say that, but the plan is for Pearl to bring Queenie. Uncle Gabe has invited her as she helped raise her."

"Oh, yes. That is perfect," says Laura Lynne.

"Okay. Quit holding off," Savannah says as she hooks her arm through her mother's and steers her to Beau. "We want to know how she handled the news."

Laura Lynne begins, "She literally said nothing. Not one word. I know she heard me. Not sure she actually processed what I said, though. Honestly, she may never be able to admit she was wrong. It might be too much for her." Savannah puffs up, ready to express her thoughts on the matter. Laura Lynne squeezes her arm. "She is complicit in this. To admit to herself or me that she was wrong will be to admit she played a role in my rape. That is a lot to ask."

Laura Lynne pats Savannah's hand and continues, "Besides, you two get to meet her tomorrow. In fact, you are going to go and pick her up from the assisted living facility at 1:30." This brought silence and staring. "Time y'all get a taste of your Grandmother Beauregard."

"Is that what we are supposed to call her?" asks Savannah.

"Hmmm, I don't know. What do you want to call her?" Laura Lynne looks at Beau. "Be nice! Listen, no need to decide right now. We have company coming for supper. I have invited the Eubanks over and they are bringing the meal. Steaks for the grill, potatoes, and a salad."

"Who are the Eubanks?" asks Savannah.

"I told you about Grace and Charlie. She is my bestest childhood friend. They have a son around Beau's age. His name is Trey. He is actually Charles the Third, but they call him Trey. You will love them. I want you to meet. I haven't had a chance to meet Trey yet, and it all just fell into place." Laura Lynne glances at her phone. It's close to 6 already. "Come on. Let's set up for company. We are keeping it informal, so the back porch works great." She looks over at Beau. "Can you let Uncle Gabe know and maybe refresh the bar?"

"On it," says Beau.

Thirty minutes later, the porch is set up. Savannah has outdone herself on the tablescape. "It's gorgeous, Savannah!"

"Hard not to be once I found the pantry of dishes and decorations. Holy cow, Momma, there is a plate for every occasion!"

"Yes, one of your Grandmother's," Laura Lynne taps her temple trying to recall which grandmother had a fondness for dishes, "I think it was Birdie's mother who loved dishes. Bought a set every time she travelled. She toured the European continent if I remember correctly."

"You do! Drove my mother crazy!" Gabe says as he goes to man the bar. "Every week or so, a crate arrived at The Residence with a complete set of dishes. She finally quit unloading them and just stacked them in the barn." Gabe starts pulling out a bottle. "I am making dry martinis since we are having steak. I hope that works."

"I have no clue. You know better than I would." Laura Lynne hears the gate buzzing. "Oh, they are here!" Laura Lynne rings them through and directs them to park in the back of the house. "Come on. Let's help them unload."

Beau heads to the passenger door to open it for Grace. She gets out and says, "My Lord, if it's not Tripp 40 years ago!" She hugs his neck and steps back. "You must be Beau."

"Ma'am," Beau says.

Laura Lynne steps up beside Beau. "Grace, my children. You have met Beau. This is my daughter Savannah. Beau, Savannah, Miss Grace, and Mr. Charlie Eubanks." Charlie comes around the front of the car with hand outstretched. He grabs Beau's hand, slaps him on the shoulder, and waits for Grace to stop hugging Savannah.

"And you are Trey," says Laura Lynne.

"Ma'am," Trey says.

Laura Lynne opens her arms and leans in for a hug and air kiss. "Grace! How did we grow such handsome and beautiful children?" Trey is gorgeous. He has blond hair and blue eyes. He is tall and strong, though not quite as big as Beau. He wears khakis and a golf shirt, as do all the men except Gabe. He is sporting seersuckers. "Trey, I am Laura Lynne. You struck the lottery when these two became your parents."

He smiles. Yep, drop dead gorgeous. "Yes ma'am."

Charlie says, "Come on, boys. Help me unload while the women rustle us up some drinks." The boys follow Charlie to the Tahoe and begin to unload. "Beau, your momma tells me you just got your MBA. Trey here has decided on law. I keep telling him the world has plenty of lawyers, but he doesn't seem to believe me."

Grace snuggles up close to Laura Lynne and Savannah. "Come on. Let's go to the kitchen. Let the boys unload. We can get the potatoes in the oven." She hugs Laura Lynne tight and then kisses

Savannah on the head. She whispers in Laura Lynne's ear, "This is how it should have been, always."

Savannah looks over at the two women. "She kisses me on the head like you, Momma."

"Yes. Well, I learned that from Mrs. Cunningham, Grace's momma. She kissed me on the head so many times I am surprised I don't have a bald spot," Laura Lynne says, laughing.

"She did. She surely did," says Grace. The three women meet the boys in the kitchen. Grace shoo's them out.

"Come on. Uncle Gabe was making dry martini's when y'all showed up," Beau says, leading the others out of the kitchen.

Charlie rubs his hands together and has a twinkle in his eye. "Sounds perfect. Y'all let me know when it's time to fire up the grill and get those steaks on."

Laura Lynne says, "Go ahead and fire it up. Uncle Gabe will show you where it is and y'all can talk manly talk about barbeque, or whatever you talk about while you are grilling."

"Whiskey, women, and hunting Laura Lynne. Whiskey, women, and hunting. Been the same since God had the good sense to put women on this earth," says Charlie. Grace takes a dish towel and swats Charlie's butt. Charlie grabs her up and swats her butt with his hand. "Careful, Grace, you know I love my woman in the kitchen!"

"Would you get out of here?" Grace wraps the towel around Charlie's neck and pulls him in for a quick kiss. "Women's work in the kitchen. Men grill." He swats her one last time and heads out the door.

Grace looks at Savannah and Laura Lynne, "I know it's stereotypical, my husband working on the grill and me in the kitchen. But it works for us. Charlie would happily work in the kitchen if I let him, though I doubt he would like me using the grill. Anyway, I am sure there are plenty of women libbers who would be appalled by our banter. Not me, though, I love it. And it works for us."

Savannah replies, "Doesn't bother me, though Chris does all the cooking in our house. Which I completely appreciate." Savannah picks out a cherry tomato from the salad and pops it in her mouth, chewing thoughtfully. "But, what is it about men in a kitchen that gets them all fired up?" Savannah is rubbing her belly. "Chris is the same way. I swear we conceived peanut here against the Frigidaire." Grace and Laura Lynne look at each other and start laughing.

"Well, they do say the way to a man's heart is through his belly," says Grace, "But the truth is, it's in food prep. Gets them all hot and bothered watching us prepare what they went out and killed. Brings out their caveman."

Savannah holds up her hand. "Okay, forget I said anything. I don't want to hear anymore." This just makes Grace and Laura Lynne laugh again.

"It's a good thing to have someone want you like that, Savannah. I am glad you have that with your husband…Chris, right?" Grace confirms.

The three women talk husbands and babies, mothers and brothers. Nothing is off limits as they put the potatoes in to roast, and Savannah takes the steaks out to Charlie.

As soon as Savannah leaves, Grace whips around toward Laura Lynne. "Okay, spill."

"What has Grady told you?" Laura Lynne asks.

"Assume he has said nothing. I know Momma and Daddy know a little of what is going on too, but they are locked boxes. I seem to be the only one out of the know."

"Brace yourself. Dr. Kenneth Butler raped me when I was 15. Dr. Goldbug was being blackmailed by Sheriff Bubba Westerman because he had a drug problem. So although they knew about it, it was never reported and happened to 20 other women."

Grace just quietly sits down on the stool. She closes her mouth which dropped open as Laura Lynne was talking. She puts the dishtowel on the countertop.

"And the woman who is supposed to be my grandmother still doesn't believe her." Savannah comes back without the steaks, catching the end of her mother's story.

"Wait. *What?*" Grace props her elbows on the island and her chin on her hands. "Start from the beginning."

Between Savannah and Laura Lynne, Grace receives a scaled-down version of events, including the latest developments. "Well, I'll be *damned*! That sorry son of a bitch!"

Savannah smiles. Watching a Southern lady swear is always so shocking to her. And cute. "Which one?" asks Laura Lynne.

"Well, all of them!" Grace's eyes tear up. "Laura Lynne, I am so sorry." She comes over and hugs her. "This whole time, I have been mad at you for leaving me our junior year! I missed my best friend. I didn't know how to *be* without you! You were my sister." She holds her tighter. "And you have been carrying this around this whole time." Then she spins away from Laura Lynne and starts pacing in the kitchen. She grabs a knife and starts heading toward the door. Savannah looks at her mother in alarm.

"Grace, *Grace*! Who exactly are you going to stab with that knife?" says Laura Lynne.

Grace turns back around, her eyes angry. She looks at Laura Lynne and then the knife. She gently places it on the island and takes a step back with a smile.

"I don't know. I really don't know. Maybe your momma?" Grace admits.

Savannah sort of spews out her water, choking and laughing. "I really like you, Miss Grace."

Grace walks over to Savannah. "I really like you too." She hugs her close. "You know you have a very brave and special mom, right?"

Savannah nods. "I always thought I knew, but now I *know*."

Charlie swings through the door. He takes one look at the hen party and does an immediate about-face. "Steaks are ready!" He shouts as he heads back out the swinging door.

Laughing again, the ladies take the salad and potatoes out to the porch. Putting them on the table, the men join them with their steaks. Trey invites Beau to go turkey hunting with him and Charlie in the morning before church. Beau is thrilled and tries to get Gabe to go, but he bows out gracefully. "No, no, you young'uns have a fine time though."

Grace and Laura Lynne clean up the dishes. Savannah is looking worn out after a full day. She excuses herself to her bedroom.

Grace says, "Laura Lynne, can I talk to Momma and Daddy about what you told me? You know they will be discreet."

"Sure. I suspect they know most of it anyway. May I ask why?" asks Laura Lynne.

"No real reason. But I don't like to keep secrets from them, especially something about someone they love."

"You have my permission."

After they finish the cleanup, Grace goes to the porch to collect her men. "Come on, Eubanks men. Time to head home."

"Trey and Beau are out by the river. Mr. Gabe, do you mind if I ring the bell to have them come back in?" asks Charlie.

"No, go right ahead." Charlie rings the mounted bell three times. Laura Lynne closes her eyes. It is the first time she has heard that sound since 1985. Grace comes over and gives her a side hug.

Grace says, "That sound brings back memories! Really good memories."

Laura Lynne sees Beau and Trey coming toward the house. "Here they come! That is two fine, strapping boys we got there." She looks out, and they are striking. Two men eating up the ground with their long strides. Warriors ready to take on the world.

"Hey, Dad. What's up?" asks Trey.

"Time to head home, kiddo. Beau, we will be by to get you at 4 AM." Charlie looks at Laura Lynne. "I promise to have him back in time to clean up for church." He takes the basket from Grace. "Boys, grab that cooler, and let's load up." He starts walking. "Mr. Gabe, Laura Lynne, see you at church tomorrow."

"See you then. It was a great evening, Charlie. Let's do it again sometime. Maybe bring Cunningham next time," says Gabe.

"Sounds like a plan! Night, Mr. Gabe," replies Charlie.

Grace walks over, hugs Gabe, and kisses him on the cheek. Gabe says, "You are a fine woman, Grace. Lovely family."

She smiles. "Thanks. God certainly blessed me."

"He did indeed," Gabe agrees.

Grace turns toward Laura Lynne and wraps her arm around her waist. "Come on, walk me to the car. You going to be okay at church in the morning? It could be brutal."

"I thought about that and then decided I really didn't care. I leave in two days, Grace. It just doesn't affect me anymore. I feel good about what I have done. If anyone is going to try and shame me or gossip about it, then the shame is theirs. I can live with it," says Laura Lynne.

"Good for you." Grace slides into the passenger seat. "Thanks for tonight, and thanks for trusting me. Love you, Laura Lynne."

"I love you back." Laura Lynne shuts the door. The window is down. "Charlie, what are you doing in the back seat?"

Charlie says, "Mr. Gabe makes a mean martini. Then he coaxed me into a bourbon while the boys went to the river. He drank me under the table your uncle did." He has a sloppy grin on his face.

"Don't worry, Miss Laura Lynne," Trey reassures her, "I only had one martini before dinner. I will get everyone home safe."

Laura Lynne steps back and waves goodbye. Beau comes beside her and does the same. "I like your friends here, mom."

"You and Trey seemed to hit it off well. You got everything you need for the shoot tomorrow?"

"Uncle Gabe said there is plenty of hunting gear. Trey and his dad are bringing the guns, so I should be good." He pets his mother's hair, a throwback from when he was a child. "You okay if I head up, Mom? I want to call Claire, and 4 AM is pretty early."

Laura Lynne lifts her hand and takes his. "Of course. But look, Beau. Isn't it breathtaking?"

The sun is setting. The sky has turned pink and purple. It is as if God decided to paint a picture just for the two of them.

Chapter 27

Laura Lynne set her alarm for 3:45 AM so that she could see Beau off. She gets to the kitchen and starts the coffee. She puts together some sausage on bread with the leftovers from yesterday's breakfast. Beau comes into the kitchen. He is decked out in camouflage from head to toe. He even has a camo hat tucked into his pocket. "Hey, Mom. I thought I heard you in the kitchen."

"Old habits die hard." She hands him a thermos of coffee and a small cooler. "Here, the Eubanks probably have some food for you, but it's always nice to make an effort to bring your own. It's just sausage on bread."

He takes it and puts the cooler in the pocket of his backpack. He zips it up. "Thanks, Mom." He looks at his phone. "That's Trey. They are at the front gate." He walks to the wall and rings them in. "Bye, Mom."

"Bye, sweet boy. Be careful and happy hunting." She follows him out the front door and watches as he joins Trey in the bed of a fully loaded Ford F150. Laura Lynne waves as they hurry on their way.

Laura Lynne watches out the front door as Beau climbs into the truck beside Trey. "Wouldn't it be wonderful if Beau and Trey became friends?" Laura Lynne thinks to herself as she climbs back up the stairs to her room. "Well," she says under her breath, "A mom can hope."

She reaches her room and decides it's just too early to start the day. Her bed beckons and Laura Lynne crawls back under the covers, closing her eyes and falling back to sleep.

Two hours later, Laura Lynne is awakened by her daughter as Savannah snuggles into the bed beside her. Laura Lynne opens her eyes and smiles at her daughter, "Hey, sweetheart. Everything good?"

Savannah rubs her belly, "Little man is active this morning and I couldn't sleep. I thought you would be up by now, but when I saw you in bed I decided to join you."

"I'm glad you did. Want me to rub your feet?"

"Oh, mom, would you? My ankles feel like they could burst most days. I can't believe how swollen they are all the time."

So, for the next hour Laura Lynne and her daughter talk and laugh, enjoying each other's company as the day wakes up. Finally, the two women go downstairs to join Gabe and wait on the return of Beau.

"Mom! Beau is back!" Savannah is on the front porch with her feet up, sipping her tea and waiting on Laura Lynne to join her. Laura Lynne comes on the porch with her mug of tea. Beau and Trey are hopping out of the bed, talking excitedly. Beau holds up his turkey for all to see. He shakes hands with Trey. Charlie rolls down the passenger window and calls out, "It was great! We each got one. Never happens! We will see you at church in a few hours!"

Waving, Beau starts up the porch steps.

Laura Lynne stops him, "Hold on, son. Where are you going with that thing?"

"I have no idea. Not sure what to do with it now," Beau says sheepishly.

Laughing, Laura Lynne directs him to the barn. "I will send Uncle Gabe to meet you. He will show you how to dress it."

***

The foursome is in the car after church, and Savannah is the first to break the silence. "That was just plain odd. Can someone explain to me what just happened?"

"Yeah, Mom. Like I expected pointing and staring. Maybe some whispers behind our backs. But not a standing ovation when we came into the sanctuary. It was like Jesus had entered the room," Beau says.

Even Gabe was stunned. "I have been attending that church for most of my life. Been a deacon since I came back from Korea. I have never once seen that either."

Savannah chimes in, "I think we handled it well. Other than Beau waving like he was a celebrity."

Beau reaches over to punches Savannah lightly in the arm. "It was instinct! I didn't know what to do. At least I didn't turn beet red like some people."

Laura Lynne interrupts the musings. "It wasn't just the applause. Somehow, they knew I was involved in the arrests. How is that possible?"

Beau replies, "I have the answer to that! Trey sent me this morning's Venice Gazette. The headline is about the arrests, but the first paragraph gives away your identity. "Newly returned local author"… Narrows it down a bit."

"Let me see," Laura Lynne says.

Gabe looks at Beau. "Start the car, Beau. No need to sit in the empty church parking lot. All that hand shaking made me tired. And hungry. Plus, we need to get ready for Eileen's party."

Laura Lynne leans her head on the back of her seat and closes her eyes. "Oh, Lord. The party. I am exhausted already. Send the article to Savannah, and she can read it to us on the way home."

For the rest of the drive, the passengers listen as Savannah reads about the arrests. "Seems like a fair and balanced article. He protects the victims."

"Who wrote the article?" asks Laura Lynne.

"Guy by the name of Ron Adams. Do you know him, Mom?" Savannah replies.

"Not personally. He is Mary's boyfriend. Helped us with some of the research. I am glad it was him. Sorry he didn't do a better job at concealing my identity, but considering what just happened at the church, I forgive him."

"I still don't get the standing ovation." Beau pulls into Tea Olive as he makes the comment.

"I believe it was to honor your Momma, Beau. A lot of people in this town turned their back on her, including her own parents. Almost like an apology," explains Gabe.

"Do you think so, Uncle Gabe?" asks Laura Lynne.

"Yeah, honey. I do. Take it as a win. I do," affirms Gabe.

"Whoa, what in the world is going on? I thought this was going to be a small celebration for Aunt Eileen. Momma?" Savannah asks.

Leaning forward, Laura Lynne sees a dozen cars parked along the drive. The front porch is full of people in their Sunday best. Pearl and Victoria are coming in and out the front door, and John seems to be setting up the bar.

"Oh dear. This could be my fault. I may have mentioned to a few people who knew my sister they were welcome to come for the celebration," explains Gabe.

"What! Oh, good grief, Uncle Gabe. Poor Pearl and Victoria!" Laura Lynne jumps into action. "Beau, drop us off at the door. Savannah, we have to help in the kitchen. Uncle Gabe, this is your mess, so you get to play host."

Laura Lynne and Savannah scurry into the kitchen. Grace and her mother are already helping Victoria and Pearl in the kitchen.

"Pearl! I am so sorry! I had no idea." Feeling no compunction whatsoever, Laura Lynne throws her uncle under the bus. "It's Uncle Gabe's fault!"

Pearl rolls her eyes. "Nothing to be done now. Most people we have had to the house since your Daddy died. Kind of nice for a change."

"What can we do to help?"

Victoria points to the plates lined up on the island. "You can start by serving up some appetizers. John is serving cocktails while we started prepping. We need to get some food in those people, or Miss Eileen's celebration might be more interesting than any of us are ready for."

Laughing, Savannah, Grace, and Laura Lynne grab a tray and start for the front door. "Savannah, you tell me if you need to sit down."

"Are you kidding? Aunt Eileen would have loved this. I think it is perfect," says Savannah.

"I love you, sweet girl. You are absolutely right. She would have loved this," agrees Laura Lynne.

Beau comes up to Savannah and plucks a deviled egg off her plate. "Come on, sissy. We need to go get Granny."

"You are on your own, Bubby. Need to help Momma host."

"Oh Lord. I need both of you here. Maybe we can just send an Uber," Laura Lynne jokes.

Grace laughs. "An Uber? In Venice on a Sunday? Let me call Charlie. He and Trey are on their way. No problem for them to pick up Miss Melanie."

"Oh, Grace. That would be so helpful." Laura Lynne swats Beau's hand as he reaches for a second egg. "Stop that, Beau! Go help John at the bar."

"Wait!" Grace hands Beau her plate. "Serve these on the way there. I need to call Charlie."

More and more people begin to arrive at the house. Melanie arrives with the Eubank men and is dressed for the occasion. Charlie drives her to the front entrance where Gabe and Beau are waiting to help her out of the car and up the stairs. Everyone stops eating and talking to watch the matriarch of the Beauregard family make her way to the top of the porch.

"Laura Lynne, come here," commands Melanie.

She looks at Grace and hands her serving platter to Trey. Trey's girlfriend, Rebecca, takes Savannah's appetizers and nudges her toward her mother. Savannah and Laura Lynne walk hand-in-hand to stand in front of Melanie. Beau comes to stand alongside his mother.

"Are these my grandchildren?" Melanie asks.

Placing her hands at the smalls of her children's backs, Laura Lynne introduces her progeny for the first time to her mother. "Momma, meet Savannah Lynne and Beauregard Cooper. Savannah, Beau, meet your grandmother, Melanie Louise Cooper Beauregard."

"Ma'am," Savannah and Beau say in unison. Both receive the once over from Melanie before she nods her approval.

"It is nice to finally meet you, and I hope we can spend some time together later this afternoon. But right now, I would like to speak with your mother."

Savannah and Beau remain standing next to their mother. Laura Lynne whispers, "It's okay. This is between my mother and me." Both reluctantly move to the side, leaving Laura Lynne standing alone with her mother. "All right Momma. Say what you need to say. Then, it's time to celebrate your sister."

Melanie is regal in her silence. She looks around the porch and into the front yard at all the guests gathered. She stops her gaze on her brother. Gabe nods his acknowledgment. "I was a poor mother to you, Laura Lynne. Any shame brought to this family in the summer of 1985 is because of me." Her voice is strong and clear. "And anyone who says differently will answer to me. The shame is mine." She walks forward and lifts her hand to cup Laura Lynne's cheek. She wipes her tears with her thumb. Dropping her hand, Melanie turns toward her brother and raps her cane on the porch. "Gabriel I could use a refreshment. Escort me to the bar?"

"It would be my pleasure." Gabe walks over to Laura Lynne with a wink and extends his elbow to his sister. Savannah and Beau surround their mother. They pull her in through the front door. The quiet from moments ago is replaced with chatter and lively conversation.

"Momma, are you okay? I am pretty sure you just got an apology," says Savannah.

Grace comes bustling in. "Okay, you two. I've got your momma. Y'all go out on that front porch, and you host all these guests. You can't be hiding in here, or people will talk."

Savannah snickers. "And they weren't before? After Granny's stunt, I will be shocked if we aren't on the front page of the Gazette again tomorrow."

"I am fine. But Grace is right. I just need a couple of minutes. Don't leave Uncle Gabe out there by himself," Laura Lynne says.

"Come on, Laura Lynne. I think you need to talk to my momma. Might explain things," Grace says. She and Laura Lynne walk to the kitchen. Laura Lynne's children keep a close eye on their mom before they go back to the porch.

Laura Lynne walks into the kitchen and sits at the island. A hot tea is waiting for her. Everyone is looking at her, and she says, "Okay, spill. What is going on? I feel like I have been set up."

Mrs. Cunningham laughs and, walking around the island, kisses Laura Lynne on the head. "My dear child, you absolutely have been! It was mostly Melanie's idea, but I helped."

"Momma?" Laura Lynne says in surprise.

Mrs. Cunningham explains, "Yesterday, Grace told me the entire story. She also told me you had gone to see your mother, and her response was…" She purses her lips. "Shall we say less than stellar? So, this morning, I skipped Sunday school and went to see her. I gave her a piece of my mind. Not that I had to do much. She had been up most of the night devastated by your news. She spoke with Gabe. He had confirmed everything you said. He told her she needed to make things right. I agreed."

"And this was 'making things right?'" asks Laura Lynne.

Mrs. Cunningham returns to her side of the island and begins slicing Victoria's rosemary bread. "In her eyes. Sweetheart, she realizes you can never forgive her. She can never forgive herself. She only has a few years left on this earth. She has to protect the next generations. She has to protect the legacy. She did that today."

Pearl chimes in, "You didn't see it, Laura Lynne, but nearly everyone had their cameras out. I am sorry to say your reel on TikTok is about to be replaced by Miss Melanie."

"Who invited all these people?"

"Your Uncle Gabe did some, but your mother and I did the rest. We made calls from your momma's room."

Grace rubs Laura Lynne's back. "You aren't mad, are you? They told me about it while we were in church. It was too late to do anything but help."

Laura Lynne says, "I honestly don't know what I am. I think the word is redeemed."

Chapter 28

Laura Lynne walks over to her desk and gently picks up the gorgeous urn that houses her aunt's ashes. For the past six years, the urn has been housed in Laura Lynne's hope chest. The urn is handcrafted and is deep blue with tea olive branches in full bloom snaking around the base. It's quite magnificent, with a horse and rider galloping through the branches. When Laura Lynne received the call from her Uncle Gabe requesting her help, Laura Lynne hastily grabbed the urn and brought it with her. Back to Tea Olive. Back home.

Laura Lynne looks out the window over the front gardens. The lawn is littered with people, and the driveway is full of cars. She sees her mother on Beau's arm as she takes him and Savannah around and introduces them. She is solidifying their place in the Cooper family legacy. And in Venice society. It is theirs if they choose to grab the brass ring. Laura Lynne is disheartened to see Scarlet has not chosen to attend. She had invited her and Buck but had received nothing but a text declining the invitation.

Laura Lynne pulls out the letter she keeps in an envelope tied to the urn with a silken chord. It is the last missive she has from her aunt.

Dear Laura Lynne,

If you are reading this, then I have gone home to be with Momma and Daddy. Don't be sad; I had a feeling this would happen sooner rather than later.

Not sure why; just a premonition. So, to cover all the bases, I made sure all the details of the farm were in order and included instructions for my passing. By now you know I want to be cremated and spread at Tea Olive in the gardens. I have loved River Oaks, but Tea Olive calls to me, and I want to go home. One stipulation, though, I want you to take me there. When you are ready. It's the one thing I have not been able to do while I was living: get you to go home. But maybe in my passing, you will gain the strength to forgive and go back to Venice. And face the stuff you have been avoiding, specifically Melanie.

Now, I don't agree with how your momma treated you, you know that, but I also know Melanie. In her own convoluted way, she thought she was protecting you, your brothers and sister, and the Cooper/Beauregard legacy. She wasn't right. But that doesn't mean you keep your momma out of your life for your WHOLE life. She only has a few more years left, if that. You need to make things right. She should be the one to do it, but it's up to you. You have to be the one. Your momma, she's not strong enough. She can't admit she was wrong.

Enough about Melanie. I have deeded River Oaks to your Uncle Gabe for many reasons. None of them matter, really, because the final decision on all things River Oaks is yours to make. I hope you will finish the dream Gabe and I talked about over the years, somehow merging River Oaks and Tea Olive, making the two properties become one estate. Or if everyone agrees, including Mabel and Ben, to sell

River Oaks and purchase more property in Venice. To expand Tea Olive closer to its original acreage. A place for orphan animals, a sanctuary of sorts. The property is yours. Tripp will be the executor of Tea Olive and you, River Oaks. I expect you to do right by Scarlet and Avery. Scarlet, she needs more help than most. And Avery's namesake, 'Rhett'. We have to look out for that sweet boy too.

The family has been broken up long enough over silly things. First, it was me, my marriage, and my divorce. My parents just couldn't take it. Gabe, too, was kicked out of Daddy's will for no good reason. Then you, baby girl, sent away for reasons beyond your control. Scarlet never comes back to Tea Olive unless she is forced by obligation to visit. Tripp ran off and joined the military, and Avery, well, Avery, has his family in North Carolina. Scattered to the four winds. The dream is to bring everyone back together. Tea Olive is home for Coopers. It's in our blood. We all have to stop hiding from it and instead CLAIM it. If not in this generation, then you and Tripp see fit to make it happen for the next generation.

The money, well, there is plenty to care for River Oaks for the next ten years. I set up a trust with DeeDee and that second husband of mine. Well, he never changed his will. When he died, I got it all. Crazy man. I should have never married him. I never loved him, but he did treat me good. Keep the farm running. Help out Gabe if he needs it (he won't; he's a cagey businessman), but you need to have a handle on what is going on...it will be your responsibility one day.

And, you Laura Lynne, you are an amazing woman. I am so proud of you. You did it. You made a life for yourself. You raised two amazing children under less-than-ideal circumstances. You were the very best gift I ever received. You know, I couldn't have children. Not that I didn't want them; just never happened for me, and I think that was so because God knew you were going to need me to be your momma, at least for a little while. I loved it all. I loved you. And I have one final thing to tell you. Stop doing what you are supposed to do and start doing what you want to do. You told me when you were a teenager that one day you wanted to write a book. You were always writing in your journals and sending letters to Queenie. It's time. Quit putting it off. You have done all you need to do for everybody else. It's time you chase your dream and do you!

I love you, baby girl. You are the best part of me.

Aunt Eileen

Eileen was right about everything. Everything except her mother. It was not exactly an apology, but Laura Lynne believes even her aunt would have been surprised by Melanie's actions. She folds up the letter and places it back in the envelope. She removes the chord from the urn and places it on her desk. One last glance out the window and Laura Lynne sees Pearl has arrived with Malcolm and Queenie. Smiling delightedly, Laura Lynne goes down the stairs to join in the festivities. This time, she is bringing Eileen with her.

Laura Lynne spots Savannah talking to Trey's girlfriend, Rebecca. They seem to be getting along splendidly. Catching her daughter's eye, Savannah disengages and walks toward her mother. They stand next to each other, watching as Melanie commands the festivities.

"She's rather impervious, isn't she? I can't decide if she realizes we are her grandchildren or if we work for her." Savannah says as she starts walking toward the garden with Laura Lynne.

"Well, it's probably a little of both. What do you think overall?" asks Laura Lynne.

"Well, there is no question where you get your spine from, Mom. She is what I think of when I think of a Steel Magnolia."

Laura Lynne pats her hand. "Like it or not, she is your grandmother. As Chris said, we come from good, strong stock. I will never forget what my mom did. Ever. But I do forgive her. I think I forgave her a long time ago."

"I think it might take me a little while."

"Fair enough. Enough talk about my mother. Let's celebrate your real grandmother. The grandmother of your heart."

The ceremony is brief. Laura Lynne looks at the large group gathered around in the garden. The gorgeous garden was created by her very talented uncle using a design over 100 years old. Laura Lynne sees John facetiming Avery and his family so he can be a part of the festivities.

Laura Lynne has a moment to miss her brother and sister before she steps forward. "I really don't know what to say. Aunt Eileen would not appreciate long and flowery speeches, so I am just going to speak from my heart." She looks around at the group gathered. "When I was little, I loved it when Aunt Eileen visited. She always brought the fun with her. There was never a dull moment when she was around. Then, when I was broken and scared, Aunt Eileen became my very air. She was my light. She believed in me. She supported me. She helped me to heal and became a mother to me and a grandmother to my children. I could tell her anything, and I did. She never shied away from my weaknesses, from my faults, and I loved her for that." Laura Lynne opens the urn. At her signal, Malcolm begins singing "Into the Garden" in a deep baritone voice. Pearl and Victoria join in, and to everyone's surprise, Queenie begins singing. Her voice gains strength as the verses continue. Laura Lynne and Pearl meet each other's eyes. Tears flow.

Laura Lynne secures the lid in place and then places the urn in a hole in the ground. She covers the hole with dirt and whispers, "You are home now. I love you."

Standing, Laura Lynne finishes. "She told me to bring her home when I was ready. That Tea Olive had always called to her. And it would do the same for me. At the time, I didn't understand it, but I understand it now. Uncle Gabe?"

He clears his throat. "Please bow your heads. Lord, we are so grateful for the time we had with Eileen. She was light and love— a beautiful creature who never shied from living life to the fullest. May we all learn something from her love. I miss my baby sister, but I am so glad she is back home. Continue to bless our home. Give us peace and safety. Allow your arms to surround us with your protection in the coming months and years. In your name, we pray, Amen."

On that final note, the party began to disband. People head to their cars, saying their goodbyes. Others go back to the front porch for a mint julep as one last gesture of celebration. Beau and Savannah stay with their mother while she covers the hole and secures the grave marker.

Brushing off her hands, Laura Lynne stands with her hands on her hips.

"Mom?" Beau questions.

"Hmm, what is it, sweet boy?"

"Can we come back, like, and visit? I want to bring Claire and show her Tea Olive. I really like it here. It's like a puzzle piece that has been missing for me was found and finally slid into place." He shakes his head. "I don't really know how to describe it."

"No, Beau, I get it. It's like this chunk of who we were was missing; now it's there. Makes me want to explore it more."

Laura Lynne smiles. "You would have to check with your Uncle Gabe, but I am certain he would love to have you and your families visit anytime. Tea Olive was meant to be for all generations of the Coopers and Beauregards. There is no reason I need to be here for you to visit. Unless you just want me here." She links her arms through her child's arms. "You're right, though; a puzzle piece has been put into place." She smiles at both of her children. "I like that thought."

Savannah stops walking and tugs her arm. "Wait! Who is that man walking down the driveway?" She points. "Do you see him?"

"No, where?" Laura Lynne squints.

Beau spots him too. "Next to the Magnolia tree. He has on army fatigues and is carrying a duffle bag."

"What?" Laura Lynne walks toward the drive leading to the house. The figure walks down the driveway, looking like the ghost of the boy she once knew.

"Tripp?" She starts running down the drive and straight into his arms.

He laughs and spins her around. "Hey, baby girl. I came back just like you asked."

Made in the USA
Columbia, SC
07 February 2025

91151a6b-f50b-49db-91ab-b8a1dff69377R03